D

Forbidden Love

Her father had brought his shotgun on the ride with him. Even now she could see that his hand rested on it in the gunboot at the right side of his steed.

Realizing that he had not yet seen her with Bold Wolf, Shanna fell to her knees in the canoe and scrambled over to Bold Wolf. She frantically grabbed him by the arm. "Turn around!" she cried. "Oh, Lord, please turn around! It's Father. Don't you see him? It's Father."

But it was too late. Her father had wheeled his horse around and was glaring at Shanna and Bold Wolf.

Bold Wolf's skin prickled at the nape of his neck when he saw the anger in Shanna's father's eyes, yet he continued onward, for he knew that fate had drawn her father there. It was time to set things straight.

BOLD
WOLF

by

Cassie Edwards

A SIGNET BOOK

SIGNET
Published by New American Library, a division of
Penguin Putnam Inc., 375 Hudson Street,
New York, New York 10014, U.S.A.
Penguin Books Ltd, 27 Wrights Lane,
London W8 5TZ, England
Penguin Books Australia Ltd, Ringwood,
Victoria, Australia
Penguin Books Canada Ltd, 10 Alcorn Avenue,
Toronto, Ontario, Canada M4V 3B2
Penguin Books (N.Z.) Ltd, 182–190 Wairau Road,
Auckland 10, New Zealand

Penguin Books Ltd, Registered Offices:
Harmondsworth, Middlesex, England

Published by Signet, an imprint of New American Library, a division of
Penguin Putnam Inc. Previously published in a Topaz edition.

First Signet printing, February 2000
10

With much affection I dedicate *Bold Wolf,* the thirteenth book of my Topaz Indian Series, to my sweet editor, Audrey LaFehr, who because of her insight into how readers crave to know more about our Native Americans, suggested I write the Topaz Indian Series for Penguin Putnam. Audrey, I thank you. My *readers* thank you!

Always,

Cassie Edwards

POEM

A long time ago, when the world was new,
God and the Great Spirit had a dream for me and you.
They placed together on Grandmother Earth . . .
Children of two colors to earn their worth.
A river placed between the two,
They did all this for me and you.
Carefully planned, their lives commenced. . . .
All the odds seemed stacked against.
Struggling every day to just survive,
The weather, the animals, and human nature
    connived,
It seemed though this could not be . . .
But they did it all for you and me.
The children of the dawn, we are,
We have all traveled so very far.
With us we have brought our love. . . .
God and the Great Spirit smile on us from above!

—Harriet Lucas Garnett,
Poet and Friend

1

Oh, fair she is!
Oh, rare she is!
—GEORGE SIGERSON

Old Town, Maine, 1874.
June—the muskhogi-gizus, "Seals Ride
on the Water Moon"

The distant low mountain domes to the south and east
lifted their dense forest slopes heavenward. From the
base of the mountains, forests of beech, maple, birch,
and hornbeam reached wide and far. Fir and spruce
grew stately tall along the low swampland.

The breeze was warm and velvet against twelve-
year-old Shanna Sewell's face and arms as she skipped
along the sandy shore of the Penobscot River.

Behind her, up a slight slope, lay Old Town, and
across the bay she could see Indian Island, which was
occupied by a band of Penobscot Indians.

Corber Sawmill was a short distance upriver, where
a good portion of Old Town's population of men
were employed.

Bernita Sewell, Shanna's mother, sat on a blanket
on the beach with her four-month-old twins, Tommie
and Terrie, enjoying the early morning sun. "Shanna,
don't go far," Bernita said, watching Shanna. "Stay
where I can see you. You never know when one of

those Penobscot Indians will suddenly grab you and take you hostage to Indian Island."

"Mama, you know the Penobscot never do things like that," Shanna said over her shoulder as she kept skipping away from her mother, her red, waist-length curls bouncing along her back. She clutched a small basket that was already half filled with beautiful seashells. "I must go farther. I want to find more shells."

"Shanna, why on earth do you wish to have so many?" Bernita fussed.

"Mama, I've told you before . . . I am searching for that perfect one," Shanna said. She stopped and picked up a delicate, bluish white shell and carefully placed it in the basket with the others. "It will have surely traveled far. Just imagine where it might have been. As I look at my shells I dream of distant places. I would so adore finding a *conch* shell, all pink and shiny."

"Just hurry up, Shanna, the sun is getting too hot too quickly this morning," Bernita said, folding the corners of the blankets over each of her sons as they lay in her shadow.

"I won't be too much longer now, Mama," Shanna said over her shoulder, the skirt of her long, blue ruffled dress tangling around her legs as the breeze picked up strength.

"Your father would say you are wasting time today walking along the beach," Bernita said. "He would expect you to be practicing your violin."

"Papa is too busy now to notice," Shanna said, shuddering when she thought of her father and what he might be doing at this very moment. The only mortician in town, he was more than likely preparing a body for burial.

Suddenly Shanna saw something else besides shells that intrigued her. It was a butterfly. Its flight was so smooth and even; it seemed only to be floating through the air instead of flying.

And she had never seen such lovely colors: a mixture of blues and blacks, with a lacy trim of white at the very tips of the wings.

Wanting to get a better look, Shanna glanced over her shoulder at her mother and was glad to see she was occupied with one of Shanna's brothers. She had moved from the beach and was now resting beneath the shade of an oak tree, sliding a breast free to feed one of the babies.

Taking this opportunity, when her mother surely wouldn't notice, Shanna followed the butterfly from the beach into a stand of snowy-white birch trees.

After she had been gone for only a scant minute, she heard her mother yelling for her. She sighed and ran back to the beach so her mother could see that she was all right.

"Mama, *please,* I'll be gone from the beach for only a *moment,*" she said. "I've seen the most beautiful butterfly. I want to watch it for a moment or two longer."

"Just hurry up and don't go far," Bernita said, giving her a stern look.

"I shall not go far, Mama," Shanna said, then ran back into the birch forest and stopped short when she found the butterfly. It had landed on a low tree limb.

Scarcely breathing, not wanting to frighten it away, Shanna stepped slowly closer to get a better look.

She then took a quick step backward and gasped when the butterfly was startled away by a young Indian brave, who stepped from the forest and now stood only a few feet from Shanna.

Shanna recognized the brave and knew she had no reason to be afraid. She had seen him often in Old

Town. Yet she felt awkward standing there eye to eye with him, especially after her mother's warning.

That puzzled Shanna, for her mother had never been given any reason to distrust the Penobscot. That their skins were different and that they were *Indians* seemed enough for her mother not to want Shanna near them.

Shanna hated that prejudiced side of her mother—and her father, for that matter—for Shanna saw everyone as equal. She had been taught that in Sunday School class, so wasn't it true?

"I know you, but I do not know your name," the brave said, his dark eyes locked with Shanna's. "I have seen you in Old Town."

"Shanna," she said softly. "My name is Shanna Sewell." She felt suddenly timid in the presence of this young brave. Although probably only about seventeen, he had already developed into a man. She could tell by how his fringed buckskin leggings strained at the seams that his legs were powerfully muscled.

With his smooth, copper skin, his face was handsomely sculpted, his cheekbones pronounced, his features pleasing. And his hair! Sleek and black, it hung in long, loose locks past his waist.

But it was his eyes that mesmerized Shanna most. They were dark and deep like midnight, inviting and friendly.

"Shanna?" Bold Wolf said, as though testing the way her name felt as it was breathed across his lips.

Yes, he thought, her name was beautiful. And he could not help but be enamored of her in her presence. Always before he had watched her from afar, in awe. Yet up this close, he saw just how delicately beautiful she was, with her tiny wisp of a figure, her sweet, heart-shaped face, and her frail cheekbones.

Her eyes, large and shiny, were like the violets that grew in the blowing grass on his island. They were so unique and beautiful, they almost stole his breath away.

But it was her hair that had first attracted him to her when he had seen her that first time in Old Town. It was reddish orange, the color of the wild strawberries that grew in clusters along the riverbanks in the spring before they were ripened enough to eat.

And unlike the women of his village, whose hair was straight, Shanna's hair lay across her shoulders and far down her back in swirls of soft, beautiful curls.

"*Your* name is . . . ?" Shanna said softly, quite uncomfortable now over the way he was studying her so intently, as if she were some expensive painting that people looked at but never touched.

"Bold Wolf," he said, their eyes meeting and holding. "I am Bold Wolf of the Bear People band of the Penobscot Indians. I am from Indian Island. My father is Chief War Eagle."

"Your father . . . is chief?" Shanna said breathlessly, her violet eyes widening. "Your father is a powerful Indian chief?"

Seeing just how entranced Shanna was that his father was chief made Bold Wolf's chest swell with pride. "Yes, my father is chief," he said. "And your father—what does he do?"

"My father is the mortician in Old Town," Shanna said guardedly, having always shied away from confessing that truth about her father to anyone. She hated her father's occupation, for it did seem so morbid, especially since he practiced it in the very house in which his family lived.

"Mortician?" Bold Wolf said, raising an eyebrow. "Explain to me what that word means. I know English well enough, but there are some words that are a mystery to me. The word *mortician* is new to me."

Shanna cringed. She sighed heavily, for she dreaded having to tell this handsome brave what her father truly did. She knew that Indian customs varied much from the whites'. What if the Penobscot didn't approve of the way white people prepared their dead for burial? Talking about it certainly made Shanna uncomfortable.

"A mortician, well, they . . . my father . . . he . . . prepares the dead for burial," she stammered awkwardly.

Seeing how speaking of her father's chosen occupation made Shanna uncomfortable, Bold Wolf quickly changed the subject. "What do *you* want out of life?" he asked. His gaze moved to the shells in her basket. Then he gazed into Shanna's eyes again. "What do you dream when you dream?"

"I am going to be a famous violinist," Shanna said, smiling at him. Then her smile faded. "But that is not so much my dream as it is my father's. The violin I play was once my aunt's. Just before she died at age seventeen, her future as a concert violinist was almost a reality. My father wishes that I continue *her* dream."

"I am not familiar with the instrument called a violin," Bold Wolf said. "Please tell me what it is."

She tried her best to tell him about the violin and how drawing the bow across the strings created such beautiful music.

"I do love playing the violin," she murmured. "But it is not something that I would die for."

"I would hope not," Bold Wolf said, his eyes widening.

"You must have your own dreams," Shanna said, laughing softly to herself over his innocent expression.

She shifted her basket from one hand to the other. "Please share your dreams with me."

"I wish to one day be the chief *kwsiwa*, Runner, for my people," he said. "Runners are also called Pure Men."

"A runner? A pure man?" Shanna said, watching him reach out for the butterfly as it came fluttering close again to the tree limb.

"A Runner is chosen because of his fleetness of foot," Bold Wolf said, talking more softly as the butterfly landed on the palm of his hand. "A Runner can cover large tracts of land and run down moose, deer, and other game. He can kill animals in their tracks faster than any other brave in his village. It is a social honor to be given the title of Runner of one's Penobscot village."

"How interesting," Shanna said, mesmerized not only by what he had told her, but also by how the beautiful butterfly trusted him enough to stay on his hand. She so badly wanted to touch the butterfly herself.

Bold Wolf saw Shanna gazing at the butterfly with a soft longing in her eyes. He knew she wished to be the one holding it. Slowly he moved his hand close to hers.

"Ease your hand up close to mine," he said in almost a whisper. "When the sides of our hands touch, I will lean mine sideways so that the butterfly will move over to yours."

"Do you truly think it will?" Shanna whispered back, her heart pounding with excitement.

"Yes. Just do as I say and you will soon enjoy, as well, the velvet touch of the butterfly's wings against your skin," Bold Wolf said, a feeling of warmth threading through him when her hand touched his.

It was at this moment that he knew he had found

something in his life besides being the village Runner that would please him. It would be wonderful to be able to steal moments like this with Shanna Sewell.

But he knew better than to believe it could happen again. Surely she would not want to meet him again, and even if she did, he doubted that her parents would allow it. Most *webala-giks,* white-eyes, avoided contact with the Penobscot unless it was for the sake of business . . . business that would always benefit the *webala-giks.*

And he knew it was foolish to let anything stand in the way of him being his people's Runner! He had aspired to it for so long!

Shanna looked quickly up at Bold Wolf when their hands touched. Never had she experienced such a delicious sweet feeling inside as the touch of his flesh against hers had caused. It had awakened strange sensations inside her heart, as though the butterfly were *there,* madly fluttering its wings, instead of resting peacefully on Bold Wolf's hand.

Somehow she knew that it was not right to have such feelings, especially for someone so much older than herself—and especially an *Indian.* Her parents would never allow her to have him for a friend.

She felt the butterfly's softness against her palm now and gasped with delight as it moved from Bold Wolf's hand to hers. "It's so soft and beautiful," she whispered.

Bold Wolf wanted to tell Shanna that *she* was *far* more beautiful than the butterfly, but he knew he shouldn't. She was much too young to understand the infatuations of a young man.

Yet he knew he must see her again, even if in secret rendezvous, at least until he became his people's Runner—for he was certain that he would be. His chieftain father had already spoken in council of how Bold

Wolf deserved such an honor. Bold Wolf had proved to be the fastest of all men his age.

"Why do you have shells in your basket?" Bold Wolf asked, eyeing their beautiful colors. His people used shells to decorate their clothes and lodges. Surely she did the same, yet the dress she wore had none of it.

"I just find them so pretty, that's all," Shanna said softly, sighing with disappointment when the butterfly took wing and fluttered away. "I would hope one day to find a conch shell. They fascinate me even more than butterflies."

"Meet me again?" Bold Wolf quickly asked, taking her hand, holding it.

"My parents would forbid it," Shanna said, her breath catching, her knees weakening with the bliss of his hand actually holding hers!

"We would do nothing shameful," Bold Wolf said, his voice softly pleading. He raised his eyes and nodded toward a bluff that overlooked Old Town and the river. "Meet me there tomorrow when the sun is at the midpoint in the sky."

Shanna's eyes followed his gaze. What a thrill it would be to meet him there. It would be as though they were the only two people on the earth. They could share their most hidden secrets there!

"I will be eating dinner then," Shanna said, her heart pounding as she realized she was actually considering meeting Bold Wolf in private!

When she saw an instant disappointment shadow his beautiful, dark eyes, she quickly blurted, "But I can come shortly after."

There! she marveled to herself. She had said it! She *was* going to meet him!

In truth, she could hardly believe that any of this

was happening. Surely it was a dream, and she would soon awaken and only find herself in her dreary bed!

But when Bold Wolf spoke again, she knew it was true . . . every wonderful moment of it was absolutely true!

"I will be there," Bold Wolf said, his eyes now lit with excitement.

"Oh, *no*! Shanna!"

When Shanna heard her mother cry out behind her, she turned quickly and saw her standing just inside the clearing with the baby buggy, in which her two brothers lay.

She saw the utter shock in her mother's eyes. With a gasp, paling, Shanna took a quick step away from Bold Wolf.

"Mama, I . . . I . . . have made friends with Bold Wolf," Shanna stammered out. "Mama, Bold Wolf's father is the chief at Indian Island."

"Shanna, I *told* you . . ." her mother said, stopping short of ranting and raving at Shanna about ignoring her warning.

Instead, her round face red with anger, her mother reached a hand out. "Come with me, Shanna," she said. "Come *now*."

Shanna gave Bold Wolf a wavering, apologetic look, then ran away from him and walked in haste beside her mother as they made their way toward town.

"I told you never to get near those Indians," her mother scolded. "Especially one of their boys." Her mother stared at her. "You could have been raped, Shanna. Raped!"

Shanna swallowed hard. She looked quickly over her shoulder at Bold Wolf as he walked toward a beached birch-bark canoe. She was taken by how sure he was in his movements. Although her mother kept fussing at her to turn around, to pay attention to what she was saying, Shanna continued to watch Bold Wolf. He shoved his canoe into the water, then went knee-deep into the river and climbed aboard, paddling across the bay toward Indian Island.

She heard her mother using the word *rape* in the same breath as Bold Wolf's name. Shanna ignored her. She knew that no one as gentle as Bold Wolf could ever rape anyone.

And she knew that she would be his friend as long as he wished her to be!

She could hardly wait until tomorrow, when they would be with each other again—for nothing would stand in the way of her going to the high bluff to meet him.

Thinking of being together with him in secret gave her a strange thrill that made her blush.

2

The thirst that from the soul doth rise,
Doth ask a drink divine,
But might I of Jove's nectar sip,
I would not change for thine.
                                    —BEN JONSON

July—the adji-tae-gizus,
"Berry Ripe Moon," 1880

The evening sun was losing its strength as Shanna
stood high on the bluff that had been hers and Bold
Wolf's secret meeting place until he had come to her
one day, brimming with excitement, with the news that
finally he had been appointed the Runner for his
village.

Shanna had not shared his exuberance. And he had
a short while later become sad himself, realizing that
because the rules of his people forbade their Runners
from speaking or being with women, Shanna and he
would no longer be able to have their rendezvous.
They had shared so much! Especially innocent, wonderful kisses after Shanna had become sixteen and felt
it was not a shameful thing to be kissed by the young
man she adored.

It had been two years now since she had been able
to speak to, or be with, Bold Wolf. Whenever they
had met in town, they had gazed into each other's
eyes with a longing only they understood.

And then Shanna had become ill with pneumonia,
so ill that she had not recovered as quickly as she

should have, and she had been taken to a warmer climate to recuperate at her Aunt Bessie's house in New Orleans, until her lungs were strong again. She had been completely taken away from the man she loved.

She had been back at Old Town now for a month and she had only now come to this place of rendez-vous. She had not been here, in fact, since the evening Bold Wolf had told her their meetings had to stop. She had not been able to bear being here without him.

But now she could not stay away. She hadn't seen Bold Wolf since her return from New Orleans. She had earnestly looked for him every time she shopped in Old Town, hoping to see him as he bought supplies.

But not once had she seen him.

She had recently heard gossip about the failing health of Bold Wolf's father. She knew that Bold Wolf stayed closer to home now to see to his widowed father's needs, since he was the only child and thought so highly of his father.

"I miss you so," Shanna whispered, gazing intensely at Indian Island. It was a physical hurt, this need she felt for the man she loved. "Oh, have you missed me as much? Two years, Bold Wolf. Two long years. I don't know if I can stand to wait much longer."

When she thought that she was going to die during the worst of the pneumonia that had robbed her of her strength, she had wondered: If she were lying on her deathbed, would Bold Wolf have been allowed to come and say last words to her?

She knew that a "custodian" had been appointed for Bold Wolf, someone who watched his every move. Bold Wolf's custodian was his grand-uncle He Who Watches. And he guarded Bold Wolf well, to make sure that his grand-nephew did nothing that might weaken his endurance and fleetness.

Worst of all, Bold Wolf was denied the pleasures of women. That was why the Runners were also called "Pure Men."

"We are still young," Shanna whispered, always trying to convince herself that she should be able to endure their separation. "I am now eighteen, Bold Wolf is twenty-three. We have a lifetime ahead of us."

But that lifetime also included the time he still would spend as a Runner. She wondered now if he would ever be free to marry her.

She had tried to pour her heart and soul into her violin playing. She had wanted to feel passionate about it. But nothing surpassed Bold Wolf in her heart. Her passion was only for him.

Still weak from her illness, Shanna knew she must sit down and rest before venturing back down the side of the hill, to return home before night fell with its cloak of black. She spread the skirt of her dress beneath her and sat down on a soft cushion of moss, becoming lost in thought, her mind drifting back to that day when Bold Wolf had said good-bye.

Tears misted her eyes as she felt the despair rise again. That day of their last meeting, Shanna rushed through the forest at the edge of Old Town, and then up the steep hill to the secret meeting place. When she saw him standing there, waiting for her, her heart pounded with excitement. Yet as she drew closer, her smile and her excitement faded. Bold Wolf had a solemn look on his face that she would never forget. He looked as though someone close to him might have died.

She hurried to him and flung herself into his arms. She could remember now, as though it were yesterday, the desperation in his hug. And when he kissed her, she felt a sense of desperation, as though the kiss would be their last!

Then she eased from his arms and asked what was wrong.

He had told her he was feeling torn. He was proud and happy, yet on the other hand, his heart was steeped in sadness . . . for he could no longer meet with her, nor could they speak if they did see one another in Old Town!

She would never forget the despair she felt at the thought of being denied their private moments together. She had always known that this day would come, but that made the reality of it no less painful.

She was strong enough that day to keep herself from begging him to reconsider being his people's Runner. She knew just how long he had aspired to this honor.

And when he asked for her to wait for him, promising her that he would not be the Runner forever, she vowed to him her undying love.

Yes! she had told him. Yes! She would wait for him. And despite how her parents would feel about it, whenever Bold Wolf was free to marry her, she would be proud to become his wife.

The splashing of ash paddles in the river below brought Shanna from her deep reverie. Her heart leaped with a quick, hot passion when she saw it was Bold Wolf in his canoe, crossing over to Old Town!

Her pulse racing, her cheeks suddenly hot with excitement, Shanna leaped to her feet and began waving at Bold Wolf. He finally saw her, and her insides melted as their eyes locked in a silent message of love and adoration.

And then she saw another canoe. Bold Wolf's grand-uncle He Who Watches was coming up behind Bold Wolf.

Had he seen Bold Wolf looking up at Shanna? If so, would Bold Wolf be punished?

Shanna paled at the thought. But perhaps He Who Watches hadn't yet seen her standing there.

She hurried from the edge of the bluff and hid in a thick stand of birch trees. When she thought Bold Wolf and He Who Watches might have gone on past, she inched back to the edge of the bluff and looked down at the river again.

She was torn. She would have loved seeing Bold Wolf for a while longer, yet she knew it was best that he was gone. She didn't want to be responsible for Bold Wolf being stripped of his Runner status. She knew how much it meant to him. He had temporarily chosen it over her.

Tired and aching inside over missing Bold Wolf, Shanna walked down the hill. She could not help but be bitter toward He Who Watches. Those few times when she and Bold Wolf had seen each other in town before her illness, and they had come close to actually speaking, Bold Wolf's grand-uncle had stepped into view to act as a reminder of Bold Wolf's vows.

Shanna saw He Who Watches as no less than a spy. His wrinkled, leathery face always had a perpetual look of stern disapproval, almost a scowl. She didn't see how Bold Wolf could stand having him around, spying on him both night and day.

With violin practice ahead of her, having put it off long enough today, Shanna hurried to her home, which sat stately tall at the top of Stillwater Avenue Hill.

As she started up the steps of the two-story house, with its lovely gingerbread lace trim around a large, circular porch, she dreaded going inside. She despised her father's profession no less now than when he was new at it. It made her shiver even now to think of where his preparation room was. The room where he prepared bodies for burial was in back on the lower floor, just beneath Shanna's bedroom.

A local woman, Nancy Bramlett, had died yesterday. Her body had been prepared earlier this morning and now lay at rest in its casket in the viewing room, awaiting the funeral tomorrow.

As Shanna stood on the front porch, she stared at the window behind which lay the dead woman. Only a filmy, sheer curtain hid this fact. She dreaded going past the room, where the casket sat on a bier in a circular groove under the front window in what was once the parlor of the grand mansion, but she had no choice. She had to pass that room to get to the stairs that took her up to her room.

Shanna shuddered, then went inside.

She closed her eyes as she ran past the viewing room. Then she opened them and made a mad dash upstairs, hurrying into her bedroom.

After closing the door, she rested against it, panting. Then she went to the window, drew back the sheer white curtain, and peered toward Indian Island. It was growing dusk and she could see a huge outdoor fire on the island. She was able to forget the morbid thoughts of a dead body in her house when she thought again of Bold Wolf. Was he also thinking of her?

"Shanna, where on earth have you been?"

Her mother's voice behind her drew Shanna quickly around. Her mother had opened the door and was walking toward her, her hands on her thick hips.

Shanna's mother had given birth to the twins late in her life; the twins were twelve years younger than Shanna. Bernita's hair was all gray now and was swirled atop her head in a tight bun. There were tiny wrinkles at the corners of her eyes and mouth. There was a feathering of a mustache above her lips, and she now weighed nearly two hundred pounds.

"I needed to take a walk," Shanna said, moving away from the window. She lifted her violin case from the floor to her bed and opened it. "You know how before practicing sometimes I love to walk in the forest. It seems to prepare me somehow for the long hour of practice."

"*Must* you practice this evening?" Bernita said. She closed the lid of the violin case. "That racket is enough to wake the dead. Poor Mrs. Bramlett downstairs. Surely she would not enjoy hearing the squawking of your violin."

"Mama, when I play the violin, it does not 'squawk,'" Shanna said, sighing heavily. "And, Mama, Mrs. Bramlett is . . . is dead."

"Now, don't get smart with me, young lady," Bernita said with a loud snort. "Certainly Mrs. Bramlett is dead." She took her hand away from the violin case as Shanna slowly began lifting the lid again. "But do you still have to practice, Shanna? The boys have been fussing something terrible. I have just prepared them for bed. I hope they will be asleep soon so I can have a few moments to myself."

"Mama, if Father knew how you so often tried to persuade me not to practice my violin, he would be appalled," Shanna said, lifting the violin from the case and laying it on the bed.

"You don't share his love for the violin," Bernita said over her shoulder as she waddled toward the door.

"No, but neither do I only play it to make Father happy," Shanna said, taking the bow from the case, slowly tightening its horse hairs. "I do enjoy playing. I just don't aspire to go as far with it as Father wishes. I shall never be a world-renowned concert violinist."

She wanted so badly to tell her mother that she would only continue playing the violin until Bold Wolf told her he was free to take her as his wife. But she knew telling her mother this would absolutely mortify her—far worse than a mere moment or two of fussing over violin practice.

Bernita turned and gazed at Shanna, then stepped toward her and gently placed a hand on her brow. "Shanna, are you all right?" she murmured, the soft side of her personality surfacing. "You are somewhat flushed." She stepped back and eyed Shanna more closely. "And there is something in your eyes I haven't seen since before your illness. What has caused it? What happened today while you were out getting a breath of air? Did you overdo it? Did you walk too far? Did you get too much sun?"

"No, it's none of those things, Mama," Shanna murmured, glancing at the window, again thinking of Bold Wolf. It had been so wonderful to see him again. It made her feel warm inside and it had even given her the desire to play her violin again. While playing, now she would think of how their eyes had locked and held and how in his she saw the same promise she had seen before.

Yes, he still wanted her!

One day she would be his wife!

"What, then, is the matter with you?" Bernita said, kneading her pointed chin as Shanna slowly ran her tightened bow over the small, golden cake of rosin. "I haven't seen you this pink-cheeked for some time now."

"I'm just so glad to be well again, Mama," Shanna said, placing the rosin inside her case. She lifted her violin and tucked it beneath her chin.

She reached for her bow and hesitated before placing it on the strings. She gave her mother a wavering

look. "I truly must practice now, Mama," she murmured. "Just close my door *and* yours to your bedroom. I won't disturb you as much with two doors
closed between us."

"If you insist on practicing, then get in a full hour,
for you know that your father is in his office down
the hall and will be timing you," Bernita said, then
went on out and closed the door behind her.

"Mama, Mama," Shanna whispered to herself.

She went to the window and gazed toward Indian
Island.

Placing the bow on her strings, curving the fingers
of her left hand up over them, she began playing, still
gazing over at the island, the fire's glow in the center
of the village now lighting up the dark heavens with
its wavering, golden light.

"Is he thinking of *me* now?" she whispered as she
played something soft, beautiful, and filled with tenderness, yet with a deep, haunted longing.

3

An Image gay,
To haunt, to startle, and way-lay.
—WILLIAM WORDSWORTH

Only half aware of his grand-uncle beaching his canoe a few feet away from where he had secured his own, and most definitely ignoring the sparkle of anger glinting in his grand-uncle's old eyes, Bold Wolf walked away from the river and up the slight hill toward his village, where in the center the flames of a huge outdoor fire leaped high into the sky.

Bold Wolf's mind was still on seeing Shanna standing so beautiful on the bluff. He had not seen her for a couple years. When their eyes met, if only for a few lingering moments, he had still seen in hers her silent, deep promise of enduring love for him. Now he knew that she still cared . . . that she still waited for him!

Today his purpose for crossing the bay was to break his vows as the village Runner and go to Shanna's house to inquire about her welfare, to ask her outright if she had fallen out of love with him.

It was as though fate had drawn her to the bluff today. Actually seeing her was the only thing that could have stopped him from doing something that would have stripped him of his title of Runner.

Now that he knew she was all right, he felt he could hold on for a while longer, without hearing her voice and feeling her sweetness in his arms.

But he was still puzzled about why he had not seen her for so long. He was most certainly puzzled over why she suddenly appeared on the bluff *now*. As far as he knew, she had not been there since their parting words on the day he told her it was time for him to live the life of a Runner.

Yes, it must have been fate that had sent her to the bluff today. Surely she had been guided there by the heavy medicine of *M-teoulin*, the Penobscot's Great Spirit. The mighty one above knew that now was not the time for Bold Wolf to abandon his life as Runner. If Bold Wolf had spoken even one scarce word to Shanna, he would have broken the sacred vows he had made in the presence of his chieftain father and the people of his village!

Bold Wolf was not sure if he could have lived with the humiliation of letting his people down in such a way—especially his chieftain father. If he had broken his vows, he would have felt too ashamed to take Shanna as his wife—not when everyone knew it was because of her he had brought shame upon himself.

But no shame was brought upon anyone this day, he thought proudly. Even if his grand-uncle had seen him gazing up at Shanna, that in itself was not breaking his vows. Exchanged looks of longing were not the same as words spoken aloud *of* such feelings.

Yes, he was still the Runner, and Shanna was still patiently waiting for him.

Feeling relieved now, Bold Wolf hastened toward his father's dwelling. The sky was dark. Stars shone like tiny dancing moonbeams against the velveteen backdrop. Casting its silvery sheen over everything, the moon was full.

Yes, Bold Wolf thought, it was a beautiful night filled with magical, whispering shadows, and he felt at peace with himself. Always when he looked into the future he felt good about it, for in that future lay the moment he could once again hold and kiss his Shanna.

But when Chief War Eagle's cabin came into sight, Bold Wolf was reminded that not everything was as he wished it to be. A sadness quickly gripped his heart. His father's health had worsened these past several weeks. He had not been well since a skirmish with a faction of Indians the Penobscot were not familiar with.

It had happened when Chief War Eagle accompanied several of his warriors in their canoes to harvest fish in the larger waterways away from Penobscot River. The ambush had been quick and deadly. More than one Penobscot warrior had died. Several were wounded.

The arrow shaft that had embedded itself near Chief War Eagle's heart could only be partially removed. Cloud Racer, the village shaman, had warned that disturbing the arrow so close to the chief's heart might be instantly fatal, whereas if it was left alone, War Eagle could live for a while longer.

Infection had now set in and War Eagle had refused to give Bold Wolf permission to bring a white doctor with his healing medicines from Old Town. War Eagle had told Bold Wolf that he welcomed death over being touched by the hands of a white witch doctor.

Chief War Eagle had also told Bold Wolf that he welcomed death for another reason. He would be joining his wife in the hereafter. After his wife had been bitten by a deadly snake, she had died some moons ago.

Bold Wolf knew his father had never accepted his wife's death. He especially had not been able to fight off the loneliness that ate away at him as each day passed without his Orenda.

Bold Wolf walked through his village, gazing at the

dwellings that comprised it. They varied in structure. Some were made of logs, their roofs of elm or sheets of evergreen bark. But the most common dwelling in his village was the conical birch-bark wigwam.

Because of their status in the village, both Bold Wolf and his father lived in more elaborate dwellings. Living separately, theirs were rectangular single-room log houses with gabled roofs made of cedar shakes.

Now at the door of his father's house, Bold Wolf stopped and inhaled a deep, shuddering breath. He dreaded his father's death. When War Eagle was gone, a piece of Bold Wolf would die with him. Because Bold Wolf was the only child—the only *son*—the two had bonded closely in thought and deed.

Yet Bold Wolf would endure. As it was when he lost his precious, gentle mother, he would accept his father's death and move on with his life.

Shanna would then be a part of that life, for once his father was gone, Bold Wolf would no longer be the Runner for his village. He would be chief. He would then be free to marry.

Bold Wolf lifted the east-facing, tanned moose-hide door flap and stepped quietly inside his father's lodge. He paused for a moment just inside and gazed at his father, noting how quietly he lay on his bed. His father's back was to him. He could not tell if War Eagle was asleep or . . .

He swallowed hard and would not allow himself to think the worst. Yet he hesitated going over to his father. If he was soundly sleeping, Bold Wolf did not want to awaken him. At least while his father was asleep he was not conscious of his grueling pain.

Still hesitating, Bold Wolf looked slowly around him. The interior was lit not only by the lodge fire, but also by the soft glow of a kerosene lamp that sat on a hand-hewn table at the right-hand side of the door.

A feeling of melancholy swept through Bold Wolf, for before he had grown old enough to have his own private lodge, he had shared this home with his parents.

As it was those long years past, there were still three bed spaces in the large room. Separated into spaces on the wooden floor by three logs, the beds were made of evenly laid spruce and fir boughs covered with tanned skins.

There was scarcely any other furniture in the cabin. When people came for a visit, in the winter they sat on blankets or birch-bark mats before the fireplace. In the summer they sat outside, where the breezes were filled with the fresh scent of river water and pine.

He took one last look around him and wondered if Shanna could accept such a house as this over the huge mansion she was accustomed to. Certainly this cabin was nothing in comparison. Supplies such as wooden dishes, cooking ware, food, and spare blankets were kept in a separate wigwam not far from the cabin.

Valued drums, medicine bundles, shields, and weapons were kept inside the cabin.

Rarely did anyone find a Penobscot lodge that appeared cluttered. The Penobscot were a people who believed in neatness and cleanliness.

His Shanna was both neat and clean, so surely she would see the good of how the man she would marry lived.

"Is that you, Bold Wolf?"

His father's voice brought Bold Wolf from his thoughts. He hurried across the room and sat down beside his father's bed of boughs and blankets. It tore at Bold Wolf's heart to see his father's sunken cheeks, his eyes two dark pools in his face.

It was evident to Bold Wolf that his father's temperature had risen. His face was flushed. His eyes were red and bloodshot.

A blanket drawn up only to his father's waist revealed how tightly his copper skin was now drawn over his bones.

Bold Wolf wanted to turn his eyes away when he saw the puckered, festered skin that clung around the arrow shaft that protruded from his father's chest. Something whitish green oozed from the wound tonight.

The terrible stench of it reached up inside Bold Wolf's nose, giving him a sick feeling at the pit of his stomach.

"Father, I wish you would allow me to—" Bold Wolf began, but stopped when his father began slowly shaking his head back and forth.

"Do not say the words again to me that you know I do not wish to hear," War Eagle said, his voice weak and drawn. "I want no white doctors ever in our village, my son. My death might be coming slow, but it is a peaceful one. My Orenda, your mother, smiles just on the other side. I see her beckoning to me with her delicate hands. I can even hear her soft laughter."

"It is a lovely night," Bold Wolf said, fighting back tears. Hearing his father speak of such things tore at Bold Wolf's very being. He knew his father was only hearing and seeing his wife because of the poisons flowing through his veins, into his brain.

"The stars are bright tonight, my son?" War Eagle murmured. He gazed toward the closed door flap, and then to a window where the buckskin covering had been drawn aside so that fresh air could waft into the room. "Ah, I see the brightness of the moon. I hear the night sounds. There is such peace here on our island for our people." He turned his eyes back to Bold Wolf. "Is that not so, my son?"

"Yes, there is much peace for our people," Bold Wolf said. He placed a gentle hand on his father's brow, grimacing when he felt the heat there. "Because of *you,* Father, there is such a peace. Your leadership has led our people into a time of harmony with the *webala-giks,* white-eyes. Our people can go to Old Town and gather supplies without feeling threatened. It is because of you, Father, that this is possible."

"And it will be so when you are chief, my son," War Eagle said thickly. "As you know, the office of head chief, *sa-ngama,* strong man, is held for life. The hereditary chieftainship continues with you. Someone else will be named Runner as you will be named chief."

"I do not wish to talk about anyone being chief besides you, Father," Bold Wolf said, his eyes wavering. "This thing that has you down now will pass. I know it. The wound will soon heal. You will rise again and walk among your people."

War Eagle laughed throatily. "Yes, I would walk among our people with an arrow shaft protruding from my body," he said. "Would not that be an amusing sight?"

"Not amusing," Bold Wolf said tightly. "It will be a thing of wonder. It will be proof of your strength, not only as a man, but also as a chief. Father, you will live. You will!"

"You try so hard to convince yourself of that, you almost succeed at convincing your tired old father," War Eagle said, sighing heavily. He reached for Bold Wolf's hand and clutched it. He gazed intensely up at Bold Wolf as the fire's glow shadow-danced across his son's handsome face. "My son, was the *webala-giks phe-nam,* white-eyes woman, standing on the bluff? Did your eyes meet? Was there still promise in hers? Has she stayed true to her promise to you, as you have stayed true to your vows as Runner?''

Bold Wolf was so taken aback by what his father said, he felt the color leave his face. Speechless, he stared at his father for a moment longer.

"How could you know?" he asked guardedly, his eyes wide in wonder. His father wasn't strong enough to leave his bed, much less travel to the riverbank to look across at the high bluff on Old Town's side of the river. So how *could* he know about Shanna?

"I saw her in a vision," War Eagle said, slowly nodding. "As I saw her in a vision with you before you became Runner for our people. She is as beautiful now as then, is she not?"

"You know about Shanna?" Bold Wolf gasped. "You even knew about her before I became Runner?"

"My visions reveal everything to me," War Eagle said proudly.

"Then you know of my love for Shanna," Bold Wolf said, swallowing hard. "You also know that I gazed up at her today, nothing *more.* I am still true to my vows."

"Yes, I know all of those things," War Eagle said, releasing Bold Wolf's hand. He pulled his blanket up over his aching chest, leaving it to rest just beneath his chin. "As I know that soon you will be free to choose a wife. When I am gone, and you are chief, your confined life as a Runner then only a memory, you *will* want a wife to lay with you in your blankets. If you choose a woman for this honor who is white, you have my blessing."

"But you have never been fond of any *webala-giks,*" Bold Wolf said, again guardedly. "Why would you feel different about Shanna? Her skin *is* white. She has been raised by parents who are prejudiced against our people."

"Yes, all of that is true," War Eagle said. "But I can look past that, since I know of this woman's gentleness and her deep love for you. Such a love can only happen once in a lifetime. I knew such love. It was fate that led my heart to a woman of my same skin coloring. It was fate that led you to someone of a different culture. You are no less blessed than I, for to love and to be loved in such a way as I know you are loved is a blessing from high above. It was M'Teoulin, Great Spirit, that brought you and this gentle-hearted woman together those long years ago when she was but a child and you were a young brave who would one day be the leader of your people."

"Father, had I not met Shanna as I did when we were younger, and had I not bonded so quickly with her, I, too, would never have considered a white woman for a wife," Bold Wolf said softly. "But I *did* meet her. I *did* bond with her. There is no other woman like her, red- or white-skinned. I, too, believe M'teoulin brought us together."

"Then she *is* the right woman for you," War Eagle said softly. "When you are free to do so, love her openly. Bring her among our people. Let them grow to love her as you do."

War Eagle paused, sighed, then continued. "You will have many sons and daughters with this woman." He slowly closed his eyes. "Oh, if I could but have lived to see and embrace your children . . . my . . . grandchildren."

"There will be many children born of our love?" Bold Wolf asked softly.

"Many, many . . ." his father said, his voice trailing off.

Bold Wolf was truly in awe of his father's skills in

seeing the future. Never before had his father talked of such things to Bold Wolf, especially of having visions that gave him such knowledge. Bold Wolf had to believe it was not so much visions that gave him such insight, but the fever adding strength to his hallucinations.

Yet that truly could not be the answer, Bold Wolf argued to himself. His father knew too much that was true for it to be brought on by hallucinations!

"Father, will I ever have the power of visions such as you?" Bold Wolf asked—but knew, when his father did not answer him, that he had drifted off to sleep again.

Bold Wolf leaned over his father and brushed a soft kiss against his cheek. "Sleep, Father," he whispered. "Find peace and relief from your pain in your dreams."

He hesitated before rising to leave.

Then hunger gnawing at the pit of his stomach reminded him that he had not yet eaten his evening meal. He rose quietly and left his father's lodge.

When he arrived at his own cabin, not far from his father's, he found He Who Watches sitting outside on a blanket, his head down, a red blanket wrapped around his shoulders, his long gray hair nestled around him on the ground.

The way the old man's head bobbed, Bold Wolf could tell he was fighting sleep so that he could be sure Bold Wolf would not follow his heart back to Old Town where the white woman who had stolen Bold Wolf's heart lived.

At this moment, Bold Wolf saw his grand-uncle as a lonely *ktcialna-be,* old man, whose wife had passed on to the other side too soon, leaving He Who Watches sad and empty inside.

Bold Wolf now filled the empty spaces of his grand-uncle's heart and he would never resent He Who Watches when he sometimes became a little adamant in his viewpoints concerning Bold Wolf.

He Who Watches raised his head and looked up at Bold Wolf through eyes that were narrowed to wrinkled slits.

"Come inside, *Ah-Koh,* Grand-Uncle, and share food with me," Bold Wolf said, holding the entrance flap aside. "Then we shall both get our sleep."

He Who Watches smiled and nodded. His long gray hair swept the ground as he rose to his feet. Nothing was said between them about that brief moment when Bold Wolf's eyes had met and held Shanna's. For now it was forgotten between blood kin who were also friends.

Bold Wolf found food warming in the hot coals of the fireplace along his far back wall. The women of the village took turns bringing food to his lodge. To-night he found *nsa-boen,* soup, made from *maso-sied,* fiddle beans from the village garden, and *penak,* wild potatoes from the forest, cooked with deer meat.

In silence, Bold Wolf and He Who Watches ate their fill. Bold Wolf knew what was on He Who Watches's mind as he kept gazing at him, yet still not one word was said about Bold Wolf's shared gaze with Shanna.

But Bold Wolf knew enough to avoid tempting fate too often, or he would get an earful from his uncle— or worse. There were punishments that were handed out to a Runner before going so far as to strip him of his honorable title!

4

I love your arms when the warm, white flesh
Touches mine in a fond embrace.
                    —ELLA WHEELER WILCOX

The plate of scrambled eggs that sat before her on the
table, and the untouched toast that was heaped with
butter and jelly on a separate plate, made Shanna
wrinkle her nose and turn her eyes away.

She started to leave the breakfast table, but the firm
hand of her father on her arm as he reached over
from the other side of the table made her quickly
change her mind.

"Shanna, you've got to eat or you'll never get all
of your strength back," Jordan said in his low, yet
authoritative voice. He eased his hand from her arm.
"I don't want you having a setback."

Shanna gazed over at him and felt herself shrink
beneath his commanding violet eyes. A tall and lanky
man with delicate features, he was always dressed im-
maculately in his black fustian suits. His hair was the
same color of reddish orange as Shanna's and lay just
above his stiffly starched white collar.

She cringed when she got a slight whiff of embalming fluid that seemed always to cling to his skin,
hair, and clothes.

Twisting and untwisting the napkin on her lap,
Shanna found the courage to speak her mind, yet always felt she was on dangerous ground to do so. Al-

though her father was not a strict disciplinarian, when he spoke his mind, he meant for his children to listen and obey.

"But Papa, nothing has tasted good since I was so ill," she said guardedly. "Everything tastes like cardboard to me."

"Shanna, your father is right," Bernita said, reaching over to scoot Shanna's plate closer to her. "Shanna, eat. Eat *now*. If you don't, you will be late for your violin lesson."

"Daughter, I heard you practicing last night," Jordan said, dabbing at his lips with a white linen napkin. "If I hadn't been so immersed in my journals, I would have come and told you to retune your strings. The E string was flat. Couldn't you hear it? Or is playing the violin like eating these days . . . you just don't care?"

Shanna paled. "Papa," she gasped. "I *do* care. And I . . . I . . . didn't hear the flatness of the E string. I thought I had it tuned perfectly."

"Listen more closely next time," Jordan said stiffly. He rose from his chair and walked away from the table.

"Eat, Shanna," he said over his shoulder. "Eat everything on that plate and then hurry on over to Mr. Lovett's. I don't pay him for your violin lessons only to have you arrive late for them."

"Yes, Papa, I shall hurry," Shanna said, grimacing as she plucked up a bite of eggs with her fork. She was scarcely aware of her brothers leaving the table, laughing and playfully hitting one another as they left the bright and sunny breakfast room. She was forcing herself to concentrate on eating . . . only eating. . . .

"I shall sit with you until you are through," Bernita said, setting down beside Shanna at the table. She poured herself a cup of tea from a beautiful silver tea service. She took a slow sip, then set the cup down again as she watched Shanna struggling with her breakfast. It made her uncomfortable to see her daughter struggle with each bite.

Finally she pulled Shanna's fork away with one hand, the plate of food with the other.

"Go on, child," Bernita said softly. "Go to your violin lesson."

"But Mama, I didn't eat everything," Shanna said. Eyes wide, she watched her mother take her plate and scrape the uneaten eggs and toast into a wastebasket. "Mama, if Papa found out—"

"He won't," Bernita said, her jaw tight as she turned and gave Shanna a determined look. "Now go on, Shanna. Forget this happened. Your father need never know."

Smiling, relieved that her mother understood, Shanna hurried from her chair. "Thank you, Mama," she murmured, embracing her. Then she stepped away from her mother and started for the door.

"How is Jennifer these days?" Bernita asked as she gathered the other soiled dishes from the table. "Is she still able to be at Mr. Lovett's for her violin lessons? Is her crazy father allowing it?"

"Yes, Jennie is still allowed to be there for her lessons," Shanna said, in her mind's eye seeing her best friend, whose life was nothing like Shanna's. Her family was poor and her father was an abusive man.

At times Shanna had even feared for her friend's life, especially after Jennie Anderson had told her how her father would beat her mother after he came home from a night of drinking whiskey at one of Old Town's saloons.

"And how *is* she, Shanna?" Bernita asked, removing her apron and hanging it on a peg on the wall. "I worry so about her. It's no secret around town about her father and what he is capable of."

"As far as I know he hasn't touched Jennie, but he curses her terribly and threatens her," Shanna said somberly. "And Mama, thank you again for taking food to Jennie's mother. Jennie says she hopes that one day she will find a way to repay you and Papa for everything, especially for paying for her private violin lessons."

"I just wish there was more we could do for her family," Bernita said. She took Shanna gently by the arm and walked with her from the kitchen. "Jennifer has so many brothers and sisters. The food baskets I take over there surely last for only one or two days."

"What you have given them is quite a blessing," Shanna said, grimacing when she was forced to walk past the room in which Nancy Bramlett still lay. The services for her were later in the day. The flowers were now standing with their sickening sweet smell around the casket.

Shanna was glad to have an excuse to leave the house today. Soon people would be arriving for the funeral. The house would be filled with the mournful sounds of organ music and people crying.

Shanna hoped that no one else would replace Nancy Bramlett in the parlor for many days. It would be wonderful to know that for at least one week no dead bodies lay beneath the roof of their home!

Shanna lifted her violin case by the handle and started for the door. "I'm so glad that Jennie's mother had the violin in her family, or Jennie would have never known her love of the instrument," she said over her shoulder. "I've never seen anyone so passionate about playing the violin as Jennie is."

"Your father would love for you to have such passion over your violin," her mother said, opening the front door, breathing in the fresh air as it wafted in from outside.

Shanna stopped and gazed at her mother, so badly wishing that she were free to share with her just where her true passions lay. It was a secret that Shanna had shared with no one but Bold Wolf.

Shanna would never forget how her mother had looked at Bold Wolf that day so long ago when she had found Shanna and Bold Wolf talking among the white birch trees. There had been a look of utter disgust in her mother's eyes, as though Bold Wolf were nothing more than a mouse that everyone abhorred having in their homes.

Shanna wondered just how her mother was going to react when Shanna eventually married Bold Wolf. Surely Shanna would be disowned by both her mother and father. She hoped not, but nothing, no one, would force her into giving up Bold Wolf. Not even her parents.

Dressed in a lovely violet cotton dress, with white eyelets around the wide collar and the cuffs of her sleeves, and her hair held back from her face with a matching violet velveteen bow, Shanna gave her mother a quick hug, then stepped out onto the wide porch and hurried down the front steps.

Although she loved her parents dearly, she could not help but truly enjoy these moments of freedom away from them. She hated the fact that, though she was old enough now to be married, she had to behave like a child under the thumb of her parents. If only Bold Wolf were free, she could be with him.

Sighing, knowing that she must be patient for a while longer, Shanna carried her violin to Main Street, grimacing at the thought that Roscoe Lovett's music studio was only a few doors down from the town's places of ill repute.

Even now Shanna's insides tightened as she walked past something new that had sprung up on a vacant lot between two brick establishments. It was a large tent that was being used as a new brothel.

Shanna's face became hot with a blush when several women stepped outside of the tent in their skimpy attire and started taunting Shanna, calling her a rich Miss Prissy!

Not even wanting to think of what went on inside the tent, Shanna rushed onward. She raced up an outside staircase that led over the Old Town General Store to the music studio, which was known to be the "only true culture for miles around."

Not having eaten enough breakfast to keep a flea alive, Shanna was breathless after the steep climb.

Jennie had seen her coming. She opened the door just as Shanna reached the landing at the head of the stairs.

"Shanna, I had begun to think you were going to miss your lessons today," Jennie said, taking Shanna's violin case from her as Shanna brushed past and went inside the studio.

Jennie, short, slender, her hair as black as a raven's wing, laid Shanna's violin case on a long table. She reached a gentle hand to Shanna's flushed cheek. "Are you all right? I would hate to think that you are not well enough yet to be here with me to take our lessons."

Shanna laughed softly. "I'm just fine," she said, taking Jennie's soft, long-fingered hand from her face. She squeezed it affectionately before releasing it. "I just haven't quite regained all of my strength."

Shanna gazed at Jennie's faded cotton dress. Because of Jennie's loveliness, few noticed the true signs of her family's poverty; her slippers' heels were worn flat and her clothes were faded.

The same age as Shanna, Jennie was petite yet well endowed. Today her breasts strained beneath the dress that Jennie had outgrown two years ago yet was still forced to wear because her father spent most of his lumberjack's pay in saloons and gambling halls. Shanna had even seen him leaving a brothel or two, with fancy women hanging on each arm.

"Are you two ready for your lessons?" Roscoe Lovett asked as he stepped from a small room where he kept his spare instrument parts. He had brought out a G string for Jennie's violin, her string having popped as she tuned her delicate, lovely instrument.

"Shanna, have you practiced an hour a day since your last lesson?" Roscoe asked as he carefully restrung Jennie's violin. "You know I encourage you to practice as much as possible. Only by practicing will you one day find yourself on a stage before throngs of people who will listen raptly to your playing."

"Yes, I have practiced enough," Shanna said. She most certainly was not going to admit to him that she never went beyond the one hour that was required of her. Too often it was a chore to get in the one hour that she knew she must admit to.

She gazed at Roscoe as he stood between her and Jennie. A bachelor, a man who was quite skilled at playing the flute, he was of average height, yet tall enough that both Shanna and Jennie had to look up at him.

His hair was the color of winter wheat and lay long down past his shoulders. His features were as lovely as a woman's, yet he was all brawn and muscle otherwise.

His blue eyes were piercing, especially when he was seriously teaching the fundamentals of the violin to his students.

"Let me check Jennie's other strings and then we shall get into our lessons for today," Mr. Lovett said, giving Jennie a smile that only recently Shanna had begun to notice was quite different from the smile he gave Shanna.

There seemed to be more to his feelings toward Jennie than merely being her teacher.

Yet it didn't seem that Jennie noticed it. She was too involved in her violin to think of anything else.

Finally the practice began. Shanna and Jennie stood side by side sharing one piece of music that was spread out on a stand before them. Shanna was always confident about her playing. She knew well the true sound of her strings and when she would or would not play a sour note. Rarely did she play off-key. And her fingers seemed born for the strings as they lifted and slid from place to place, string to string, as her right arm so masterfully drew the bow across them.

Suddenly Roscoe tapped his small wooden baton on the music stand so hard it snapped in two.

Startled by Roscoe's manner—he was usually so gentle and understanding—and seeing that he seemed to be focusing his sudden burst of displeasure on her, Shanna lifted her bow from the strings, held it down to her side, and took a slow step away from her violin teacher.

"Shanna, your fingers are too stiff today," Roscoe snapped, stooping to retrieve the other half of his broken baton from the floor. "You are even holding your bow too tightly. Surely you haven't practiced enough. Shanna, it takes practice, practice, practice to be a concert violinist."

"Sir, you know that Shanna hasn't been well," Jennie was quick to interject in defense of her best friend. "She has only recently resumed playing the violin after her pneumonia. Please don't ask so much of her."

Shanna smiled weakly over at Jennie, touched by

her genuine caring. Then she gasped when Roscoe took her violin away from her and lay it in the green velvet-lined case.

"I'm sorry," he said thickly. "I was wrong to scold you like that, Shanna." He glanced over at Jennie, then looked away from her and busied himself locking Shanna's violin case. "It's a beautiful day today. You two go on outside and enjoy the sunshine. We'll just make our lessons longer next time. And if you wish, leave your violin here for now, Shanna. Take a stroll, Shanna, you can come back later for your instrument. I'll be here for the rest of the day."

He looked nervously from Shanna to Jennie, then smiled awkwardly. "I'm sorry for my behavior," he said, sighing deeply. "I've . . . I've got a lot on my mind today besides music lessons."

Shanna and Jennie exchanged quick glances, but accepted his apologies and then left together, rushing down the steep stairs and past the brothel tent. Shanna didn't feel uncomfortable leaving her violin in her teacher's care. Jennie's violin never left the music room for fear of her father breaking it in a drunken rage if it were where he could find it at Jennie's home. Jennie arrived early at the music studio in order to practice.

"Mr. Lovett is in a strange mood today," Jennie said, looking up at the music room. "I wonder what's wrong. He seemed much too eager to get rid of us, don't you think, Shanna? While I was there before you, I watched him. I've never seen him so restless."

Shanna shrugged. "He's only human, Jennie," she said. "I guess he has problems just like everyone else."

"Yes, I guess so," Jennie said. "Shanna, let's take a walk through the forest." She took Shanna's hand. "Come on. It's been a while since we've done that. Do you feel like it? Do you?"

"Yes, I do, and, Jennie, I have a special place that I would like to show you," Shanna said, her thoughts on the bluff and how wonderful it had been to see Bold Wolf yesterday, if only from a distance.

Shanna had never thought she would share this special place with anyone but Bold Wolf. But if sitting there long enough would give her the opportunity to see her beloved again, she saw no harm in taking Jennie with her. It would be wonderful to sit there in the warm sunshine and talk.

She had missed her friend those longs months she had been away at New Orleans. They had a lot of catching up to do!

"A special place?" Jennie asked, her eyes wide with excitement. "Do you mean the pond where we used to swim all the time?"

"No, not there," Shanna said, her eyes dancing. "I'm taking you to an even more special place than that."

"Where, Shanna?" Jennie said excitedly. "Where are you taking me? You've never spoken to me of a special place before."

"That's because I shared it with only one other person," Shanna said. She heard Jennie suck in her breath, and realized her friend was assuming Shanna had another best friend besides herself.

"The person I have shared this with is a man," Shanna said. She felt Jennie's hand tighten in hers, and smiled when she saw the utter shock in her friend's eyes. "Yes, a man, Jennie. I have been in love with him for some time now and no one but he and I know it."

"But we have always shared secrets with one another about everything," Jennie said.

"Not *this* secret, Jennie," Shanna said, leading Jennie into the shadows of the forest, then on toward the bluff. She gave Jennie a skeptical gaze. "If I tell you about it, will you keep my secret? Your promise never to tell anyone?"

"You know that I wouldn't," Jennie said anxiously. "Oh, do tell me, Shanna. Tell me about this man. Where does he live? Do I know him?"

"Wait until we get to the bluff and then I shall tell you everything," Shanna said, now running as she saw the hill that led to the bluff through a break in the trees. "Come on, Jennie. It's not far now. Follow me. Oh, it is such a special place, with beautiful flowers and a view that is breathtaking."

"Shanna, this hill is so steep," Jennie cried as she lifted the skirt of her dress. "Are you certain you are strong enough? Should you be climbing the hill?"

"It is not the best thing for me, but I shall do it anyhow," Shanna said, puffing as the top of the bluff finally came into sight. "Just a little farther, Jennie. Then we can take all of the time we wish before heading back to Mr. Lovett's studio to get my violin."

"Have you noticed how Roscoe Lovett seems to be staring at me of late?" Jennie said, sighing with relief when they reached the top of the hill.

"Yes, and how do you feel about that?" Shanna asked, giving Jennie a quick glance as she took Jennie's hand and led her out to where moss ran thick and green to the edge of the bluff.

"He is such a handsome man I cannot feel anything but pleased at his sudden special attention," Jennie said, giggling. "But he is so much older than me. Surely he has no intentions toward me besides admiring, perhaps, how I play my violin, or perhaps even how I might hold my fingers on the strings." She shrugged. "Or whatever."

"He was quite cranky today about how I held *my*

fingers," Shanna said, frowning. "But, yes, perhaps he is admiring how you play your violin so skillfully."

"Perhaps," Jennie said, settling down on the mossy ground beside Shanna. She gazed in all directions, then looked over at Shanna. "This is such a perfect place for lovers to meet. Shanna, tell me about him. Did you . . . uh . . . you know. Did you?"

Shanna's cheeks grew hot with a blush. "No, we never went that far," she murmured as she stared across the bay at Indian Island. Oh, how she longed to see Bold Wolf again, if only a glimpse. "But Jennie, we did kiss, and he held me so tenderly!"

"Truly?" Jennie said, breathless. "He kissed you? He held you? Tell me how it felt. Tell me *who*. Who is this man you have fallen in love with?"

"You truly promise never to tell?" Shanna asked warily, looking intensely into Jennie's eyes.

"Never," Jennie said. She crossed her heart with a quick motion of her forefinger. "Cross my heart and hope to die, I promise, Shanna. Now please tell me. Please?"

"You have seen him, I am sure, in Old Town, as he came from Indian Island for supplies," Shanna said in a rush of words.

"From . . . Indian Island?" Jennie gasped, her eyes growing wider. "Only Penobscot Indians live on Indian Island. Are you saying that . . . you . . . ."

"Yes, I'm in love with an Indian," Shanna said, lifting her chin proudly. "His name is Bold Wolf. His father is chief. One day Bold Wolf will be chief."

"Bold Wolf?" Jennie said, in her voice the awe that she felt, knowing such a secret as this. "He's the one? You've actually kissed him?"

"Yes, and we are in love and plan to marry once he is free to marry," Shanna said dreamily. "That is, when he is no longer his people's Runner."

"You are going to marry him? And what is a Runner?" Jennie asked, so quickly she did not give Shanna a chance to answer.

Shanna took Jennie's hands. They sat facing one another as Shanna told Jennie everything. She told Jennie about the earlier years, how she and Bold Wolf had met and how they had continued to see one another in secret.

Shanna explained why she and Bold Wolf couldn't see one another at this time, and how long it had been since they had actually spoken.

"Jennie, never tell anyone what I have told you today," Shanna said, sliding her hands free and turning to stare with a longing at Indian Island. "Especially not my father. My father doesn't know that I will give up my violin playing for Bold Wolf, for, in truth, it is my father who wants my future as a concert violinist, not me."

"I can understand that," Jennie said, drawing Shanna around to gaze at her. "I think Bold Wolf is oh, so handsome. Even I would give up my dream of being a concert violinist if ever a man such as Bold Wolf would love *me*."

"You truly would?" Shanna gasped. "I thought you loved the violin so much that you would give up everything for the chance to play before a concert audience."

"Shanna, I do love my violin, but after having dreams of Bold Wolf, his arms reaching out for me, his lips so warm on mine, I could not honestly say that the violin is as important to me as it once was," Jennie said softly.

Shanna paled. She inched away from Jennie. "You have truly dreamed of Bold Wolf?" she asked, her voice breaking. "You would give up everything to have him? Do you love him, Jennie? Do you love Bold Wolf?"

Jennie burst into soft laughter. She reached out, grabbed Shanna by the waist, and drew her over to hug her. "I was only teasing you," she said, still laughing softly. "I have never dreamed of Bold Wolf. And no, I certainly don't love him. How could I? I have never actually met him . . . and you *know* that I can put nothing first before my love of my violin."

Relieved, and now feeling foolish, Shanna giggled and returned Jennie's hug. "Oh, but how special you are to me," she said, sighing. "I so value our friendship. Let's let nothing ever come between us, Jennie. Promise?"

"Promise," Jennie said. Then drew away from Shanna, her smile fading. "But Shanna, I do hope to meet someone someday who will take me away from my abusive father and my mother who allows it. Perhaps one day, while I am playing my violin on the stage before an audience, the man of my dreams will be there, watching."

Again Shanna hugged Jennie. "It will happen," she murmured. "You will have all that you wish for—a career as a famous violinist, and a man who adores you. Yes, it will happen."

"Promise?" Jennie said softly.

Shanna giggled. "Yes, I promise," she murmured. "Who knows, Jennie, it might even be Roscoe Lovett."

Jennie smiled, then her eyes were filled with a deep, haunting sadness. "Sometimes I think I would do anything to get away from my father," she said somberly.

Shanna heard the hate and desperation in her friend's voice and felt suddenly sad, *and* afraid for her.

5

Kiss me sweet, with your warm, wet mouth,
And say with a fervor born of the South,
That your body and soul are mine.
                    —ELLA WHEELER WILCOX

Her one hour of practice behind her for the evening, and so restless she could only pace her bedroom floor, Shanna's thoughts were torn between two people: Bold Wolf, whom she had not seen again since nearly a week ago when he had been crossing from Indian Island, and Jennie, whom she had not seen since the day Shanna had shared so many of her treasured secrets with her friend on the bluff.

Jennie had now missed five days of violin practice and lessons. There had been no note sent with an explanation for her absence.

Shanna was haunted by Jennie's bitter words about her father. Shanna could not help but think that Jennie's father was the reason Jennie had not been seen or heard from!

The moon spilling its silvery light through Shanna's bedroom window drew her attention. She moved to the window and, gazing up at the sky, marveled over just how bright the moon *was* tonight. It seemed twice as bright as normal.

She saw just how lit up everything was outside. Except for dark shadows here and there, it was so clear one surely could move around freely without carrying a light.

"Should I go and check on Jennie?" Shanna whispered to herself.

She peered into the distance, where Jennie's house sat among those homes that were in the poorest section of town. She had walked past Jennie's house more than once since Jennie had skipped violin lessons, and she had not seen any signs of her anywhere.

Knowing how Jennie's father was so cruel, Shanna had not worked up the nerve to knock on the door. Through Shanna's entire friendship with Jennie, Shanna had never gone to Jennie's house. They had always met elsewhere.

Surely going to Jennie's house at night, with lamps lit in the rooms, she would be able to see enough inside the house to discover whether or not Jennie was safe.

Her heart pounding, Shanna turned and stared at her closed bedroom door. She would never have a better opportunity than now to sneak from the house. Her mother had gone to bed early with a headache brought on by her two rambunctious twins. And her father was occupied preparing someone for burial. When he was involved in this sort of activity he heard nothing. He got completely wrapped up in doing the best job possible on those who had passed away.

"Yes, I shall do it," Shanna whispered, firming her jaw.

The excitement brought back many memories of when Shanna had daringly fled her house and met Bold Wolf beneath the moonlight. She had done this only a few times, for the most part meeting him during the day, but those times beneath the moon were the most cherished of all for her.

If only tonight that was where she could be going, with Bold Wolf waiting for her, she thought sullenly as she walked to her door and paused a moment before opening it. "If only his arms could hold me," she whispered as she dared to slowly open the door and peer down both sides of the dimly lit corridor, the candles in the wall sconces almost burned down to pools of melted beeswax.

Knowing that she must concentrate on her escape—her brothers surely were still awake and ready to pounce on her should they discover her out in the corridor tiptoeing toward the staircase—Shanna moved stiffly past her mother's closed bedroom door, then past her brothers' door, their giggles escaping from the crack beneath it proof of their mischievous mood.

Finally at the staircase, Shanna rushed on down the steps, stopping with a start when she heard movement at her left side.

Her father.

If he was finished with his tasks and he was coming toward the stairs to retire for the night and he caught her there, what could her excuse be?

"An apple," she whispered. She could tell him that she was going to the kitchen for an apple, for again, tonight, she had scarcely touched her evening meal. She could not help but feel the hunger gnawing at the pit of her stomach even now, yet still nothing tasted good to her. And until it did, she only ate enough food to get by on.

No longer hearing anything, deciding it had only been her imagination working overtime, Shanna tiptoed toward the front door.

She cringed when she had to walk past the parlor where a casket already sat on an oak bier, awaiting the arrival of the body of Reverend Anthony Siegel, an elderly priest who had passed away from a heart attack in the middle of his sermon a couple of days ago.

Shanna's father was taking special pains to prepare him for burial, for Reverend Siegel had been a man loved by everyone.

Finally outside, and past the shadows that her huge home cast along the ground, and now out in the road, Shanna walked quickly away, seeking the shadows of the other tall houses to keep herself from being seen.

She walked from one street to another, up one hill and down the other, and then had no choice but to walk in the open when the houses became small and insignificant, among them Jennie's tiny, unpainted bungalow.

Just as Shanna began to cross the street to get a closer look at Jennie's house, she was stricken by a sudden bout of dizziness. She stepped from the board sidewalk and grabbed at a tree, then leaned her back against it and held her face in her hands until the dizziness passed.

Her pulse racing, her color ashen from the fear of possibly fainting, Shanna swallowed hard. This was the first time she had experienced this and knew now the importance of eating a well-balanced meal. Surely the dizzy spell had come from her having only picked at her food.

Now no longer dizzy, yet no less alarmed from having the experience, Shanna raised her head just in time to see someone move quickly from Jennie's house into the looming shadows beside it.

It was a man. Shanna could tell by his size that it was Jennie's father!

Feeling suddenly vulnerable, Shanna felt a desperate fear rush through her. She knew now the foolishness of having come here tonight. If Jennie's father caught her snooping about, what would he do to her?

Her knees trembling, her heart pounding, and knowing that she now had to abandon her plans,

Shanna stayed in the shadows of the trees as she re-treated in the direction of her home.

But when she came close to a section of trees that were familiar to her, where she had so often traveled through them to get to the bluff, Shanna could not deny herself the temptation of going to the secret meeting place. She wouldn't have to stay long, only long enough to peer wistfully over at Indian Island and allow herself to dream of being in Bold Wolf's arms.

Perhaps she might again even see him in his canoe. What Penobscot warrior could resist going for a ride in his canoe on such a lovely moonlit night as this, even if this warrior was a Runner who was not able to share the night with the woman of his dreams?

"Yes, I shall go there," Shanna whispered.

She took a quick turn and made her way through the dense woodland, for the moment lost to the guiding light of the moon. But she had been there so often she would know the way to the bluff even blindfolded.

She said a soft prayer beneath her breath. One look at Bold Wolf tonight was all she asked for, then she would return home feeling as though everything she attempted tonight were not in vain.

If only she could have gotten one glimpse of Jennie and know she was all right!

Tomorrow, if Jennie didn't show up for her violin lesson again, nothing would stop Shanna from going to Jennie's house. She would boldly knock on the door. She would demand to see Jennie.

If Shanna wasn't allowed to see her, she would make further, angry demands to know why.

In broad daylight Jennie's father would not be as frightening should he be there.

At night, however, a man such as he, who seemed

a part of the dark himself, who was no less than an animal, could frighten the stripe from a skunk.

Shanna hoped that if she did go to Jennie's house tomorrow, Jennie's father would be away, working for the Corber Sawmill with the other lumberjacks, far from his home, busy felling trees.

Shanna certainly was not afraid to confront Jennie's mother. From the few times Shanna had seen her, she seemed a timid soul whose spirit had been beaten out of her by a husband who took delight in seeing his wife cower and cry.

Shanna had wondered often how Jennie might get away from the environment forced on her by questionable parents. Yet it was not only Jennie who was trapped there. There were seven brothers and sisters who also were at the mercy of such abuse.

Finally at the foot of the bluff, Shanna stopped to get her breath.

When she proceeded up the challenging slope of the hill, her heart raced. Halfway there, she had to stop and inhale another deep breath. And then, as she resumed going up the hill, she experienced another quickly passing spell of dizziness.

Afraid that she might pass out, Shanna started to turn around and head back toward home . . . but she was so close! She just couldn't go until she took one look across the bay at Indian Island.

Oh, for just one *glimpse* of Bold Wolf! Surely that could sustain her just a while longer until he could come to her and tell her that he was free to marry.

Each step was an effort for Shanna now, and as she finally reached the summit, she saw Bold Wolf sitting there, the moonlight bright on him and his handsomeness.

Shanna gasped. And as she started to speak his name, the only word that breathed across her lips was

"Bold . . ." before her knees buckled and she found herself lost in a world of black as she fainted.

Never thinking in his wildest dreams that he would find Shanna there, especially not this time of night, Bold Wolf had been so immersed in thoughts of Shanna, he had not heard her approach.

When he heard her start to speak his name, his heart stopped for a moment. He turned and saw her fall to the ground in a dead faint.

Not even considering the fact that He Who Watches was close by watching his every move, and at this moment not even caring, Bold Wolf rose quickly to his feet and ran to Shanna.

In the moonlight, his gaze took in Shanna's utter loveliness. He saw all over again why he loved her so much. She was such a tiny, delicate thing! Her face was so perfect in its features . . . her beautiful lips that knew so well the art of kissing him, and her long, thick lashes, which covered her cheeks now like veils.

As he gathered her into his arms, he knew she had only fainted, and wondered why. Was it over the shock of her seeing him sitting there? Or was she ill?

Although He Who Watches had stepped out into the open and was now standing where Bold Wolf could clearly see him, and knowing that he could be stripped of his title of Runner, Bold Wolf still lifted Shanna into his arms and began carrying her from the bluff. Surely his grand-uncle would realize that it would be less than honorable to ignore someone who was in need of help. Surely even He Who Watches would not have been able to leave Shanna lying there defenseless and vulnerable in the dark.

Bold Wolf carried Shanna down the steep hillside, his gaze never leaving her face. He watched carefully for signs of her awakening. When she awakened, he would place her on her feet and hurry on away, even though his heart would be aching to hold her and whisper to her how much he still loved her.

Yet knowing that he had carried her to safety would be enough for tonight.

As Bold Wolf reached the street, where he had only a short distance to go to get to Shanna's house, she was still unconscious. Bold Wolf did not hesitate to travel onward. If he was questioned by her parents, how he had happened to be near when she fainted, he would not hesitate to tell them.

He was tired of all of this secrecy! He was tired of fearing the taboos! Perhaps he was even ready to give up his status of Runner.

For Shanna, yes! He was!

Knowing that his father blessed his future with Shanna made Bold Wolf feel confident about sending the bride price to Shanna's parents, then later, after they accepted it, facing them to hear their answers to the question that had waited too long to be asked.

Perhaps, even, it was best if it happened that way. It would be wonderful if his father could witness the marriage between him and Shanna before he passed over to the other side—which could be any day now. His health had worsened to the point of no return.

Finally at Shanna's house, Bold Wolf gently took her up the steps. When he reached the porch, he stopped. Before he laid her down and left her, he wanted to gaze down at her again.

It was then that her eyes fluttered slowly open.

His heart melted when she looked up at him, their eyes instantly locking.

Shanna was touched deeply to know that Bold Wolf had risked everything to bring her safely home. And knowing that He Who Watches had to be someplace close by, witnessing everything, Shanna knew not to say anything to Bold Wolf.

Not even a thank-you, even though she so badly wanted to hold him to her heart and tell him how much she had missed him . . . how much she wanted him!

She knew that she must not endanger him further, for the spy He Who Watches had just stepped out into the open for them both to see.

Bold Wolf smiled down at Shanna. Their eyes held for a moment longer, then he eased her from his arms and left her standing on the porch, watching him slip away into the darkness.

Tears streaming down her cheeks, Shanna reached a hand out for Bold Wolf. "Thank you, my darling," she whispered. "I *love* you."

Now weak, not only from her hunger but now also from rapture, Shanna went slowly inside her house.

She was relieved to find that her father still seemed busy in the preparation room. She was almost certain that her bone-weary mother was still asleep upstairs in her room.

She crept to the kitchen and grabbed a handful of cookies from the cookie jar, gobbling them up quickly as she went quietly up the stairs to her room.

She was scarcely aware of closing the door behind her and leaning against it. Her thoughts were on what had happened tonight. She was not amazed that Bold Wolf had been on the bluff, as though destiny had led him there to see to her welfare.

She went to the window and gazed at the river. Her heart skipped a beat when she saw two canoes crossing over to Indian Island. She knew that those in the canoe were Bold Wolf and He Who Watches.

She was afraid for Bold Wolf . . . that he might be punished somehow for what he did tonight. Her eyes narrowed at the thought of how He Who Watches was in charge of Bold Wolf's life. She had not actually met the man, so she did not know if the punishment he would choose for Bold Wolf would be light or severe. She just hoped that Bold Wolf wouldn't be stripped of his Runner's status. She would feel responsible, for had she not foolishly gone to the bluff tonight she would not have placed Bold Wolf in this position.

Shanna could no longer see the canoes. Bold Wolf and He Who Watches must now be in Bold Wolf's lodge.

She could not help but tremble inside over her deep concerns for the man she loved. She *did* feel responsible for everything that might happen to him now. Had she not wandered to the bluff tonight, all would be well with Bold Wolf!

But now? she thought sullenly. What now?

6

O, beauty, are you not enough?
—SARA TEASDALE

He Who Watches went with Bold Wolf to his cabin. Bold Wolf was surprised that his grand-uncle had yet to say anything about what had happened tonight.

Instead his grand-uncle just sat on the floor beside the door near Bold Wolf's bed and stared into the darkness as Bold Wolf undressed and stretched out on his blankets and pelts.

Just as Bold Wolf found himself drifting comfortably off to sleep, he was awakened with alarm when He Who Watches struck the soles of his feet with a stick.

Bold Wolf suddenly realized that this was to remind him that Runners do not sleep with their legs outstretched, as this marred their running qualities. Runners were to sleep with their legs drawn up to their knees.

Realizing that his grand-uncle was purposely being more strict with him tonight because of what Bold Wolf had done with Shanna, Bold Wolf tried not to show that he was disgruntled. Without a word, he drew his legs up to his knees.

Bold Wolf now knew to expect his grand-uncle to be more strict tomorrow and the day after that. He would find as many ways as possible to torment Bold

Wolf, thinking that might make him more obedient to his vows.

Bold Wolf expected He Who Watches to watch closely how Bold Wolf sat while eating, making certain that he would sit with his knees drawn up, which would keep his tendons stretched.

Also, his grand-uncle would make sure Bold Wolf chewed no spruce gum, which was said to impair one's breathing. Bold Wolf recalled when He Who Watches told him the story about spruce gum. He had told Bold Wolf that spruce gum had originated from scabs from a myth woman's crotch. Should any man chew the gum, it would make his testicles clack when he ran, and so forewarn the animals he was hunting of his approach.

As Bold Wolf obediently lay there with his knees drawn up, he thought further of the woman of the myth. Her name was Jug Woman. She was a hag who had roamed the woods many years ago, uttering weird cries and seducing children.

On one occasion, several young men had teased her because of her scabs and her ugly looks. She became angry and declared thereafter they would chew her scabs.

Then she climbed up a spruce tree and scraped off her scabs against the bark. The scabs now appeared in the gum exuding from all spruce trees.

As Bold Wolf drifted off to sleep, however, he didn't dream of Jug Woman.

His dream was filled with Shanna.

In the dream, he saw her dancing amid clouds, her violet eyes beckoning to him. In his dream, he went to Shanna. But just as he started to reach out for her, to draw her into his tender embrace and kiss her, a flock of blackbirds flew between them, squawking and flapping their wings.

When the birds disappeared in the dream, Shanna was also gone.

Bold Wolf awakened with a start. He felt suddenly lonely and empty. Aware of a presence, he felt no less alone, for it was only He Who Watches.

Bold Wolf knew now that, after tonight, and after having been with Shanna for those stolen, treasured moments, he could not go on much longer without the woman his heart now desired most.

His Shanna!

7

Clasp me close in your warm,
young arms.
—ELLA WHEELER WILCOX

Shanna had never struggled through a violin lesson like she had today, for after discovering that Jennie had missed another lesson, she could not just stand by and wonder about it any longer.

Her violin lessons finally over, and having left her violin at the music studio for safekeeping, Shanna was now on her way to Jennie's house. Shanna *must* know why Jennie was staying hidden like some dark sin!

Shanna's heart pounded with fear as Jennie's house came into sight. She hoped that the person coming to the door would not be Jennie's father. Shanna wasn't sure if she would be able to stand there facing the brutish man.

When Shanna left the shade of the trees and stepped out into the sun across the street from Jennie's house, she realized how extremely hot it was. She was glad she had eaten a good breakfast, or she might by now be feeling faint again as the sun beat on her brow.

She lifted her hair back from her shoulders so that it would hang long and loose down her back, then hesitated a moment before going on up the rickety steps to the porch of Jennie's house.

The front door was open and flies buzzed around a

dog that lay sleeping beside it. She could hear a baby crying inside the house, and children arguing.

Fighting off any fears that still threatened to cause her to turn and hurry home, Shanna went up the termite-infested steps, steadying herself as they squeaked and threatened to cave in beneath her.

When the dog awakened and its dark eyes found her there, Shanna's insides froze. She stopped and stood still just as she reached the porch, waiting being pounced upon.

But instead the short-tailed mixed breed of a dog rose slowly, stretched one of its rear legs, then lumbered over to Shanna, sniffing, its tail wagging.

"Good doggie," Shanna said softly, daring to reach down and pat it on the head.

"Whatcha doin' here, Shanna?"

The scratchy voice of Jennie's mother made Shanna jump. She turned quickly and stared down at the woman, who was holding a basket of wet clothes.

Shanna looked past Jennie's mother at the side yard, where a clothesline stretched out from tree to tree.

She then gazed at Jennie's mother again. "Good morning, Mrs. Anderson," she said, forcing a smile. She extended a hand of friendship, then dropped it awkwardly to her side when Jennie's mother seemed less than impressed over her show of politeness.

"Shanna, tell me why you're here and be quick about it," Bonnie Anderson said, blowing out of the side of her mouth at a wisp of dirty, black hair that had fallen out of the tight bun that swirled around her head. "I've got work waitin' to be done."

Shanna felt a tightness in her throat as she gazed at Jennie's mother. There was a bruise beneath her left eye and a cut healing on her chin. No one had to be smart to know what, and who, had caused the bruise and cut on the middle-aged lady's face.

Shanna looked further than that. Unkempt, wearing shoes that were broken at the sides, and with her faded cotton dress shabby and stained with food at the front, Jennie's mother was nothing like Shanna's, who was fastidious to a fault.

"Ma'am, I'd like to speak with Jennie, if you please," Shanna finally murmured. "She's missed several violin lessons. Ma'am, is she ill?"

"No, she ain't ill," Jennie's mother grumbled, setting the basket on the ground.

Shanna gasped in surprise as she watched the woman take a cigarette and a match from her apron pocket. As she lit the cigarette and began smoking it, Shanna's earlier impression of Jennie's mother faded. This woman no longer seemed meek, but instead, more like the bawdy-house women, who smoked openly for everyone to see as they stood outside their establishments making eyes to all men who passed by them.

Never would Shanna have thought a mother would smoke, especially a mother who rarely had enough money to put adequate food on the dinner table for her children. But remembering why she was there, she decided not to condemn this poor woman for smoking.

Shanna cleared her throat and glanced toward the house, then slid a slow gaze back at Bonnie. "If Jennie isn't ill, then why has she missed her violin lessons?" she asked warily. "You know that with each lesson and practice she misses, she gets further and further behind. Mr. Lovett is very disturbed by her absence."

Shanna glanced at the house again and tried to see through the open door, unable to now because several of the children were clustered around the door now in their skimpy, dirty attire, staring at her and blocking the way.

"Jennie ain't home," Bonnie said, with what seemed to Shanna an urgency. She flicked ashes from her cigarette onto the ground. "She's gone to visit an ailing aunt in a neighboring town. She's volunteered to care for her. She'll be there for a few weeks."

"An aunt?" Shanna said, raising an eyebrow, finding this hard to believe. Jennie had never mentioned any aunts, especially one she would be so fond of that she would put her ahead of her love of her violin.

And the last time Shanna had been with Jennie, speaking openly to one another about their feelings about so many things, Jennie had not said anything about an aunt who was ill, nor anything about going to stay several days with one.

And Shanna knew that Jennie would have confided that to her, for it was the very next day that Jennie was suddenly, strangely missing.

Shanna stared at Bonnie, aware now of how the woman's eyes would no longer meet hers, which to Shanna was how a person would behave who had just lied. Shanna had no choice but to leave the matter alone, however, for it was obvious that she wouldn't be able to see Jennie today.

Tomorrow she would try again. She would not take no for an answer over and over again before she would go to the authorities and tell them that she was afraid something horrible might have happened to Jennie Anderson.

"Get on home, Shanna," Bonnie said, picking her clothes basket up and walking away from Shanna. "Mind your own business."

Stunned, afraid for her friend yet feeling helpless to do anything about it, Shanna turned and walked away.

No matter how hard she tried, Shanna couldn't get

Jennie off her mind. She was such a dear friend; she deserved so much more in life than what she had gotten.

And Jennie's dream to be a concert violinist, a dream that could get her away from her family, was now in jeopardy. If she no longer took lessons or practiced, she would compromise the skills she had honed.

Sighing disconsolately, and again aware of how oppressive the heat was today, Shanna sought the shade of the trees. She smiled when she remembered the swimming hole, where she and Jennie had so often enjoyed getting cooled off on the hottest days of summer.

Making a sharp turn, Shanna hurried through the dense forest and made her way through the thick brush toward the pond, which was not that far away, yet was private enough for two young ladies who loved swimming without their clothes on.

Shanna blushed even now at the thought of being so carefree. She and Jennie had swum like fishes in the pond, nude, giggling and splashing one another, and the differences in how they lived never mattered.

They had grown to be the closest of friends, and it ate away at Shanna's heart to think that something bad might have happened to Jennie. It had been hard to walk away from Jennie's house without rushing inside to search for her. The thought of her possibly lying there all battered and bruised from a beating made shivers race up and down Shanna's spine.

No, she wouldn't think about such things as that. Surely she was wrong to think the worst. Perhaps there *was* an aunt. Surely Jennie *was* there, being the sweet person she was and caring for the ailing woman!

But if Jennie had been harmed in any way, Shanna would not stop until she saw the man responsible locked behind bars! "Even if I endanger myself doing it, I shall see that Jennie's father is punished!" Shanna whispered as the shine of the glimmering pond came into view through a break in the trees.

The thought of the cool water against her body made Shanna hurry more quickly onward.

If only Jennie were there to swim with her. If only she knew where Jennie *was*.

When she came to the banks of the small pond, where water lilies bloomed in clusters of bright pink and yellow, Shanna plopped down on the ground and started to yank off a shoe, then stopped and scarcely breathed when she heard something that sounded like . . .

Her eyes widened and she jumped back to her feet when she heard it again.

It sounded like a soft whimper . . . a *baby's*.

It was coming from somewhere close by!

Her pulse racing, Shanna frantically began folding back the weeds that grew tall and gangly beneath the shade of the oak trees that circled the pond, and searched for the baby, who no longer made any sounds.

"Where is the baby's mother?" she whispered, still searching. "Oh, where is the *child*?"

She parted some taller grass and she found the baby girl laying there, so tiny, so vulnerable, and without a stitch of clothing on it. Shanna could hardly believe her eyes. She could tell it was a newborn child; the umbilical cord was still bloody. And this child was so tiny, surely it had been born prematurely!

But something else that grabbed at her heart was the fact that the child was an Indian . . . and . . . one tiny hand was terribly deformed and twisted.

As the child's dark eyes gazed trustingly up at Shanna and it made another soft, whimpering sound, Shanna was lost heart and soul to her.

"Oh, just look at you," Shanna whispered, falling to her knees beside the baby. "Aren't you the sweetest thing?"

She looked around her again for the mother, again seeing no trace of anyone. It was apparent now that the child had been abandoned.

Shanna was almost afraid to pick the child up, the infant looked fragile—as though it were made of porcelain and might break if handled wrong.

But Shanna would not leave the child lying there any longer, as though it were from a discarded litter of puppies. Her hands trembling, her heart pounding, she slid one hand beneath the tiny baby's head, then slid her other hand beneath the baby's body. Slowly she lifted the child up from the ground.

Then she held the child—a baby girl—in her arms against her chest and began slowly rocking her back and forth. "Lord, who would have been this heartless?" she whispered. "You are so sweet, so tiny, so helpless!"

The baby snuggled trustingly against Shanna, as though seeking warmth from her clothes, making Shanna aware that the baby needed to be wrapped. Although the temperature was near ninety degrees today, a child still needed the comfort of clothing around its newborn body, especially a child *this* small.

Shanna thought quickly about what she could use for wrapping the child and smiled when she thought of the petticoat beneath the skirt of her dress. It was clean. It was made of a soft cotton. Surely that would do!

Laying the child down on a soft, spongy hill of moss, Shanna lifted the hem of her dress and ripped her petticoat away up to her waist.

Carefully, oh, so gently turning the child from side

to side, Shanna wrapped the child within the soft fabric and once again held her and rocked her.

"I would never have abandoned you," she murmured. "If you were mine, I would adore you!"

She stretched her legs out before her, lay the baby on them, and slowly unfolded the petticoat away from the child.

Once again she gazed at the child's tininess, the color of her skin, and then at the limp, deformed hand.

She reached for the hand and almost choked from emotion when the tiny fingers curled around her forefinger.

"You certainly do trust me, don't you?" Shanna whispered, tears streaming from her eyes. "Oh, sweet child, you *know* I would never hurt you. If only you were mine, I would show you how much love I would give you."

The child's tiny lips quivered into a smile, touching Shanna's heart even more sincerely, even though Shanna had heard people say that when a newborn child smiled, it was not because it was happy, but because it was gassy.

But Shanna would not believe that, not now that she had experienced seeing such a smile. She knew that she was making the baby happy! She was giving love to her, love that her mother had obviously not felt for the child.

"Who would do this to you?" Shanna whispered, then gasped when she wondered if it might be the custom of some Indian tribes to throw deformed babies away at birth.

Shanna felt so much at this moment—anger and disgust that this might be the reason the child was abandoned. But most of all she felt a sudden surge of protective love for the baby. She so badly wanted to take her home and keep her, but she knew her parents wouldn't allow it.

Shanna knew the child needed quick nourishment. Who could say how long she had been there? Who could say how long ago she had been fed . . . if ever? Surely a mother who would throw a child away this easily would not have taken time to feed her first.

Frantically, Shanna searched her mind for someone who might take the child. Yet how could she take her to anyone, when she so badly wanted to keep her, herself? She needed to find someone who would care for the baby at least until Shanna found a way to make a home for her.

Yes, she *would* claim the baby as hers. She felt such an instant bonding with the child.

"Mr. and Mrs. Diepholz!" Shanna suddenly said, recalling a wealthy family on the far side of Old Town who already had a house full of children, twelve in all, some of whom were adopted, the others theirs.

Yes, they loved children and they were rich enough to see that each of them was cared for and treated properly. And Emily Diepholz had recently had another baby. Her breasts could surely feed two.

"Would she?" Shanna whispered, raising an eyebrow. She gazed down at the child again. "Sweet thing, if Emily and her husband Samuel have adopted so many children already, surely they would care enough to take in one more child, at least for a little while."

Knowing that she must give it a try, and anxious to find a way to get this child nourishment quickly, Shanna wrapped the baby in her petticoat again and hurried from the pond, so glad that the outer fringes of the forest reached almost to the front door of the Diepholzes' grand mansion at the edge of town so that Shanna would not be seen carrying the baby to the door.

She knocked and stood at the door, breathless until someone opened it.

She was relieved when no stiffly-collared butler was there at the opened door, but instead Mrs. Diepholz herself. Shanna found herself in the presence of a woman who was elegantly dressed in silk. She was tall, stately, and proud. Her golden hair was swirled neatly in a bun atop her head. Her green eyes twinkled as she pleasantly smiled.

Shanna quickly explained the dilemma to Emily, and was near tears when Emily gently took the child in her arms.

"Come to the sitting room with me, where we can have privacy," Emily murmured, her eyes never leaving the tiny Indian child as she walked ahead of Shanna.

Shanna followed her through a long corridor where fancy, gilt-framed paintings lined the walls on both sides. She could hear children playing upstairs, and laughter was the chief sound she heard.

"Shanna, please come on into the sitting room with me and close the door behind you," Emily said, walking gracefully over to a thickly upholstered chair and sitting down, her eyes still on the child.

Shanna nodded, gently closed the door behind her, then sat down on a divan close to Emily and looked quickly away, embarrassed by how quickly Emily had unbuttoned a portion of her bodice and slid one of her thick breasts free.

"Don't be shy, child," Emily murmured. "Watch the child feed from my breast. It is a wonderful sight, a sight to behold."

Shanna slowly turned eyes to the suckling child. Tears streamed down her cheeks when she saw just

how hungrily the child fed from the breast, her lame
hand kneading the breast almost desperately.

"She was starved," Emily murmured, a sob lodging
in her throat. "And she is so tiny, surely prematurely
born. How could anyone have abandoned her?"

"You are so kind to feed her," Shanna said, wiping
tears from her cheeks.

"You should allow me to keep her," Emily said,
locking eyes with Shanna. "A child is quite a responsibility for such a young thing as you. Surely you truly
don't want to have such a responsibility. Child, you
aren't even married."

"I will be, *soon*," Shanna was quick to interject.

She paled, knowing that she had confided something
to this lady that might endanger her chances of marrying Bold Wolf, should Shanna's parents get wind
of it.

She quickly explained her situation, as Emily listened and the child continued to suckle.

"So you see, ma'am, I will have a home for her one
day soon," Shanna said, after telling this lady more
than she had ever even told her best friend.

"I can see just how much you do want the child,"
Emily said, now holding the baby up to her shoulder,
softly burping her. "I promise, Shanna, that I won't
tell anyone except my husband what you told me
today. I will protect the baby and love her until you
can make a home for her. And come, Shanna, as often
as you wish. You need to make sure the child is familiar with *your* arms and voice. That will form the special bond that is usually felt between a mother and
child."

"From the bottom of my heart I thank you,"
Shanna said, stifling a sob of relief behind her hand.

Samuel Diepholz, dressed in an expensive black

suit, with a diamond stickpin glistening from his fancy ascot, came into the room.

Shanna turned and gazed at him. She knew almost instantly that he would also approve of the plan, for when he bent down on a knee before Emily and watched the child feeding again as his wife explained everything to him, Shanna saw the acceptance in his smile and how he reached up and stroked the child's tiny head.

Samuel rose to his feet and held out his hands for Shanna. "Come, Shanna, I will walk you to the door," he said softly. "And don't you fret one moment about the child, or that word might spread that she is here, or how she got here. My wife and I will care for the child until you are ready to take her."

Shanna flung herself into his arms and hugged him. "Thank you," she cried. "Thank you so much."

She turned when Emily came to her and held the child out for her. "I'm sure you want to hold her one last time before leaving," Emily murmured. She carefully placed the baby in Shanna's arms. "She's asleep now. When she awakens, I will bathe her and put a soft gown on her. She will never be neglected again."

Shanna slowly rocked the child back and forth in her arms and gazed at the baby's peaceful face as she slept. "Elizabeth," she murmured, having that quickly decided on a name for her. "My sweet, adorable Elizabeth."

Then, with a full heart, she hurried home, feeling good about saving the child, yet still troubled over not having helped her friend Jennie!

8

Shanna was hardly able to wait until her violin lesson was over for another day, so that she could go and see Elizabeth. She raced down the steps from the music studio, her eyes lit with excitement. She couldn't wait to hold Elizabeth again. Shanna was an instant mother! Ah, what a wonderful secret to have!

Having Elizabeth to think about helped lighten the concern for Jennie inside her heart, for another day had passed now without hearing from her friend.

Shanna had noticed Roscoe Lovett was moodier today. He had said he was concerned for Jennie's welfare, but he had also said he couldn't go to Jennie's house to inquire about her. It was less than professional for a man such as he to interfere in one of his student's family affairs.

Shanna had heard more in his voice today than mere concern when he talked about Jennie. She saw that Mr. Lovett's feelings for Jennie went deeper than those of a teacher for a student. Shanna truly thought he might have fallen in love with her.

Rushing now along the wooden sidewalk in town, the sun behind clouds today, making the day more tolerable than yesterday, Shanna flipped her long hair back from her shoulders and smiled a silent hello to those who nodded to her along the walkway.

Everyone she saw today seemed happy, and everything *could* be so wonderful for *Shanna* . . . *if* Jennie was all right, and *if* Bold Wolf would be able to send some sort of word about when he might find an end to his Runner duties.

Since Shanna had finally been able to enjoy eating again, her full strength had returned. And today she was glowing over the child that she had rescued and now called her own. She would not think about what would have happened had she not found the child. She found it hard to think that Elizabeth might have died!

Now rushing along the board sidewalk before Old Town's various business establishments in quicker, more eager steps, Shanna was finally able to see the tall roof of the Diepholz house. Soon she would be holding Elizabeth! Almost in the same heartbeat that she thought this, she again thought of Bold Wolf.

She could not help but fantasize about marrying Bold Wolf.

She could take Elizabeth to Indian Island. The child would not only have a mother and father, but a home where she would be raised with much love. And Bold Wolf's people . . . oh, how *they* would love the beautiful child.

Something came suddenly to Shanna's mind that made her stop with a cold feeling inside.

Bold Wolf's people!

If they saw Elizabeth's deformed hand, how would they react? What if Bold Wolf's people believed in the custom of throwing handicapped children away? What if it was one of the Penobscot women who did this terrible thing to Elizabeth?

Such thoughts brought a strange emptiness to the pit of Shanna's stomach, casting a dark shadow of

gloom over her plans to eventually marry Bold Wolf.
How could she marry him when she was not sure how
Elizabeth would be treated once she arrived at the
Penobscot village?

How could Shanna tell Bold Wolf about the child
when she could not trust *his* feelings about her having
Elizabeth? How could Shanna chance losing the child?

She was torn with feelings—loving both Bold Wolf
and Elizabeth so much!

Feeling less exuberant, Shanna walked onward,
cringing when she had to go past one of the worst,
most indecent bawdy houses in town. She was always
afraid of being grabbed and forced inside one of those
terrible places and made to perform sinful acts with
men. She *had* heard tales of young girls being abducted and forced into a life of corruption and
prostitution.

Shivering from such a thought, Shanna stepped out
into the street to walk on the other side, away from
the bawdy houses, but stopped and grew pale when
suddenly Jennie rushed from one of the buildings, all
gaudied up, and in an indecent skimpy attire that
showed almost all of her breasts and also revealed her
bare legs up to just past her knees.

Shanna was so shocked, she felt as though her feet
were frozen to the street. She wasn't even aware of
horses and buggies traveling dangerously close to her
in the street. All she could see was Jennie and how
she was dressed, and then she saw the utter fear in
her friend's eyes when Jennie saw her standing there.

Breathless, Jennie ran to Shanna, grabbed her by a
hand, and yanked her over to stand in an alley between two buildings. "Hide me, Shanna!" she cried.
"We mustn't let Al Adams find me! You've got to
help me get away from here!"

Her heart pounding, shaken by the knowledge of

where Jennie had been these past several days, wondering how this had come to be, Shanna started to run with Jennie behind the building. From there they dashed toward the dark depths of the forest, but a bald man with a black mustache and thick eyebrows was suddenly there in the alley, blocking the way.

"Al Adams," Shanna gasped, paling.

"Come on to papa," Al said, snickering, his gray eyes gleaming as he beckoned mockingly toward Jennie. "You're bought and paid for, Jennie. You ain't goin' nowhere 'cept back inside my establishment." His eyes shifted to Shanna. He slowly looked her up and down, then smiled coyly at Jennie again. "If you don't come with me willingly, Jennie, by God I'll yell for some of my men to come out and help me take your *friend* inside and she'll *also* be entertainin' gents at the midnight hour in my establishment," he threatened.

"No! You can't do that," Jennie cried, her hand tightening desperately around Shanna's. "I won't let you."

"And how are you gonna stop me?" Al said, laughing boisterously.

Shanna looked over her shoulder, hoping that someone out in the street or along the boardwalk might see what was happening.

But no one noticed the drama in the alleyway.

"You paid Papa for me," Jennie cried, tears streaming from her eyes. "You paid no one for Shanna. Leave her be, Al. Let her go home."

Jennie slid her hand from Shanna's. She turned and embraced Shanna, then ran over and stood beside Al.

"Jennie, you don't have to go with that man," Shanna cried, a sob lodging in her throat.

"Please go on home," Jennie cried. "My father sold me to the brothel owner. Father received three hundred dollars and two good horses as payment. I must now live the life of a whore. But you don't have to, Shanna. Leave. Forget what you saw." She swallowed hard. "Forget *me*."

Shanna was stunned speechless by what she'd just heard. Jennie's father had actually sold his daughter to this evil man? How could he be so heartless and cruel . . . so uncaring?

And although Jennie was begging Shanna to go, to forget what she saw, Shanna could see the desperation in her friend's eyes. She saw a silent plea for help!

Not wanting to get Jennie into any more trouble with the brothel owner, Shanna didn't come right out and tell Jennie that she was going to make sure she was released from that hellhole, and *soon*.

Shanna gave Jennie a lingering, somber look, then sobbed and felt empty as she watched Jennie being dragged back inside the terrible den of iniquity.

Still too stunned to move, Shanna continued to look at the two-story brick establishment. Now she understood why she hadn't seen Jennie for so long, and why she had not been able to get answers from Jennie's mother.

"Jennie's mother," Shanna whispered, turning to rush back out onto the boardwalk.

She was no longer headed for the Diepholz mansion. She was going to see Jennie's mother and shame her into freeing her daughter from such bondage.

These past two days, Shanna was discovering just how lucky she was to have such parents as hers. Although sometimes they grated at her nerves something fierce, they loved her and would never treat her as less than human, as she'd seen others being treated lately.

First the child and how its mother had abandoned it. And then *Jennie,* whose abandonment by her parents was perhaps the worst kind of all! To know that their very own daughter's body was being defiled over and over again by strange men?

Her jaw tight, her spine stiff, her hands doubled to fists at her sides, and fighting off the initial fear she always had of possibly coming face-to-face with Jennie's horrible father, Shanna went up the rickety steps to Jennie's porch.

Before she had a chance to knock on the door, it opened with a jerk and Jennie's mother was standing there, balancing a baby on a broad hip, a hard, stubborn look in her eyes.

"How could you?" Shanna blurted out, angry at herself when she could not stop her tears from flowing. "Your very own daughter? Do you truly know what she is forced to do at that . . . place? Do you not care at all that she is now a . . . a . . ."

Shanna didn't get the chance to complete her scolding. Jennie's mother was suddenly jerked out of sight and in her place Jennie's father stood with a shotgun aimed at Shanna.

The blood drained from Shanna's face.

Her knees grew weak.

Nervous sweat trickled down her ribs.

Yet she stood her ground and glared up into the most evil eyes she had ever encountered, on a face that was covered with a thick, wiry, black beard. His eyes glowed like flames as the sun suddenly broke through the clouds overhead and shone into them.

Up this close to the man, truly fearing him, Shanna gaped openly at George Anderson. He was a tall and thickset man who wore his long, black, greasy hair tied in a knot at the back of his head.

A deep, livid gash ran from the corner of his left eye to well past the left corner of his mouth.

His red plaid flannel shirt was faded almost colorless and reeked of perspiration.

His large stomach hung out over the waist of his soiled denim breeches, gaping open to reveal thick spirals of black hair curled around his navel.

"Our family's had their fill of you, little miss busybody," George growled. "Now *git,* do you hear? Get on home. Stop stickin' your nose in where it don't belong."

"Jennie is such a dear person," Shanna managed to say between heavy heartbeats. "How could you do this to her?"

"I'm tellin' you to leave," George said, his eyes narrowing. "Never show your face here again." He inched the barrel of the shotgun closer to Shanna's abdomen. "And don't you tell your pa and ma none of this. I'd as soon shoot your ma and pa as look at 'em."

"You . . . wouldn't . . . dare," Shanna said, her voice a shocked whisper.

"You don't think so?" George said, then held his head back in a roar of laughter.

Scared clean to the bone by this man and his threats, Shanna backed down the steps.

When she felt her feet on the ground, she broke into a breathless run and didn't stop until she was at the sheriff's office at the center of town.

Panting, her side paining her, Shanna gazed down at the man sitting behind the desk. The badge on his stiffly starched white shirt looked as though he spent most of his day shining it instead of taking care of serious business in the town. He was a tiny man who wore gold-framed eyeglasses, and his bald head glistened nearly as much as his badge.

"Hello there, young lady, what can I do for you?" Sheriff Wisler asked, cocking an eyebrow as he gazed up at Shanna. Locking his thumbs around his bright red suspenders, he scooted his chair back, placed his feet on the edge of his desk, and crossed his legs at his ankles.

"Aren't you aware of what's happening in those bawdy houses?" Shanna asked, her breath having finally returned. "My friend Jennie has been wrongly placed in one of those terrible places. Her father . . . he . . . actually sold her to Al Adams, the brothel owner. For money and . . . and . . . horses he sold his very own daughter to a life of indecency. I . . . I . . . want her *out* of there. Sir, you've got to help me. You've got to go and get her out of there!"

"Whoa, slow down," Sheriff Wisler said, dropping his feet from the desk. He slid his hands away from his suspenders, stood up, and walked around the desk to stand before Shanna, his height no greater than hers. "Now tell me again. Who is this Jennie? Where is she?"

Unable to *not* speak fast, so anxious to get Jennie out of that place, Shanna told the sheriff all she knew, then was appalled when even then he wasn't willing to help her set Jennie free.

"Nope, I don't interfere in family affairs," he said, going to sit down behind his desk again. "Now, if that's all you came here for, I'd say you'd best go on home. But let me give you a piece of advice, young miss. Quit sticking your nose in other people's affairs. You'll live longer that way."

"You . . . aren't going to help me?" Shanna said incredulously. "You are going to just sit there and tell me to mind my own business . . . when it is your business to protect the citizens of this community? What about Jennie? If you don't help her, no one will."

Suddenly she thought of someone who *could* help Jennie! Bold Wolf!

Then she remembered his vows as a Runner and

became discouraged and downhearted all over again. Jennie was a woman. Bold Wolf could not speak or do anything that had to do with women!

"Ma'am, I learned long ago, when I first came to Old Town, that I wasn't hired so much to protect the citizens of the community as I was just to sit here for show," Sheriff Wisler grumbled. "Now, take the Indians over there on Indian Island, for example. If I had the true authority that was supposed to be invested in me when I was given this badge, I'd see to it that there were no Indians for hundreds of miles, whereas there they sit on that island and wander about this town like they own everything."

He laughed and leaned back in his chair. "But that don't matter much anymore, especially now," he said. "The one Indian I hate the most kicked the bucket this morning. Yep, old Chief War Eagle died this morning. I don't have him to reckon with any longer. But hell, I doubt things will change much, because his *son* is now chief. I'm sure his son has the same stubborn streak as his father, and Lord knows I'd be wasting my time trying to convince him to move elsewhere with his throng of savages."

He shrugged. "No, it don't matter none," he said dryly. "As long as I get paid to wear this badge, that's all that matters."

Shanna was listening to him ramble, yet scarcely heard him.

Bold Wolf was no longer the Penobscot Runner!

Bold Wolf . . . was now *chief*!

That meant that as soon as he got past the mourning period for his father's death, he would be free to marry her!

For so long she had dreamed of the time she knew she would be Bold Wolf's wife. Now she couldn't be happy about it all that much. Too much was standing in the way of her happiness!

Oh, poor Jennie! What about Jennie? And Elizabeth! Would Bold Wolf truly accept Elizabeth in his life?

Dispirited, Shanna left the sheriff's office. She stopped and stared toward Indian Island. Her heart went out to Bold Wolf for the sadness he must be feeling at this moment.

She wanted to rush to him and hold him and help him through this, but she knew that must wait. He would send for her when he felt that enough time for his mourning had passed.

But what then could she say to him? *Could* she tell him about the baby? Was she going to be forced to make a choice between them?

Could she even do that?

At a time when she should see such promise ahead of her, because the man she loved would soon be free to marry her, she could not help but feel forlorn and torn.

Never had she felt as torn about so many things as now!

9

Drink to me only with thine eyes,
And I will pledge with mine.
                              —BEN JONSON

In the sun's rays, spider webs, moistened and glittering with dew, fluttered in the breeze. Bold Wolf looked out across the river toward Old Town. It had now been two weeks since his father's burial and it was time for the Penobscot to put the mourning for Chief War Eagle behind them. In a sense Bold Wolf had been forced to do this the very day his father had died, for he had quickly assumed the title of chief.

But now it was time to make it official. Tomorrow there would be a ceremony, followed by a great feast that would celebrate Bold Wolf's true initiation as chief. Out of respect for his father, Bold Wolf had not yet sent word to Shanna about the changes in his life.

Today he would. She would be invited to the celebration. That would not only begin his true reign as chief, but also Bold Wolf's and Shanna's lives together.

"She has known," he whispered. Being the understanding woman she was, she surely understood why he had not been able to come for her the moment he put his title of Runner behind him. She had been waiting patiently for him, as he had as patiently waited for these two weeks to pass before he could go to her and claim her as his.

"It has been so long, my Shanna," he whispered, now looking up at the bluff across the river, remembering their many moments there together.

He frowned, though, when he thought of the last time they had been there. She had fainted. And he still had no idea why.

But he had seen her since and was assured that she was all right. In fact, the last time he had observed her when she was not aware of being watched, he had seen a luminous look about her, a radiance that had somewhat frightened him.

As he recalled, he had only seen her appear that happy when she had been with him.

He could not help but wonder if she might have found someone else who made her happy now besides himself. If so, and he had lost her due to their long separation, he would die a slow death inside, because now was the future they had always sought. Now they could finally be together.

If she refused him, and he discovered there was someone else who had been holding her and speaking words of forever in her ears, he was not sure if he could live with knowing that he had caused her to turn away from him by placing his status as Runner over the chance to marry her.

But she *had* promised him that she would wait for him, that she could never love anyone but him! She was not the sort of person who made promises and then broke them.

Yes, he decided, surely she still loved him. Yes, she still waited to receive word from him.

"Bold Wolf, are you certain you want me to go to the white woman today and speak on your behalf?"

He Who Watch's voice behind him startled Bold Wolf from his troubled thoughts. He turned and saw the old man with his flowing silver hair standing there.

He also saw the wariness in his grand-uncle's tired eyes.

"You ask me this question when you already know the answer?" Bold Wolf said. "I told you early this morning what you are to do for me today. Are you still questioning my ability to choose a wife for myself? Is that so, He Who Watches?"

"You know that I have always questioned inside my heart your choice of women," He Who Watches said somberly. "It is only now that I openly speak my mind of it."

"Then please question it no more, not in your heart or across your lips," Bold Wolf said. "Today you must approach Shanna for your chief in the way in which it is done for the Penobscot men who pursue the woman of their choice. I have assigned you to be the go-between for myself and Shanna. Go now. Seek her out. Tell her of my desire to have her with me tomorrow during our people's special celebration. After the ceremony, you will have only one more duty as go-between. After you take the bride price to Shanna's father, that particular duty will end. I will then speak for myself to Shanna, alone, of special things . . . of our future together."

"I will do this for you, but I urge you to think deeply about your decision while I am gone," He Who Watches said. "It is still not too late to change your mind about this woman."

"Ever since I saw Shanna that first time, I knew that my destiny is to be with her," Bold Wolf said. "Hers is to be with me. We have waited long enough to fulfill this destiny. Go. Make haste. Take my message to her."

He Who Watches nodded, then walked stiffly down to the beach and boarded his canoe.

Bold Wolf's jaw was tight as he watched his grand-uncle's canoe move slowly across the bay. His heart raced at the thought of seeing Shanna so soon and holding her.

"Soon, my woman," he whispered. "Soon."

Smiling, he turned and walked back to his village. He had called a council to discuss the events of tomorrow. He could hardly believe that finally tomorrow also included his woman.

10

Why have I put off my pride?
Why am I unsatisfied?
                    —SARA TEASDALE

Shanna stood before Roscoe Lovett in his music room, her fingers skipping and sliding over her violin strings, but, as so often lately, her heart was not in her playing.

Two weeks!

Two whole weeks had passed and she had heard nothing from Bold Wolf!

She understood that Bold Wolf had to honor a mourning period, yet she could not understand why he couldn't have broken away long enough to come to her and tell her when they could be together.

She had begun to doubt his love for her. Had it died during their separation?

And besides her concerns about Bold Wolf, Shanna was worried about Jennie. Jennie was still in that terrible place where men had no respect for any women.

Even Roscoe Lovett had forgotten his hesitation to become involved in one of his students' personal lives. He had gone to the brothel and spoke in Jennie's behalf, asking Al Adams to release her.

Roscoe had even offered Al money, but the brothel owner had laughed in his face. He had told Roscoe that someone as young and beautiful as Jennie brought in far more money than the music instructor would ever earn in a lifetime.

"Shanna, your heart is not in your lesson today," Roscoe said, laying his baton aside. He gently took Shanna's violin from her arms, and then her bow. "Mine isn't, either."

"You're worrying about Jennie, aren't you?" Shanna asked, watching him lay her violin, and then her bow, in her velveteen-lined case. She knew that the lesson was over when he closed the case and locked it.

"It's impossible to think of anything else," Roscoe said solemnly. "I feel like taking my shotgun over to Jennie's father's house and blowing a hole through his gut."

Shanna paled. "Sir, I have never heard you talk like this before," she murmured. "I suspected you cared for Jennie. Now . . . I know."

"Yes, I care," Roscoe said, slumping down into a chair. "I regret now not revealing my feelings to Jennie before . . . before . . . her father sold her to that evil man."

He nervously raked his fingers through his long, golden hair. "But my age and Jennie's are so different, and there *is* the matter of my being her instructor," he said thickly. "It would have looked scandalous should I have made advances toward Jennie, although they would have been honorable."

"Yes, I'm sure they would have been," Shanna said, surprised that her instructor would be this open with her. He was revealing to her how even *he* could feel helpless . . . perhaps even vulnerable.

"And now she has slipped through my fingers so quickly I shall never have the chance to let her know just how special she is to me," Roscoe said, slowly shaking his head.

"I think she knew," Shanna said, going to kneel before Roscoe, her eyes meeting his as he gazed at her.

"She did?" Roscoe said, his eyes wavering.

"She mentioned feeling that something might be developing between you," Shanna murmured. "Sir, I believe she cared as much for you."

"Had I but known," Roscoe said, lowering his eyes.

When he said nothing else, Shanna rose slowly to her feet. She gazed down at her teacher for a moment longer, then grabbed her violin case by the handle, turned, and left.

She was still surprised at having seen such a different side to her teacher. Although he had always been kind enough—strict only when he felt she needed scolding in order to improve her violin playing—she had never seen him this emotional.

And it was over Jennie!

Oh, if only Jennie knew, Shanna thought sullenly. If only someone could *do* something about Jennie.

Shanna had decided never to ask Bold Wolf to help Jennie. Getting him involved in such matters could only bring trouble to his people. She never wanted to do anything to cause tensions between the Penobscot and the white community.

It gave her the shivers to recall how Sheriff Wisler talked about Bold Wolf's people. She knew that the sheriff would grab the first opportunity to run the Penobscot off the island, and even from Maine, if possible.

Shanna started to go and see Elizabeth, to find some solace as she held her, then stopped with a start when He Who Watches stepped from between two buildings and stood there blocking her path, his eyes cold as he gazed at her.

"He . . . Who . . . Watches," Shanna gasped. "What are you doing here? What do you want?"

"You are to come to Indian Island tomorrow," He Who Watches said in a low rumble. "Bold Wolf has sent me to you to request your presence on our island. Tomorrow Bold Wolf will be initiated as chief. There will be a celebration. Bold Wolf wants you to participate."

"Truly?" Shanna said, her eyes widening. Her heart was pounding so hard from excitement she could hardly breathe.

She could hardly believe this was *happening*.

She had truly begun to think that Bold Wolf no longer cared for her, since he hadn't been in touch with her at all since his father's death. And Shanna had been too proud to go to Indian Island to ask him why.

And now? He truly had sent for her? He truly still cared?

"You will come?" He Who Watches asked guardedly.

Although Shanna knew there could be many obstacles making it difficult for her to go to Indian Island—mainly her *parents*—she knew that she would find a way. Nothing would stop her from going to Bold Wolf now that she knew he still wanted her and was free to follow their plans to be together.

"Yes, oh, yes," Shanna said, trying to hold her excitement down. "Please tell Bold Wolf I will be there."

"I will bring a canoe for you tomorrow morning when the sun is halfway in the sky between sunrise and the noon hour time," He Who Watches said, showing an obvious disappointment in her decision. "If you are not at the river when I arrive there, I shall wait for you until you do come."

"Thank you," Shanna said. "Please tell Bold Wolf I can hardly wait to see him."

He Who Watches nodded and walked away, his, long silver hair dragging the ground behind him.

Although excitement bubbled inside Shanna, she could not help but be uneasy. She had to find a way to get away from her parents' house for several hours without arousing their suspicions.

There was one thing in her favor. She would not have to deal with Mr. Lovett over her lessons, for tomorrow there were to be no lessons.

As for her mother, Shanna could tell her that she was going to visit friends, or go swimming, or *something*. Her mother was so often occupied by the twins she scarcely was aware of Shanna's comings and goings, anyway.

And her father?

These past several days he had been swamped with his mortuary duties. As usual, the hot summer months were claiming some of the elderly.

Her father now had two funerals to prepare for. He had even resorted to using more than one room in the house to keep up with the demand.

"Elizabeth," she whispered, her eyes gleaming happily as she hurried onward to the Diepholz mansion. "Oh, Elizabeth, I have such a *wonderful* secret to share with you!"

Then she stopped dead in her tracks, her face ashen. She was now faced with a very important decision.

Could she have both Bold Wolf and the baby? *Could* she chance telling Bold Wolf? *Could* she chance taking Elizabeth to Indian Island, where the child's true mother might be?

If the mother saw Elizabeth, would she ask to have her back, but only this time because she wanted to make sure that she killed the baby?

"I can't think about that now," Shanna whispered. She hurried onward. She would hold Elizabeth today,

then go and be held in someone's arms tomorrow—
Bold Wolf's! She had waited so long for this moment,
how could she deny herself the joyous bliss of being
with him?

And she *would* find a way to have both Bold Wolf
and Elizabeth in her life. Somehow! Yes, she *would*
find a way, for she loved them both from the very
bottom of her heart.

"Why must life be so difficult for me?" she whispered as she stopped in front of the Diepholz mansion.
Then she felt ashamed for having so selfishly thought
herself unlucky. Compared to Jennie's, Shanna's life
was sheer paradise.

Humbled by that thought, she walked up the stairs
and knocked on the door.

As the door opened, she found Emily Diepholz
standing there with Elizabeth. She sighed when she
saw how Elizabeth was dressed . . . in a beautiful white
dress trimmed in pink lace.

Then her smile faded, for the contrast of the dress's
color with the copper of Elizabeth's skin was another
reminder of who the child's true mother was, and how
the child's life might be in danger should the mother
ever know she was alive. Oh, what *was* she to do?

"Shanna, you seem so distraught about something,"
Emily murmured. She stepped aside as Shanna went
on inside to the foyer. "Do you want to talk about it?"

"I'd best not," Shanna murmured, knowing that this
was something she had to work out.

And she would—soon! But only after she spent tomorrow with Bold Wolf.

Nothing and no one, especially her own *fears,* would
keep her from going to Indian Island!

11

Her beauty lights the day
With radiance of her chastity,
And innocence doth slumber now
Upon her candid brow.
—EDWARD J. O'BRIEN

Shanna felt as though she were in the midst of a fantasy as she sat among Bold Wolf's people. She had wished for this day for so long, she could hardly believe that it had finally arrived.

And it was far more wonderful and intriguing than she had ever dreamed it would be. The tribe—men, women, and children—were assembled in the *gwundawun,* dance hall, a huge, cylindrical, domed wigwam made of birch bark.

A row of cauldrons brimming with assorted foods filled the very back of the lodge. Two fattened oxen had been slaughtered and were roasting on the outdoor fire. Rice, beans, and garden vegetables were boiling in huge copper pots over outdoor fires. Loaves of bread were abundant, as were other countless sorts of meats and vegetables awaiting the time of feasting, their mouthwatering aromas scenting the air.

The people were dressed in their most special attire—some in buckskins, others in bright broadcloth. They all wore an oblique bar of black paint across their faces as a sign of mourning for their last chief.

Shanna's gaze went to Bold Wolf. He wore the buckskins familiar to Shanna, but the rest of his attire was different and fascinating, especially a ceremonial cape of red cloth decorated with white beadwork. He had explained to Shanna earlier that the red background of the cape signified war, while the white beadwork meant peace.

He also wore a necklace of deer antler prongs and deer hooves bored and strung on leather, a sign of success, and a decorated headband fastened with a circlet of rigid gull, great blue heron, eagle, and hawk feathers.

With his own black bar of mourning painted wide across his face, Bold Wolf was seated in the center of a semicircle of people on a platform facing them.

So proud of Bold Wolf, so *happy* for him, Shanna watched one of the old councilors, a leading man of the tribe, as he began to address the assemblage. He spoke of the purpose of this occasion and reviewed the history and the government of their tribe.

When he was through, another elder of the tribe came forward and set a vial of red paint before Bold Wolf, while another man brought a basin of water and a soft cloth.

There was a hushed silence as the elder meditatively washed the black paint from Bold Wolf's face. The basin of water and soft cloth were then passed around the room so that everyone else's face could be washed as clean as their new chief's.

When that was finished, another elder knelt before Bold Wolf and just as meditatively painted his face again, this time with red paint.

Shanna watched as the man painted Bold Wolf's face between his eyebrows and above the nose, from the corner of his mouth to his chin and his cheeks.

Then a bar of red paint was applied across Bold Wolf's forehead, denoting renewal of joy and life.

Seeing the intense pride in Bold Wolf's eyes as he slid his gaze slowly over to Shanna, she smiled back

at him, so proud herself that finally his life would resume a more natural pace, which she so badly hoped
would include her.

Despite her vow to simply, at long last, enjoy Bold
Wolf's presence, she could not help today searching
the women's eyes time and again, wondering if one of
them might be Elizabeth's mother. She was torn about
how to face Bold Wolf with the truth. She wondered
again how she could take the chance of bringing Elizabeth to the island. The worry was almost driving her
crazy.

The ceremony continued, and two other elders
spoke about Bold Wolf's strengths and courage. Bold
Wolf was no longer looking at Shanna, but meeting
the eyes of his people. Shanna's thoughts went back
to earlier in the day, when she faced the problem of
leaving home without worrying her parents.

Her plan was so ingenious she found it hard to believe that she had thought it up. Although she could
not deny being devious these past several years when
she had met secretly with Bold Wolf, and of late after
having found beautiful Elizabeth beside the pond, she
was not truly someone who enjoyed deceiving her
parents.

But today it had become necessary again and she
had devised the best possible plot. At the proper time
she had brought her violin out of its case and had
begun practicing. She had chosen the most monoto-
nous music, to cause her mother to *wish* Shanna were
somewhere besides her room, playing the violin.

She had worried that perhaps her father might not
cooperate with this scheme she so badly wished to
work, for he *did* want her to practice and become a
famous violinist. But there were to be three funerals
that day at their home. She knew her father would

not want her playing the violin during the solemn, quiet ceremonies.

Shanna smiled as she recalled how perfectly the plan had worked: how her mother was the first to come into her room and ask her to please find something else to do today besides practice the violin. Every time Shanna played, the twins seemed to be more rambunctious. Only moments after her mother had left her bedroom, Shanna's father had come and told her regretfully that today she must put her violin away. The families of the deceased were already arriving. The violin music seemed out of place with the mourners' grief and despair.

So sweet, *so* understanding, Shanna had placed her violin in its bed of green velvet in the case. She had given her father a long hug and had said that she understood.

Moments later she chose a pretty, soft yellow cotton dress and fled the house, then met with He Who Watches down by the river.

Her heart racing, she clung to the sides of the canoe until they reached Indian Island. She had almost leaped into Bold Wolf's arms when they had reached the other side. His lips had quickly claimed hers. His arms had held her in a long, tight embrace.

Now she awaited the moment they could be together again, alone. But they still had the rest of the ceremony to get through, and then the festival of food and dancing.

She hoped the festival didn't last too long, for she so badly wished to be alone with Bold Wolf before returning to Old Town. She wasn't sure when she could see him again—if ever. If her parents ever learned where she had been today, they might hire a bodyguard to keep watch on her and keep her from Bold Wolf.

Now another elder stepped up to Bold Wolf, carrying a silver medal. It was attached to a ribbon, which
he solemnly placed over Bold Wolf's head and around
his neck. After delivering a brief speech about Bold
Wolf serving his people faithfully, the elder announced
that Bold Wolf was now officially the *sa-ngama*,
"strong man," the head chief, a position that was held
for life.

Shanna listened intently to the man as he now
talked about how their band of people came to be
known as the People of the Bear Family, The Bear
Clan. An ancestor had been abducted by a bear and
treated as one of its cubs. Afterward, after the man
was recovered by his human relatives, he and his descendants became known as "Bears."

From that moment on, their descendants never
killed bears. They held them in a supernatural kinship
and reverence. The likeness of a bear always appeared
on their possessions and in pictographic carvings.
Whenever they visited different camps, they always
drew a picture of a bear on a piece of birch bark with
charcoal and left it at their camps.

The story told, as it had been repeated countless
times before, and the medal now around Bold Wolf's
neck, he rose to his feet and gave his own impressive
speech. It was full of promises and native patriotism,
thanking the tribe for the honor of being chief, and
asking for their help and cooperation.

When Bold Wolf was finished, there was much applause and handshakes as the warriors of the tribe
walked past him.

And then Bold Wolf sat down on a blanket beside
Shanna as young people rose to their feet and began
dancing to the rhythm of rattles shaking and drums
drumming. Shanna's insides rippled warmly when
Bold Wolf slid a hand over and clasped one of hers.

She smiled into his eyes, then her eyes were drawn to the medal. She was surprised to see that it bore a facsimile of Andrew Jackson and was dated 1827.

"This was a gift to my father's father," Bold Wolf said, noticing Shanna's interest in the medal. "It is now worn only by those who are chief of our people."

Shanna started to say something, but an elderly woman carrying a walking cane and leading a file of women dancers to the central dance floor caused her to become quiet.

Bold Wolf leaned closer to Shanna and whispered into her ear, "Now you will be entertained by a dance ceremony called *mowia-wegan,* the Chief's Dance, he said. "I have only witnessed such a dance one other time . . . when my father was ordained as chief."

Shanna could hear a deep sadness in Bold Wolf's voice when he spoke of his father. She knew that although he was proud today, being honored in such a way, he must also feel sad about the reason he was now his people's chief.

His father was dead.

Shanna wanted to hold him and comfort him. She hoped her presence at his side was comfort enough.

Shanna looked quickly away from him and gasped when one of the women threw a handful of angelica incense on the fire and then others threw other various substances that made the fire leap as if it wanted to devour everyone, flashing, then sparkling, then bursting into the colors of the rainbow.

The women then began dancing. Shanna became mesmerized by the dancers, hoping one day she would be dancing among them, as one with them.

She watched carefully so that when there was another celebration she might be able to join them. It became apparent to Shanna that the dancers' rattles, singing, and steps were not in the same rhythm, the

effect so uniform to the ear that it was with difficulty
that one was brought to realize that all three were
moving in independent rhythms.

It fascinated Shanna to see the complexity of the
dance. It seemed so much more difficult then white
people's dances.

Just as she was thinking she understood more about
the dance, it changed. The whirling dancers reached a
peak of frenzied activity, intoning, throwing the last
of the incense into the fire, shouting, and waving
their arms.

Suddenly the rattles and drums ceased. Instead the
women dancers were keeping time with the men of
the village, who shouted in regular rhythm.

This went on for a long period, then just as suddenly
they stopped.

The women then moved to the back of the room
and lifted birth-bark and wooden dishes and began
passing them around.

After everyone had an eating vessel, Bold Wolf
shouted, "*Kewalade-wal,* your dishes"—the signal for
everyone present to help themselves from the row of
prepared foods.

Food was brought to Shanna and Bold Wolf in
heaping platters.

Shanna gazed down at the varied assortment. She
saw wild potatoes, *penak,* and artichokes that had
been baked in the ashes of the outdoor fire and were
now covered with maple sugar.

Sand plums, *abediu-mkiminal,* which had been
found growing on low bushes in the sandy places of
the northern end of Indian Island, had been gathered
and stewed.

There was much more on Shanna's plate than she
could identify. One meat, however, absolutely repelled
her. Muskrat! A large chunk of it now lay skewered

on a forked stick on her plate. She would never forget
seeing it for the first time as it cooked over the fire
today. Large forked sticks, called *psaphi-gan,* had been
pushed into the legs so that the carcass hung down,
while the end of the stick was stuck into the ground
near the fire. The carcass had been slowly turned all
morning until it was nicely roasted. But still it looked
less appetizing to Shanna as it lay among the other
foods on her plate.

"Are you not hungry?" Bold Wolf asked, seeing
how Shanna stared at the food. "Does not the food
look appetizing to you?"

"All but one thing . . ." Shanna said, still staring at
the muskrat on her plate.

Bold Wolf followed her gaze, then laughed softly.
"And so you have never eaten muskrat before," he
said, reaching over to take it from her plate, placing
it on his own.

"I think a muskrat is a hideous animal," Shanna
said, shivering. "It's . . . it's . . . no less to me than
the horrid *rats* that are killed in the buildings along
the riverfront."

"Muskrats are a delicacy," Bold Wolf said, sinking
his teeth into the sweetness of the meat. He chewed
for a moment, then swallowed. "It tastes good." He
held a bite close to Shanna's mouth. "Try it. I am
certain you will like it. It has the taste of the bird you
whites call chickens."

"No, thank you," Shanna said, shuddering. "I shall
be content enough eating what else is on my plate."

Bold Wolf shrugged and continued eating the muskrat. "Perhaps the meat should have been cooked dif-
ferently today for the celebration, masking it for you,
our only white guest," he said. "Muskrat can be fixed
many ways."

His eyes gleamed mischievously as he leaned closer

to Shanna. "But the best way to cook this animal is not one in which it can be readily disguised," he said, laughing softly. "Although its body is cut up and stewed, like a fricassee, with other ingredients, called *sikpe-su,* and is one of our warrior's favorites, it is its head that is cooked with this fricassee that makes it special." He chuckled. "Whoever takes the muskrat head from the dish has to tell a story."

"The head is actually eaten?" Shanna gasped, paling. "How horrible."

Bold Wolf reached for something else on his plate. "This is my favorite tidbit of all," he said, drawing the long piece of meat between his teeth, sucking the bone clean.

"What is *that*?" Shanna asked, eyes wide. "It does look somewhat good."

"Muskrat tail," Bold Wolf said nonchalantly. "The tails are fried between layers of fat. The tails become soft and juicy and are very sweet."

Her appetite now truly gone, and feeling queasy, Shanna dropped her plate to the ground, rose shakily from the blanket, then rushed from the huge dwelling, leaving behind a silence as everyone stared after her.

Bold Wolf dropped his own plate. He went outside and searched frantically for Shanna, feeling bad now for his teasing. He had not truly thought it would affect her in this way. He had hoped she would see the lighthearted side of his jesting. Instead, he had ruined everything for her.

Feeling wretched, he searched until he found her behind the council house. He could tell by her paleness and by the way she held her face in her hands that she might retch at any moment.

This made him feel doubly bad and a hundred times sorry that he was so thoughtless. He took Shanna's hands from her face, then drew her against him and held her in his arms.

"I'm sorry," he murmured. "I do not know how I could be so thoughtless."

"I understand what you were trying to do," Shanna murmured, already feeling better. His arms were all she had wanted, this whole day through. And now she had them. "I'm sorry for not being strong enough to laugh along with you."

"I should have known better," Bold Wolf said thickly. "You are such a delicate thing. I will never forget the time you fainted on the bluff when you saw me standing there."

"You were like an apparition that night," Shanna murmured, turning her eyes up to his. "Bold Wolf, oh, Bold Wolf, I have waited so long for this moment. Please, oh, please kiss me."

Their bodies straining together hungrily, their lips met in a frenzy of kisses.

Bold Wolf then lifted her into his arms, and with a pounding heart he carried her to his cabin.

As sunlight streamed across his bed, he slowly disrobed Shanna. Lost in bliss, Shanna then slowly disrobed Bold Wolf, his muscled body and his throbbing readiness soon revealed to her.

Not even thinking about the red paint that was still on his face, looking past it and seeing his utter handsomeness, Shanna tremored with ecstasy as his hands caught her about the waist and brought her beneath him.

"It has been forever, Shanna, since our first kiss," Bold Wolf whispered against her trembling lips. "I have wanted you . . . your *body* . . . ever since."

"Take me now," Shanna whispered, sinking into a chasm of pure joyous rapture. "I am yours, Bold Wolf.

Oh, my darling . . . I am yours. I always have been. I always will be."

He placed his heat against her soft folds. "The pain will be brief," he said huskily, his eyes holding hers as she silently nodded for him to go on.

Their lips met in a long, deep kiss as he slowly shoved his throbbing need into her.

12

Oh, pale dispensers of my Joys and Pains,
Holding the doors of Heaven and Hell,
How the hot blood rushed wildly through the veins,
Beneath your touch, until you waved farewell.
— LAWRENCE HOPE

Shanna scarcely breathed as Bold Wolf's manhood slid slowly into her hot, moist folds. She tightened her arms around his neck and gasped when a searing pain made her realize why he had warned her.

But soon her mind was splintered with wondrous sensations that made her relax and sigh with pleasure as her body moved with his toward a place she had never known existed. As he moved faster inside her, in quicker, surer movements, he gently kissed her, his hands searching her body, stroking.

Then he slid his mouth away from her lips and he leaned just far enough away so that he could peer down at her. The way he looked at her, with such passion clouding his eyes, caused strange, fluttering sensations deep in Shanna's belly.

"Do you feel it?" Bold Wolf whispered, his body still rhythmically moving. "Do you feel the passion? The intense pleasure?"

"I feel so many things," Shanna whispered back, overcome with a feverish heat. "And they are all wonderful."

"It will always be this way for us," Bold Wolf said, his steel arms enfolding her, his lips now resting against the slender column of her throat. He was growing hotter and hotter, as if a fire were consuming him. "My woman, my Shanna, feel how I want you."

"Yes, yes," Shanna breathed.

Her eyes closed in ecstasy when he slid his mouth lower and swirled his tongue around one of her nipples, then sucked it into his mouth and nipped it with the edges of his teeth.

Her body tightened when he slowed his movements inside her. She looked at him questioningly when his hands went to her waist and he moved her to another position, on her hands and knees.

Quiet, her eyes wide, thinking this to be an odd way to make love, Shanna waited as he moved behind her. Then she gasped with renewed pleasure when Bold Wolf thrust his manhood back into her swollen folds and again began his rhythmic thrusts.

When he reached around and filled his hands with her breasts, his fingers tweaking her pink-crested nipples to hardness, she was left shaken with desire.

Feeling the pressure building somewhere deep inside him, Bold Wolf found it hard to think any longer. Wanting to hasten Shanna's pleasure, he slid a hand down to touch her and caress her woman's center, the tiny rosebud of flesh swollen and pulsing against his fingertips. He caressed her until he could hear her moans and gasps of rapture.

He then turned her again.

Stretching his hard, taut body over hers, he once again shoved his manhood inside her and resumed his strokes within her.

"Kiss me?" Shanna whispered, twining an arm around his neck, bringing his mouth to her lips. She gave him a frenzied kiss and locked her legs around his waist. She arched her back and met his thrusts with eagerness, her hips moving with his as though she were practiced in the art of lovemaking.

Suddenly Shanna felt a tremor going through her body, swelling inside her into an incredible spasmic heat.

She cried out against Bold Wolf's lips as the pleasure overwhelmed her, then she sighed when his body quaked against hers, their pleasure intertwining as though they were one mind, one soul, one heartbeat.

Afterward, lost in a tempest of emotions and still breathing hard, Shanna watched Bold Wolf roll away from her and stretch out on his back beside her. She turned on her side and gazed in wonder at him as he lay there, breathless, his eyes closed.

Her gaze went to that part of his anatomy that had just taken her to paradise and back, in awe of how it had happened. She reached a trembling hand to his manhood and slowly wrapped her fingers around it, the heat of his flesh surprising her.

"Move your fingers on me," Bold Wolf whispered huskily as he reached down and guided her hand in how to pleasure him.

He sighed and stiffened as he felt the coolness of her hand against his heat, the ecstasy once again swimming through him in bursts of white light.

When he spilled his seed into Shanna's hand, she gasped and drew her hand away, puzzled, afraid that she had actually hurt him.

Bold Wolf sat up quickly, took her hand, and held it out before her. "What you have in your hand are seeds that could make many babies," he said, his eyes locking with hers as she looked quickly over at him. "Yes, I sent many such seeds into your womb moments ago. One is all it takes to make a child. We will soon marry. We will have a home for the baby when it slides from the protective cocoon of your womb."

"Me? I might be pregnant?" Shanna whispered, paling.

He cradled her face between his hands. "Yes, it is possible that you might be with child," he murmured. Then he chuckled. "And I see how it might frighten you to think of becoming a mother so quickly. Do not fret about it. Just because I planted seeds today inside your womb does not mean that you will become pregnant. The time has to be right in a woman's body for this to happen. Chances are this is not the time of the month that you could conceive."

"Then you don't think I am pregnant?" Shanna asked, her eyes wide as she peered into his.

She felt foolish now for having made love so easily without thinking about the chances of getting pregnant. It had just happened so quickly . . . this desire for him that sent her into his bed so easily.

And there was their long absence from one another. It had made her hunger for him twofold.

She cast her foolish feelings aside, knowing that if she had it to do over, she would once again go to bed with him this easily and make love. She could not have waited another moment for what they had denied themselves those long years they had met in secret and had only held and kissed one another.

"No, I do not think you are with child," Bold Wolf reassured her. "But once you are my wife and we make love every night, perhaps sometimes even in the mornings, you will then know that a baby will be conceived."

She heard him, yet her mind was suddenly elsewhere . . . on another baby. She hoped that by the time she could come to him to be his wife he would know and accept Elizabeth and promise to protect her from anyone who might still want to harm her.

"Shanna?" Bold Wolf said, bringing her face close to his, forcing her eyes to lock with his.

He suddenly recalled how he had earlier thought

she had looked radiant when he had seen her at Old Town, as though she might have found a new lover. Had she falsely come to Bold Wolf today while all along thinking of someone else?

Yet he knew that she had not made love with another man, for her woman's line of defense inside her body had not been tampered with or broken.

"What?" Shanna said, shaken from her thoughts when she found Bold Wolf staring into her eyes. "What did you say?"

"Your mind was somewhere else," Bold Wolf said thickly, dropping his hands away from her face. "Do you wish to talk about it? Is there something troubling you that you need to tell me? You soon will be my wife. There should never be any secrets between us."

"And there won't be," Shanna murmured, her eyes lowering. "Once we are married, I shall be open with you about everything."

"But till *then,* will you?" Bold Wolf said, sensing in her words that something wasn't right.

"What do you mean?" Shanna said, his question causing her heart to leap inside her chest. She gazed guardedly into his eyes.

"Is there something you aren't *telling* me?" Bold Wolf insisted. He left the bed and pulled on his fringed breeches. "I sense something about you, Shanna." He tied the leather thongs at the front of his breeches, then reached for his buckskin shirt. "I hope your distant behavior is only because you are concerned about how to tell your parents that you will soon leave them for me."

"Yes, I have worried so often about that," Shanna said, slowly sliding from the bed, grabbing her dress from the floor. "I must have time now, Bold Wolf, to prepare them for the marriage."

"You have had time while I was in mourning," Bold

Wolf said, watching her dress flutter down across her body as she slipped into it. "You had to know that my father had passed to the other side. You knew then that it would not be long before we would be together. You had to know that I would have wanted to marry you soon."

"Yes, I knew all those things, yet still I have not told my parents," Shanna said, hating to see the disappointment in his eyes. "You don't know my father . . . how . . . how ambitious he is for me to be a concert violinist. And . . . you *know* that he is a prejudiced man. When he hears that I am going to be your wife, I dread thinking what he might do."

She didn't think this was the right time to tell Bold Wolf about Elizabeth. She had to sort things out one at a time. It was enough now to think about the chore of telling her parents.

But it was time now to act, not to worry.

Yes, she had to go to her parents and tell them things she knew would enrage them. She shuddered especially to think of her father's reaction.

Glancing through the window, Shanna saw that the sun was dipping lower in the sky. If she did not arrive home by suppertime, her parents would be aware that she had done more today than just swim or meet with friends.

The twins were surely settled down now, probably exhausted after having played so hard all day. Her father would soon put his day's activities behind him. It was the family custom, while eating the evening meal, to discuss their day's activities with one another.

"I truly must go," Shanna said, slipping her feet into her shiny leather slippers. She ran her fingers through her hair to smooth out the tangles. "I had no idea it was so late."

"I will escort you across the river," Bold Wolf said, yanking on his moccasins.

He then went to Shanna, slid his arms around her waist, and drew her against him. "Meet me tomorrow in midafternoon at our secret place," he said thickly. "I hope you will then tell me that you have told your parents about us. Once that is done and they understand that nothing will stop our marriage, I will send He Who Watches with my bride price for your father."

Shanna paled. "No, don't do that," she blurted. "Father might insult He Who Watches."

"It is the custom of the Penobscot that bride prices will be paid to fathers for daughters, so Bold Wolf *will* send a bride price," Bold Wolf said flatly. He swung an arm around her waist and walked her toward his door. "Do not fret so. The time has come for us to be together. It is our *destiny*. No one will stand in the way of such a thing that has been written in the heavens as our being together as man and wife has been written."

Shanna became quiet as they walked outside. She saw that the celebration was still in progress.

"The games, the feasting, the singing and dancing, will go on far into the night," Bold Wolf said. "Once I have you safely across the river, I will return to my people and once again join the celebration."

Shanna scarcely heard what Bold Wolf was saying. Her thoughts were so scrambled with her concerns, these precious moments with Bold Wolf were almost ruined.

This made her know that she must straighten things out soon, for she did not want to build disappointment upon disappointment in Bold Wolf's mind, or he might decide he did not want to have her after all. If his trust in her wavered, so might his love!

The river was calm, the breezes were soft, and the sun was only barely peeking through the thick tapestry of birch leaves overhead when Bold Wolf helped Shanna into the canoe.

She sat behind him while he sat in the middle of the canoe, his muscled arms rhythmically lifting the paddle and pulling it through the water.

Shanna tried to center her thoughts on other things besides her concerns. She clung to the sides of the canoe, noticing, as she had before, how the Penobscot canoe rode so low in the water. The sides of the craft curved inward, and the upturn of the ends was not very high.

Bold Wolf had told her that the brown and white triangular decoration along the bark insert at the middle of the canoe was considered a Penobscot mark of distinction, as were also the series of double-curve ornaments etched on the bark flaps at the ends.

Bold Wolf told her that *Gluskabe,* the culture hero of the Penobscot, was credited with introducing the canoe to the tribe and with instructing them in how to make it.

Shanna was drawn out of her reverie as they approached the other side. She stiffened when she saw activity at the waterfront as some fishermen docked and shouted at one another excitedly over their day's catch.

Shanna became unnerved about being seen with Bold Wolf. She was afraid that word would spread quickly to her father even before she got the chance to explain things to him.

And she was afraid that others could see on her face the awakened feelings of a woman. She did feel as though she were glowing!

She was glad when Bold Wolf steered his canoe far to the right, so that Shanna could disembark on a strip of shore where she could say good-bye to her beloved without anyone watching her with condemning eyes.

But in a moment, Shanna's color drained quickly from her face and she gasped with fear. Her father was riding along the shore, his horse kicking up rocks and sand beneath its hooves. She knew that he sometimes went horseback riding before supper. He did this to work off emotions that sometimes overwhelmed him after working with the dead all day.

She knew he had worked harder then usual lately, so she should have known he would take his horse along the shore, the river breeze soft and sweet against his face.

There was one difference tonight. He had brought his shotgun on the ride with him. Even now she could see that his hand rested on the weapon in the gunboot at the right side of his steed. She wondered why he had the gun.

Realizing that he had not yet seen her with Bold Wolf, Shanna fell to her knees and scrambled over to Bold Wolf. She frantically grabbed him by an arm. "Turn around!" she cried. "Oh, Lord, please turn around! It's Father. Don't you see him? It's Father."

But it was too late. Her father had drawn a tight rein, wheeled his horse around, and was glaring at Shanna and Bold Wolf.

Bold Wolf's skin prickled at the nape of his neck when he saw the anger in Shanna's father's eyes, yet he continued onward, for he knew that fate had drawn her father there. It was time to set things straight between father and daughter and the man who would soon be this man's son-in-law. Bold Wolf had known that it was going to be a hard task for Shanna to handle alone. Now she wouldn't have to. He would help her through this thing that he knew was like a heavy weight on his woman's delicate shoulders.

Shanna's eyes were wide and her pulse raced as Bold Wolf beached the canoe only a few feet away from her father.

Her eyes met and held with her father's and she shrank away from the accusation in his stare. She felt ashamed now for having gone behind his back today. Not only had she gone to be with Bold Wolf during his celebration, she had also made love with him.

But how could any of this be wrong? she thought in despair. Her future was with Bold Wolf. He *was* her future.

No. She would not allow her father to make her feel sordid and small over what she had done.

"Shanna, Shanna," her father said, his voice thick with disgust.

She had expected him to reach for his firearm and threaten Bold Wolf with it. Instead he held out a hand for her, beckoning her to come to him.

Shanna scampered from the canoe, leaving Bold Wolf alone in it. She gave Bold Wolf a wavering glance over her shoulder, then hurried to her father and allowed him to grab her and yank her up on the saddle before him. She knew that she *had* to cooperate now or never get her father to understand.

"Bold Wolf, I know that you are now chief and feel you have the right to do as you please about many things, but don't think that includes my daughter," Jordan said, his eyes narrowing as he glared at Bold Wolf. "She has a bright future ahead of her and that does not include sneaking around with a savage. I'm sure she can explain away why she did it today. But don't expect her to do it again. She knows better than to spoil her future over some whimsical notion of being infatuated with a savage! By damn, I've taught her better than that."

Enraged over being called a savage and having been

talked down to as though he were no more than a child, Bold Wolf held his temper at bay. He stared up at Jordan, but said nothing.

Then Bold Wolf looked into Shanna's eyes. He saw a deep apology and knew that she was not there in her father's saddle because she wanted to be.

And Bold Wolf knew now just what a chore Shanna *did* have ahead of her in convincing her father that her life was with a Penobscot chief, and *not* the lonely life of a concert violinist.

Understanding so much and not wanting to create any more problems for his woman, now knowing that there was nothing he could say at this time to alter this white man's feelings about him, Bold Wolf kept his silence. Shoving his canoe back out in the water, he began his return to his island.

Tears spilled from Shanna's eyes as her father held her possessively against him and rode off toward home.

She gazed over her shoulder at Bold Wolf as he slowly crossed the river. She was so afraid that she might not see him again. Her father had actually called Bold Wolf a savage and said things that surely cut deeply into Bold Wolf's heart.

Surely Bold Wolf's humiliation ran deep.

"How could you have done this, Shanna?" her father quickly said, "How long have you been involved with that Indian? How many times have you gone to Indian Island when I thought you were with friends? When did you become a sneak, Shanna? When?

The more he said, the more Shanna's shame and humiliation turned to anger.

But she still said nothing. She knew that she had to be careful not to rush into anything or Bold Wolf's life could be endangered. It was obvious today that her father's hate ran deep, and she knew that it was not entirely because Bold Wolf was an Indian. It was because Bold Wolf had interfered in her father's plans for her future. He would have hated any man who had done this!

She looked again toward the river, her spirits plummeting even more when she no longer saw Bold Wolf. He was back among his people. She was among hers. Strange how now it seemed as though they had never had this special day together!

Would they ever again? Right now she felt only despair.

13

You may stretch your hand out towards me—
Ah! You will—I know not when—
I shall nurse my love and keep it
Faithfully, for you, till then.
                    —ADELAIDE ANNE PROCTER

A loud explosion, and then loud blasts of the whistle at the Corber Sawmill upriver from Old Town awakened Shanna with a start.

When the whistle continued to blow, one continuous blast after another, tearing through the panes of Shanna's bedroom window like loud thunderclaps, she sat up and covered her ears and closed her eyes.

She understood well enough what the continuous blasts from the sawmill meant: that the explosion she had heard only moments before had not been a minor one. Surely several men had been injured . . . or killed.

Now she heard her twin brothers wailing. The loud blasts of the whistle surely had awakened and frightened them. Shanna opened her eyes, lowered her hands from her ears, and became quickly aware of the scampering of footsteps out in the corridor.

Her father's strained voice as he spoke to Shanna's mother just outside Shanna's door made her realize that her father had to prepare himself for the worst. If the explosion had killed several of the lumberjacks, then he, being the only mortician in town, would soon be overwhelmed with bodies.

"Oh, Lord, let it not be so," Shanna whispered, slipping into a soft silk robe. She shuddered at the thought of the house being turned into one huge morgue. It had happened one other time. Right after they had moved to Old Town a paddle wheeler riverboat had sunk and several people had drowned in the Penobscot River.

Then another thought came to her that made her heart skip a beat. If lumberjacks had been injured or killed at the sawmill, might one of them be Jennie's evil father?

No. She would not allow herself to wish for someone's death, not even the man who sold his own daughter into slavery at the terrible brothel.

Shanna started to go out of her room to inquire about what had happened, then stopped and decided not to. Her feelings were still too raw to face her parents just yet after being reprimanded last night by not only her father, but also her mother, after she and her father had arrived home. Shanna had been treated like a child and sent to her room without supper.

That had made Shanna even more adamant about marrying Bold Wolf as soon as possible. She was old enough to know her own mind. She was definitely old enough to get married and marry the man of her choosing.

Today, though, she would still play the role of daughter and try to draw her parents into an understanding with her instead of just going off half-cocked and getting married to spite them. Shanna had seen enough of life to know that, for the most part, her parents had been good to her. She owed them respect, in return.

Yes, she would bide a little more time until she found a way to make them understand that she loved Bold Wolf more than life itself. Surely they would want her true happiness! It would be so ideal if they would give her their blessing. And to get it, she would do as they wished for a while longer. Today she would take her violin lessons. She would come home afterward like an obedient daughter and practice her violin before supper.

Yes, she would try just a while longer to make things right between herself and her parents before giving them the news that no matter what, she *would* marry Bold Wolf.

She was glad for one thing. Last night, after Shanna's father had gone to bed, her mother had slipped into Shanna's room and had brought her some cold chicken and fruit. Without saying anything to Shanna or giving her a hug of reassurance, she had left the room. Yet the gesture of love had been enough for Shanna. Content for the moment that her mother still loved her, she had eaten her belated supper.

Then, content enough, she had gone to bed and dreamed of Bold Wolf and the wonder of feelings he had brought out in her.

Dressed, her hair combed and drawn back from her face with a velveteen ribbon the same color of pale green as her fully gathered cotton dress, Shanna left the bedroom to have breakfast with her family before leaving for her lessons.

But soon she realized that nothing would be the same today around her house. She stood at the railing at the top of the staircase and watched, her eyes wide, as scorched, unrecognizable bodies were brought through the front door and taken to the holding room, the room where bodies were kept before they were taken to the preparation room.

The stench of the bodies wafted up the stairs and into Shanna's nose, causing her to flinch. She had never smelled anything as vile and unbelievable.

"Oh, Shanna, isn't it horrible?" her mother cried as she came and stood next to Shanna, staring down at the macabre scene below. "There was an explosion. So many men were killed. They are . . . all being brought here."

Shanna started to reply, but stopped when her twin brothers came running past and started down the stairs in giggling leaps.

"Oh, no!" Bernita cried, paling. "I told them to stay in their room! Shanna, help me get them! I can't allow them to see the morbid sight down below."

Shanna raced after one of the twins while her mother went after the other one. Soon they had them in their bedroom, their crying filling the air, their fists pummeling their mother's legs.

"Tommie! Terrie! Stop that this instant!" Shanna cried as she yanked one twin away from Bernita and held him tightly in her arms, while her mother knelt down and grabbed the other child and held him.

"What am I to do with these children?" Bernita cried, her eyes frantic as she gazed up at Shanna. "They are so out of hand, Shanna. They are nothing like you were when you were a child their age."

"Mother, you know that you have spoiled the twins terribly since they have been old enough to know how to get their way with you," Shanna said amid their relentless crying. "I'm not sure what you can do about them now."

"Shanna, you've always been such a good girl," Bernita said, tears flooding her eyes. "Until . . . until . . . yesterday, I have never had one moment of trouble with you. Shanna, what were you thinking, going to Indian Island and being with Bold Wolf? It would be scandalous should that get around town."

"Mother, I . . ." Shanna said, then stopped. She had started to tell her mother that she loved Bold Wolf. She wanted so badly to go ahead and tell her mother that she was going to marry Bold Wolf. But her mother was already distraught over the children's behavior and what was happening down below—*and* surely feeling as though Shanna had deceived her.

"Mother, if I don't hurry along, I'll be late for my violin lessons," Shanna said, releasing little Tommie, who took advantage of his freedom by rushing to the door and trying to open it.

Shanna grabbed him, carried him to his bed, and placed him on it. "Stay there, Tommie," she said, her voice firm, her eyes filled with anger. "You've caused enough trouble for Mother today. Behave. Do you hear me? Behave!"

She felt a slight sting of regret over scolding her brother like this, the very first time she had ever done it. He looked up at her with tear-filled eyes, his body racked with deep sobs. She gazed at him for a moment longer, then sighed and hurried from the room.

She was glad when she heard the door lock behind her, knowing that was at least one way for her mother to temporarily control the children.

As Shanna started to go down the stairs, she stopped and stared in disbelief at what she saw below. She paled and felt faint when she saw that her worst fears were confirmed: The whole downstairs *was* being turned into a morgue as bodies lay stretched out on all the open spaces, blankets and articles of clothing covering them.

Shanna turned and fled to the back of the house, where a set of stairs led down to the kitchen, and then to the back door, where she could make a quick, unseen escape. She knew that the wives of those fallen men would be arriving soon. She was glad she would not be there to hear the wails and screams of those who would sort through the bodies, most of which were scorched unrecognizable.

Shanna was so glad to be outside, but found no

reprieve of fresh air. The stench of the explosion had sent a huge, billowing black pall of smoke over Old Town. The whistle still blasted eerily into the air. Screams and cries were heard as people scrambled in all directions, their eyes wild, their faces tear-streaked.

Rushing onward, wanting to get to the music studio to find momentary escape there, Shanna was breathless as she finally arrived and climbed the stairs in a mad rush.

But when she got to the top of the stairs and started to open the door, she stopped, her eyes wide. The door was locked, a note tacked to it beside the window.

She read the note and discovered that Roscoe Lovett had gone to the sawmill to help with the disaster. "*Now* what am I to do?" she whispered, turning to stare at how the town had been turned into a frantic melee. She wondered what she might do to help, yet knew that someone as inexperienced as she with tragedies such as this would only get in the way.

Then her eyes lifted and she stared farther, past the town, toward Indian Island.

Her heart stopped for a moment and she went cold inside when she saw great palls of smoke rising from the *island*.

"How can that be?" she whispered. She didn't see how the sawmill explosion could have anything to do with Indian Island. The sawmill was upriver and on the opposite shore from Bold Wolf's island.

Yet there it was! Smoke *was* rising in great black clouds from the island!

"How *can* that have happened?" Shanna cried, lifting the skirt of her dress, rushing back down the stairs. "Bold Wolf, oh, Bold Wolf, are you all right?"

She held her skirt up past her ankles and ran breathlessly to the waterfront, maneuvering to avoid crashing into the frantic townspeople blindly hurrying about.

When Shanna got to the river, she rushed up and down the embankment searching for an idle canoe. When she found one, she shoved it out into the water, ran knee-deep into the river, then tumbled in and grabbed the paddle.

Not caring now what her parents would say when they discovered that she had gone against their wishes and was again going to Indian Island, knowing that she could not rest until she saw that Bold Wolf was all right, Shanna drew the paddle incessantly through the blue water, shuddering as debris from the burning rubble of the sawmill fell from the heavens.

Shanna found herself immersed in great bursts of black smoke, some wafting from the sawmill, some wafting from Indian Island. The smoke was so intense, she couldn't get a clear view of the Penobscot village.

But she could envision it in her mind's eye as burning, with people left homeless and dying. This made her find the strength to pull the paddle through the water until she finally reached the other side.

Panting, her arms trembling from the unfamiliar effort of paddling, Shanna jumped from the canoe and dragged it up to dry land. Then she turned and ran up the hill toward the village.

She stopped short when she got past the worst of the smoke and she found the village intact, the people casually about their morning chores.

Inhaling a deep breath or relief, Shanna looked past the village and saw, at the far side, far past the lodges, the cause of the smoke on the island. She could see several of the warriors tending to fires and some starting new fires along ground where she now recalled having seen berry fields.

She knew that the island produced an abundance of

blueberries, blackberries, and huckleberries. They were an important crop to the Penobscot. But why were the warriors burning them?

"Shanna?"

The soft voice of a woman drew Shanna around to see Pale Star coming toward her. Shanna had been introduced to the lovely Penobscot woman prior to the celebration yesterday. Sweet and friendly, Pale Star was Shanna's age.

Shanna looked once again at the smoke rising in great, black plumes from the berry patches. "Why are they burning the berry bushes, Pale Star?" she asked, turning to gaze into Pale Star's midnight-dark eyes. "I saw the smoke. I . . . I . . . thought the Penobscot homes were burning."

"This is an annual chore for our men," Pale Star said, turning to watch the activity herself, where the fires were spreading through the bushes. "They burn off our berry fields to replenish the soil. Then when the berries grow again, they will be larger and juicier."

Then Pale Star turned and looked across the river at the smoke rising in great black puffs from the destroyed sawmill. "The fires on your land were not lit purposely, were they?" she said softly.

"No, Pale Star. The people of Old Town are experiencing a true tragedy today," Shanna said. She turned and stared across the river, where people were frantically dealing with the disaster, still taking bodies out on slabs of wood that had been quickly prepared to act as stretchers. "It's horrible, Pale Star. So horrible."

She turned again to Pale Star. "But I am so glad that everything is all right here," she murmured, now taking the time to admire the lovely woman in her doeskin dress, beads resplendent at the front. Pale Star was somewhat shorter than Shanna. Her raven-black hair was coiled up into a tight knot at the top of her head. She had a beautiful, slender face, with luminous brown eyes that were slightly slanted at the corners.

Shanna was glad to know that this woman was Bold Wolf's blood kin, a cousin, or she would have seen her as a rival, since Bold Wolf always looked at Pale Star with much admiration.

"Yes, things are fine on Indian Island," Bold Wolf said as he came through a screen of smoke and walked toward Shanna. His clothes and his face were smudged from the smoke.

Shanna melted inside when their eyes locked and held.

Pale Star slipped silently away, leaving Bold Wolf and Shanna alone.

Bold Wolf took Shanna's hand and swept her away to his cabin. Once again, he drew her into his arms and gave her a long, deep kiss, then laughed softly and leaned away to gaze down at her.

"Did my kiss taste of smoke?" he said, reaching up to wipe a smudge of soot from Shanna's cheek, only succeeding in rubbing it more into her skin, since his fingers were smoke-blackened from tending to the fires.

"Your kiss tastes of heaven," Shanna murmured, caught up in the wondrous feelings she only felt while in his presence. "Although we have only been apart for a few hours, it seems an eternity."

"It does not have to be that way," Bold Wolf said huskily, reaching down to slide a hand up inside her dress.

He watched her eyes cloud with ecstasy as he caressed her. "Stay," he said huskily. "Be mine. We can exchange vows as early as tonight."

"I so wish that was possible," Shanna said, her heart pounding as his fingers awakened her senses. "But I

can't betray my parents in such a way. They don't
deserve that. I will, in time, find a way to make them
understand. Please be patient a while longer, Bold
Wolf. Oh, please be patient. I so long for nothing
more than to be with you. Only you."

"I have already waited for so long," Bold Wolf said,
taking her by a hand, leading her down to his bed.

"But that was not my fault," Shanna whispered, becoming languorous as he lifted her dress and he bent
low to kiss her throbbing center through her silk undergarment. "It was . . . because . . . of your duties
as Runner that we were apart for so long."

She closed her eyes in ecstasy, welcoming this way
to forget the mayhem at Old Town, at least for the
moment. He removed her undergarment and she felt
his lips and his tongue directly on the flesh of her
swollen bud. She gasped with pleasure and soon forgot
what they had been discussing. The pleasure was fore-
most on her mind now as he sent her mind spinning
with rapture. His mouth was so hot, his tongue so wet,
his fingers so demanding as he reached up and caressed her breasts through the cotton material of her
dress.

Finding the pleasure almost too much to bear, and
realizing she was close to the ultimate of ecstasy,
Shanna opened her eyes wildly and placed her hands
at his cheeks. "No, Bold Wolf," she said, her voice
sounding strangely husky to her. "Please . . . please . . .
not in that way. That way . . . doesn't seem right."

Bold Wolf smiled up at her, then stood beside the
bed as he took his clothes off. Shanna sat up and
yanked her own clothes over her head.

Bold Wolf soon blanketed her with his body. He
crushed her to him so hard, she gasped. Everything
but this moment, their love for each other, their
yearning, was forgotten. Bold Wolf sought her mouth

with a wildness and desperation as he thrust himself
into her and began his rhythmic strokes. The blood
pulsed hot and rapid through his veins and he felt her
heat fusing with his. He wrapped his arms around her,
and with a fierceness, held her close as he plunged,
over and over again, into the yielding silk of her body.
He rained kisses on her eyelids and her face, and then
bent low and sank his mouth over a breast, his tongue
flicking over the tight nub of nipple.

Lost in ecstasy, Shanna thrashed her head back and
forth, tears of pure bliss streaming from her eyes.

With quick, eager fingers, Bold Wolf's hands were
in her hair, stilling her so that he could kiss her again.
His mouth bore down, exploding with raw passion.
His tongue forced her lips apart as his kiss grew more
and more passionate. His hands were on her throat,
framing her face. His body moved rhythmically against
hers, her hips responding, moving as he moved, then
lifting to bring him even closer.

A cry of sweet agony tore from the depths of Shanna's being as the ultimate of pleasure came to her in
great bursts of heat.

Trembling, her whole body quaking, she arched
against Bold Wolf. She clung to him as she felt his
release coming in great, explosive bursts as he groaned
and shoved endlessly into her.

Afterward a great silence vibrated between them.
Shanna lay beside him, her body locked against his.
Their breaths mingled as they gazed into one anoth-
er's eyes.

"I shouldn't have done this," she murmured, breaking the euphoric moment. "I shouldn't have come."

"You belong here," Bold Wolf said flatly. He
stroked her hair back from her face.

"I know," Shanna said, choking back a sob that was

suddenly there in the depths of her throat. "And I *will* be with you, as soon . . . as soon as I work things out."

She knew he thought that she only meant with her parents, while in truth she still had doubts about what his feelings would be toward little Elizabeth. She would not confide in him just yet about Elizabeth, but knew soon she would have to tell Bold Wolf everything.

For now, she felt the urgency to get back on the other side of the river without her father discovering that she had been with Bold Wolf. She felt wrong about having taken advantage of the moment, when her father would be so immersed in the disaster that had claimed the lives of so many innocent men.

Yet, she reminded herself, it was not *that* that had sent her across the river. It was the smoke she had seen wafting from Indian Island. Her concern for her lover's safety had lured her there. She had thought tragedy had also struck Bold Wolf's people.

"When can we see one another again?" Bold Wolf asked, brushing a soft kiss across her breasts. "I live for these moments with you, Shanna. Although I am now chief to my people, *you* are my true life."

"As you are mine," Shanna whispered, closing her eyes when once again he stroked her tender woman's center with his deft fingers. She found herself being too aroused; she knew that she should hurry back home.

Finding the willpower, Shanna watched his eyes as she slid his hand on away from her. "I truly must return home," she murmured. She laughed softly as she gazed at the smudges of black on his face, knowing that so much of that had to have rubbed off onto hers. She knew that would be no cause of alarm should her parents see it. Everyone in town at this moment would

look the same, for the whole town was filled with the
smoke from the explosion.

"I will not be able to wait long for you to come
and join me as my wife," Bold Wolf said solemnly as
he left the bed and yanked on his breeches. His eyes
looked haunted as he gazed into Shanna's. "I love
you, Shanna. I alone can fulfill your every need."

"Yes, you alone," Shanna said, yet in her heart
knowing that Elizabeth now fulfilled her as well, but
in a much different way.

Shanna hurried into her clothes, then became
breathless all over again when Bold Wolf yanked her
into his arms and gave her a deep, long kiss.

Bold Wolf then stepped away from her. "Take that
with you and think of it when you still do not find the
courage to tell your parents that you are mine," he
said, then stalked out of the cabin, leaving her alone
with her wonder.

She wrenched herself out of the sensual reverie and
hurried from the cabin. She rushed to the canoe and
made the journey back across the river, soon to be
immersed in the reality of just how bad the explosion
had been. The whole town of Old Town seemed
turned upside down because of it.

She rushed home and mustered the courage to offer
her help, although it cut deep into her heart to see
the dead and the agony of those who loved them.

She felt eyes on her and looked up to find her
mother standing on the staircase, frozen, it seemed,
with the shock of it all. Shanna went to her, and felt
a wave of compassion when her mother turned and
clung to her, crying.

For the first time in her life, Shanna felt she was
the stronger of the two. She helped her mother to her
room and saw that she was snuggled in bed before
she left to see about the twins.

When she got to the twins' room, she discovered that her mother had finally hired a nanny, a large, stout woman who would soon have the twins in tow.

Smiling, Shanna left the room and went back downstairs, helping again with the grieving women who had lost their world today.

That made Shanna realize just how quickly the world could stop for people. She hoped she could get on with her own life the way she wished to live it.

She wondered just how long Bold Wolf would continue to patiently wait for her. Was it possible she could lose her chance forever?

14

Both of her parents slept in exhaustion between funerals. Shanna had found her own reprieve from these past two morbid days by going today and seeking the wonders of being with Elizabeth. She had been told that her violin lessons would be postponed until things got back to normal in Old Town; Roscoe Lovett was involved in helping his fellow townspeople.

Shanna wished he could have been as effective where Jennie was concerned. But everyone seemed unable to help Jennie. Everyone seemed frightened to death of the vile man who owned this particular brothel. Even Sheriff Wisler had not interfered. It was obvious to Shanna just how ineffective a sheriff he was for Old Town.

Shanna discovered soon after the explosion that, of all the people to escape the sawmill explosion without a scratch, Jennie's father was still around to wreak havoc on the lives of his family.

As Shanna held Elizabeth in her arms in the stately oak rocker at the Diepholz mansion, slowly rocking her back and forth, she tried to forget the ugly side of life and concentrate only on her beautiful child. Elizabeth had grown so much since the day Shanna had found her tiny and helpless beside the pond. It

made Shanna's heart fill with gratitude toward Emily
Diepholz for having so generously taken the child to
her breast for nourishment.

Shanna gently folded the blanket away from Elizabeth. Today she wore a soft gown. Shanna scooted the
sleeves up and gazed at Elizabeth's wrists. She smiled
when she saw the rolls of fat. She then raised the
gown up and marveled over the rolls of fat on the
child's smooth, copper legs. Yes, Emily's milk was
working wonders on Elizabeth. She was no longer that
forlorn baby Shanna had found by the pond. She was
healthy. She was content.

"You *are* so beautiful," Shanna whispered, gazing
into Elizabeth's shining eyes as the child studied the
one who held her. "I'm your mother, Elizabeth. Your
mother. Can you feel it in the way I hold you? Can
you hear it in my voice? Elizabeth, *I* shall *solely* care
for you soon." She swallowed hard. "I *must* be able
to take you with me to Indian Island. I must."

"Indian Island?" Emily said as she came into the
room, so stately and dignified in her maroon silk dress,
with lace in deep gathers around the collar. Her hair
was worn in a fancy chignon atop her head and dia-
monds sparkled on her fingers. "Have you worked
things out with Bold Wolf? Has he assured you that
it isn't his people's custom to do away with children
who are handicapped?"

"No, I haven't yet talked with Bold Wolf about
Elizabeth," Shanna said somberly as she slowly drew
the blanket back over Elizabeth, leaving only her tiny
face exposed. "There have been so many things that
have gotten in the way." She sighed. "My father. He
found me with Bold Wolf the other day. He laid down
the law. He doesn't want me around Bold Wolf. I
truly am afraid to tell Father that I can't stay away
from Bold Wolf . . . that I love him so dearly."

Emily sat down in a plush, brilliant red velveteen chair next to Shanna. "But, child, you are planning to *marry* Bold Wolf," she said, reaching a gentle hand over and resting it on Shanna's arm. "Dear, don't let your father stand in the way of your happiness." She glanced down at Elizabeth. "Or Elizabeth's. Life can be so short, Shanna. So very, very short."

"Yes, I know that, especially after witnessing the recent tragedy in Old Town," Shanna murmured. "But I just can't run off to Indian Island and marry Bold Wolf. I can't hurt my parents in such a way."

Shanna recalled these past two days and how she had worked side by side with her father, doing things she never would have thought herself capable of, helping her father prepare the dead for burial. She had felt a bonding between herself and her father. Now, especially, she wanted to avoid causing him heartache.

She *had* to find a balance between the two men she loved. And she *would*. She didn't want to hurt one in order to give to the other!

And then there was her mother. Of late Shanna had seen her mother's vulnerable side, and she worried about her state of mind. No, she couldn't do anything to bring any more stress into her mother's life. Shanna had to find a way to feed her own happiness without taking away from those she loved.

"What *are* you going to do, Shanna?" Emily asked, reaching a hand to Shanna's face, gently smoothing a fallen lock of hair back from her eyes.

"I don't know," Shanna said, a sob lodging in her throat. "But I *will* work it out. I can't lose Bold Wolf. I love him so much."

"I'm sure you will find a way, child," Emily murmured. "I'm sure you will."

Elizabeth began to whimper, then began to cry.

"It's time for Elizabeth's feeding. Later, after you

are gone, I am going to church to help the ladies prepare food for those who have lost loved ones," Emily
said softly, unbuttoning the front of her dress.

Shanna had a deep respect for this woman who
was always ready to give of herself for those who
were in need. She had so much wealth and could
have done nothing but sit in her house and be
comfortable.

Shanna was inspired by this lady every time she
was around her. Unspoiled by her riches, Emily was
the sort of woman everyone aspired to be like. She
was kind, considerate, and heartwarming to be
around.

No longer embarrassed by Emily's breast-feeding,
Shanna handed Elizabeth over to her. She settled back
in the rocker and slowly rocked back and forth as she
watched Elizabeth suckling from the nipple, her tiny
fingers kneading the breast.

"I wish *I* could be feeding her," Shanna murmured.
"Would you tell me how it feels?"

Emily looked at Elizabeth and smiled. "How does
it feel?" she murmured. "Spiritual, as though the hand
of God reaches down and touches your heart."

"That's beautiful. *I* hope to experience those feelings one day," Shanna said, recalling how she and
Bold Wolf had discussed having children. Without
even being conscious of what she was doing, she
placed her hand over her tummy and stroked it.

When she caught Emily staring at her, Shanna
blushed and realized what she was doing. She drew
her hand quickly away.

"Yes, Shanna, one day, after you are married to
Bold Wolf, you *will* grow a child within your womb,"
Emily said, smiling at Shanna. "You will feel the wonders of pregnancy, and then of holding the child to
your breast and feeding it."

After I am married, Shanna thought, knowing that it was possible she was pregnant even now, for she had not waited for marriage vows to make love with Bold Wolf.

Sometimes shame filled her when she thought about what she had allowed herself to do. Yet she felt as though she were already married to Bold Wolf. She had loved him for so long!

"Elizabeth is through feeding," Emily said, folding the blanket snugly around the child, then handing her over to Shanna. "Hold her, dear, while I go and see that tea is being prepared for us."

Shanna held Elizabeth to her bosom and slowly rocked her back and forth. She glanced over at the open window, enjoying the breeze. The sheer, lacy curtains were softly shimmering, the air cool and refreshing after the recent hot days, the smell of smoke from the explosion finally dissipated.

Elizabeth emitted a sweet cooing sound, bringing Shanna's eyes back to her. "Darling daughter," she said, lifting the corner of the blanket to give Elizabeth a soft kiss on her brow. "You are mine, Elizabeth. Oh, my darling daughter, how I love you. Soon I will be able to take you with me. I will give you a wonderful home. You will never want for anything."

A movement at the window drew Shanna's eyes there again. She jumped with alarm and held Elizabeth even more closely.

Emily came back into the room. "What is it?" she asked, her eyes following Shanna's startled gaze to the window. "You are white as a ghost. Did you see something?"

"I saw someone at the window," Shanna said, almost afraid to get up to see, for she remembered now that she had felt as though she'd been followed as soon as she had left her home today.

"Who would be there?" Emily asked, going to the window. She held the curtain aside and peered out in all directions. "No one is here, Shanna. *No* one." She went back and sat down in the velveteen chair.

"I'm certain I saw someone there," Shanna murmured. "And, earlier, on my way here, I . . . I . . . felt as though someone were following me."

"After all that's happened these past few days, I'm certain you are just edgy," Emily said. She nodded a silent thank-you to the maid as she came in with a tea service and tray of petit fours. "Now, Shanna, tell me about your twin brothers. Are they a handful for your mother? I have one child the age of your brothers, and my, oh, my is *he* a challenge for his nanny."

Shanna slowly turned her eyes away from the window. She was certain she *had* seen someone. The glimpse had been fleeting, yet there had been someone there all the same, spying either on her or Emily Diepholz.

Her jaw tightened when she thought of only one man she had labeled "spy" these past several years. He Who Watches! Could it have been?

"Your brothers," Emily repeated, bringing Shanna again from her thoughts. "Are they well-behaved?"

"Tommie and Terrie?" Shanna said, nervously clearing her throat. "No, I wouldn't say they were well-behaved. They are quite a challenge for my mother. She very wisely recently hired a nanny. I wish she would have done so earlier, for mother's nerves are quite frazzled."

"Yes, I'm sure," Emily said, nodding.

They continued with small talk awhile longer, yet Shanna couldn't get over having seen someone at the window. Could it have been He Who Watches, up to his usual spying games?

Or had it been someone else?

It made her somewhat afraid to walk home by herself! The whole town seemed to have turned into something unfamiliar to her.

The scent of death and the sense of dread was everywhere.

15

I will not let thee go.
Have we not chid the changeful moon?
—ROBERT BRIDGES

"You witnessed what?" Bold Wolf said, finding it hard to stay calm after what He Who Watches had told him. Not only had He Who Watches taken it upon himself to spy on Shanna, he had come back with news that had to be a lie.

Yet Bold Wolf had never known He Who Watches to lie to anyone. Especially not his very own grand-nephew, his *chief*.

He Who Watches repeated himself. "I saw Shanna holding a baby," he said guardedly, his old eyes gleaming as he came closer and knelt on his haunches before Bold Wolf inside Bold Wolf's cabin. "I heard Shanna calling the baby her *daughter*. A woman does not call a child 'daughter' unless she is the child's mother."

Bold Wolf stared incredulously at He Who Watches, stunned numb by what he was saying. "It cannot be true," he said, his voice drawn. "Shanna a mother? How . . . can that be? How could she keep such a secret from me?"

He thought back to when they had made love. His eyes brightened with hope when he remembered that Shanna definitely had been a virgin when they'd first made love. Yet perhaps it was not the same for white

women. Perhaps the small barrier of skin that proved
her virginity had been broken and then healed after
the child had been born.

He was so confused, his head was spinning.

"Tell me everything," Bold Wolf said somberly,
fighting the anger he felt for He Who Watches's interfering ways. He didn't think the old man opposed
his marriage to Shanna just because she was white. It
had to be because Shanna had always threatened Bold
Wolf's vows while he had been a Runner.

But Bold Wolf had stayed true to those vows. He
had turned away from Shanna many times when he
had been tempted to speak to her at Old Town. So
why should his grand-uncle resent her over something
that had never happened?

He Who Watches gathered the tail end of his robe
up into his arms and sat down on a blanket next to
Bold Wolf before a slow-burning fire in the fireplace.
This August day felt cooler, more like September.

"I decided to follow Shanna because I didn't trust
her reason for delaying marriage to you," He Who
Watches said, leaning closer to Bold Wolf. "I followed
her, hoping to find something about her that I could
bring back to you, to make you know the true person
she is. I have always felt it is best that you not want
her. I had hoped to find a reason to put her from
your mind."

"And so today you bring me news that tears at my
heart?" Bold Wolf said, fighting the ache that encom-
passed his entire being.

"I bring news today that you should be glad to
know, so that you would not marry a woman who
betrayed you," He Who Watches said, nodding.
"Shanna held the child as a woman holds her own.
She called the child her *daughter*. That has to mean

that Shanna is the mother of an illegitimate child, for you know as well as I that she has never married."

Bold Wolf inhaled a deep, bitter breath, as he again recalled the radiant look on Shanna's face that day he had observed her unawares. Had she even then come from a rendezvous with her lover? Had she told her lover that she had given birth to his daughter?

He hung his face in his hands and groaned. These possibilities cut deeply into his heart, as though someone were stabbing him repeatedly.

"I stood at the window at the Diepholz grand white house and saw and heard all of this," He Who Watches said. "When I saw Shanna glance toward the window, I went quickly into hiding. Then I came to you with the news about her and the child."

"Bold Wolf, this woman Shanna has proved to be no better than whores who work at the white man's brothels," He Who Watches dared to say.

Instead of strangling the man for such impertinence, Bold Wolf sat there, as though drained of feeling.

"Bold Wolf, must I remind you that Shanna was gone for some time," He Who Watches said relentlessly. "Perhaps she went away to have the child so that no one would know of her whorish ways. Surely she brought the child back for someone else to raise until she is married, and can make a home for her. That child, Bold Wolf, is why she hesitates to marry you. Surely she hopes the true father will marry her instead."

"The child's skin is white?" Bold Wolf asked solemnly.

"The child was wrapped in a blanket, so I could not see the color of the skin, but I doubt Shanna slept with a Penobscot warrior, for no warrior of our village would dare go against you in such a way. That must mean the child's skin is white, for the father is surely white," He Who Watches said.

"And you say that you saw Shanna and her child in the grand white house at the edge of Old Town?" Bold Wolf said, sighing heavily.

"Yes, in the home owned by people called Diepholz," He Who Watches said softly.

He Who Watches noted that Bold Wolf had referred to the child as Shanna's. He knew then that Bold Wolf believed his story.

Feeling triumphant, he smiled slyly.

16

The night has a thousand eyes,
The day but one;
Yet the light of the bright world dies
With the dying sun.
                                —FRANCIS BOURDILLON

Shanna was awakened by a sound in her bedroom. She stiffened and rose slowly to a sitting position, peering into the darkness.

Ever since the bodies from the explosion had been brought to her home, she had not been able to sleep soundly. Even though only a few remained for burial, she still felt as though her home were filled with ghosts. It *was* the time of month just past the setting of the partial moon, when night was at its blackest. This made Shanna's room dark as an ink spot, making it impossible for her to see who was in her room.

"Shanna, it's me. It's *Jennie*." Jennie moved quickly to Shanna's bed and knelt down beside it.

"Jennie?" Shanna whispered.

She scooted to the edge of the bed, leaned over, and hugged her friend.

"Oh, Lord, Jennie," she softly cried. "How did you get away from the brothel?"

"Al's not there," Jennie whispered. "When he's gone, the guards posted at the doors are lax in their duties. They slip into a backroom and play poker."

"Did you close my door?" Shanna whispered.

"Yes, *and* locked it," Jennie whispered back.

"Good," Shanna said, sliding from the bed. She

went to the nightstand and lit a kerosene lamp, then turned to Jennie.

The color drained from Shanna's face when she saw how pale and gaunt Jennie was. And what she wore was far different from when Shanna last saw her. She had discarded the gaudy, skimpy attire and tonight wore loose men's clothing, the large pants secured at her waist with a rope. The shirt was twice her size and almost swallowed her. Her long hair was tangled and frizzy as it hung down to her waist.

"I know I look horrible." Jennie sighed, going to stare at herself in a mirror on the wall. "I've been so disheartened over what I've been forced to do in that hellhole, I have no appetite. I've lost a lot of weight. And I had no idea where Al put my clothes from the day Father sold me. I . . . I sneaked into Al's room tonight and stole one of his shirts and a pair of his pants."

She stuck her bare feet out for Shanna to see. "I have no shoes, Shanna," she said, her tears flowing. "I hated those things they forced on me at the brothel. "I . . . I just couldn't wear them any longer. They are as cheap-looking as the clothes I've been forced to wear."

Shanna grabbed Jennie and hugged her. "I'm so sorry I couldn't do anything to get you out of that horrid place," she cried. "Father wouldn't interfere and Sheriff Wisler is worthless."

Jennie stepped away from Shanna and plopped down on the bed. "I saw Roscoe Lovett come one day to the brothel," she said, her voice drawn. "I . . . I . . . had no idea he frequented places like that. Imagine, Shanna, a man like him paying for the services of—"

Shanna sat down beside Jennie and gently placed a hand over Jennie's mouth, stopping her from saying anything else about Mr. Lovett, since Jennie was absolutely wrong about why he had been at the brothel.

"No, Jennie," Shanna murmured, now slowly sliding her hand away from her friend's mouth. "Roscoe wasn't there to be with those women. He tried to reason with Al about *you.* He asked for your release. He even tried to pay your way to freedom. But Al refused him. I guess he just laughed at Roscoe, then told him to leave."

"Mr. Lovett . . . Roscoe . . . truly did that for me?" Jennie said, breathless with the knowledge that her music instructor would care this much for her.

"Yes, he *is* such a kind man, you know," Shanna said, recalling these past few days when lessons were set aside so that Roscoe could assist those whose lives had been torn apart by the explosion.

Then, afraid her father might hear her and Jennie talking, and unsure what he would do if he discovered Shanna preparing to do something dangerous, she rose quickly from the bed and began dressing. She chose a simple black skirt and gray blouse, to blend in with the dark night.

"What are you doing?" Jennie asked, slowly rising from the bed.

"We've got to find a place for you to hide," Shanna said, buttoning her skirt at her waist.

She rushed back to her chifforobe and chose a skirt and blouse for Jennie, and a pair of shoes. She shoved these into Jennie's arms. "Hurry up and get dressed," she whispered. "I will see that you are well hidden. Damn that Al Adams. He won't have the opportunity to abuse you any longer."

Shanna went to her dresser and grabbed a brush. As Jennie hurried into the clothes, Shanna brushed her hair, then tied it back from her face with a dark maroon ribbon.

"Where are we going?" Jennie asked, a tremor in her voice. "Who can you trust? Who is willing to help me?"

Shanna handed Jennie the hairbrush. "While you were in that horrid place I have tried to think of someone who would be willing to help you," she said solemnly, watching Jennie wince as she struggled to get the brush through her tangled hair. "I so badly wanted to ask Bold Wolf, yet I didn't want to take a chance of getting him involved in something that might bring harm to his people. The sheriff hates the Penobscot. So I didn't ask Bold Wolf's help. He's chief now and has the responsibilities of his people to tend to."

"But now?" Jennie asked, searching Shanna's eyes. "You are going to ask him now?"

"Yes," Shanna said, her jaw tightening. "If you can get hidden well enough on Indian Island, no one will ever suspect you are there."

"Indian . . . Island?" Jennie gasped. "For how long, Shanna? Must I stay there forever in hiding?"

"There's got to be a way to make people understand that what has happened to you is wrong," Shanna said angrily, placing her hands on her hips. "But it will take time, Jennie. I'm not sure who I can go to. But until I figure something out, you *will* be safe on Indian Island."

"What if Bold Wolf doesn't want to help me?" Jennie murmured, lowering her eyes.

"Bold Wolf is a kind man who knows injustice when he sees it," Shanna said stiffly. "He knows this, it seems, far better than most whites."

"What if your parents discover that you are gone tonight and punish you for helping me?" Jennie asked, watching eagerly as Shanna went back to her chifforobe and fell to her knees to sort through the shoes at the bottom.

"My parents know my loyalty to you," Shanna said, turning to hand her friend a pair of slippers. "I just wish I could have done something earlier so that you . . . you wouldn't have had to spend one night in that sordid place."

Shanna didn't want to think about how Jennie's body had been used—soiled, perhaps, for a lifetime. Shanna wasn't sure if any man would want Jennie now, since she was no longer an innocent virgin.

And although Roscoe Lovett had spoken of his feelings for Jennie, surely he no longer felt the same, not after thinking about her nights at the brothel.

Shanna brushed such thoughts from her mind and slipped into her riding boots. She had not worn them for ages; horseback riding had become less important in her life. She hadn't gone for a long ride since before she had become so weakened by pneumonia. And now she had more important things on her mind.

She turned to Jennie and so badly wanted to tell her about Elizabeth, but decided that now was not the time. Perhaps later, when Jennie's life had gained some semblance of normality, Shanna could tell Jennie. They had many secrets to catch up on, yet Shanna doubted that Jennie would want to ever tell of hers, for surely they were too horrible.

"Ready to go?" Shanna asked, her eyes finding Jennie's.

"Yes, I'm ready," Jennie whispered back, wiping tears from her eyes. She grabbed Shanna's hands. "Do you truly believe I can hide well enough on Indian Island that Al can't find me?"

"I'm certain of it," Shanna said, giving Jennie a fierce, reassuring hug.

Shanna then stepped away from Jennie, blew the lamp out, and gingerly unlocked the door.

She held her breath as she slowly opened it; then,

eyes wide, she stepped cautiously out in the corridor,
looking up and down the hallway.

She grabbed Jennie by the hand. "Come on," she
whispered. "The coast is clear. We'll go down the
back stairs."

Knowing that her father could awaken at any moment, Shanna's heart was thudding inside her chest.
She and her father had become closer these past few
days, and she knew he would not want her taking risks
with her own life, no matter what.

And she did know the risks of doing this tonight.
When Al Adams realized Jennie was gone, he would
begin an adamant search. If he found them before
Shanna could get Jennie safely to Indian Island, who
knew what he would do? She knew he was devious
enough to do away with both herself and Jennie. Their
bodies could be thrown into the river or hidden in the
ashes of the explosion, and no one would be the wiser.
Shanna gave Jennie's hand a yank. "Hurry," she
whispered.

"How are we going to get across the river?" Jennie
asked as they rushed out the back door into the black
shroud of night.

"There are always canoes beached along the riverfront," Shanna said. She lifted the hem of her skirt
and ran breathlessly down the steep hill toward the
river.

The hour was late. There was no one anywhere.
There was no warm, friendly glimmer of lamplight
from the dozing houses. The only sounds were those
of the reedy tree frogs and the cadence of crickets.
The blackness of the night was as tangible, warm, and
humid as the breath of an animal.

"Hurry, Jennie," Shanna said, giving Jennie a quick
glance. "At any moment now Al could return and

discover you gone. If he does, you know he'll come looking for you."

"I haven't seen him now for two days," Jennie said, as she ran exhaustedly beside Shanna. "I've heard the women whispering among themselves that something might have happened to him. He's never been gone for this long. He doesn't trust anyone enough with his brood of women to venture very far from town."

"It would be such a blessing if something *has* happened to that man," Shanna said tightly. "But I'm sure it's only hopeful thinking. Men like him surely don't die easily."

The soft lapping of the river came to them in the night. Shanna squinted as she searched for, then found several canoes beached together at the waterfront. A lot of white men chose canoes over the other boats when they wanted to take a leisurely trip along the river to hunt or fish.

"I'm so weak I can't help you paddle across the river to Indian Island," Jennie told her, slipping on wet rocks as she ran with Shanna toward the canoes.

Shanna ran ahead, chose the sturdiest of the canoes, and shoved it out into the water. "I'll paddle," she said, giving Jennie a glance over her shoulder. "Just sit down and relax. We'll soon be on Indian Island. I know you'll be safe there."

She knew, though, that she had to return home as quickly as possible after seeing that Jennie was safely hidden. She hated to lose her father's newfound trust. She was close to feeling confident enough to tell him about her intentions toward Bold Wolf . . . *and* about the baby.

She was even feeling confident enough, as well, to tell Bold Wolf about the baby. Surely the child would not keep him from wanting to marry her. Surely he would fall in love with the child immediately, as she had, and would promise to keep Elizabeth safe.

Once they were out on the river, Shanna's arms aching as she drew the paddle through the water, she kept glancing at the street that led from Old Town to the river. So far she saw no one. Everything was quiet. Out this far in the water, all she could now hear was the sound of the paddle dipping in and out of the water and the occasional call of a loon in the far distance.

"We're almost there," Jennie said, her eyes wide as she saw Indian Island drawing closer and closer. "Oh, Shanna, what if Bold Wolf doesn't want to be bothered with me? What if his people don't want him to help?"

"He will help you, and his people won't have a say in the matter," Shanna said, gazing at Indian Island. "Remember, Jennie, he's now the chief. His word is law on Indian Island."

"I hope so," Jennie whispered, only loud enough for herself to hear.

Shanna kept moving the paddle, her brow pearling with cold sweat. Finally she heard the crunching of rocks beneath the canoe as it scraped against shore. She dropped the paddle to the bottom of the canoe and leaped out into the water.

"Come on, Jennie," she said, dragging the canoe to the shore. "Bold Wolf's cabin isn't far from here."

"I hope not," Jennie said, her knees almost buckling beneath her.

"You'll be all right," Shanna reassured her, putting her arm around Jennie's waist to steady her. "You'll get all the food you want here at the village." She laughed softly. "But just say no to muskrat if it is offered to you."

"Muskrat?" Jennie said, gasping. "They actually eat muskrat?"

"Bold Wolf finds their tails a delicacy," Shanna said, laughing again when she heard Jennie let out another sharp gasp. "Seriously, Jennie, the food *is* good here. And they don't eat muskrat unless they are having a celebration."

"Thank goodness," Jennie said, laughing softly. "For I doubt they will feel like celebrating having *me* among them."

"We're almost there," Shanna whispered. They were among the lodges now.

"Does he live in a tent?" Jennie whispered, gazing at a tent at her right side, then also seeing wigwams and log cabins.

"No, he lives in a cabin," Shanna whispered back. She nodded toward it as they approached. "That one, Jennie. The larger one."

Shanna stepped away from Jennie as they came to the door of Bold Wolf's cabin. She took a deep breath, then lifted the moose-hide entrance flap and held it aside. "Go on," she whispered. "Since there is no door to knock on, we'll just make our presence known in this way."

Jennie nodded and stepped past Shanna, then stood aside as Shanna knelt over Bold Wolf's bed of blankets and pelts.

Shanna lingered a moment, looking at Bold Wolf in the soft light of his lodge fire.

He looked so peaceful in his sleep, like a little boy. She could see how sculpted his shadowed features were. His long black hair lay around his head on the blankets like a huge halo.

His lips fluttering into a soft smile made her wonder what he might be dreaming about. Her? Could he be dreaming of them being together making love?

Overwhelmed with love, she bent over him and brushed a soft kiss across his lips.

She flinched and drew back when he awakened with a start. When he saw her there, she expected him to smile and greet her with outstretched arms. Instead, she was taken aback when she saw an instant anger, a coldness, enter his dark eyes.

"Bold Wolf?" she said, her voice drawn. "I hope you don't mind that I came tonight like this. You seem angry about me being here."

Bold Wolf felt a soft despair as he gazed at Shanna. He loved her still, yet he resented her, for she was a woman who had betrayed him in the worst way possible.

Then he looked past her and saw Jennie standing in the shadows. His eyebrows rose when his gaze swept over her and he saw how gaunt she was. And then he noticed the fear in the woman's eyes and knew this must be the friend Shanna had told him about, and that she must have escaped from the brothel where her father had sold her into the life of degradation.

Shanna took Jennie by the hand and brought her out into the firelight for Bold Wolf to see her better. She tried to forget Bold Wolf's strange reaction over seeing her at his bedside.

"Jennie escaped from the brothel tonight," she murmured. "I brought her to Indian Island. Please hide her, Bold Wolf, so that Al Adams can't find her!"

Bold Wolf left his bed, holding the blanket around his shoulders as he stood before Jennie and Shanna, his eyes again studying Jennie.

Shanna was hurt and confused by his continued aloofness. She couldn't think of anything she could have done or said to anger him. When she had told him that she must work things out with her parents before marrying him, he had seemed to understand. So that couldn't be why he acted as though she wasn't even there.

But, wanting to think solely of Jennie's welfare at this moment, Shanna brushed her concerns about herself and Bold Wolf from her mind.

"Yes, I will take you into hiding," Bold Wolf said, placing a gentle hand on Jennie's ashen cheek. "You will be safe here for as long as you wish to stay."

Jennie flung herself into Bold Wolf's arms. "Thank you, thank you," she cried, clinging to him. "I will find a way one day to repay you. Oh, thank you!"

Jennie stepped away from him and hugged Shanna, then went and stood over the warmth of the fire.

"*I* thank you," Shanna said, trying to draw Bold Wolf's eyes to her, stunned speechless when he didn't look at her or respond to her in any way. It was as though she weren't there! As though she were a nobody and worthless to him!

"Bold Wolf, what's wrong?" she blurted out, then grew cold inside when he gave her a look of utter contempt. "Bold Wolf, what have I done? Why are you angry?"

"You have brought your friend to my island for safekeeping, and she will be kept safe, so is that not all that matters now?" Bold Wolf said thickly. "Shanna, return home."

Dispirited, hurt, and confused, Shanna backed away from Bold Wolf, their eyes locked in a strange sort of battle.

Then she looked over at Jennie, who seemed also aware that something was awry. "Jennie, Bold Wolf *will* make things right for you," she murmured, then turned and ran from the cabin, sobbing.

She couldn't believe how Bold Wolf had changed since the last time they were together. It was as though he had given up on her! He had even ordered her from his home! And he had not escorted her to the canoe.

She wanted to go back and pull answers from him. She wanted to demand to know why he was treating her so coldly. But she knew that now was not the time. She had to return home before her parents discovered she was gone. She must remember that all that mattered now was that Jennie was safe. She was no longer in that terrible brothel.

"I fear I've lost him," Shanna sobbed as she shoved the canoe back out into the water. "Oh, Lord, I know that I've lost him. But . . . why?"

When she returned safely home and returned to her bed, she couldn't sleep for wondering about Bold Wolf's cold aloofness.

What could I have done to change his feelings toward me? she worried over and over again, so glad when finally her eyes closed and she found escape in the dark void of sleep.

17

The waiting angels see and recognize
The rich crown jewels, Love, of Paradise,
When life falls from us like a withered husk.
                    —MARY ASHLEY TOWNSEND

Arriving at Mr. Lovett's music studio after all the canceled lessons, Shanna was filled with many emotions. As she waited for Roscoe to step from his small cubicle of an office to get started, Shanna tuned her violin and thought of last night.

She was so glad Jennie was no longer at the brothel and was safely hidden on Indian Island, but Bold Wolf's attitude toward Shanna herself still confused and hurt her.

She had slept only fitfully, often lying awake, trying to think of what she had said that had caused Bold Wolf to treat her as though he despised her.

She had asked him to wait until she had a chance to prepare her parents for their upcoming marriage. Had he thought further about it and decided her request was not fair?

"How could he forget that I was also made to wait?" Shanna whispered to herself now, plucking her violin strings to be sure they were tuned accurately.

Yes, *she* had been forced to wait to marry Bold Wolf, and all because Bold Wolf put his status in the tribe before *her*.

Her troubled thoughts were interrupted when Roscoe stepped from the back room with his easy gait.

He was carrying his flute in one hand, a cloth in another. It was apparent that he had been shining his prized instrument.

Before Shanna arrived today, she wondered if she should tell Roscoe about Jennie's escape from the brothel. She concluded that it was much safer if she told no one. She especially felt uneasy about telling Roscoe. In the search for Jennie that was sure to come, Roscoe Lovett might be one of the first questioned by Al Adams, since he had made a fuss at the brothel over Jennie. If he didn't know where Jennie was, the information could not be forced out of him.

Yet Shanna knew how much Roscoe wanted Jennie out of that place. Surely it would only be fair to him to know that she was now safe.

"Good morning, Shanna," Roscoe said, laying his flute and the rag aside. He began sorting through a stack of sheet music, to choose one for this morning's practice. He gave Shanna a glance and smiled, then resumed his task. "I do apologize for having to ask you to skip a few lessons. But we will make it all up. Today we can extend your lessons from one hour to two."

He smiled at Shanna again. "Today I plan to accompany you with my flute," he said, pride showing in his eyes.

Shanna knew he had performed in concert before he had settled down to become an instructor. Sometimes, Shanna knew, he hungered for that applause and might pursue it one day again.

For now, he seemed content just to share his talents with his students.

Shanna had heard him playing his flute in the forest more than once. Before her pneumonia and her stay with her aunt, she remembered hearing Roscoe's music wafting through her bedroom window from the depths of the forest, sweet and beautiful on the night breezes.

"You do not mind an extra-long practice today, do you, Shanna?" Roscoe asked, arranging the music on a stand before her.

Shanna frowned at that idea, yet she did not voice her feelings. She had planned to go and hold Elizabeth. The child always seemed to tranquilize her when she felt so torn. But she did not want to disappoint Roscoe. Lately, especially the day he had tried to save Jennie from the brothel, he had seemed to her heroic, the sort of man who would be good for Jennie.

"Mr. Lovett, I—" Shanna blurted out, ready to tell him about Jennie, after all, but stopped when she heard a rush of footsteps coming up the outside steps.

Shanna looked quickly at Roscoe and saw an instant guarded fear enter his eyes. He turned abruptly and stared at the closed door. He quickly went to the window in the door, edging the curtain aside to see who was approaching the landing. When he dropped the curtain back in place, he went to Shanna and grabbed her by an arm. Hurriedly he led her to his windowless office at the back of the large music room. She almost dropped her violin when he shoved her behind a stack of boxes.

"Stay hidden," Roscoe said, his voice drawn. "No matter what happens, don't you come out until I say it is safe to."

"But why?" Shanna asked, her heart thudding. "What's wrong?" She stiffened when she heard loud banging at the door. "Who is there that you don't want me to see?"

"I don't want them to see *you*," Roscoe said. "It's best not to question why, *ever*. As soon as they are gone, I think it would be best if you leave and don't come back again until I send word that it is safe."

"But . . ." Shanna said, her words dying on her lips when he blew out the kerosene lamp, then left the room, closing the door behind him.

Shanna clung to her violin in the dark, her pulse racing, her throat dry from the mounting fear. Who had put such fear into the heart of her music teacher? Whoever it was, was now in the outer room shouting at him.

She scarcely breathed as she tried to hear what was being said, then gasped and went cold all over when the voices grew louder. She could hear very clearly that these men were from the brothel.

They were demanding to know if Roscoe knew anything about Jennie's disappearance from the brothel, and furthermore wanted to know if he knew anything about Al's disappearance.

Since Roscoe had voiced a threat to Al before storming from the brothel the day he had gone there to demand Jennie's release, the men said, he was the first person who came to mind when it became obvious that Al was missing.

"A threat?" Shanna whispered, her eyes widening. Her music teacher had threatened Al? The man who was usually so gentle and meek had actually threatened the powerful, cruel Al Adams?

That made her smile. Then her smile quickly faded when she heard a loud crash and the noise of a scuffle.

When she heard someone cry out with pain over and over again, she knew that it had to be Roscoe, for she could tell Roscoe was outnumbered.

Suddenly she heard a door slam shut, followed by silence. Shanna stiffened as she waited for the door to the office to open.

When Roscoe didn't come, Shanna was almost too afraid to open the door herself, for fear of what she might find. Her pulse racing, her knees weak, Shanna stepped from behind the boxes and felt her way to the door. Her heart throbbing, she slowly turned the knob.

Slowly she inched the door open, then almost dropped her violin with alarm when she saw Roscoe stretched out on the floor, his eyes closed and swollen. Blood streamed from a cut on his upper lip and from his nose, which was turning purple and obviously broken.

"Oh, Mr. Lovett," Shanna cried.

She lay her violin aside, then fell to her knees beside her teacher.

When he didn't immediately respond or open his eyes, she grew pale, afraid that he might have been killed. Slowly she reached a trembling hand to his throat, so glad when she found a pulse there.

When Roscoe began to groan, and his eyes slowly opened, Shanna gently placed a hand on his arm. "Should I go for Doc Rose?" she asked, a sob catching in her throat when he gazed up at her through his pain-filled eyes. "Should I go for Sheriff Wisler?"

"No, don't go for anyone. Just get out of here, Shanna," he managed to say, his voice low and raspy. "Shanna, take your violin and get . . . out . . . of here. But watch out for those men. They are from the brothel. There's four of them."

"They almost killed you," Shanna said, gulping hard.

"Just do as you are told, Shanna," Roscoe said, groaning as he pushed himself up to a sitting position. He reached for his bleeding lip, then touched his flattened nose. "Those sons-of-bitches. They'll pay. They . . . will . . . pay for this!"

Having never heard Roscoe Lovett speak so crudely, his vicious, threatening tone frightening her,

Shanna moved slowly to her feet, then spun around and secured her violin in its case.

"Are you certain I can't send the doctor back to see to your—"

"Just leave," interrupted Roscoe. "I need to be alone."

"All right," Shanna murmured. "But if you need anything, please don't hesitate to go to my father. You know how much he thinks of you. He'd do anything to help you."

"Like he helped poor Jennie when he heard that she was forced into the life of a whore?" Roscoe growled, finally standing on his unsteady feet. "No, thank you, Shanna. This is my own fight. I'll fight it alone."

"Please be careful," Shanna murmured, now regretting that she had not told Roscoe where Jennie was. It was because of Jennie, after all, that he had gotten the terrible beating.

But Shanna still could not find it in herself to tell him, not with men like those who had come today out there somewhere, ready to kill over Jennie. She still thought it best to keep Jennie's whereabouts absolutely secret.

Slowly Shanna opened the door. She hesitated, then took a shaky step out onto the landing, stopping long enough to stare down at the people walking along the boardwalk, and at those men who were loitering at the foot of the stairs, gossiping and smoking.

She didn't see a cluster of four men who seemed intent on tearing the world apart today. Those men she could see appeared friendly.

What she truly feared was that at the foot of the stairs the four men could be standing in the shadows, watching. . . .

Breathless, her heart pounding, Shanna made a mad

dash down the stairs. She didn't stop to look around her. She ran blindly through the crowd and was relieved when she was finally away from the main part of the town and now saw the Diepholz mansion only a short distance away.

When she got to the door of the grand two-story house, she didn't even stop to knock. She burst through the door, closed it behind her, then leaned against it, panting.

When Emily came rushing from the parlor and saw how frantic Shanna was, she went to her and pulled her into her arms. "What's wrong?" she asked, holding Shanna, who burst into deep, throaty sobs.

"I . . . was at Mr. Lovett's," Shanna cried. "Four men came and . . . and beat him. I've never been so afraid!"

When she heard other footsteps coming from the parlor, Shanna looked up slowly, then stiffened and stepped quickly away from Emily. Bold Wolf was standing there, in his eyes a tenderness she had not seen the previous night.

18

Let us hope the future
Will share with thee my sorrows,
And thou thy joys with me.
—CHARLES JEFFREYS

Emily stepped aside and gestured toward the parlor door with a hand. "Shanna, go into the parlor with Bold Wolf," she murmured. "You can have your privacy there. He has something he wishes to tell you."

Shanna's eyes held Bold Wolf's as she moved toward him. If Bold Wolf was at the Diepholzes' house, that had to mean that he knew about Elizabeth, for Shanna's relationship with the Diepholz family had only to do with the child.

Shanna thought back to last night when Bold Wolf had treated her so coldly. Had he known even then about Elizabeth and, not understanding why Shanna had chosen to deceive him, especially not understanding why she had claimed the child as hers, had been too angry about it to question her then?

After thinking about it all night, how did he feel *now*? He still hadn't said anything to her, yet she could tell by his gentle expression he was at least no longer angry.

But how had Bold Wolf discovered her secret? It had been so carefully kept. Not even her parents knew about the child.

Wanting so badly to know how he knew, and to have the chance to tell Bold Wolf everything now in her own way, Shanna slipped past him and went into the parlor. Her heart pounding, she turned to him as he came in and Emily closed the door behind him. The sun through the window gave the lovely room a soft, golden glow.

"How did you find out?" Shanna blurted out.

"About the child?" Bold Wolf said, going to Shanna, gently taking her hands. "He Who Watches brought the news to me."

Shanna's breath caught. She recalled the moment she had felt certain someone was spying on her through Emily's parlor window. She had even guessed it might be He Who Watches. But there was no way he could have known about her and the child. Unless . . . unless he had followed her from her home to the Diepholz mansion. Yes! She now recalled feeling as though someone had followed her that day!

She grew angry now, knowing it *had* been He Who Watches. It was obvious he was still trying to find ways to tear her and Bold Wolf apart. And she felt he had come close to succeeding.

"And how did He Who Watches know?" Shanna said tightly. Then she gasped with pleasure as he pulled her into his arms and held her against him.

"Let us not speak any longer of my grand-uncle or why he does what he does," Bold Wolf said. He placed a finger beneath her chin and lifted it so that their eyes could meet and hold again. "I know everything, Shanna. *Every*thing. Before you arrived, Emily explained everything to me: how you found the child . . . how you fell in love with the child . . . how you have claimed her as yours."

"How could I not?" Shanna said softly, feeling so many tumultuous emotions now she could hardly help but shed tears of pure joy, for she could tell by the tenderness in his voice that Bold Wolf approved of her feelings toward the child. Surely he was enamored, himself, with Elizabeth.

"Yes, how could you not?" Bold Wolf said thickly. He gazed more intensely into her eyes. "You, with the heart of an angel, would never have left a child to die."

"My love for the child was instant," Shanna murmured. "I wanted her as quickly. I want her *still.* And even though someone else's breasts have nourished her, it makes her no less mine. I have held her often. I have talked to her so that she would be familiar with my voice. I wanted her as a part of my life, forever, Bold Wolf."

She lowered her gaze and swallowed hard, then looked again into the dark depths of her lover's eyes. "I want her as a part of *our* lives, Bold Wolf," she said softly. "But . . . but I was afraid you might not want her or love her as instantly. I . . . was afraid . . ."

He slid a hand up and placed it gently over her mouth. "I know how you felt about everything—your fears, your desires," he said softly. "Emily told me how you were afraid the child might have been abandoned by a Penobscot woman. She told me that was why you were afraid for anyone at my village to know that you found the child."

She reached up and gently slid his hand aside. "Yes, I was afraid it might be your people's custom to do away with children who are born handicapped," she said, her voice breaking.

"Do you truly believe that I, the chief of my people, would ever approve of such a practice?" he said thickly. "That my people, whose hearts are gentle and warm, could ever do such a thing to any newborn child? My people see all children as special."

"Bold Wolf, I tried *so* hard to make sense of this," she said, giving him a soft look of apology. "Thinking someone had abandoned this child because it was a custom, instead of for lack of caring, was easier for me to accept."

"You could have trusted me enough to confide in me," Bold Wolf said, an instant hurt showing in his wavering eyes.

"Oh, I'm so sorry I didn't," Shanna said. A sob lodged in her throat as she flung herself into his arms, hugging him tightly to her. "I'm sorry, Bold Wolf. Please forgive me. But the child! Everything I did was for the child."

"Yes, I know," Bold Wolf said, holding her close, his nose burrowed into the depths of her perfumed hair. "But now you can stop worrying about everything. I want both you *and* the child. Leave now for the island with me, Shanna. Let us have a true marriage ceremony. Let us give the child a home together."

The thought of going with Bold Wolf, with the baby in her arms, made Shanna's head swim with an overwhelming happiness. She could hardly believe this was happening . . . that he was there and that he forgave her ignorance and lack of trust, and that he had so quickly accepted the child.

She smiled, thinking how He Who Watches's plan had gone awry. He, in fact, had brought Bold Wolf and Shanna more closely together than ever before. She wished she could see his face the moment he was told what he really accomplished. But she knew that was not possible. There were still issues that had to be ironed out.

"Bold Wolf," Shanna said, easing away from him. She moved to the window, drew back a sheer, lacy curtain, and gazed outside. "I can't go with you today."

She turned quickly and faced him as he came to her

with a look of bewilderment. "The child still needs milk from Emily's breasts," she murmured. "And . . . and I truly have the battle of my life ahead of me. I *still* need more time. The recent explosion and how it wreaked havoc in everyone's lives has postponed my talk with my parents about my loving you and wanting to marry you. Soon things will get back to normal. Please understand why I want to wait until then to tell them."

She swallowed hard. "And there is the utter disappointment my father is going to feel once he realizes that I will abandon a future as a concert violinist the moment I cross the river to live with you on Indian Island," she murmured.

Bold Wolf didn't say anything, but this time Shanna did not see frustration in his eyes. She again moved into his arms and hugged him.

"I love you so much," she said, her voice breaking. "Soon all of this will be behind us. We will be together for a lifetime."

"I will wait for a short while longer, and then I *will* be sending a bride price to your father," Bold Wolf said softly. "So make your peace with your parents soon, Shanna, for I cannot . . . I *will* not . . . wait much longer. My lodge needs your laughter and sunshine. My bed needs the warmth of your body."

He stepped away from her and framed her face between his hands. "And as for Elizabeth, my sweet Shanna, there is a woman in my village who can feed her. The child will be as well nourished on Indian Island as here."

"Then I will try to find a way to talk with my parents soon," Shanna murmured. "My father is the worst obstacle. His ambitions for me blind him of too many truths."

Then she recalled what she had just experienced at

Roscoe Lovett's music studio. She hurriedly told Bold Wolf. "It was so awful," she said, shuddering. "Roscoe's nose was broken and his lip was split open. What if they discover that Jennie is on your island? It would be my fault should anything happen to you or your people."

"Jennie will be kept hidden from the white men," Bold Wolf reassured her.

"How is she?" Shanna asked anxiously. "I mean, is she going to be all right?"

Bold Wolf nodded. "She will be just fine. But she is still traumatized over all that has happened to her. She is haunted by the nights she spent at the brothel."

Bold Wolf grabbed Shanna's hands. "Once your father knows about your plans to marry me, can you trust that he will not prefer selling you to the brothel rather than allow you to marry a Penobscot chief?"

"Never," Shanna said, her jaw tightening. "My father is a decent, God-fearing man. He would never sell me into slavery." She hoped he did not think this was a common practice among white people.

Shanna eased her hands from Bold Wolf's. "Have you held Elizabeth?" she asked, a flush of pink filling her cheeks. She wanted to see Bold Wolf and Elizabeth together.

"Yes, before you came, I held the child," Bold Wolf said.

Shanna rushed to the door, opening it. "Isn't she just so adorable?" She left the room and found Emily already standing there with the baby.

"I knew that you would want her," Emily said, holding Elizabeth out for Shanna.

Shanna's heart warmed when she saw how Elizabeth was dressed so special today. She wore a white dress adorned with pink bows and lace, with pretty, matching pink booties. Emily had even managed to get a tiny pink bow in a lock of Elizabeth's black hair.

And when Shanna drew Elizabeth into her arms, she could smell the wondrous scent of soap and baby powder. She melted inside as Elizabeth smiled up at her, her dark eyes dancing with contentment.

"I have already fed her," Emily said. "So take as long as you wish with Elizabeth. It will be good for Bold Wolf to start bonding with her as her father."

Shanna smiled at Emily, then held Elizabeth in her arms and went back to the parlor. Bold Wolf stood over her and gazed at the child, beaming. Shanna knew he already loved Elizabeth. She didn't have to ask him if he wanted to hold the child. She knew.

Gently she slid Elizabeth from her arms into Bold Wolf's. She stood back and watched as Bold Wolf gently talked to the child, while Elizabeth intensely gazed into his eyes and listened.

Shanna now regretted with all her heart that she had not told Bold Wolf about Elizabeth earlier. The child and Bold Wolf had missed so much by not having known one another until now.

Shanna drew in a quick breath when Bold Wolf lifted the child's lame hand into his. Tears sprang to her eyes when Bold Wolf then bent low and kissed the hand.

When he looked over at her, Shanna was touched deeply by the compassion she saw in Bold Wolf's eyes.

Never could she have loved him as much as now.

19

We both can speak of one love
Which time can never change.
                    —CHARLES JEFFERYS

Lightning sent great, lurid flashes of white through Bold Wolf's bedroom window, the ensuing thunder awakening him with a start.

Propping himself up on an elbow, he listened to the waves thrashing against the shore and knew that the approaching storm was going to be a fierce one. He needed to go and help those who lived in wigwams fasten them down better. He hurried from his bed and slipped on his fringed breeches.

Just as he slid an arm into a sleeve of his shirt, loud pops of gunfire and shouts made him jump with alarm. He hurried into his shirt, grabbed his rifle, and, barefoot, ran outside just in time to see several of his warriors at the banks of the river, firing their weapons at canoes that were sweeping quickly away from the island, soon lost in sight in the darkness of night.

When Bold Wolf reached the river and another great burst of lightning filled the heavens with its silver, lurid light, he got a quick glimpse and saw that those who had stolen into his village at this midnight hour were the *Me-gwak,* the Mohawk.

It puzzled him to know the Mohawk had come to

his island in such a way. Before Bold Wolf's father had died, the Penobscot and the Mohawk had signed a treaty that promised against such attacks.

Bold Wolf found it hard to believe the Mohawk would be foolish enough to break the treaty, for Bold Wolf's warriors numbered twice those who lived in the Mohawk village one mile downriver. The *Me-gwak* had to know that Bold Wolf could attack and disable their entire village in one blow.

No, it made no sense, and he had to believe only a few had been ignorant enough to come tonight and chance making war between Bold Wolf and Chief Bent Arrow. It was surely renegades who came tonight, who did not know better than to see after their own greed, ignoring the danger they brought to their people.

"They stole food from our supplies for our long winter!" one of Bold Wolf's warriors said, running to him, his dark eyes filled with panic. "I was awakened by the thunder and when I went outside to see the approaching storm, I saw them! There were four of them in two canoes! They found our storage shed! They stole from it!"

Pale Star came rushing toward Bold Wolf, waving her hands and screaming. "They took Jennie away with them!" she cried. "The storm awakened both of us. She was restless. She went outside to take a walk. She did not return! Surely the *Me-gwuk* saw her and took her!"

Seeing the panic in Pale Star's eyes and hearing it in her voice, Bold Wolf pulled her into his arms and held her close. "Do not cry so," he said, staring angrily down the long avenue of the river. "It is not your fault." He gazed into her tear-filled eyes. "Go back to your lodge. We warriors will go for Jennie. She will be all right."

Just as he said that, as though huge buckets of water had overturned in the heavens, the rain started in thick, blinding torrents. The wind howled. The waves were great, white peaks in the river, crashing incessantly against the shoreline.

"No!" Pale Star cried, reaching out for Bold Wolf as he ran away from her toward the beached canoes. "Do not go down the river now! Can you not see how treacherous it is?"

Bold Wolf knew the dangers of being on the river when the waves were so high, yet he didn't want Jennie with the Mohawk renegades any longer than was necessary. Although the Mohawk were not known for their mistreatment of women, the fact that they had dared take Jennie troubled Bold Wolf.

Taking food supplies was one thing. Taking a defenseless woman was another!

Bold Wolf fought against the onslaught of rain. As he tried to shove his canoe out into the river, several of his warriors joined him, wrestling their canoes into the water between the leaps of waves.

But soon Bold Wolf realized the foolishness of their attempt. They could not get far without the danger of capsizing, now that the storm had worsened. Bold Wolf decided against going now. They had no choice but to wait until the storm had passed.

He dragged his canoe to safer, higher ground, his warriors following his lead and bringing their own vessels up past the line of danger. Bold Wolf stared at the river, wondering if Jennie would make it safely to the Mohawk village. Or would the canoe that was carrying her be torn apart in the demonic waves?

His heart sank, for Jennie had come to him for safekeeping, and he had let her down. And by letting

Jennie down, did he not also do the same to Shanna, who had trusted him to keep Jennie safe?

He doubled a fist and looked heavenward through the blur of rain. "Jennie had better come through this alive or the Mohawk will pay!" he cried.

20

My true-love hath my heart, and I have his,
By just exchange one to the other given,
I hold his dear, and mine he cannot miss.
> —SIR PHILIP SIDNEY

The storm, and what had sounded like gunfire over on Indian Island, had awakened Shanna.

Bolting from her bed, she hurried to her bedroom window and looked through the flashes of lightning toward the island, just as some Indians hurried toward the river from Bold Wolf's village.

She knew they were not Penobscot, for those leaving were being fired upon by those who were still on the island. And those who were in the canoes were firing back!

"The Mohawk?" she whispered, paling at the thought. In all the time she had lived in Old Town, she had never heard of an enemy attack on the Penobscot.

And even tonight it seemed surreal. The lightning! The thunder! The gunfire! It seemed to be something that she would only read about in a novel, not witness firsthand from her bedroom window.

She leaned closer to her window to see if anyone in Old Town was going to lend a hand to the Penobscot. When she saw no one, everyone obviously not caring one iota about the welfare of their neighboring Indians, she felt a bitterness rise into her throat.

How could the people be so callous about the Pen-

obscot? Did they all feel the same hate toward them
as Sheriff Wisler?

Then another thought came to Shanna that made
her knees grow weak. If there had been an exchange
of gunfire on Indian Island, could Bold Wolf have
been injured? Could Jennie have been harmed in any
way? Could any of the Penobscot have been killed?

"I must go and see," she whispered, already pulling
her gown over her head.

The rain had already hit, loud like gun pellets
against her windowpane. The wind was thrashing the
trees close to her window, threatening to snap them
in half as though they were nothing more than
toothpicks.

Shanna dropped her gown back down over her body
and looked again toward the river. Now she couldn't
see *anything* through the heavy falling rain! Never had
she seen such torrents.

There was no way she could get across the river.
She could hear the thrashing of the waves. She could
almost feel the throb of them beneath her bare feet
in the board flooring!

Then she heard something else and groaned. The
frightened wails of her brothers. She turned and stared
at her closed door.

Then she heard both her mother and father out in
the corridor as they each carried a child back and
forth in an effort to comfort their sons.

Sighing, knowing that she was trapped in her room
now until her brothers calmed down and her parents
could return to their own bed, Shanna turned and
again watched the island.

For a moment the rain let up and her heart went
still when she saw several Penobscot attempting to put
their canoes into the river, surely to go after those

who had fled. She was relieved when she saw them
decide against it and retreat to higher land.

The earth seemed to quake with the thunder. She
covered her eyes when the lightning flashes became
more lurid and frightening.

"Shanna? Are you awake?" she heard her mother
say through her door. "Are you all right?"

Shanna went to the door and opened it. The candles
in the wall sconces along the corridor gave off enough
light for her to see. She saw how protectively her
mother and father held their twins in their arms, her
brothers' tiny arms clutching so tightly around each of
their necks, and it was at this moment she knew the
intenseness of her parents' feelings toward their
children.

Shanna had always felt it, but a night like tonight
made it a keen reality to her. Surely no one could
hold children more endearingly and protectively in
their arms than her parents were holding their frightened twins.

And her parents' concern for her own welfare made
Shanna feel guilty for ever having done anything in
her life that might have worried them.

She was quickly reminded of so many things she
had recently done: helping get Jennie safely to Indian
Island, adopting Elizabeth, making love with Bold
Wolf, promising to Bold Wolf that she would marry
him soon!

But she wouldn't change any of it. She loved Bold
Wolf and Elizabeth as endearingly and protectively as
her parents loved her and her brothers. She would die
for both the man who would soon be her husband
and the child she loved as if it had been born of her
own womb!

"Mama . . . Papa . . . I'm fine," Shanna said
reassuringly.

Yes, she was fine, and yes, she felt so dearly loved tonight, and protected. Yet she knew also that once the storm abated and her parents returned to their room to sleep, she would slip away into the night and go to Indian Island to see if Bold Wolf and Jennie were all right.

Shanna would not allow herself to feel guilty again for things she did out of love. She could not just return to her bed and pretend what she had seen and heard tonight had not happened. It was all too real, the sickening blasts from the firearms sending shock waves through her even now as she thought of them.

No. Sleep would never come to her again if she didn't go and see if Bold Wolf had been among those fired upon tonight. If he should die, a part of her would die along with him.

"Do you wish to come with us to our room until the storm is over?" Shanna's father asked, reaching out to gently touch her cheek. "We're taking the twins there. They will be sleeping the rest of the night with us."

"Shanna, we can make room in our bed for you," Bernita said softly. "Please come with us."

"Mama, there is no need in me crowding your bed," Shanna said. "Papa, I'll be all right. Please go on with the twins. I'm sure they will feel much better beneath the blankets with you and Mama."

"All right, then," Jordan said, giving Shanna another soft smile. He started to walk away, then turned and looked at her again. "But if you should change your mind, come ahead. Do you hear, Shanna? Come ahead. There is always room in our bed for our little girl."

Shanna laughed softly. "Your little girl is not so little any longer," she said. She again felt guilt tugging at her heart over planning to deceive them again as soon as they were asleep. She blew her father a kiss. "Good night, Papa." She gave her mother a lingering soft gaze. "Good night, Mama."

She watched them walk away, the twins already asleep in their arms. Only after they had their door closed and she knew they were in bed did she return to her own room.

Going to the window, Shanna again looked over toward Indian Island. The rain was no longer coming down in blinding sheets. She could see the island, but saw no activity.

"Bold Wolf, *are* you all right?" she whispered. "Jennie, are *you*?"

Shanna paced the floor. She wanted so badly to go to Indian Island, yet she knew how distraught that would make her parents if they discovered her gone. She stopped and stared at her closed bedroom door. Surely everyone was asleep in her parents' room.

She then looked outside, where the rain was now scarcely falling. She could no longer hear the river, which meant the waves had calmed.

"I've just got to," Shanna whispered, jerking her gown over her head.

She prayed that she could get to the island without being seen. She would go to the island and see if everyone was all right, then return home before dawn.

Even then, she knew that her parents and her brothers might sleep past their normal time. Tonight might exhaust them all. And her father had no burials to prepare tomorrow. For a while, at least, the rooms downstairs were empty.

Shanna hurried into a skirt and blouse, then yanked on her leather boots. Her hair hanging loose around her shoulders, she slowly opened her door.

Her pulse raced as she listened closely to be sure no one was moving about in her parents' room. When she heard nothing except her father's soft snore, she smiled and felt safe enough to continue. Shanna hurried on down the back stairs and outside.

The rain had stopped, but the breeze was still shaking the limbs of the trees overhead, occasionally spending sprays of rain from their leaves onto Shanna as she ran down the hill toward the river.

She was relieved that no one was on the streets of town. There was no lamplight in the windows. She could only hear the occasional bark of a dog in the distance, and then a coyote responding somewhere farther away, its long howl eerie in the damp darkness.

Shivering from the chill of the night, her skin prickling as another spray of rain splashed down on her from the trees overhead, Shanna was glad to finally run free of them, the river shimmering now as the clouds swept away and revealed the full moon overhead.

So glad that the water was calm enough to cross over to Bold Wolf's island, Shanna found a canoe and quickly boarded it. Rhythmically pulling the paddle through the water, she worried about what she might discover once she arrived at Bold Wolf's village. She paddled more determinedly, then stopped when she saw movement on the island.

Her heart sang with gladness when in the moonlight she could make out Bold Wolf shoving a canoe into the water, followed by several of his warriors with their own canoes.

Bold Wolf was alive and well, and tears of joy welled in Shanna's eyes. He *had* lived through the attack! She could still hold him and tell him of her deep love for him!

She was shaken from her reverie when Bold Wolf and his warriors began paddling their canoes away from the island in the direction that the invading Indians had traveled as they had escaped into the rainy darkness on the river.

She realized that in his determination to pursue his enemies, Bold Wolf hadn't seen her crossing the river toward his island. She was tiny and unnoticeable in the darkness, the moon once again having slipped behind a cloud.

Having come this far, and wanting to be with Bold Wolf so badly, no matter where he might be headed, Shanna began waving her arms. "Bold Wolf!" she cried. "It's me! It's Shanna! Can't you see me?"

Again the clouds floated away from the moon. The white light flooded down onto Shanna. She again shouted Bold Wolf's name, and began paddling as quickly as she could toward him.

Hearing what he thought was Shanna crying his name, Bold Wolf stopped paddling, startled, and turned quickly and gazed over his shoulder.

"Shanna?" he whispered, stunned to see her coming toward him in a canoe, her reddish orange hair like sunshine beneath the bright light of the full moon.

21

A hundred years from now, dear heart,
We shall not care at all,
It will not matter then a whit,
The honey, or the gall!
                                    —JOHN BENNETT

Bold Wolf rowed quickly to Shanna. He reached out, grabbed the side of her canoe, and brought it next to his. "Why are you away from your home at this late hour?" he asked thickly. "Why were you canoeing toward my island?"

"I wish I could say it is only because I've missed you," Shanna said, her eyes holding with his. "But, Bold Wolf, I heard gunfire coming from Indian Island. From my bedroom window I saw canoes leaving the island. I guessed that the Mohawk had come to attack. I . . . I feared for your welfare. I worried about Jennie."

She reached over and gently touched his cheek. "You don't know how relieved I am to know that you are all right," she murmured. She looked toward Indian Island, then gazed at Bold Wolf again. "Is *Jennie* all right?"

Bold Wolf's gaze wavered. He looked suddenly away from Shanna, searching within his heart how to tell her what had happened to Jennie. If he could reassure her that the Mohawk wouldn't harm Jennie, that was one thing. But he couldn't, for he was not even certain why she had been abducted.

"Bold Wolf, what about Jennie?" Shanna asked, a

quick panic seizing her as he hesitated. To Shanna that could only mean one thing. Surely Jennie *wasn't* all right. Perhaps she had been harmed during the exchange of gunfire.

Bold Wolf looked quickly and apologetically into Shanna's eyes. "Jennie was abducted by the Mohawk," he said in a rush. "We are on our way to the Mohawk village to rescue her."

Shanna was stunned. She covered her mouth with a hand and looked away from Bold Wolf. She bit back an accusation. He had not taken care of Jennie well enough after promising that he would! But several of his warriors were waiting in canoes, watching and listening to what was being said between Bold Wolf and Shanna. She would not say anything that would make Bold Wolf look shamed in the eyes of his warriors.

"You must return home," Bold Wolf said thickly. "Shanna, even if I believe it was only a few renegades, the Mohawk treaty was broken tonight by those who came to my island, who stole not only from our food supplies, but who also fired upon me and my warriors and stole an innocent woman. Even if I have to enter into war with the Mohawk over these things, I *will* get Jennie back."

"But will she be alive?" Shanna asked, her voice breaking. "If gunfire is exchanged again between your men and the Mohawk, might the Mohawk not place Jennie in the midst of it purposely? She is nothing to them!"

"I do not anticipate warring with the Mohawk, or the Mohawk using Jennie as a pawn," Bold Wolf said. "I think what happened tonight was done by renegades who did not have the blessing of Chief Bent Arrow. Once I arrive at Chief Bent Arrow's village and he hears what happened at Indian Island, he will make all wrongs right. Chief Bent Arrow was my father's enemy, but he has always known who is the strongest tribe and will not seek trouble with the Penobscot."

"I want to go with you," Shanna said, stubbornly lifting her chin. "I *must* go with you, Bold Wolf. No matter how much you try to reassure me, I'm afraid for Jennie. Jennie needs me. When you arrive at the Mohawk village, I think it would give Jennie much encouragement if she sees me with you. She will know that you wouldn't have allowed me to come with you were it not safe enough to rescue Jennie from those who abducted her."

"I cannot allow you to accompany me and my warriors there," Bold Wolf said, just as stubbornly. "I will ask one of my warriors to escort you back to shore. Return home. Then meet me tomorrow before the noon hour at our secret meeting place. Jennie will be with me."

"Bold Wolf, you can't expect me to return home and worry myself sick the rest of the night over both you and Jennie," Shanna said. "*Please* allow me to go with you tonight. I promise not to do anything that might jeopardize what you have planned. Just let me go and be there for Jennie. She has already been through enough. She needs me, Bold Wolf. She *needs* me."

Bold Wolf kneaded his chin. He thought deeply about what she was asking of him. He truly didn't expect an altercation between himself and the Mohawk. He truly believed that the Mohawk chief would be appalled by what some of his warriors had done tonight.

And when Chief Bent Arrow discovered Jennie in his camp, he would more than likely hand her over gladly to Bold Wolf to rid himself of the trouble she could bring his people. Unaware of Jennie's status in

life, that only a few people cared for her welfare,
Chief Bent Arrow would surely believe the whole
white community could be brought in on this also and
cause his people much harm.

But Bold Wolf was thinking as well about the consequences if Shanna's parents discovered he had allowed
her to accompany him to the Mohawk camp. He
wanted to win over her parents so that he could soon
marry her, not antagonize them and give them cause
to keep her away from him forever.

But here before him was Shanna's intense, pleading
stare as she awaited his answer. That and her true,
undying friendship for Jennie made him cast all worries from his mind.

"Yes, you can go with me," he decided, leaning
over to brush a soft kiss across her lips. He took her
hands and he gazed into her eyes. "But once we arrive
at the village, you must do everything I say. Only by
doing that can I be assured of your safety."

Shanna reached over and gave him a tight hug.
"Thank you, thank you," she murmured. She smiled
through her tears at him. "I'll do anything you ask of
me. Just tell me and I will do it."

She was especially grateful because she knew just
how much he *didn't* want her to go. She knew she was
pushing him into this decision. But she wanted to be
there for Jennie so badly she would not be denied.

"Come over to my canoe," Bold Wolf said. He
steadied the boats as she moved from one to the other.

Shanna settled on the small seat behind Bold Wolf,
then watched the canoe she had stolen drift away in
the slow current. She then turned and watched Bold
Wolf as he took her farther away from Indian Island
in his canoe, his warriors following.

Anxious for her friend's safety, Shanna clung to the
sides of the canoe and peered through the night as

they slid through the dark waters, the moon again covered by clouds. She gazed at Bold Wolf and admired how he so masterfully drew the paddle through the water. She could see the determination in each of his strokes. They traveled incessantly onward, sliding across the water as quietly as eels.

Shanna was beginning to wonder if they would ever arrive at the Mohawk camp when she noticed that the Penobscot warriors, with Bold Wolf in the lead, were now hugging the banks of the river, well hidden by the thickets and stands of cottonwood.

Knowing they must now be near the Mohawk camp, Shanna's pulse raced. She kept telling herself, deep inside her heart, that things would be all right. Soon they would have Jennie and would be on their way back home. Shanna would then return to her bed and hope that her parents would never realize what she had done tonight.

She held her breath as she watched the Penobscot warriors beach their canoes. She clung more tightly to Bold Wolf's as he took one more stroke with his paddle that led them onto the rocky shore of the river. She watched as he jumped from the canoe and started yanking it farther toward dry land, soon beaching it with the others along the rocky shore.

"Come," Bold Wolf whispered, reaching for Shanna, lifting her from the canoe. He grabbed his rifle. "Stay close beside me."

They hadn't gone far when suddenly many Mohawk warriors stepped from behind boulders, their arrows drawn.

Shanna's heart seemed to stop as she stared at the Mohawk and the threat of their arrows. Her knees shook as she breathlessly watched Bold Wolf raise his right hand in the accepted gesture for peace among Indians, then she listened to one of the Mohawk warriors talking to Bold Wolf in language she did not understand.

But she understood well enough when Bold Wolf took her by the elbow and led her along with his warriors into the Mohawk camp of several lodges. The Mohawk warriors now stood aside as a bent old man wrapped in snug red blankets, his skin drawn tight as leather across his face, stepped from the largest lodge.

When Shanna heard Bold Wolf speak to the man as they clasped hands in a friendship that looked forced, she knew she was in the presence of the Mohawk chief, Bent Arrow. She couldn't understand what was being said between Bold Wolf and the Mohawk chief, but all was peaceful so far.

Chief Bent Arrow turned and went back inside his lodge, then soon emerged again, and this time not alone. Shanna's eyes widened and she gasped when she saw Jennie with him, unharmed but stiff with fear.

Jennie broke away from the chief and flung herself into Shanna's arms. "Shanna!" she cried. "Shanna!"

Feeling the desperation in Jennie's grip, Shanna clung to her. "It's going to be all right," she whispered. "We've come to take you away from this place."

Shanna eased Jennie from her arms. She looked her slowly up and down, relieved that her dear friend showed no signs of having been ravaged by the Mohawk. She was wet from traveling through the fierce storm, but was well and untouched. She wore a buckskin dress and moccasins that she had been given after having arrived at the Penobscot village. Her hair hung in wet, frizzy curls down her back.

The Mohawk chief surprised Shanna by speaking now in English, so clearly she could understand everything he said as he spoke directly to Bold Wolf.

"This white woman is not at my camp because I

wish her to be," Chief Bent Arrow said in a low, gravely voice, giving Jennie a glance. Again he gazed at Bold Wolf. "Nor did I send warriors to steal from your food supply. Bold Wolf, when I made a reasonable peace with your father, where treaties were signed between us, it was not one made falsely. Tonight it was restless young braves from our camp who went against all they have ever been taught."

Chief Bent Arrow turned and began to walk away in a shaky, unsteady gait, as warriors held up burning torches to light his way. "Come, Bold Wolf, and I will show you the punishment those restless young braves must endure for their foolish deeds tonight," he said, looking over his shoulder at Bold Wolf, gesturing with the wave of a frail hand. He glanced over at Shanna and Jennie. "Bring women. It is important that they see, also, that what was done tonight to the white woman was not something taken lightly by this Mohawk chief."

Shanna grabbed one of Jennie's hands and walked beside Bold Wolf behind the Mohawk chief. Although Shanna realized that many Mohawks were coming from their lodges, staring and whispering among themselves, she looked straight ahead.

When she saw four young braves staked to the ground by ropes that were straining at their ankles and wrists, Shanna stared at them for only a moment, then turned her eyes away. She couldn't help feeling embarrassment for the braves, for they were stark naked, their legs spread wide.

Chief Bent Arrow stood over the young braves and glared down at them. Torches were held over them so that everyone could see those who were being punished.

He then turned to Bold Wolf. "And so you see that what I said was true," he said thickly. "You now believe me when I say that none of this that happened tonight was from my commands?"

"Yes, what I see is proof enough," Bold Wolf said, staring down at the young men, recognizing them. They were known to go into Old Town and frequent the brothels and cause trouble. He had seen them drinking firewater. They seemed to be lost young men whose future was dim. He was proud that none of his young braves walked such a troubled road in life. He, as did his father before him, made sure that the young men of his village always had goals that made them eager to rise each day with the morning sun.

"You will come again to my island and join me in a peace council?" Chief Bent Arrow asked, turning his back to the young braves.

"Yes, and soon there will be a seven-year Grand Fire Council celebration at my island," Bold Wolf said. "I personally extend you an invitation to participate."

"Chief Bent Arrow has never been asked to participate in the Grand Fire Council on your island before," the chief said, openly touched by the invitation. "Yes, I will come."

"Bring warriors of your choice, and also your wife," Bold Wolf said. He got a quick glimpse of Chief Bent Arrow's lovely Mohawk wife, Running Deer, as she momentarily lifted the entrance flap of their lodge, then dropped it and went back inside by the fire.

Bold Wolf knew all about Running Deer. A beautiful woman forty years younger than her chieftain husband, she was known to have married him for the honor and privileges of being wife to a powerful Mohawk chief. It was known by only a few that during a war between another faction of Indians, he had been wounded in the worst way possible for a man who, until then, had been virile and boasted of having many children and wives. He now had to be satisfied just to have the pleasure of looking at his young wife and sleeping with her amid the blankets.

"Thank you, Bold Wolf, and we will gladly come and bring gifts," Chief Bent Arrow said.

Chief Bent Arrow lifted a hand toward one of his warriors. "Return the food that was stolen from the Penobscot tonight to their canoes," he flatly ordered.

Bold Wolf reached a quick hand to the chief's frail shoulder. "No, that is not necessary," he said, his voice filled with kindness. "The earth has been good to us this year. Our food supply is enough, even with the loss of what was taken tonight. Keep what was taken tonight as gifts from the Penobscot."

Chief Bent Arrow nodded a silent thank-you, then gazed at Jennie. "Young woman, do not think badly of all Mohawk over what a few did tonight," he said, his voice drawn.

"I was not harmed," Jennie murmured. "Frightened . . . but not harmed."

"Go and be frightened no more," Chief Bent Arrow said, humbly lowering his eyes.

Shanna's grip on Jennie's hand strengthened. She smiled at her friend. "Let's go and get in the canoe," she murmured.

Jennie nodded, then hurried away with Shanna.

"I don't want to return to Indian Island," Jennie suddenly blurted out. "I want to go home with you. Surely your parents will allow it. I'll stay hidden so that Al will never know."

"You dislike being on the island with Bold Wolf and his people so much?" Shanna murmured as they waited inside the canoes for Bold Wolf and his warriors.

"I miss playing my violin," Jennie said, her voice filled with longing. "While I practice at your house no one will know it is not you. We play alike, Shanna. You know that no one would be able to tell that it's not you."

"Yes, you can go home with me," Shanna said softly. "Father and Mother will just have to understand. But Jennie, perhaps you won't have to stay in hiding much longer. Al has disappeared."

"Disappeared?" Jennie gasped, her eyes wide. "Truly? He's gone?"

Shanna explained how the brothel's men had beaten up Roscoe Lovett, and why.

"Oh, no," Jennie groaned. "How *is* Roscoe? Is he hurt bad?"

"Bad enough," Shanna said, sighing. "But—"

She stopped when she saw Bold Wolf coming from the Mohawk camp. She broke away from Jennie and ran to him. He took her into his arms and hugged her.

"Thank you for everything," Shanna murmured. "If not for you, who is to say whether or not the chief would have let Jennie go? There is something about that man that makes me distrust him."

Bold Wolf eased her from his arms, took her by her hand, and led her toward the canoes. "Yes, he has always been a man of deceit, but tonight I believe he was being truthful," he said, helping Shanna into a canoe. He reached a hand out for Jennie. "It might be the beginning of a friendship that I never thought possible."

He helped Jennie into the canoe beside Shanna, then shoved it out into the water and boarded it himself.

Shanna pulled Jennie close and they hugged as the canoe moved back in the direction of Indian Island. Shanna was relieved that this was behind them, yet knew that now she had perhaps much worse to face.

When her parents discovered Jennie at their house, she would have to come out with the truth about so much that she had been afraid to tell them.

This time there was no getting around it!

22

It is not while beauty and youth are thine own,
And thy cheeks unprofaned by a tear,
That the fervor and faith of a soul may be
   known,
To which time will but made thee more dear.
                              —THOMAS MOORE

So glad to be home safe and sound with Jennie, and
certain that no one had seen them, Shanna plopped
down on a chair beside the bedroom window and
sighed.

"How can I ever thank you for what you continue
to do for me?" Jennie whispered. She fell to her knees
beside the chair and gently rested a cheek on Shanna's
knee. "Oh, Shanna, my world is so torn apart. It shall
never be as I wished it to be." She closed her eyes
and shivered. "Those horrible men at the brothel.
Their groping hands . . . their foul breath . . . their . . ."

Unable to tell Shanna the depths of despair she
truly felt over having her body defiled and spoiled for
the husband she'd hoped to have one day, a sob
lodged in Jennie's throat.

Feeling Jennie's despair, feeling it inside her heart
as though it were her own, Shanna placed a gentle
hand on Jennie's head and softly stroked her damp,
tangled hair. "Things will work out for you, Jennie,"
she whispered, hoping they were talking softly enough
that her parents wouldn't be awakened. "Eventually
all of those men who own brothels will be dealt with.
The townspeople will grow tired of such an embarrassment in their proud little town."

"It's no use," Jennie said, easing away from Shanna. She stood and stared down at her wet, clinging clothes and the muddy moccasins. "Just look at me." She pulled her fingers through her tangled hair, then ran a hand down her slight figure. "I am only a mere image of what I once was." She held her hands out before her. "My fingers. They may never play the violin as they did before I was wrenched from my lessons!"

Sobbing, she threw herself on the bed. "I hate everything about me now," she whispered harshly. "Everything!"

Tears stinging her eyes, Shanna went to her friend. "You mustn't talk like that," she said, sitting down beside her. She gently drew Jennie into her arms. "Once things are straightened out, you will resume your violin lessons."

She leaned back and looked into Jennie's eyes. "And, Jennie, I truly know that Roscoe loves you," she murmured. "Surely once he feels less threatened, he will marry you. He will probably even take you away to a new town where no one knows about the brothel *or* your horrid family."

"I will only bring hardships into Roscoe's life," Jennie said softly, wiping tears from her face with the backs of her hands. "What I should do, Shanna, is sneak away on the next paddle wheeler and go to St. Louis or New Orleans. I can start my *own* new life."

Jennie took Shanna's hands. "You are the true lucky one," she murmured. "Shanna, Bold Wolf is such a special man. Do you know just how lucky you are that someone like him loves you? And it would not be hard at all to adjust to life on Indian Island. I already made friends with Pale Star. It was fun sitting and talking with her and watching her make bread, and sew beads and shells on dresses and skirts."

"Yes, I feel very lucky to have Bold Wolf," Shanna said, sighing. "And I must find a way to break the news to my parents soon about marrying him or, Jennie, I might lose him to another woman. His patience can only last for so long."

"Don't let that happen, Shanna," Jennie said, gripping Shanna's hands more tightly. "That man has so much love to give a woman. And he is so kind, so gentle and understanding!"

The more Jennie talked about Bold Wolf, the more Shanna became wary of it. It appeared that Jennie might have fallen in love with Bold Wolf herself during the short time they had been thrown together on Indian Island. Jennie spoke so fondly of Bold Wolf, while she hardly said anything about Roscoe Lovett.

Jennie drew her hands away from Shanna's and stretched her arms over head, yawning. "I'm so sleepy," she announced. "And my bones ache so badly from being yanked around by those Mohawk scoundrels."

"Let's go on to bed," Shanna said. "I'll bring a basin of hot water and soap into my room tomorrow morning so that you can bathe." She went to her chifforobe and slid two gowns from pegs. "You'd best get out of those clothes, Jennie, and wear a gown until your bath tomorrow."

"When are you going to tell your parents about me?" Jennie asked, taking the gown and laying it over the back of a chair until she removed her wet clothes.

Shanna sat down in a chair and yanked one boot off, then the other. "I've got to tell them tomorrow, but I'm not sure yet what I'll say, or how far I'll go into explaining everything," she murmured, standing now, sliding the skirt off. "They *have* to be told, though, for I cannot hide you in my room forever."

"Your father, more than your mother, will be upset

over my being here," Jennie said, stretching her damp buckskin dress over the back of a chair to dry. She then drew the gown over her head, relishing its warmth as it clung to her body.

Knowing just how much Jennie loved to practice her violin, Shanna laughed softly. "Well, I'm not so sure about that," she murmured. "Jennie, you don't know how violin practice irritates my mother. She will go to any lengths to keep me from it."

"Truly?" Jennie asked, eyes wide. "She truly doesn't approve of you playing the violin?"

"It's not that so much—it's the music itself that she doesn't like," Shanna said, pulling the gown over her head. She hugged the warm fabric to her body, then pulled back the bedcovers, the warm blankets inviting her between them. "My mother says my violin 'squawks,' " she said, smiling at Jennie. "She will just die once she knows there will be *two* people practicing violins in her house."

"I don't want to do anything that will upset your mother," Jennie said softly. "I'd best not practice, Shanna, while I am here." Tears streamed from her eyes once again. "Oh, Shanna, I can't stay here forever and I can't go home. I no longer *have* a home. What am I to do?"

"You have a home here as long as you wish to stay," Shanna murmured. "I know my parents will welcome you. And I truly believe someone has done away with Mr. Big Mouth Adams."

"You do truly think he has met with foul play?" Jennie asked, yawning.

Shanna watched Jennie crawl onto the bed, curling up on her side in a fetal position, her eyes slowly closing. "I'm not certain what might have happened to him, but the world sure would be a much better place without him," she said, crawling into bed beside Jennie. "Especially *yours.*"

"Please stop worrying about me so much, Shanna," Jennie whispered. "Let's go to sleep. I know you must be as tired as me."

Shanna pulled the blanket up and made herself comfortable, her back to Jennie. Just as she was about to close her eyes, a reflection of fire on her ceiling, coming from somewhere outside, made her gasp and bolt from the bed.

She hurried to the window, and drew back the curtain, and gasped when she saw a huge fire sending bursts of black smoke and flames heavenward from the downtown district.

From this vantage point, her bedroom window being higher than the buildings in the town, she could see well enough which building was burning.

"Al . . . Adams's . . . brothel!" she gasped, her pulse racing. "Jennie, the brothel! It's on fire!"

Jennie rushed to her side. "Truly?" she said, clasping Shanna's arm. "Is it truly burning?"

"I *know* it's the brothel," Shanna said, the horrific screams of women and men now filling the air.

The town's firehouse had been built on the steepest point of Stillwater Avenue Hill so that the firemen could see the town and better assess the situation before responding to fires. Holding hands, Shanna and Jennie watched the fire wagon dash past them, the bells clanging, the team of horses straining at their bits as they tackled the steepness of the hill.

"Lord have mercy, what is happening now?" Shanna heard her mother crying out in the corridor. "I do believe it must be the end of the world! When will things ever stop happening in our town?"

A sudden fear gripped Shanna that her mother might come on into her room and catch Jennie there.

She needed time to tell her mother about Jennie in a way that would not upset her! Shanna needed time to find the right way to tell her *father*!

When Shanna heard her brothers wailing, and then her father's heavy footsteps as he raced from his bedroom, she grabbed Jennie by the hand and ran her over to the chifforobe.

"Get inside!" she whispered shakily. "Hide!"

Her eyes wide with fear, Jennie climbed in and hid herself behind the clothes.

Shanna closed the door to the chifforobe just in time. Clutching her robe around her, her graying hair hanging long and loose to her waist, Bernita came into the room and rushed to the window.

"It's the brothel, Mama," Shanna said, hurrying to her mother's side. She nervously glanced at the chifforobe, then held the curtain aside for her mother. "See, Mama? You can tell that it's Al Adams's brothel."

"Hear the women screaming?" Bernita said, trembling. "Do you think many died in the fire? If I wasn't a God-fearing, Christian lady, I would say it serves them right, the trollops."

Shanna's heart skipped a beat. She looked over at the chifforobe, hoping Jennie hadn't heard her mother, for Jennie had been one of those women, but absolutely not of her own choosing.

The twins came bouncing into the room in their pajamas. "Let me see!" Tommie cried, shoving Terrie aside as Terrie tried to squeeze in between Shanna and Bernita.

"You children should not want to see the fire," Bernita scolded, turning to put herself between her children and the window, shielding them from the sight. She took their hands and led them toward the door. "Children who watch fires wet the bed. Do you want to be bed-wetters? Do you?"

Shanna sighed with relief when her mother left the room with the boys. But then her father came into the room and stood at the window watching the fire.

"I should go and offer my help," he said thickly. "But being it's Al Adams's establishment, I wouldn't bend a finger helping him. Let the goddamn place burn to the ground. Good riddance."

He turned to leave, then stopped quickly, staring at the buckskin dress stretched out on the back of the chair, and turned slow, accusing eyes to Shanna.

The color drained from Shanna's face when she realized he had seen Jennie's dress. Her eyes wide, her throat suddenly dry, she edged slowly away from him.

"Explanations are in order, don't you think?" Jordan said, yanking the dress from the chair. He turned it over in his hands, studying it.

Then he shoved it in Shanna's arms. "Where did this goddamn thing come from?" he growled, his jaw tight, his eyes filled with an angry fire.

Scarcely breathing, Shanna clung to the dress.

Then she turned with a start when Jennie stepped from the chifforobe, tears streaming from her eyes, as she looked slowly from Shanna to Shanna's father.

"Sir, that's *my* dress," Jennie murmured, then waited for the world to crumble around both herself and Shanna.

23

Last night, ah, yesternight,
Betwixt her lips and mine,
There fell thy shadow!
—ERNEST DOWSON

Except for Tommie and Terrie giggling as they played
with their bowls of oatmeal instead of eating, everything was strained and quiet at the breakfast table.

As Shanna took a bite of her toast, she glanced over
at Jennie, who sat beside her, her eggs untouched, and
with only one bite taken from her toast. Jennie and
Shanna had bathed and washed their hair early in the
morning. Shanna had let Jennie sort through her
clothes and choose something to wear today. Jennie
had chosen a simple skirt and blouse over a dress, as
had Shanna. Their hair was now dry and clean and
hung in long, perfumed streamers down their backs.

Jennie slowly turned her eyes to Shanna and smiled
weakly, then resumed watching Shanna's father, who
had his face hidden behind the morning paper.

Shanna was relieved that her parents knew about
her trip to the island and the rescue of Jennie—although when her father heard about her daring night,
she thought he was going to explode, his anger was
so intense. It was not just that she had disobeyed his
orders and had gone to Indian Island. It was that she
had placed herself in danger while going to Jennie's
rescue that had seemed to be the final straw.

But Jennie had broken down and cried—at just the

right time—and nothing anyone could say to her could stop her heart-wrenching sobs. It was at that moment Shanna's father had realized just how traumatized Jennie had become over all that had happened to her. Tears had come to Shanna's eyes when he drew Jennie into his arms and comforted her.

After that, the shouting had stopped and her father had at least listened to reason, actually *commending* Shanna for being such a devoted friend.

But when the conversation had turned to Bold Wolf and Shanna had told her father that she would soon marry him, he had again become outraged and unreasonable.

At least in the end both of her parents had agreed to let Jennie live with them, taking her under their wing as though she were their daughter.

But everyone had agreed that until more was known about Al Adams's whereabouts, *and* those men who had beaten Roscoe Lovett unmercifully, Jennie was to stay inside the house. No one was to know she was there. That was the only certain way to keep her safe.

Shanna's plans with Bold Wolf were not mentioned again, both her mother and father acting as though, if they said nothing more about it, the problem would just go away.

"Jordan, *must* you keep your nose in the paper at the breakfast table?" Bernita said, reaching over to pour her husband another cup of coffee. She gave Tommie a frown when he nudged Terrie with an elbow. "And *must* you boys start the day being so ornery?"

"It says here in the *Bangor Daily News* that no one was hurt in the fire at the brothel," Jordan said, still holding the paper up. "But listen to *this*. It says that the fire was purposely set. It was *arson*. Also it says that those men who ran the brothel with Al Adams have run scared from Old Town after receiving death threats from an unknown source. The paper says it seems the one who sent the note also is suspicioned of having set the fire."

Shanna's eyes brightened. "Then that has to mean that it's safe for Jennie to leave the house," she said, giving Jennie a quick, reassuring smile.

Shanna's smile waned when she saw that Jennie was not showing any signs of relief about the news. "Jennie, didn't you hear?" she murmured. "Those terrible men have run like scared cats from Old Town. Surely it is safe for you to do as you please now." She took one of Jennie's hands and gently squeezed it. "Jennie, you are *free.* Isn't that wonderful?"

"The fact that those men have disappeared doesn't mean anything," Jennie said solemnly. She shoved her untouched dish of food away from her. "I still have to worry about Al Adams. Surely he's still somewhere ready to kill the one responsible for the fire. That means that if he sees me, he'd just as soon kill me as let me go free like those other women."

Jennie's eyes wavered as she looked over at Shanna. "And there is my father," she said, gulping hard. "After he reads about the brothel burning down, he will surely come looking for me. If he finds me, he will surely sell me again to one of the other hideous establishments in town." She shuddered. "I'd hate to have to live in that . . . that dreadful tent with the painted ladies I've seen coming and going from there."

"It always amazes me how news can get into Bangor so quickly about Old Town, so that the *Bangor Daily News* can report every seedy thing that happens in our town, even when it happens in the wee hours of the morning," Bernita said, obviously ignoring Jennie's frightened statements. She rose from the table, gathered the dishes, and carried them across the room to a counter. Dishwater was heating in a teakettle on the wood-burning stove.

"The next thing you know, those paper people will come nosing around here, especially if they hear about Shanna being in love with an Indian," Bernita said, giving Shanna a scolding frown over her shoulder. "That's news, you know, a pretty white thing like Shanna being infatuated with a redskin so much she wants to marry him."

Shanna paled as she waited for her father to lower his paper and explode all over again about her loving Bold Wolf.

Instead, he seemed intent on reading something else, something so interesting he had not heard his wife.

"Good Lord," Jordan said. He quickly lowered the paper and stared over at Jennie, then at Shanna. "It says here that another body was uncovered down at the sawmill. Since the ashes have finally cooled enough from the sawmill fire, they have resumed searching for bodies. They found one late last evening and it wasn't one of the lumberjacks or anyone who worked inside the sawmill offices. It was—"

Tommie suddenly fell from his chair and hit his head on the edge of the table with a loud popping sound, wailing to high heaven. Jordan dropped his paper, shoved his chair back, and pulled Tommie up from the floor. After he studied the purplish lump that was swelling on the twin's forehead, he held him closer and rocked him back and forth in his arms.

"Terrie shoved me," Tommie cried, reaching up, howling even more loudly when he touched the knot on his brow. "Send him to bed, Mommy. Send him to bed!"

"I'll do no such thing," Bernita said, lifting Terrie from the chair and holding him in her arms. "I saw you pinch him. Will you boys ever learn to just love one another? Will the fighting ever stop?"

Curious to know whose body *had* been found in the ashes at the sawmill, Shanna left her chair and picked up the newspaper.

Standing beside a kitchen window, where the morning sun was pouring through the windowpane like liquid gold, Shanna searched the page that her father had been reading, then found the headline about the discovered body.

"A body was discovered yesterday . . ." she began aloud, then read the rest to herself until she came to the name of the dead man. Her heart leaped inside her chest and her eyes widened.

Wanting to be sure she was reading the right name, finding it hard to believe that the vile man *could* be dead, Shanna jerked the paper closer and read it again.

Then she laid the paper aside and turned and smiled at Jennie. "Jennie, the man they found dead yesterday?" She sat down beside her. "Jennie, it's Al. Al Adams is dead!"

For the first time today, Shanna saw a sparkle in Jennie's eyes. "He . . . is . . . truly dead?" Jennie murmured. "They truly identified him?"

"That's what the article says," Shanna said, sighing. "He was murdered, Jennie. He was *shot*."

"He surely had many, *many* enemies," Jennie said, then flung herself into Shanna's arms. "The vile creature will never touch me again! He was the worst of them all!"

Bernita paled and turned quickly to Jennie. "Hush," she said, putting Terrie down. She held her hands over Terrie's ears. "Don't talk about such things in the presence of the twins."

"I'm sorry," Jennie said, paling.

Then Jennie rose from her chair and went to stare

out the window. "Perhaps it is safe enough now for
me to go for my violin lessons today," she murmured.
"I have missed playing so much."

"No, I don't want you leaving the house just yet,"
Jordan said, placing Tommie on his feet. He went to
Jennie and drew her into his comforting embrace.
"You must let things cool down a bit here in town
before you go out and face the world again." He released her and gazed into her eyes. "And let's never
forget your father."

He dropped his hands to his sides, stared at Jennie
for a moment longer, then left the room.

Shanna took Jennie by the hand and led her from
the kitchen, toward the staircase. "Papa is right, you
know," she said softly. "Rest today, Jennie." She
gazed at Jennie's gaunt figure. She placed a gentle
hand to her cheek. "And, Jennie, you must start eating
better. You'll be ill if you don't."

"Yes, I know," Jennie murmured. She lowered her
eyes. "All I want now is to play my violin."

"Since yours is always left at the music studio so
that your father can't sell or destroy it, you can play
mine," Shanna said. "Come on upstairs. I'll give you
mine to use for now."

"It's not the same as playing my own," Jennie murmured. "We seem bonded, my violin and I, as though
it is a person with a heartbeat and breath that are a
part of mine."

"If it's that important to you, Jennie, I will go to
the music studio today and get your violin for you,"
Shanna said, rushing toward the door. "Anyhow, I'd
like to know when I'm to be there again for lessons."

Jennie followed Shanna to the door. "Are you going
to tell Roscoe about me?" she asked, eyes wide. "That
I am here, safe, at your house?"

Shanna opened the door, then turned to Jennie.

"No, I don't think so," she said softly. "You know what Father said."

"But it's only Mr. Lovett," Jennie said, sighing. "He would want to know that I'm all right. Surely he's worrying about me after the fire. He'll wonder where I am, since he will know that I am no longer at the brothel."

"Of course, you're right," Shanna said, nervously raking her fingers through her hair. "And he will most certainly know that *I* am aware of where you are if I come purposely to get your violin. He will know that only you would send me for it."

"Then you will tell him?"

"Yes, but I will make him promise not to come here to see you for a while, and not to tell anyone that you are here."

"Hurry back," Jennie murmured, giving Shanna a big hug.

"I shall," Shanna said, returning Jennie's hug.

She hurried from the house and ran down the steep hill toward town. She looked down at where the brothel had once stood, where now only ashes and rubble were strewn along the ground, smoke still spiraling from it.

It gave Shanna an uneasy feeling to know that someone had purposely set the brothel afire, and that someone had murdered Al Adams. It made her feel uneasy, knowing that someone could take it upon himself to burn and kill so easily.

"Who could have done it?" Shanna whispered to herself, running to the opposite side of the street so that she could avoid the ashy remains of the brothel.

She hurried onward and rushed up the stairs to the music studio, then stopped on the landing and stared at a posted note on the door. She quickly read it, then stared at the closed, locked door.

"He's gone," she whispered. "He's gone to tend to business in another city."

She started down the steps slowly, her mind troubled by Roscoe's sudden absence. He had not given any warning that he was leaving.

"Strange that he leaves just as . . ."

Her heart skipped a beat. She stopped on the steps and turned and stared up at the door. Her face drained of color as she recalled that day when the men from the brothel had come and beat Roscoe as Shanna hid and listened. Afterward she had seen a side of Roscoe that she had never seen before . . . such an intense anger and hatred. He had even voiced threats against the men, as well as Al Adams.

"But wasn't Al already missing by then?" Shanna whispered, trying to sort all of this inside her mind.

Her eyes widened. Yes! Al's disappearance was the reason the men tried to force answers out of Mr. Lovett. It was as though they had known that Roscoe Lovett might have done something to Al because of Jennie's imprisonment in the brothel.

"Did Mr. Lovett kill Al Adams and . . . and bury him in the ashes?" she whispered, paling even more at the thought of such a kind man as Roscoe Lovett being forced into such an act as murder.

She turned and stared at the burned brothel. "Did he do *that*?" she whispered, covering a gasp behind her hand.

Not ready to go home just yet, unsure of what to tell Jennie and not wanting to alarm her about Roscoe Lovett, Shanna decided to visit Elizabeth. Too much had taken her away from Elizabeth much too often!

But soon nothing at all would keep them apart, for Elizabeth would be hers.

Hers *and* Bold Wolf's!

24

All paths lead to you
Where e'er I roam.
You are the lark-song
Calling me home.
—BLANCHE SHOEMAKER WAGSTAFF

Bold Wolf stood on the banks of the Penobscot River, gazing across at Old Town. He had not been able to sleep last night and he had not been able to eat his morning meal.

After Shanna had left for home with Jennie last night, the fire in Old Town had quickly alarmed him. He had hurried to Old Town to make sure Shanna was not affected by the fire in any way, and he was relieved when he saw it was only one of the brothels.

But later, after he arrived home and sleep eluded him over thinking endlessly of Shanna, he knew he could not wait any longer to bring her over to his island to protect her. Of late, Old Town had become a place where no one seemed safe. He felt that the only place for Shanna to truly be safe was with him.

And although Jennie had been abducted from his island by the Mohawk, that had been achieved only because Bold Wolf had not seen the need to have sentries posted around his island.

If Shanna were on his island, no Mohawk *or* white man would dare come like a thief in the night to attempt stealing from the Penobscot. They would pay dearly for their transgressions. Sentries were now posted around the outskirts of his village, keeping watch.

"Today," he whispered to himself, doubling his hands into tight fists at his sides. "Yes, I *must* send my bride price *today.*"

He remembered, then, how Shanna had asked him not to do anything just yet, especially not send a bride price to her father, for she still asked for more time.

"Time has been my enemy for too long now," Bold Wolf whispered, turning sharply and walking in stiff, quick strides toward his village. "Time has just run out."

No, he would wait no longer. No one would protect Shanna and cherish her as much as he.

Not even her father.

Bold Wolf had listened often to Shanna speaking about her father and his plans for her future. He felt that her father's plans for her career as a violinist overwhelmed his true feelings for Shanna as a person.

Her father saw her as an object. Bold Wolf saw her as a woman, sweet and wonderful.

Bold Wolf hurried into his cabin and knelt down on the floor beside his bed. Reaching beneath it, sliding his hands inside the storage space, he brought out a soft buckskin bag, then gently placed it on his bed and opened it.

Reverently, Bold Wolf slid his hands inside the bag. When he touched the smoothness of the conch shell, he was reminded of those many years ago when he had first met Shanna and she showed him her basket of shells.

He had seen her love of shells then and remembered how she wished to find the perfect one. As far as he knew, she never found the one she had been seeking and had given up long ago searching for it.

"I found it *for* you, Shanna," Bold Wolf whispered.

He smiled as he held the large conch shell out before him, its pinkish hue picking up the sunbeams as they danced through his window, giving the shell a soft, translucent look.

When Bold Wolf had been far from his village on a fishing expedition only a year ago, he had discovered this shell lying on the shore, alone, away from the many other shells that the water constantly washed in from its depths.

Bold Wolf had known the minute he had seen it that he would save it for Shanna and give it to her on their wedding night. He had brought the shell home and cleansed and polished it until it glistened.

The shell shone so much now he could see his reflection in it.

Smiling, he lifted the shell to his right ear and listened to the faint roar, as if the ocean resided in the depths of the shell.

Yes, his woman would be ecstatic that he had found what she had wanted to find when she was a child maturing into a woman. Yes, the shell was for his woman.

But the bride price he had prepared was something even more valuable than the conch shell. It was a precious article never intended to be used as money, but as a pledge of honor.

He lay the conch shell aside on his bed, then reached under his bed and took out another soft buckskin bag.

Scarcely breathing, he lay the bag on the bed.

He reached inside and removed a soft, rolled-up red handkerchief.

He lay this on the bed and slowly unrolled it, soon revealing a wampum band, two hands wide and twenty-one hands long. He had collected quahog and conch shells, both white and purple, from many different shores, and had woven them into a *wa-babi,* white band, for the sole purpose of a bride price.

Bold Wolf had spent many nights before his lodge fire preparing the shells for the wampum band. He had rubbed gritty stone on them to shape them. An awl had been used to make the holes. Making the holes had been the slowest part of the work, for he made sure they were smooth, finely bored, cylindrical.

And now, as he gazed proudly at the band, he knew it was perfect in every way. It was something no man could refuse. Such bands had been used for generations of Penobscot, recording negotiations and history of their people, and kept by council. Belts of wampum were handed out after peace talks. Treaties were recorded on them.

Running his fingers slowly over the smooth beads of this band, Bold Wolf felt confident that today, when Shanna's father gazed upon this beloved article and realized the many hours and the care that had been put into it, he would not be able to refuse it.

Many daughters had been exchanged for wampum in such a way. The bands were always accepted anxiously because the person receiving them had been given something precious and honorable.

To the Penobscot, the wampum was of more value than the white man's gold. Surely it was the same for white men. He knew that Shanna's father could not possibly turn down such a grand gift.

"Bold Wolf, you sent for me?"

He Who Watch's voice broke through Bold Wolf's deep thoughts. Before Bold Wolf had gone to look across the river at Old Town he had sent a young brave to his grand-uncle's lodge with the message to come to him.

Bold Wolf rolled the wampum up in the red handkerchief again and slid it inside the bag. Gently, carefully, once again with reverence, he lifted this into his hands, rose to his feet, and turned to He Who Watches.

"Today is the day for you to *keluwewangan,* negotiate, with Shanna's father. You will take the bride price to him," Bold Wolf said, trying to ignore the disappointment that came into his grand-uncle's eyes. "It is in this bag. Protect it with your life, He Who Watches, until it is safely in the hands of my woman's father."

"For so long I have tried to make you see the wrong in wanting the white woman," He Who Watches grumbled. "Her father will bring trouble to our people should you take her from him. I have watched. I have seen. I know this father has plans for his daughter other than being a wife. Should you interrupt such plans, you will bring the wrath of this man upon our people. Is she worth it, Bold Wolf? This man, her *father,* has power among the white community. Surely he possesses supernatural powers, as well. His hands touch the dead every day, do they not?"

"I have so often, for so long, wondered why you did not want me involved with Shanna, and now I know," Bold Wolf said, sighing. "You are afraid of her father, and perhaps of even Shanna herself. Grand-uncle, if you would have told me before why you held such hostility toward my woman, I could have helped you cast it aside. Her father is not involved in supernatural practices. He is a *mortician. Only* a mortician. His duties are to prepare white people's bodies for burial, not to use them in some sort of supernatural way."

He sighed. "And Shanna?" he said. "How could you ever suspect her of being anything but sweet and innocent?"

"I did not tell you earlier about my feelings because

I hoped that in time she would forget *her* infatuation with *you*," He Who Watches said somberly. "I had hoped that she *would* become more involved in her violin playing than in the idea of marrying you, our people's chief."

He Who Watches leaned closer to Bold Wolf. "Can you say, Bold Wolf, that she is not now intrigued with you because you *are* chief?" he said, trying one last time to plant seeds of doubt inside his chief's head.

"She loves me because she *loves* me," Bold Wolf said, frowning at He Who Watches. He held the bag out closer to his grand-uncle. "I spent many long dedicated hours preparing this bride price. Deliver it, grand-uncle. Deliver it *now*. You know the procedure in which it should be done."

He Who Watches lowered his eyes, then sighed deeply, lifted his hands, and gazed at the bag as Bold Wolf relinquished it to his safe care.

"Go," Bold Wolf said, his heart pounding at the thought that finally he was proceeding with his plan to have Shanna with him for the rest of his life.

Surely once Shanna saw how anxious her father was to have such a gift, she would not be angry with Bold Wolf for proceeding before she sent word to him that the time was right.

Bold Wolf *knew* that by tonight he would be free to go for Shanna. He *would* soon marry her in the Penobscot tradition!

He could hardly wait to begin a family with Shanna, to make brothers and sisters for Elizabeth—for Elizabeth would come also tonight and forever be a part of their lives.

Bold Wolf walked down to the beach with He Who Watches. He held his breath as his grand-uncle placed the bag with its precious cargo at the bottom of the canoe on a padding of pelts. Clasping his hands tightly behind him, Bold Wolf watched his grand-uncle make his way slowly across the river.

He badly wished his grand-uncle could share in Bold Wolf's exuberance. Instead, He Who Watches acted as though he were on his way to something dreadful, perhaps one of the white man's funerals.

Planning not to move from the banks of the river until his grand-uncle came back with his answer, Bold Wolf sat down on the sandy shore and drew his knees up before him. Tightly locking his arms around his knees, he stared endlessly toward Old Town, his heart pounding so hard inside his chest he felt threatened by it.

Never in his life had he been as anxious as now!

25

I will not let thee go,
I hold thee by too many bonds.
—ROBERT BRIDGES

Having knocked on the door of the grand, two-story mansion, He Who Watches stood stiffly waiting for someone to come. He knew it wouldn't be Shanna. As he approached the house he had seen her leave. He had seen her go to the Diepholz mansion and knew she would be there at least long enough for He Who Watches to get through with this transaction that his grand-nephew had forced upon him.

He was glad Shanna was gone. He did not wish to face her, knowing that he had lost the battle with Bold Wolf over her, *she* the true victor.

He wanted to get this chore finished and return to his lodge so that he could be alone with his defeat. No matter what Bold Wolf said to try to reassure He Who Watches, he still felt uncomfortable about who Shanna's father was. And since she had the same blood flowing through her veins, surely she was no less a person of supernatural means than her father.

His only chance to still be victorious in this battle of the heart was for her father to refuse the gift of wampum. Yet if he *did* refuse it, He Who Watches did not like thinking about how Bold Wolf would react. Rejection would be the worst of insults for Bold Wolf.

Loving his grand-nephew so much, feeling as close

to him as if he were a son, He Who Watches was torn. He wanted Bold Wolf to look away from this woman, yet he did not want his chief to carry the insult of rejection inside his heart.

When the door opened, He Who Watches found himself suddenly face-to-face with the man he could not help but fear. His leathery skin covered by a sheen of nervous sweat, He Who Watches searched inside his heart for the courage to carry on with this mission, knowing that Bold Wolf would be anxiously waiting.

"Good Lord, what are *you* doing here?" Jordan gasped, his spine stiffening. "Get out of here. I don't want any savages seen at my doorstep. It's not good for business. Do you hear? Go back to your island. I don't give handouts to Indians."

"I have not come today for . . . as you say, 'handouts,'" He Who Watches said tightly, insulted by the man's attitude. He held the buckskin bag out for Jordan. "I have brought something for *you.* I am here in behalf of my chief, Bold Wolf. I am here to offer Bold Wolf's bride price for your daughter."

"What?" Jordan said, blanching. He took an unsteady step away from He Who Watches. "Did . . . you . . . say a bride price?"

"Bold Wolf spent many hours preparing the wampum band that is inside this bag for you," He Who Watches said, nodding. "Take it. It is yours. It is tradition for the father to keep the bride price for a short while to think on it. He Who Watches will return later today for your answer."

When Jordan didn't reach his hands out for the bag, He Who Watches quickly removed the band from inside it. He lay the bag aside on the porch, then slowly unfolded the red handkerchief from around the band and held the lovely band closer to Jordan. "Now you can *see* what I have brought," He Who Watches said. "Surely you can see its value."

When Jordan didn't even glance down at the band, but instead suddenly slammed the door, loudly cursing, He Who Watches was so stunned he was not sure what to do. He certainly couldn't just walk away with the bride price still in his possession. It *was* tradition to leave it with the father, then return shortly to receive the answer!

He Who Watches knew that he *must* leave the bride price, whether or not he actually placed it in the hands of Shanna's father. Surely after Shanna's father had more time to think about what lay on his porch, he would be tempted to take a look at it.

And once the man saw just how precious the wampum was and realized its true worth, He Who Watches expected a different reaction when he returned for his answer. Although He Who Watches didn't want this man to accept this gift, he felt Shanna's father wouldn't be able to resist something that had been so honorably made by Bold Wolf's own caring hands.

He Who Watches gently placed the wampun band on the bag beside the closed door, stared at it for a moment, then looked slowly around, hoping it would be safe enough there until the white man opened the door and retrieved it.

Then knowing that he had no other choice but to leave it, He Who Watches left and walked awhile, then entered the shadows of the forest and sat down beneath a huge oak.

Unnerved about what had happened, he lifted his eyes heavenward and began a low, droning chant. His voice carried high into the trees. Birds fluttered from the limbs in all directions. His voice carried along the land. Squirrels scampered away. A deer, hidden in the brush, its round, black eyes wide, stood quietly by, watching and listening.

He Who Watches prayed for a while longer, then sat quietly, then decided that it was time to go and face the white man again.

Slowly he made his way back into town and trudged breathlessly up the steep hill to Shanna's house.

When he came close enough to see the porch, his heart skipped a beat. He couldn't believe his eyes. The precious wampum was no longer there, but not because the white man had decided to accept it as the bride price for his daughter. The wampum, its bag, and the red handkerchief lay in a heap on the ground besides the porch steps.

Sharp prickles of anger crept along He Who Watches's flesh to see something so valuable, so utterly precious, treated in such a way, and to know the insult that Bold Wolf would soon know and feel.

Bold Wolf's bride price—and so Shanna herself—had been denied Bold Wolf in the worst, most degrading way!

So angry he could hardly see through his old eyes, He Who Watches retrieved the wampum belt from the ground. He gently brushed dirt from it, wrapped it tenderly with the red handkerchief, and slid it back inside the safety of the bag.

Glaring at the house, and holding the bag near his heart, He Who Watches walked away, his gait stately and proud even though he himself had been treated as though he were no better than a snake by the white-eyes!

26

Do you think, because you fail me,
And draw back your hand today,
That from out the heart I gave you
My strong love can fade away?
—Adelaide Anne Procter

Bold Wolf was standing inside the privacy of his home
so that none of his people could see by the solemn
look on his face that his bride price had been rejected—and that Bold Wolf carried the insult deeply
inside his heart.

He felt hollow inside as he stared at the buckskin
bag in his hands. Then he looked quickly up at He
Who Watches. "How could he have rejected my bride
price?" he said thickly. "He did not see the worth of
that which I offered him? You left it with him long
enough to study it? You gave him time to see its
worth?"

"I doubt that he ever did take a serious look at the
wampum," He Who Watches said, gazing down at the
bag, then looking apologetically up at Bold Wolf.
"When I took the band from the bag for him to see,
he ignored it, as though it were a worthless object, as
though the beads on the wampum band were worthless *rocks*."

Bold Wolf gasped. "But still you left it with him so
that he could study it more seriously and know that
it is something far more valuable than rocks?" he said,
his voice tight. "He was holding the band when you
left? He was . . . actually holding it?"

A quick alarm leaped into He Who Watches's eyes. "No," he said guardedly. "He would not accept it in his hands. I . . . I left it on the porch. I truly thought that once I was gone he would pick it up, hold it, study it, then realize its value and know that it was a gift offered from the heart."

"And so the white man's hands never actually touched it," Bold Wolf said solemnly.

"No, I did not say that," He Who Watches quickly interjected.

Bold Wolf's eyes widened. "How do you mean, then, that he never held it and studied it?" he asked, his voice weary.

"He did hold it, Bold Wolf, but for only long enough to take it from his porch and place it in the dirt on the ground in front of his home," He Who Watches said, stiffening. He swallowed hard. "I am not sure, even, if he did this with the gentleness due the wampum. He might have thrown it to the ground. But . . . I am not even certain *he* took it from his porch. Perhaps he asked someone else to do it for him."

"My wampum was left on the ground like something unholy?" Bold Wolf gasped, paling. "You never should have allowed that to happen, grand-uncle. You should have foreseen what would happen because of the man's attitude toward the wampum. You should have, with much dignity, walked away with the wampum and brought it back to me."

"But that would not have followed protocol," He Who Watches said sullenly. "I was to leave it for him to consider. I left it. How was I to know to what extent he truly abhorred the bride price?"

"Yes, how could you have known?" Bold Wolf said, his shoulders slumping as he sank into a chair. He lay the bag on his lap and slowly opened it, then gently

removed the wampum band, unfolded the handkerchief from around it, and gazed down at it.

The sun pouring through the window over Bold
Wolf's left shoulder revealed to him only a few specks
of dirt on the precious object. Otherwise, it was still
as beautiful as the day he had finished it with hopes
of it being accepted.

Bold Wolf slowly ran his hands over the shells, remembering when he prepared each of them for the
band. Oh, the time he had spent making certain that
each shell was perfect before placing it on the band.
Oh, the hours he had spent shining each shell, knowing just how much Shanna would enjoy looking at
them once her father accepted the band as his and it
became a part of their family.

"He was wrong to make a fool of Bold Wolf," Bold
Wolf said in a hiss.

He slowly wrapped the band again, placed it back
inside the bag, then went to his bed and slid it under-
neath, next to the bag in which still lay the lovely
conch shell that would yet soon belong to Shanna.
What her father had done today had only made Bold
Wolf more adamant to have her.

Even if a bride price was not accepted for her, she
would be his!

"What are you going to do now?" He Who Watches
asked warily.

"For now I am going to sit in my lodge and be
alone for a while, to think through everything, and
then later I will join our warriors, who are preparing
to soon poison the water close to our village for an
eel kill," Bold Wolf said, sitting back down in a chair,
his hands clutched to the arms so tightly his knuckles
were white.

"Grand-nephew, you do know that I earnestly tried
to make the white man keep the bride price, do you

not?" He Who Watches asked warily. "You do not hold me personally responsible for his refusal?"

Bold Wolf looked into his grand-uncle's eyes. "I know that you did as you were told because it was your chief telling you to do it," he said, his voice tight. "The true person I hold responsible is not even Shanna's *father*." Swallowing hard, he looked quickly away from He Who Watches. "It is Shanna herself."

Stunned, He Who Watches took an unsteady step away from Bold Wolf. "You blame . . . the woman?" he gasped.

Bold Wolf turned his head in a jerk and looked sharply at He Who Watches. "Would she have talked to her father and told him that she was going to marry me, then today he never would have turned down such an offer of a bride price," he said sullenly. "He would have known that no matter what he said or did, she would still be my wife. He would have eagerly taken the gift, for he would know how foolish it would be to turn his eyes away from something so valuable. Why would he, if he had known that Shanna was going to be my wife anyway? What I offered him in return was valuable!"

Bold Wolf doubled a hand into a fist and slammed it down hard on the arm of the chair. "Valuable, He Who Watches!" he shouted. "I put my all in making that wampum band for Shanna's father, and he would not even look at it."

He Who Watches stared at Bold Wolf for a moment longer, then crouched down on his haunches before him. "Are you saying that your anger toward Shanna is so great that you no longer will pursue her?" he asked guardedly.

The question cut like a knife into Bold Wolf's heart. At this moment he felt as though Shanna herself had slammed a knife into his body!

He was so angry at how this had turned out, he found it easy to think he could turn his back on *her* as insultingly as her father had turned his back on the wampum band—for to Bold Wolf, the wampum was Bold Wolf's pride . . . his honor!

Bold Wolf stared straight ahead, avoiding He Who Watches's gaze now, refusing to say any more about Shanna, the wampum, or Shanna's father. For now he would force his thoughts elsewhere. That was the only way he could survive, mentally *and* physically, this that had been done to him today.

Yes, he could not help but hold Shanna at least partly responsible. She had put off telling her father for far too long and the consequences were what had happened today.

"You will not still pursue the woman Shanna, will you?" He Who Watches asked, stiffening when Bold Wolf still said nothing more to him.

He Who Watches backed away, then turned and rushed from the cabin. When he was outside in the warm air and sunshine, he still did not feel that the burden of what happened today had lessened any inside his heart. He felt responsible for his chief's grief.

He Who Watches began to pace back and forth, his long hair whipping around his ankles with each turn. He knew he must do something to help his chief. But what?

It was true that He Who Watches could not help but, deep down inside, be glad that Shanna had finally done something to dishearten his chief and lose favor in his eyes. That could mean that the white woman might never be a part of the lives of the Penobscot.

But he wanted his chief, his grand-nephew, to be happy.

There had to be a way!

Still pacing, He Who Watches desperately sorted

through the turmoil of his feelings for an answer. If he *was* going to find a way to make Bold Wolf happy without Shanna, then would not another woman be the answer?

He stopped suddenly. His eyes gleamed when he thought of another woman who, for a short while, had brought some sunshine into his grand-nephew's heart.

And since Bold Wolf had no qualms about the women he married being white, why *not* approach another white woman with the offer of marriage?

And this time no bride price would have to be offered. The woman He Who Watches was thinking about no longer lived with her father.

She had no ties!

Except for Shanna's friendship, this woman was, in a sense, alone in the world.

She would surely come to Indian Island and eagerly accept Bold Wolf as her husband. Then she would finally have a true home. She would have what white people called "roots"!

"Yes, I must go and talk to *Jennie*," He Who Watches whispered to himself.

In his mind's eye he saw Jennie. Ah, yes, she was as beautiful as Shanna, perhaps even *more*. She would be enough to make any man look forward to those times shared between the blankets.

His heart pounding, as though he were going to ask a woman to be *his* bride, He Who Watches walked quickly toward the river, where the Penobscot warriors were busy preparing for the eel harvest.

Only last week several warriors had camped along the streams, gathering pokeberry and Indian turnip, which grew in the moist ground along the streams.

The berries of the poke plants were, during the summer months, the richest, and contained more of the poison that was used to stupefy the eels so that they would be easily caught.

The first two days for those warriors who would participate in the eel harvest today had been spent digging the roots and crushing them, together with purple pokeberries, on flat stones.

Enough had been prepared, and today the Penobscot men would strip to their skin and distribute themselves in the river all around Indian Island.

They would plunge into the water and spread the poisoned pulp thickly upon the surface and then dive to the bottom, where they would stir up the muddy sediment with sticks and poles.

When the water was so strongly impregnated with the juices that the men were driven ashore with inflamed and smarting skins, about thirty minutes would then be spent dressing and rubbing the inflamed spots with fresh plantain leaves.

By this time the agitated water would have settled somewhat. Torpid eels would begin to appear upon the surface, and before an hour had passed, the top of the water would be spotted with the bodies of dead or dying eels, floating belly-up.

With large nets, the Penobscot would bring the eels to shore, where they would be skinned and salted by the women. There would be a great eel feast today, while the rest would be placed upon spread out buckskins to dry in the sun for two days. They would then be hung up in a tent and smoked until there was no drip from the suspended bodies.

Another feast would then be enjoyed by all.

The remaining eels would be kept to be eaten during those cold days of winter when ice would freeze over the river.

Nodding to one and then another warrior, glad to see that some younger braves had joined the warriors this year to learn the art of the eel harvest, He Who Watches shoved his canoe out into the water, then climbed in and started pulling his paddle earnestly through the splashing waves.

He hoped that he would not fail twice in one day in bringing a woman back to his chief for a wife!

He knew that Jennie would see the honor in being asked. She had lived among his people for only a short time, yet it had been enough for her to gain a respect for all that she had learned of the Penobscot customs.

Yes, and He Who Watches had seen even more about her that was in his favor. He had seen her admiring glances at Bold Wolf. He had seen in her eyes how she might even love Bold Wolf, yet would never voice this because Shanna was her best friend and she thought that Shanna would move heaven and earth by now to be Bold Wolf's wife.

"Shanna cared too little for Bold Wolf or she would even now be with him!" He Who Watches mumbled to himself.

He gazed over at Old Town and with his old eyes sorted through the houses until he came to the one in which Jennie was staying. Shanna's. He knew it would not be an easy thing to knock on the same door twice in one day and be humble enough to speak a second time in behalf of his chief over a woman.

And should Shanna's father slam the door in his face when he saw He Who Watches standing there, He Who Watches would find a way before sunset today to talk to Jennie. He would relentlessly stalk the house if necessary.

He only hoped Shanna was still at the Diepholz home so that she could not interfere with his ingenious scheme. He would check to see if she were there before going on to her home to speak with Jennie.

He must not fail this time.

He must not allow anything or anyone to stand in his way. He must show Bold Wolf that his grand-uncle *had* succeeded in bringing him a woman today who would soon become his wife.

Smiling, feeling confident, He Who Watches drew his paddle through the water at a more feverish pace.

He could already see his grand-nephew commending him for being astute enough to think of Jennie as his wife.

"I will erase his frown forever," he whispered.

27

The heart that has truly loved never forgets,
But as truly loves on to the close,
As the sunflower turns to her god when he sets,
The same look which she turned when he rose.
                                    —Thomas Moore

He Who Watches waited stiffly after knocking on the door of Shanna's house. He was prepared for her father to answer and was taken aback when, instead, it was Shanna's mother who opened the door and gave him a quizzical stare.

"Didn't my husband tell you to leave?" Bernita said, lifting her chin haughtily. "Our daughter will *not* marry Bold Wolf."

She started to close the door, but stopped when He Who Watches spoke up suddenly, saying something that completely puzzled Bernita. Her lips parted and her eyes widened as she listened to him.

"I did not come to speak with your daughter," He Who Watches said, his long, gray hair fluttering around his ankles in the soft breeze. "I have come to speak with *Jennie.*"

"Jennie?" Bernita asked in a faint murmur, her eyes narrowing. "Why on earth would you want to speak with Jennie?"

"I have come to tell Jennie that Bold Wolf wishes to discuss plans of marriage with her," He Who Watches said, the lies slipping across his lips as easily as he breathed.

He did believe that he was doing the right thing for

his chief. If he could get Jennie to the island again, especially now when Bold Wolf's ego was so badly wounded, He Who Watches *did* believe that Bold Wolf might seriously consider marrying Jennie.

If not, then He Who Watches would deal with Bold Wolf's anger toward him for having taken on such a task without speaking first to him.

"Did I hear you right?" Jennie said, coming to the door and standing beside Bernita. "He Who Watches, did you say that Bold Wolf wants to . . . marry *me*, not Shanna?"

"He is a man scorned," He Who Watches said, ignoring Bernita's snort of displeasure as he spoke openly with Jennie. "Bold Wolf has forgotten Shanna."

"Jennie, don't say another word to this savage," Bernita said. She took Jennie by the arm and tried to move her away from the door.

But Jennie did not budge.

Instead, she stood wide-eyed, staring at He Who Watches, stunned by what he had said.

And, oh, it would be so tempting to say yes, that she would go to the island and marry Bold Wolf, she thought. Never had she known anyone as handsome, or as intriguing, as Bold Wolf. He was so gentle and warmhearted.

His good qualities even surpassed Roscoe Lovett's!

While she was in hiding at Bold Wolf's village, he had treated her as though she were no less than a precious jewel. Why, he had even chanced a war with the Mohawk when he rescued her from them.

"Jennie, go to Shanna's room," Bernita said, her face flushed red with anger. "Now. Do you hear me, Jennie? Now!"

Then a thought came to Bernita that made her stop making such heated demands. If Jennie were to go to the Indian's island and marry Bold Wolf, wouldn't that mean Shanna would no longer be pestered by the Penobscot chief?

Wouldn't Shanna then be free to pursue her violin career?

Jennie was still lost in her own thoughts, thinking how wonderful life would be with Bold Wolf. In her heart she thought of how long she had hungered to have a home of her own . . . to be loved solely by one man!

She had never had a happy childhood.

With Bold Wolf her life as an adult could be sweet and fulfilling.

Fulfilling, she thought quickly, knowing that the only true thing that could fulfill her was to go on the stage and play her violin.

That was her true dream, not marrying a man just because she had never had a decent home or parents who truly cared for her.

Her thoughts wandered again to Roscoe Lovett. He was her true love, always and forever. If she could marry him, they could go together on a world tour with her violin. That was where her true fantasy lay.

"Yes, I will go with you to Indian Island," Jennie blurted, surprised when Shanna's mother seemed suddenly not to care. Puzzling Jennie most was the strange smile on Bernita's face.

Jennie started to tell Bernita the true reason she was going to Indian Island, but she saw Shanna's father coming down the long corridor toward the door and realized that she must hurry and leave or be stopped by him.

And she *had* to go and talk to Bold Wolf. She had things to say to him about a friend she adored!

Lifting the hem of her skirt, Jennie brushed past Bernita, ran outside, and went down the steps with

He Who Watches. "Hurry, He Who Watches," she said, giving a quick look over her shoulder as Shanna's father stepped out onto the porch, waving a fist and cursing. "We must get to the river before he stops me. And before he injures *you*," she quickly added. "He Who Watches, please run faster."

When Jennie was sure Shanna's father was not in pursuit, Jennie looked over her shoulder to see why. She was surprised to see Shanna's parents in a quiet conversation, Bernita doing most of the talking. She wondered why Shanna's father got the same sort of triumphant look in his eyes that Bernita had had earlier—such a look of smugness, it made her insides grow cold.

"Do not bother yourself with those people any longer," He Who Watches said. He gently took Jennie by the arm as they continued to hurry down the steep hill toward the river. "The Penobscot will be your new family. You will be much happier on Indian Island."

Jennie ran alongside him and didn't explain her true reason for going. She wanted the chance to speak with Bold Wolf, face-to-face. And if He Who Watches knew her true intentions, that she never intended to marry Bold Wolf, he most certainly would not take her to Indian Island.

Knowing that she was taking a chance of being seen by her father, and tired of worrying about it, Jennie continued on with He Who Watches and boarded his canoe with him. She held to the sides of the canoe as he paddled them away from Old Town.

The closer they came to Indian Island, the more Jennie was convinced that Bold Wolf *had* sent for her. It looked to her as though there were several warriors in the water close to the beach at the island awaiting her arrival.

They seemed to be putting some sort of petals into

the water, scattering them, surely as a way to greet her.

Now she felt as though she had gone about this in the wrong way. She didn't want to lead Bold Wolf on, not even for one moment. He had already been denied one woman today. Surely when she told him why she had come, he would feel twice scorned.

She started to tell He Who Watches to turn around, to take her back to Shanna's house. But by the way the warriors in the water were shouting and waving their arms frantically as the canoe came closer to them, she could tell that they weren't in the water for *her.* It was evident that they didn't want the canoe there because she and He Who Watches were interfering in some sort of ritual that had nothing to do with Jennie and Bold Wolf.

"Ignore the warriors," He Who Watches said, paddling past them toward the shore. "It is still safe enough to enter the water to get you to dry land."

"Safe . . . enough?" Jennie gasped. "What do you mean by *safe enough*?"

When He Who Watches didn't answer, Jennie realized now that what was being put in the river was not beautiful petals from any flowers. It was a strange sort of pulpy debris that was floating atop the water. When she looked past that and saw that the warriors in the water were naked, her face flushed hot with embarrassment.

She was glad when He Who Watches finally reached the riverbank. She left the canoe with him and walked, ankle-deep in the water until they reached dry land. She waited for He Who Watches to beach the canoe, then together they walked toward the village.

She took a quick glance over her shoulder at the activity in the water, then looked quickly away again when the men started coming from the river, their dripping-wet bodies shining in the bright sunshine.

Her thoughts were quickly taken by Bold Wolf as he came from his cabin wearing only a brief breechcloth, the wetness of his skin making it apparent that he had also been in the water for a while, surely helping the other men.

Jennie could not help but stare at Bold Wolf's muscled body. She dared to look lower and could tell by the bulge beneath the breechcloth that he was so very well endowed, he would make any woman feel faint with desire. Of all the men she had known at the brothel, none compared with Bold Wolf.

"Jennie?" Bold Wolf said, walking barefoot toward her. He gave He Who Watches a questioning glance, then went on to Jennie, drew her into his arms, and affectionately hugged her.

Then he stepped away and asked, "Why are you here?"

Jennie's heart skipped a beat. She looked quickly over at He Who Watches, wondering what on earth was going on.

"You didn't send He Who Watches for me?" Jennie asked softly. She felt foolish now for apparently having been part of a scheme thought up by He Who Watches. It was easy now to realize what He Who Watches had tried to do today by bringing her there. Surely he had hoped that Bold Wolf *might* choose her over Shanna.

Jennie should have known that nothing would ever change Bold Wolf's mind about Shanna, especially not an overbearing father who did not know the true meaning of the bride price offered to him.

Bold Wolf glared at He Who Watches. "What have you done?" he asked, his voice tight, his eyes filled with fire.

"You were scorned by one woman," He Who Watches said, trying to stay calm in the face of his chief's obvious anger. "I brought you *another*."

"You know that I was not scorned by Shanna herself, but by her *father*," Bold Wolf said, trying to keep his anger at bay, understanding now that his grand-uncle would go to any lengths to make him happy. "Yes, I blamed her for not telling her father that she was going to marry me. But, Grand-Uncle, I still plan on marrying her."

"Jennie has touched your heart, Bold Wolf," He Who Watches said, ignoring Bold Wolf's speech. "I know that by how you treated her when she was staying here among our people. It was in your eyes and the way you touched her that she was special to you. Surely she is special enough to be your wife."

"I want only one woman and I will have her," Bold Wolf said.

He slid an arm around Jennie's waist, walked her into the shade of a tall elm tree, and gestured for her to sit down.

"I am sorry that my grand-uncle has misinformed you," Bold Wolf said thickly. "I did not send for you. I did not know that he went for you."

"I'm so glad," Jennie said, sighing.

Bold Wolf's eyebrows rose. "Glad?" Then he laughed softly. "I see. You did not come to be my wife but to tell me yourself, instead of sending back the message with my grand-uncle, in a way for me to save face."

"Yes, that's why I'm here," Jennie said, lowering her eyes, so badly wanting not to hurt Bold Wolf's ego. "I . . . I was so honored to think that you might want me, for . . . for . . . Bold Wolf, it would be such a wonderful life being with you as your wife."

She looked slowly up at him. By the quiet, gentle

amusement in his eyes she knew he was not hurt by He Who Watches's scheme that had gone awry. "But, Bold Wolf, Shanna loves you so much," she hastened to say. "I would never do anything to stand in the way of yours and Shanna's love. I came to beg you, Bold Wolf, *not* to let anything dissuade you from continuing to pursue Shanna. Her parents have been good to her, far better than my parents ever were to me, but they have gone beyond what is right. They are too possessive of her."

Jennie recalled the conniving look in Bernita's eyes when Bernita thought He Who Watches had come for her to be Bold Wolf's wife. She recalled how Shanna's father had gotten the same look on his face after Bernita told him what had happened. Jennie knew now it was all because they had thought Jennie marrying Bold Wolf would set things straight in their lives where Shanna was concerned.

Because they knew that Shanna so deeply still loved Bold Wolf made their acquiescence to He Who Watches's plan an act of betrayal against a daughter. Bold Wolf was Shanna's whole future! Her life! How could they want so badly to deny her this?

"I will never give Shanna up," Bold Wolf said, reaching for one of Jennie's hands, affectionately squeezing it. "You are a good friend for Shanna. You are a good friend for *me*. Thank you, Jennie. Thank you."

Tears filled Jennie's eyes as Bold Wolf drew her into his arms again and hugged her. Oh, how foolish she was not to fight for such a man as he and give up everything to have him, for he would be so good to her!

But Shanna, oh, how Shanna deserved such a love as this! Shanna was all good that could be found on this earth. She was a devoted friend. She would be a devoted wife.

The sound of footsteps hurrying past her caused Jennie to draw away from Bold Wolf. She watched as many men and women began stacking wood in the center of the village, soon lighting it. Everyone's eyes were gleaming with excitement. The children were dancing and playing and laughing. The elderly were coming and sitting down on blankets, sharing smokes from their pipes.

"Is there going to be a celebration?" Jennie asked, now recalling all that was happening at the river when she had arrived there.

"Yes, today is a special day for my people," Bold Wolf said. He looked over his shoulder at the men who had been in the poisoned water, who were now treating their inflamed skin with fresh plantain leaves. "Soon there will be many eels for cooking today, and for storing to eat later in the winter."

He explained about the eel kill, and how the water had been purposely poisoned. It was all so interesting, Jennie forgot Shanna and how, just before He Who Watches had arrived with his scheme to have her marry Bold Wolf, she had been puzzling over why it was taking Shanna so long to retrieve her violin from Roscoe's music studio.

So caught up in the excitement of the people as they brought blankets and pelts to sit on around the fire, the explanation of the eel kill so intriguing, Jennie had momentarily forgotten that Shanna would arrive home soon. When she was told where Jennie was, and why—that it appeared to Shanna's parents that Jennie had gone to Indian Island to marry Bold Wolf— Shanna would think that she had been betrayed by her dearest friend in the world!

28

As much as love asks love,
Does thought ask thought.
—HENRY ALFORD

Having stayed away from her home for far longer than she had planned, Shanna raced up the stairs to her porch, then breathlessly hurried inside her house. It had been wonderful holding Elizabeth, watching her smile, listening to her soft laughter, and seeing her dark eyes beam with a contented happiness.

More and more Shanna was feeling the deep bond between herself and the child and so badly wanted Elizabeth with her every day instead of just for short moments.

Today had made Shanna decide to make her parents discuss with her the fact that she was going to marry Bold Wolf. She knew their reaction would be dreadful, but she had postponed her life long enough.

She started toward the library, thinking Jennie might be there relaxing in a plush, comfortable chair, reading. Or perhaps Shanna's mother might have introduced Jennie to embroidery work during Shanna's long absence this morning.

Flushed because of the run from Emily's house, her heart pounding, since she still had moments of weakness from her bout of pneumonia, Shanna went on to the library and stopped short when she found no one there.

Shrugging, she left the library and rushed upstairs
to her bedroom, truly puzzled now when she didn't
even find Jennie *there.*

"If you're looking for Jennie, you won't find her
here," Bernita said as she stepped into the bedroom.

Shanna turned with a start and stared questioningly
at her mother. "You mean she isn't here in my *bedroom,*" she murmured, seeing a strange sort of smugness about her mother, as though she were strangely
amused about something.

"No, I mean that Jennie is *gone,*" Bernita said,
smoothing her hands down the front of her blue silk
dress. "Shanna, she's gone to Indian Island."

Shanna's eyes widened. "Indian Island?" she said.
"Why would she go there?"

Bernita walked up to Shanna and reached a hand
to her face. "You are so flushed," she murmured.
"Shanna, where have you been for so long? What
have you been doing?" She dropped her hand away
and looked slowly around the room. "And where is
Jennie's violin? I thought you went for it."

"Mama, forget about Jennie's violin," Shanna said,
knowing when she was being put off, yet not understanding why. "Tell me why Jennie went to Indian
Island. Did her father discover that she was staying
here at our house? Did Jennie flee to seek safety again
with the Penobscot?"

"No, that's not the way it is at all," Bernita said.
She brushed past Shanna and went to the window.
Pulling back the sheer curtain, she stared over at Indian Island. "Jennie is there because Bold Wolf sent
for her."

"Bold Wolf?" Shanna said, now truly confused. She
went to her mother and placed a hand on her arm.
"Mama, look at me. Tell me what happened. Why did
Bold Wolf send for Jennie?"

Bernita slowly turned to Shanna.

When their eyes locked, a coldness swept through Shanna's veins, for the look on her mother's face was so unlike the mother Shanna had always known. The slow, taunting grin, the twist of her lips, made her mother look as though she had won a victory over something, and Shanna could not help but believe it was over Shanna.

"Why?" Bernita said, placing her hands on Shanna's cheeks, framing her face between them. "Darling, because Bold Wolf wants to marry Jennie, *that's* why."

Shocked by what her mother said, and the manner in which she had said it, Shanna grabbed her mother's wrists and forced her hands from her face. "Why would you lie about such a thing as that?" she cried. She stepped quickly away from her mother. "Mama, why would you want to hurt me by telling such . . . such a lie? Bold Wolf wants *me, not* Jennie."

She ran from the room crying Jennie's name, and she raced from room to room on the second floor, then almost fell down the stairs as she went to the first floor and searched there also for Jennie, going even into her father's forbidden room where the gravity percolator was even then pumping embalming fluid into a body.

The stench, the sight of the naked body of a man lying there so lifeless and pale, the fluid replacing the blood in the dead man's body, and the angry stare from her father combined with what her mother had just told her, made Shanna feel suddenly faint. She grabbed for the door and steadied herself, then fled the room.

"What's going on?" her father shouted.

Shanna opened the front door to go to Indian Island and see for herself if what her mother had said was true. Jennie couldn't be with Bold Wolf! They couldn't betray her in such a way as that!

Jordan grabbed Shanna by a wrist and stopped her. He forced her to turn around and face him. "What's happened?" he asked, his eyes imploring Shanna. "You've never burst into the preparation room like that. At all cost you've avoided it. Except for recently, when the explosion injured and killed so many people, you never had any interest in what I do. Why would you come into my preparation room today? Why do you look so frantic? Why are you upset?"

"Do you know where Jennie is?" Shanna choked out, her heart pleading with her father to say the right thing. That Jennie might have taken a walk.

"Jennie?" Jordan said, looking quickly at Bernita when she stepped up to his side and gave him a nod.

He looked again at Shanna. "Jennie?" he said, his voice tight. "She's at Indian Island, Shanna. Bold Wolf sent He Who Watches for her. Bold Wolf is going to marry Jennie. Now you can forget him. You can concentrate on your future as a violinist."

Everything she heard was like a blur in Shanna's mind. It sounded as though it were being said from a deep, dark tunnel. It echoed around Shanna, making her head spin.

She covered her ears with her hands and screamed, then jerked herself free of her father and ran from the house. She blindly ran down the front steps, stumbling, her sobs racking her body.

She ignored her father shouting her name over and over again behind her as she reached the ground and began running toward the river. All she could think about was getting over to Indian Island and seeing for herself that both her parents were surely lying! Jennie wouldn't be there! Bold Wolf would hold his arms out for Shanna! She would tell him that she was there to stay. She would marry him now, *today,* if he still wanted her.

And as soon as they were married, they would go for Elizabeth!

Behind her, Bernita was frantic. She grabbed her husband's arm, her eyes filled with alarm. "Go for her," she cried. "Lord, Jordan, when she arrives at the island, who is to say what will happen? Please, Jordan, *go* for her."

"No, I think it's time that our daughter fights her own battles," Jordan said dryly. "Surely this time she will realize just how foolish she's been to gallivant around with a savage. Thank the Lord it will be before he took her to bed and got her pregnant! The disgrace, Bernita. I'm not certain if we could live with such disgrace as that."

"Jordan, you're wrong," Bernita cried. "Go and get her. Bring her home."

"And make her a prisoner?" Jordan said. He hung his face in his hands, then looked slowly up at Bernita again. "No, I'm not going after Shanna. I'm tired of worrying so much about her and the bright future she could have as a violinist. She's made it damn clear that isn't what she wants. No matter how much we force her to practice, or how many lessons she takes, if it's not in her heart to play the violin, she won't."

Bernita stepped slowly away from Jordan. Her eyes were wild as she stared up at him. "I've never heard you talk like this before!" she cried. "It's as though you've given up on our Shanna. Don't give up on her, Jordan. Oh, Lord, don't."

Jordan's eyes wavered as he gazed at his wife. He placed gentle hands to her cheeks, drew her lips to his, and kissed her. Then he turned away from her, returned to his preparation room, and proceeded to prepare the body for viewing later in the evening.

Tears sprang to Jordan's eyes as he realized his dreams for his daughter were now futile, as they had been for his *sister* Shanna when she had died far too soon, her violin hugged to her chest as she took her last breaths.

"It just wasn't meant to be," he whispered. "I've got to let my daughter go, damn it. I'm so tired, oh, so very tired."

29

And now good-morrow to our waking souls,
Which watch not one another out of fear,
For love all love of other sights controls,
And makes one little woman anywhere.
—JOHN DONNE

Her canoe beached on Indian Island, Shanna ignored the warriors who were sitting around beneath trees, naked except for blankets wrapped around their shoulders.

Her eyes were set straight ahead as she stamped up the slight hill that would lead her into the village. She was aware of her ankles and feet starting to burn. She started to look down at them to see why, but came within view of the village and became intent on finding Bold Wolf.

What she saw made her stop suddenly and gasp. Jennie *was* there. She was sitting with Bold Wolf among his people around a huge outdoor fire, the smell of food cooking over the fire wafting toward Shanna.

Stunned, the burning of her feet and ankles now almost severe, her eyes clouded with pain and hurtful anger, Shanna covered her mouth with a hand to stifle a sob as she watched Jennie and Bold Wolf talking and laughing together.

Shanna wanted to die when Bold Wolf reached over and gently touched Jennie's face!

"No!" she cried in despair.

Shanna's voice echoed around her, sounding noth-

ing like herself. She turned and ran blindly back
toward the river. Distraught over her discovery,
Shanna dove into the river to swim across to Old
Town instead of taking the time to climb back inside
the canoe.

When Bold Wolf heard her scream his name, he
bolted to his feet and started running after her, stopping, startled, when she plunged headfirst into the poisoned river and began thrashing her way to the far
bank.

"The poison!" Bold Wolf cried, knowing that it was
now at its most potent stage, when no one should
enter the water. He ran past his warriors, who seemed
too stupefied over what had happened to react normally to it. They stared at Shanna as she swam desperately farther away from the island, then at Bold Wolf
as he dove into the water and swam after her.

"Stop, Shanna!" Bold Wolf shouted. "The poison!
You are being poisoned!"

Shanna heard Bold Wolf, especially what he had
said about poison. She wanted to avoid him, but she
knew now that she couldn't. The fire of pain rippled
across her flesh. Her body was inflamed, pulsating and
burning. It seemed as though it were on fire!

She didn't fight Bold Wolf off when he grabbed her
and swam her back to the shore, sores now spreading
across her body, the pain hardly bearable.

"What is causing this?" Shanna screamed as Bold
Wolf carried her from the water, himself now trem-
oring from the ravages of the poison. "It burns so,
Bold Wolf. It burns so!"

Fighting off his own burning pain, Bold Wolf rushed
Shanna to his cabin and lay her on his bed. "We've
got to get our clothes off," he said thickly. "Let me
take yours off and then I'll remove mine."

Shanna could hardly see Bold Wolf through her

tears, but the gentleness of his hands proved that he still cared for her, at least a little bit. She was in too much pain to question him about how he had fallen out of love with her and fallen so quickly in love with Jennie instead.

All that she could think of was the pain—the unbearable pain.

"Let me help you!" Jennie cried as she hurried into the cabin. She knelt beside the bed. "Oh, Shanna, why did you do that? What were you thinking?"

"How could you ask me that?" Shanna said between deep, gulping sobs. "I . . . I saw you with Bold Wolf. I know why you are here."

"Oh, dear Shanna, no, you *don't,*" Jennie cried, gently removing Shanna's skirt. "I now know by your reaction after having seen me with Bold Wolf that you thought what I am sure your parents *wanted* you to think."

She laid the skirt aside and started to remove Shanna's petticoat, but Shanna slapped her hand away.

"I can do it myself," Shanna murmured, cringing when she began scooting the petticoat over her blistered skin.

She looked over at Bold Wolf, who was pulling at his breechcloth, freeing the waist string as he struggled to get it untied.

When she saw the breechcloth slide down his body, leaving him standing in the nude, not only in her presence but also in Jennie's, she turned her eyes away and sobbed again.

"Shanna, it's all been a big misunderstanding," Jennie said. She stepped away from the bed when Bold Wolf came with a basin that held water and fresh plantain leaves, the concoction used to heal the sores inflicted by the poison. "I saw you together," Shanna said, her teeth gritting with pain as Bold Wolf began gently rubbing her body with the leaves.

"Yes, you saw us together," Jennie said. She slowly shook her head as she realized that Shanna's parents had done quite a job on their daughter today, filling her head with all sorts of lies as a means to get her to finally forget Bold Wolf.

"But Shanna," Jennie continued. "Bold Wolf and I are together today only because I came and pleaded your case with him."

"What do you mean?" Shanna asked, looking slowly from Bold Wolf, whose own body was covered with large red welts, and then to Jennie.

"He Who Watches came and played a little game today in an effort to get Bold Wolf to marry me instead of you," Jennie murmured. "I was not all that convinced that Bold Wolf had fallen out of love with you. I came to the island to see for sure and to tell him just how much you still loved him. The reason I stayed longer than I had planned was because the warriors had poisoned the river for an eel kill. I was going to leave later, when it was safe."

Jennie knelt down again beside the bed. "Shanna, I'm so sorry you were made to believe that Bold Wolf no longer loved you," she murmured. "I'm sorry you had reason to doubt me, your very best friend." She choked back a sob. "I'm sorry that you are feeling so miserable."

"Then it was all a lie?" Shanna said, her voice weak with pain. "My parents knew it was a lie?"

"I'm not certain how much they saw as truth and how much they merely wished to be true," Jennie said. "But surely by now they know they have lost you."

Shanna gazed into Bold Wolf's eyes and saw the same adoring look that she had seen since the first time they had met on the beach when she had been a girl just blossoming into a woman.

"Bold Wolf, oh, darling, I'm so sorry I doubted you," Shanna murmured. "I should have known better."

She turned slowly to Jennie. "Jennie, I'm sorry I doubted you," she said softly. "I should have known that you would never deceive me in such a way."

"I love only one man, and you know who that is," Jennie said, taking on a dreamy look that made Shanna know who she was thinking about. Roscoe Lovett.

"Jennie, I couldn't get your violin today," Shanna murmured. "In fact, Jennie, Mr. Lovett is gone. He left a note on his door saying that he's been called out of town for business."

"Truly?" Jennie said. "But what about my violin?"

"It will be safe enough until Roscoe returns," Shanna replied, then gasped and closed her eyes in pain when Bold Wolf ran the wet leaves over one of her worst burns.

"I'm going to go now," Jennie said, rising. "As soon as it's safe to leave in a canoe, I'll go on back to your house—that is, if I am still welcomed there. I . . . I have nowhere else to go."

"My parents wouldn't turn you out," Shanna said, opening her eyes to say good-bye to her friend. "And if they ask about me, tell them that I will soon be coming to have a talk with them. They will know that I will no longer be living with them . . . that I will soon marry Bold Wolf."

"I imagine your father will become instantly livid and come over here as soon as he knows that," Jennie said, walking toward the door.

"I doubt it," Shanna said, sighing. "After today, my

parents will think twice before trying to manipulate me again."

Jennie blew Shanna a kiss. "Get well soon, my darling friend," she said, then turned and left.

"I never should have thought her guilty of such a deceit as coming to marry you," Shanna said, gazing up at Bold Wolf.

"You never should have thought I would have asked her to," Bold Wolf said, smiling softly down at her. "My beautiful woman, you are all that my heart has ever cried for. Only you."

"I've been so foolish to put off our being together," Shanna said, swallowing hard. "But I am here now, Bold Wolf. I am here to stay."

"I wish that I could take you in my arms and hold you and tell you everything my heart feels at this moment," Bold Wolf said, his eyes filled with the deep emotions of the moment. "As soon as our bodies are healed, I will then hold you and never let you go."

"The sores hurt so," Shanna said. "How long will they hurt this badly?"

"By morning you and I both will feel *much* better," Bold Wolf said, brushing a soft kiss across her lips. "Now, my love, you must medicate *me*."

"I feel so guilty that you were burned so badly," Shanna said, cringing as she sat up on the bed and he lay down beside her. "Had I not been so foolish, you would still be outside with your people by the fire." She took a wet leaf from the water and slowly medicated his wounds. "What I saw looked like some sort of celebration. Was it?"

"Yes," he said. As she continued to doctor his burns, he told her about the eel-killing procedure and the feast they were preparing over the outdoor fire.

Then he mentioned the bride price that he had taken to her father.

"You took Father a bride price?" she gasped.

He explained what he had sent He Who Watches to take to her father and how Jordan had refused it.

"That had to have been when I was gone to get Jennie's violin at Mr. Lovett's music room, or I was at Elizabeth's," Shanna said softly. "But of course my parents never told me about the bride price. They just wanted me to believe that you loved Jennie, not I. They don't consider my happiness at all, only theirs and what my achievements as a violinist could bring them."

Even though both of their bodies were inflamed and throbbing, Bold Wolf drew Shanna into his arms. "I have never loved anyone but you," he whispered. "He Who Watches was foolish to think that another woman could win my heart."

"Where is He Who Watches now?" Shanna asked, looking into his eyes. "Is he being punished for lying?"

"He is an old man who does foolish things, but only because he thinks they are in my best interest," Bold Wolf said thickly. "So no, I did not punish him. But I do believe he finally knows that he can never change my heart. He knows you will be my wife. He will adjust to it."

"I hope he doesn't interfere anymore," Shanna said softly, settling into Bold Wolf's arms, finding such security there.

"This time I am *certain* that he knows better," Bold Wolf said, his jaw tight, his eyes filled with fire.

30

And I will make thee a bed of roses
And a thousand fragrant posies,
A cap of flowers, and a kirtle
Embroidered all with leaves
   of myrtle.
                    —CHRISTOPHER MARLOWE

Feeling a body pressed warm against hers made
Shanna awaken with a start. When she looked quickly
beside her and found Lone Wolf stretched out on his
back, asleep on the soft rabbit and elk skins of his
bed, she smiled. How could she have forgotten that
she had stayed the full night with Bold Wolf?

She inhaled the fragrant mixture of sage and cedar
that filled his cabin. She enjoyed the soft glimmer of
the morning sun as it wafted through the window beside the bed. She thrilled to the sound of a meadow-
lark somewhere in the cottonwoods that hung over
the river.

These things would always remind her of the first
night she had slept with Bold Wolf. Oh, how she loved
him. She would never forget his gentleness when she
had awakened in the middle of the night crying, when
the sores on her flesh pained her so much she could
scarcely stand it. The plantain leaves had not been as
effective for her fair skin as it was for the Penobscot.

It had seemed so natural to go to bed with Bold
Wolf without any clothes on, for he had seen her
naked before, when they had made love. Oh, how she
had wanted to make love last night. But it had been
hard enough to lie on the bed, the very touch of it

against her skin so painful she had taken forever to
go to sleep.

She was suddenly aware that her skin was no longer
burning. She looked quickly down at herself. The sun,
just rising and showing its soft, golden rays through
the window above Bold Wolf's bed, let Shanna see
that only a few sores remained on her skin.

She dared to touch one of those sores and sighed
when she discovered they were no longer tender to
the touch. The inflammation was gone.

"And how is my woman this morning?"

Bold Wolf's voice made Shanna's insides grow
warm with desire. She gazed down at him and smiled,
then stretched out beside him and ran a hand gently
over his body.

"I am so much better," she murmured. "And you?"

"I am well enough to hold you in my arms," Bold
Wolf said, reaching out for her.

His gaze swept over her nakedness, his loins growing hot at the sight of her well-rounded breasts and
the feathering of reddish hair at the juncture of her
thighs.

"I would so love for you to hold me," Shanna
sighed, snuggling against him, shivering with ecstasy
as he swept his arms around her.

"It is so right that you are here with me," Bold
Wolf said, gently cupping one of her breasts. "You
know that I can never let you go, now that you are
finally here."

"I don't want to go anywhere," she whispered. She
sucked in a deep breath when he bent low and flicked
his tongue around her nipple, then sucked it between
his lips. "Except . . . except . . . to go for Elizabeth . . .
and . . . and to go and explain things to my parents."

Bold Wolf moved away from her. He propped himself up on an elbow and gazed into her eyes. "I had

sentries watch the river all night for your father, should he decide to come for you," he said.

"I truly had expected Father to come," Shanna said. "We both took a chance that he might arrive with Sheriff Wisler."

"We cannot let our guard down just yet," Bold Wolf said. "Today the river will be watched, as well."

"*Today* we must go and explain things to Papa and Mama," Shanna said. "I want to get it over with, especially before my father does something irrational."

Now that she had turned her back on her parents, Shanna would feel like a stranger knocking on the door of her former home.

"I wonder why Father *didn't* come for me last night," Shanna murmured. "And I wonder how Jennie was received when she arrived at my house yesterday."

She sat up quickly. She placed a hand to her throat, her eyes wide. "What if they turned Jennie away?" She gasped. "Oh, Bold Wolf, what if Jennie is wandering the streets of the city all alone? In a sense it would be my fault, for had I returned home with her, my father would not have cause to be so angry with me that he would take it out on my dear friend."

Bold Wolf reached for her wrists and drew her down beside him. "Do you not realize what you are doing by allowing yourself to be alarmed about something you do not know has truly happened?" he said softly. "You are still allowing your father to interfere in your life. It is as though he were here purposely putting such thoughts into your head."

"Yes, I know," Shanna whispered. She rested her cheek on his smooth chest, savoring his nearness. "It's just that my father has always been so overbearing. How *can* I get past that so easily?"

"By being with me and concentrating on the happiness that we share," Bold Wolf said. He placed his hands on her cheeks and drew her lips to his. "Let me love you, Shanna. I will show you the ways to forget troublesome fathers."

Shanna's breath caught with a leap of ecstasy when Bold Wolf crushed his lips down on hers, his arms pulling her close against his hard body.

Shanna was aware of his heat between her legs and his hands all over her now, touching, moving, dancing.

When he slid his manhood into her soft folds and began his rhythmic thrusts, she moaned and writhed.

Bold Wolf was filled with a lethargic feeling of floating as the thrusting of his pelvis sent him more deeply within her, her own hips now responding in a rhythmic movement that matched his.

His hands swept downward and clasped her buttocks, molding her slender, sweet body against his as the pulsing crest of his passion rose within him.

His breath mingled with hers as he whispered to her how much he loved her, her eyes burning with passion as he gazed into them.

"I love you so, Bold Wolf," Shanna whispered, her throat arching backward as he buried his lips along its delicate column.

She twined her arms around him and ran her hands slowly up and down the sleekness of his back, her body turning liquid as he propped himself up and gazed down at her, his eyes darkening with the depths of his emotion.

"My woman, my Shanna," Bold Wolf whispered, then swept his arms around her as they came together feverishly, his lips covering hers in a fiery, deep kiss.

Thrusting deeply, Bold Wolf groaned huskily against her lips, the explosion of passion sweeping through him, her body trembling against his, proving that she had found the ultimate of pleasure as he had found his.

Afterward, Bold Wolf rolled gently away from Shanna and lay on his back, panting.

Shanna crept to her knees beside him and slowly ran her fingers over his muscled shoulders, down across his powerful chest, and then laughed softly as his skin rippled while her fingers crept across his flat stomach.

"It does seem that your body is healed from the poison," she murmured, now touching that part of him from which his seed had just spilled inside her. "Especially *this* part of your body is all right."

Bold Wolf's jaw tightened and he closed his eyes in ecstasy as she circled his manhood within her fingers and began slowly moving them on him again.

"You do not know just how tender I am there at this moment," he said huskily.

Afraid that she was hurting him, Shanna started to move her hand away, but his hand led hers back to him.

"Continue . . . continue . . ." Bold Wolf said throatily as desire shot through him. He reached a hand up and cupped one of her breasts, drawing a gasp of pleasure from Shanna.

Suddenly Bold Wolf reached around her and swept her beneath him and came to her, thrusting deeply, his mouth urgently on hers, drugging her.

His groans of pleasure fired her passions. She clung to his neck and felt the pleasure spreading . . . spreading . . . spreading . . .

And once again their words melted away, their bodies quaking.

This time Shanna rolled away from Bold Wolf.

She laughed softly as she twined her fingers through her hair, lifting it from beneath her. "If today is a sample of what all my tomorrows with you will be, I was right to choose you over being a concert violinist."

He reached for her and drew her against him. He kissed her long and deep, then held her. "My Shanna, soon we will share vows," he said. "Is it not a dream we have shared since that day we met on the beach, when you were collecting shells and I was already enamored of your beauty?"

"I shall remember that day for always," Shanna murmured. "I have carried the memories with me and feel blessed to have them. I knew then, Bold Wolf, that I could never be happy without you."

"So much has kept us apart," Bold Wolf said, his voice drawn. He propped himself up on an elbow and gazed into her eyes. "It was mainly I who kept us from proceeding with our future together. It was hard to choose one desire over the other. Sometimes I think perhaps I was wrong to—"

Shanna placed a gentle hand over his mouth to keep him from saying that which she knew was wrong. He wouldn't have been happy had he not performed for his people in the capacity of their village Runner. And how proud she had been of him while he had been honored in such a way. Yes, she had missed him terribly, but she had held on to his promise that someday he would be hers. He had kept that promise. And so had she kept hers. They were now finally together. No man would tear them asunder, especially not her father!

"Those shells that you collected those many years ago . . . are they still important to you?" Bold Wolf asked softly.

"Yes, I still enjoy collecting shells," Shanna murmured. "Why do you ask, Bold Wolf? Are you intrigued, as well, by shells?"

"Very," Bold Wolf said, thinking of what lay under

the bed, having kept it for her for so long. His eyes twinkled. "And have you ever found that perfect shell that you were searching for?"

"No, never," Shanna said, sighing. "And I doubt that I shall. Here, in this area, along the river, there aren't many that are extra-special. They are too small and insignificant."

"And would you say a conch shell would be called insignificant?" Bold Wolf said. He slipped away from her and reached beneath his bed, deciding *not* to wait for their wedding day to give her the beautiful shell. He had waited long enough to see the shine of delight that it would bring to her eyes.

"I have always dreamed of having a conch shell," Shanna said, watching him quizzically. "To me that would *be* the perfect shell. I have heard that you can hear the ocean in the conch shell. It would be a wonderful thing to hear."

Smiling broadly, Bold Wolf laid the buckskin bag in front of her.

"Open it," he said. "See what I had planned to give to you on our wedding day."

"A gift? For me?" Shanna asked, reaching for the bag. She stopped then and drew her hands back. "No. I mustn't," she said. "If you planned to give this to me on our wedding day, surely I shouldn't see it now."

"Please do," Bold Wolf said. He gently took one of her hands and put it over the bag. "Slide your hand inside. Tell me what you feel."

So excited that her heart was pounding against her ribs, Shanna did as he asked. When she felt around and her hand touched the smooth roundness of the shell, she gasped with surprise, then giggled and swept the shell on out for her to see.

She held it in both hands as she gazed at the pink, almost translucent shell. "It's so beautiful," she cried.

She ran her fingers over the shell, finding it exquisitely smooth. "Oh, how wonderful it feels against my hands!"

"Hold it to your ear," Bold Wolf said, pride shining in his eyes for having made her this happy. "Listen. You *can* hear the roar of the ocean."

Her eyes excitedly wide, Shanna held the opening to her ear. She gasped. "I do hear it!" she cried. "Oh, Bold Wolf, I do hear it!"

He scooted closer, swept his arms around her, and held her against him as she continued to listen to the ocean. "I had to find the perfect gift for the perfect woman," he said softly. "I do believe I have succeeded."

"Yes, oh, yes, I would want nothing more than this," Shanna murmured. "I have searched my entire life for such a perfect shell."

She drew the conch shell away from her ear, held it on her lap, then placed a cheek against Bold Wolf's chest. "I am so lucky that I didn't have to search a lifetime for the perfect *man,*" she murmured. "Thank you, my darling. Thank you for being you. Thank you for the lovely shell. I shall treasure both you and the shell forever."

"You are the true treasure," Bold Wolf whispered, then lifted her chin with a finger and gave her a long, deep kiss.

31

As Emily Diepholz stood aside, tears shining in her eyes, and Bold Wolf stood beside Shanna, his arm around her waist, Shanna held Elizabeth and gazed into her deep, dark eyes. She still found it hard to believe that the day had finally arrived when she could take Elizabeth with her to Indian Island, where the little girl would forever be a part of hers and Bold Wolf's lives.

"Today, Elizabeth, *today*," Shanna murmured. She laughed softly as Elizabeth smiled up at her from her cocoon of blankets. "Oh, precious, you will be so loved by your mama and papa."

Shanna turned proud eyes up at Bold Wolf. "Mama . . . papa . . ." she murmured, swallowing back a sob that rose quickly into her throat. "Although we are not even yet married, we *are* proud *parents,* Bold Wolf, and parents of such an adorable child. Isn't it wonderful?"

"Do your parents know yet?" Emily asked, breaking the warm, delicious spell of the moment.

Shanna's smile faded. She rocked Elizabeth slowly in her arms and looked sheepishly over to Emily. "No, I haven't told them," she murmured. "I . . . I plan to go and tell them as soon as Bold Wolf and I leave here."

"And so they have given their blessings to your plans to marry?" Emily asked, looking from Bold Wolf to Shanna.

Shanna glanced up at Bold Wolf, then looked wearily over at Emily again. "No, they haven't given us their blessings, and I doubt they ever will," she said, her voice drawn. "But at least my father is no longer *fighting* it. He knows now that nothing he does will change my mind about marrying Bold Wolf."

"And what about your violin?" Emily asked, smoothing out the sheer curtains at the open parlor window as the breeze tangled them. She looked over her shoulder at Shanna. "Will you abandon plans to become a concert violinist?"

"Although my parents never knew, and although I continued with my violin lessons, I abandoned plans of being a concert violinist the moment I met Bold Wolf," Shanna said, sighing contentedly when he drew her even closer to his side. "I could not have both. So I chose that which would make me the happiest."

She smiled sweetly up at Bold Wolf. "Only Bold Wolf could make me happy," she murmured. She then looked quickly down at Elizabeth. "And our dear *child*."

"We had best leave now, Shanna," Bold Wolf said, stepping away from her. He lifted a bag that held Elizabeth's clothes and blankets that Emily had bought for her, as well as some toys.

"Yes, I'm anxious to get the chore of facing my parents behind me," Shanna said, positioning Elizabeth more comfortably in the crook of her left arm.

"May God be with you," Emily said, coming to give Shanna an affectionate kiss on the cheek. As tears flowed from her eyes, she gazed down at Elizabeth.

"I shall miss the darling so. She is such a pleasant child. She only cries when she is wet or hungry, and even then she never actually wails. She has the most even temperament of any child I have ever been around."

"Yes, and how could anyone have *ever* abandoned her?" Shanna said, chills running down her spine as she recalled the day she had found the baby.

Again she thought about the mother and who she might be. Although Bold Wolf had assured her that none of the Penobscot women would ever abandon a child in such a way, Shanna could not get that fear behind her. The Penobscot village was far closer than any other Indian village.

The Mohawk village was the next closest. A mother who had just given birth to a child surely would not be strong enough to travel even that one mile from the Mohawk village.

Shanna was still afraid that someone on Indian Island might take one glance at Elizabeth and know she was the child that had been left to die just outside of Old Town.

Shanna knew she would always have to be on guard. She would watch all of the women and how they looked at the child. If any one of them looked suspicious, as though she resented the child in even the least way, Shanna would immediately tell Bold Wolf so that he could investigate and be sure to protect Elizabeth!

"Shanna?" Bold Wolf's voice, filled with a questioning, drew her from her troubled thoughts.

She looked quickly up at him and smiled awkwardly. "I'm sorry," she murmured. "I . . . I was thinking about something that troubled me."

"Your parents?" he said softly, placing a gentle hand to her cheek.

"No, it was something else," Shanna said, pleading with her eyes for him not to question her any further.

"Everything . . . you *and* Elizabeth . . . will be all right," Bold Wolf reassured her. "I will never let harm come to either of you again."

"Yes, I know," Shanna said, smiling up at him. "We both are so blessed to have you."

She walked from the parlor with Bold Wolf, Emily leading the way to the front door. When they got there and the door was opened, Emily wiped tears from her eyes with a delicate, lacy handkerchief, took one last look at Elizabeth, gave Shanna a long, warm smile, then went to Bold Wolf and hugged him.

"Take care of my girls," she said, her voice breaking. "They are special, Bold Wolf, so very, very special."

Bold Wolf glanced over at Shanna, smiled, and nodded. He brushed a kiss across Emily's pink cheek, then stepped back and gazed into her eyes. "We will send word for you so that you and your husband can attend our wedding ceremony if you wish to be there," he said thickly.

"We wouldn't miss it for the world," Emily murmured, then gave both Shanna and Bold Wolf a soft, apologetical look. "I'm sorry Samuel was called away on business so early this morning. He would have wanted to be here to say good-bye to Elizabeth and to give you his good wishes."

"I understand," Shanna said. "We will look forward to seeing you both on our wedding day."

Shanna and Bold Wolf left the house and made their way toward Shanna's parents' home, the autumn sun warm on their faces. As they walked past the burned brothel and then Roscoe Lovett's music studio, Shanna said, "I truly hope that Jennie is all right. I was hoping she would have found a way to send word to me that my parents either accepted her back in their home or sent her away."

She looked over her shoulder at the stairs that led to Roscoe Lovett's studio. "I hope Mr. Lovett is all right," she said warily. "There is an air of mystery about his sudden departure from Old Town. I'm afraid that Al's men might have done something to him before they fled town after the brothel was burned."

"You carry the burden of too many people's lives on your shoulders too often," Bold Wolf said in a soft, yet scolding fashion. "Starting today, Shanna, try to concentrate on what is good in life, not what is bad. I am certain that people you worry so much about will in the end find such happiness as you and I. But you must give it time. Were you and I not forced to wait until the moment was right for our true happiness?"

"Yes and the waiting was so hard, it seemed to last forever," Shanna said, sighing heavily.

"But now we are together and everything good awaits us," Bold Wolf said. But he himself stiffened with concern when Shanna's house came into view.

"We have one major obstacle yet to get behind us, and *only* then can I truly relax with our happiness," Shanna said, feeling her cheeks flush with her fear of facing her parents.

Shanna's knees shook as she climbed the stairs to her house. When she reached the porch, she stopped and sucked in a nervous breath, then stepped up to the door. Her hand trembling, she knocked, giving a quick glance to the large front window where the bodies always lay for viewing.

Today there was no one there but a little boy standing on the bier, drawing back the sheer curtain, staring out at Shanna and Bold Wolf.

"Tommie," Shanna whispered, gasping when the

child stuck his tongue out at her and left the window so quickly she had to believe that someone had yanked him away.

"Even Tommie no longer likes me," she whispered, tears filling her eyes.

Then the door opened and Shanna found herself face-to-face with her mother. Her heart ached when she saw the bitterness in her mother's eyes.

But everything changed quickly when her mother looked down at the bundle in Shanna's arms. Bernita's eyes widened and she took a shaky step away from Shanna, grabbed at her throat, then fainted.

"Mama!" Shanna cried. She handed Elizabeth to Bold Wolf. She knelt on the floor beside her mother and drew Bernita's head on her lap. "Mama, wake up! Oh, Mama, *please* wake up!"

"What have you done?" Jordan shouted as he came from the preparation room at the far end of the corridor. "Lord, Bernita! *Lord!*"

Still smelling strongly of embalming fluid, he swept Bernita into his arms, carried her into the library, and laid her on the sofa.

Jordan hurried to a table and slid a drawer open. He took out a small vial of smelling salts and took it back to his wife. After snapping it open, he waved it beneath Bernita's nose, then waited as he anxiously watched her.

Shanna looked over at Bold Wolf who stood at the door of the library holding Elizabeth, then she watched her mother's eyes slowly open.

"Mama, are you all right?" Shanna asked softly, placing a soft hand to her mother's brow.

When her mother venomously slapped her hand away and looked past her at the child, Shanna realized what had caused her mother to faint. Although her mother had to know that Shanna had not given birth to the child—for no one would know better than her mother that Shanna had never been pregnant—it had been the sight of Shanna standing there holding a baby at Bold Wolf's side that had caused her such alarm.

Bernita moved to a sitting position and began fussing with her hair, trying to replace strands that had fallen from her tight bun.

Shanna turned wavering eyes up to her father, who had yet to say anything to her or Bold Wolf. Instead he just stood there, with bitter accusation in his eyes. She shuddered involuntarily, for she could feel her father's hostility.

Shanna wrenched her eyes away from him and gently took the child from Bold Wolf's arms. Slowly rocking Elizabeth, she went back to her parents and stood before them. Gently Shanna drew back the corners of the blanket. "This is my daughter Elizabeth," she murmured.

She tightened inside when she heard them both gasp. She hurriedly explained how she had found Elizabeth, where the child had been since, and how much she loved her.

"And so, no matter how much your parents are against it, and no matter that you are giving up a bright future as a violinist, you are marrying Bold Wolf?" her father said, ignoring what she had said about Elizabeth, as though the child didn't exist.

"Papa, I love both Bold Wolf *and* Elizabeth," Shanna said, stubbornly keeping Elizabeth in the conversation. "And yes, I do plan to marry Bold Wolf. *Please,* won't you *please* give me and Bold Wolf your blessing? Don't you truly want me to do what makes me happy? I wish for nothing more than to be married to Bold Wolf and to be Elizabeth's mother. Papa, you *know* that it was never my dream to be a violinist. It was solely *yours*."

Suddenly Shanna heard footsteps behind her. She turned just as Jennie came into the room. "Jennie!" she cried. She gently handed Elizabeth back to Bold Wolf and embraced her friend. "Oh, Jennie, I was so worried about you," she softly cried. "I wasn't sure what had happened to you, whether or not my parents would allow you back in the house."

"And why wouldn't we?" her father said smugly.

Jordan took Jennie from Shanna's arms, placed an arm around her waist, and held her possessively at his side as he smiled ruefully down at Shanna. "Shanna, Jennie is going to fulfill the dream that you have so heartlessly abandoned," he said. "I am going to make certain that *Jennie* will be known worldwide for her skills at violin playing. *She* will play my sister's violin. *She* will make appearances with all of the major orchestras in the world. She will be the envy of all who wish for such success. Even *you,* Shanna. Even *you* will envy her."

Shanna's breath seemed to have frozen inside her. She was stunned by her father's absolute rejection of her and the way he so ruthlessly bragged about someone else in an effort to hurt her. But it was backfiring. Instead of hurting her, he was doing her a favor by giving Jennie the opportunities Shanna did not want. Deep inside Shanna's heart, she was glad!

This took the pressures off Shanna. Now she was free to go with Bold Wolf and live in peace!

And how Jennie's eyes sparkled, for finally she had a family, someone to care for her. All that was lacking was love, for Shanna now knew that her father did not know the meaning of the word.

Nor did her mother.

But it would be enough for Jennie to have a decent

home, a place where she was safe and warm, a place where she could dream of the day she *would* be a well-known concert violinist, for that had always been Jennie's dream.

When Jennie saw no resentment in Shanna's eyes, she broke away from Jordan and flung herself into Shanna's arms. "I'm so glad that you are happy for me," she murmured, clinging to her.

Jennie leaned closer to Shanna's ear. "Have you heard any more about Roscoe Lovett?" she whispered so that only Shanna could hear. "Whether or not he is truly all right?"

Shanna realized that her father's scheme would work only until Roscoe Lovett returned and claimed Jennie as his. Shanna knew that, if Roscoe was alive, he *would* come for Jennie someday.

"No, I haven't heard any more, but I am certain you will be the first to know if he returns to Old Town," Shanna whispered back, smiling across her shoulder at her father, who was frowning at them for whispering and keeping secrets from him.

And although Shanna was smiling and feeling more free now than ever before in her life, there was a part of her that was sad over a father who would blatantly and callously substitute someone else in his life for his daughter.

It suddenly came to Shanna that perhaps she should be more concerned about Jennie than happy for her. She hoped that if Roscoe Lovett *was* alive, he would not wait long to come for Jennie. Shanna could not help but wonder if Jennie now was at the mercy of someone who might even be more cold hearted than Jennie's own father. Jordan Sewell had proved to be a man of a questionable mental stability!

32

Blessing she is,
God made her so,
And deeds of week-day holiness
Fall from her noiseless as the snow.
—JAMES RUSSELL LOWELL

The stars were bright in the sky. The moon was a slight sliver of light. Lightning bugs flashed their tiny lanterns through the darkness as Shanna sat in a canoe with Bold Wolf and two of his warriors. Many other canoes followed them down the Penobscot River.

A *noda-sen-i,* torch—consisting of a green stave split at the end to hold a bundle of folded birch-bark strips wound with splints—was fastened in the bow of each canoe.

A man was at the bow of each canoe, standing with an *e-niga-hkw,* spear, held ready as he watched for salmon.

Shanna was amazed at the huge spears. Their shafts were twelve to eighteen feet long and were of smoothed spruce. The outside prongs were not sharp, but served to grasp the fish so that the central prong would pierce its back. The outside prongs, or grips, were of hardwood, the middle point of sharpened hornbeam.

Except for one concern, it was a night of enchantment for Shanna. She had left Elizabeth with Singing Owl, a Penobscot woman whose breasts now fed the child. She worried about leaving Elizabeth with someone else. But Bold Wolf had assured her that Singing

Owl could be trusted, that Elizabeth was safe from harm.

Yet even now, as Shanna accompanied Bold Wolf and his warriors on the salmon hunt, she could not help but worry, although from the moment she had brought Elizabeth to Indian Island, Bold Wolf had given the child over to the woman for nourishment from her milk-filled breasts, her own two-month-old child equally sharing the milk with Elizabeth.

If anything happened to Elizabeth in Shanna's absence, she would never forgive herself. Yet she came because she wanted to be with Bold Wolf tonight as he speared salmon in preparation for the Grand Fire Council celebration that was being held in his village tomorrow. They were also hoping to spear enough salmon for smoking large amounts for storage.

It was an exciting time for the Penobscot. They had held a Grand Fire Council every seven years, inviting neighboring tribes to the island for council, sports, and feasting. This year, even the Mohawk were going to join the celebration.

Tonight was special for Shanna. It was wonderful to be free of the need to sneak around in order to see Bold Wolf, as she'd had to do since she was a teenager in love with a man who would one day be a powerful Penobscot chief.

She *must* learn to relax now and take advantage of her freedom. She must learn to thank the Lord for each day with Bold Wolf and Elizabeth, for it could have been very different. Had her father truly wanted to, he could have fought endlessly for her return to his home. He could have even involved the authorities; Sheriff Wisler surely would have relished the opportunity to cause trouble for the Penobscot.

Shanna's troubled thoughts were brushed aside when she heard the rush of water up ahead. "The rapids," she whispered. She grabbed the sides of the canoe as the birch-bark vessel entered the thrashing waters where the salmon would be harvested.

A keen excitement bubbled inside Shanna as she watched Bold Wolf stand up beside the men at the bow and grab a spear. They began watching the water for the salmon.

Shanna's breath quickened when Bold Wolf raised his hand back with the long spear, the muscles of his shoulders bulging. When he hurled the spear down into the water, Shanna fell to her knees and looked into the river. She gasped with delight when she saw that his first try had been successful.

She scooted out of the way as he brought the huge fish out of the water and loosened it from his spear. Earlier she was told what to do as each salmon was brought in. She grabbed the wriggling fish and dropped it down inside a buckskin basket filled with water. Back in the village the fish would be either prepared for the feast tomorrow or placed upon pole racks over open fires for smoking.

Shanna breathlessly grabbed one salmon after another as Bold Wolf and the man in the bow handed them to her from their spears. The catch was so quick and great, Shanna didn't have time to close the lid.

Finally, with baskets overflowing with the salmon harvest in all of the canoes, the spears were put aside and everyone headed for home.

Shanna moved back to the seat behind the oarsman. She warmed inside when Bold Wolf, smiling broadly, the fire from the torch sending dancing shadows over his sculpted copper face, sat down beside her.

"And so you have shared the first salmon harvest with your soon-to-be husband," Bold Wolf said. He chuckled as he gazed at her, his eyes gleaming. "Perhaps you would enjoy learning the skills of the spear yourself?"

Laughing, reeking of fish, Shanna washed her hands in the river, then scooted over and welcomed Bold Wolf's arm around her waist. "No, thank you," she murmured. "I think I will leave the spearing to you. I saw the effort it took to sling the huge spear into the depths of the water. My, oh, my, you should have seen your muscles react to the strain."

She reached up and ran a hand over one of his arms. "I have always known you were muscled, but tonight I saw *layers* of muscles," she said. "It was something to admire, Bold Wolf. I truly admire *you.*"

"I developed my muscles early in life so that I could be the Runner for my people," he said thickly. He reached for one of her hands and ran his fingers over the calluses of her fingers. "It is almost the same as how *you* developed calluses by playing the violin strings with your fingers."

Stunned by his astuteness, Shanna gave him a quick look. "No one but you has ever said anything about my calluses and the work I put into my playing," she murmured.

"It was just something else your father took for granted," Bold Wolf said dryly. "My Shanna, I have never taken anything about you for granted."

Not wanting to talk about herself, especially about her playing the violin, Shanna looked quickly away from him and gazed at the lamplight in the windows along the shore as Old Town came into view.

"I loved being a part of tonight's harvest," she murmured. "Being there in the water, the torches reflecting in the river so mystically, the spears . . . everything was so intriguing to me."

"There are many more customs of my people that

will mystify you," Bold Wolf said, drawing her even
more closely to his side.

"I want to learn everything," Shanna said softly.
"Once I am your wife, I . . ."

She stopped and gazed up at him. "Please let's not
put off the marriage ceremony much longer," she murmured. "Anything can happen. Should my father have
too much time to think about it, he might change his
mind and come for me. If I am married, there is nothing he can do. If I am with child, surely he would
never force me to go back with him and Mama."

"The Grand Fire Council has been scheduled for
some time now, so I cannot change that, but the day
after the council meeting we can speak our vows,"
Bold Wolf said, brushing a soft kiss across her lips.
"Tomorrow, while you join my people in the council
celebration, remember that the next celebration will
be solely in honor of *us.*"

Shanna sighed dreamily. "I shall count the hours,"
she murmured. "Hardly a minute passed these past
years when I was not thinking about you and marveling over how it would be to be your wife."

He placed a finger to her chin, lifted her lips to his,
and kissed her long and deep. As the canoe made a
slow turn toward Indian Island, Shanna's heart
pounded against her ribs to know that soon she would
again be with Bold Wolf in his bed. It still did not
seem that she should be able to actually stay with him
and sleep with him.

Oh, how often had she stared from her bedroom
window, burning inside to be with Bold Wolf in such
a way?

And now? She was truly there with him to stay? It
did seem like such a dream, which sent spirals of bliss-
ful joy through her.

She was wrenched from her passionate reverie when

Bold Wolf lifted his mouth from her lips and he jumped from the canoe to help beach it.

For a while longer Shanna was just a part of the salmon harvest as she helped the warriors unload the canoes, the baskets now being heaved up the hill by the women who had rushed to the river from their lodges.

When Shanna heard a baby crying, her insides tightened. She looked quickly up and saw Singing Owl standing there in the darkness, holding Elizabeth.

Shanna paled and went cold inside when she saw that Elizabeth was no longer wrapped in a blanket, her twisted little hand quite exposed to those who might gape openly at it and realize this was the child that had been left for dead by some heartless mother.

A quick panic gripped Shanna's insides. If Elizabeth's true mother was there, helping with the baskets of salmon, oh, Lord! Wiping her hands on her skirt, Shanna hurried up the banks of the river and held out her arms for the child. She glared at Singing Owl. "Where is her blanket?" she demanded, her voice filled with an icy venom that sounded nothing like her, she was normally so soft-spoken.

"The night is warm," Singing Owl said, an instant hurt entering her eyes over Shanna's coldness. "The child needs no blanket."

Shanna took Elizabeth in her arms and held her close, still looking at Singing Owl. Shanna now felt bad for having spoken so sharply to her. By the light of the torches she could see the hurt in the woman's eyes. "I'm sorry," she murmured. "It's just . . . it's just . . ."

"Let us go home now," Bold Wolf said, sliding a gentle arm around Shanna's waist. He gave Singing Owl a soft smile. "Shanna means well. She loves Elizabeth very much."

Singing Owl nodded, then turned and ran away, softly sobbing.

"I understand why you did that, but as I said before, Shanna, you must put your concerns behind you about who the child's mother might be," Bold Wolf said, gently leading her toward their cabin. "It is not like you to inflict hurt on anyone, as you just did Singing Owl."

"I'm sorry," Shanna murmured. She gazed down at Elizabeth and found her peacefully asleep in her arms. "I *will* try harder, Bold Wolf, to stop watching for things that are not there. I'm certain Elizabeth's true mother is far away from here. I will keep that thought. I promise."

They went on to the cabin and Bold Wolf stood beside Shanna as she placed Elizabeth in her cradle and covered her with a soft blanket.

"Sleep, my darling," Shanna whispered. "Sleep."

"She *is* safe here," Bold Wolf said, gently turning Shanna to face him.

"I know," Shanna said, nodding. "Truly, I know."

He swept Shanna into his arms and carried her to their bed.

In a frenzy of eager hands they removed each other's clothes, then fell together on the bed, their bodies molded against each other, their lips on fire with eager, passionate kisses.

Bold Wolf slid his lips from Shanna's mouth. "Right now, Shanna, *we* are the only two people on the earth," he whispered, his hands kneading her breasts. "But not selfishly. Tonight we will make a brother for Elizabeth."

He blanketed her with his body and pressed gently into her, then gave one deep thrust and began his rhythmic strokes within her.

Shanna's gasps of pleasure as she clung to Bold

Wolf's sinewed shoulders became long, soft whimpers. She lifted her legs around him, and locked them together at her ankles, and rode him, flesh moving against flesh.

Bold Wolf was aflame with longing, his breath ragged as the pleasure spread in hot, smoldering waves through him. He framed Shanna's face between his hands and plunged his tongue into her mouth to touch his tongue to hers.

And then he slid his mouth lower and his body turned to instant fire when he flicked his tongue over her nipples, tasting her sweetness, savoring it. The tip of his tongue traced the outline of both of her nipples and then he nibbled them until Shanna moaned and arched her body even more closely into his.

"My woman," Bold Wolf said huskily, then tilted her head up and brought his mouth down hard on hers just as their bodies vibrated, jolted, and quivered.

Shanna clung to Bold Wolf and she felt the warmth of his seed spilling out inside her.

Afterward they lay together, still in each other's arms.

Shanna leaned up and flicked her tongue along his lips, moaning throatily when he locked his fingers through her hair and gave her another hard, deep kiss.

Shanna became lost again in the moment as Bold Wolf made love with her a second, and then a third time.

33

The huge fire still burned bright, flaring up into the sky as day turned to night. The excitement of the Grand Fire Council celebration was still in high gear as the children from various neighboring tribes competed in games, proud adults watching, mothers rocking babies in their arms, fathers smoking long-stemmed pipes.

To Shanna it was like living in a different world at a different time. Everything she had experienced today was so new and awesome. Had she ever doubted for even one moment her decision to live with Bold Wolf and his people, learning their ways, being a part of them, what she had experienced today had wiped all doubt from her mind and her heart.

Her jaws ached even now from smiling so much, her laughter bringing pride to Bold Wolf's eyes, for from her laughter came his knowledge of her true happiness. She was glad to prove to him in such a way that she did feel as though she belonged.

Except for one thing that kept ebbing into her consciousness, she had shared everything with him and his people today with a happy heart.

Elizabeth.

Elizabeth, and whether or not among those women

present for the celebration might be the child's mother.

While sitting beside Bold Wolf on a platform strewn with beautiful wildflowers, and dressed in a beautiful doeskin dress with beautiful tiny shells and beads sewn onto the skirt, Shanna had found herself often scanning the crowd, searching for a woman who might be paying her more interest than the others.

Although Shanna had asked Singing Owl to stay with Elizabeth in the cabin instead of bringing her out among the crowd, hoping to keep interest in the child to a minimum, Shanna knew that gossip had spread among the visiting women about Elizabeth. It had happened so quickly, when those who came today had been told of Shanna's and Bold Wolf's upcoming marriage. Their interest piqued, they had then wanted to know everything about this white woman who was marrying a Penobscot chief.

Of course, that for the most part always led to Elizabeth. Many had asked to see Elizabeth, but Shanna always declined the offer, saying that she was sleeping, or eating, or *anything* that would give her a reprieve from such questioning eyes.

Shanna so far had been successful in keeping everyone away from Elizabeth. She knew she had only a few more hours before the council was over and the guests would board their canoes and return to their own villages.

"And how do you find the way we Penobscot treat our guests?" Bold Wolf asked, leaning closer to Shanna.

His gaze swept over her, seeing her as nothing less than radiant in the dress Pale Star had sewn for her, and with her hair swept back and hanging in long braids down her back. Around her neck was a necklace made of shells that matched those on her dress.

She wore knee-high moccasins, also decorated with the same type of shells.

Shanna leaned closer to Bold Wolf so that their shoulders touched. "It's all been so breathtaking," she murmured. "Even Chief Bent Arrow seems to be enjoying himself."

Shanna gave the chief's wife a lingering look, feeling somewhat apprehensive about this woman whose eyes had often met Shanna's today. . . .

Her thoughts were interrupted when Bold Wolf began talking to her again. She turned her adoring eyes to him and listened.

"For many years, the Mohawk hosted the Grand Fire Council, entertaining the visiting tribes," Bold Wolf said, his voice drawn. "Neither my father nor I ever went then. That was when we were not friendly with the Mohawk."

He laughed scornfully as he looked over at Chief Bent Arrow, the Mohawk's arrogant smugness even now proving that he scoffed at how today's celebration had been handled by the Penobscot. "It seems that Chief Bent Arrow was too bossy when the celebration was held at his village, and for the most part the other tribes said they would not return there," he said dryly. "They came to my father, one by one, requesting that the Grand Fire Council be held here on Indian Island. Everyone admired my father. They knew that if he hosted the council, everything would be shared equally among those who attended."

Bold Wolf lowered his eyes and swallowed hard, then looked over to Shanna. "My father did not live long enough to be able to experience the Grand Fire Council held here among his people. I am the first host on Indian Island for this great event."

"He would have been so proud," Shanna said, reaching over, taking one of Bold Wolf's hands. "You have done well today, Bold Wolf. Everyone will want to return here for the next council."

"Seven years will pass before the council meets again before the huge outdoor fire," Bold Wolf said, sliding an arm around her waist. He smiled into her eyes. "We could have *sons* competing in the games then."

"Sons," Shanna said, the thought of having sons in Bold Wolf's image filling her heart with warmth. "Yes, we will have *many* sons."

She laughed softly. "But we should have at least one daughter so that Elizabeth will not be over-whelmed by her brothers," she said.

She thought of Tommie and Terrie. Although they were mischievous and aggravating, she could not help but miss the little scoundrels. She wondered if they missed her, or if they had accepted Jennie into their lives as their sister.

She wondered how Jennie was faring. She wondered if Roscoe Lovett had returned. If so, was Jennie resuming her violin practice with him as a student, or as his love interest?

"Your thoughts have strayed," Bold Wolf said, placing a finger to her chin, turning her eyes up to his.

"Yes, I was thinking of Jennie," Shanna said softly. "Did you send someone today to my parents' house with invitations for my parents, Jennie, and my brothers for our wedding tomorrow?"

"The messenger was sent, but was ignored," Bold Wolf said thickly. "No one opened the door to him. Eagle Wing said that he saw Jennie looking through an upstairs window, but she, too, ignored him."

"I'm sure Jennie had no other choice but to behave in such a way," Shanna said, sighing. "If she is to stay in good standing with my parents, she must do as they ask."

"But as you know, Eagle Wing also went to Emily and Samuel Diepholz's home and they eagerly opened the door to him and sent word that they will most certainly be here tomorrow for the ceremony," Bold Wolf said, glad to see that brought a quick smile to Shanna's face.

Shanna turned abruptly when she heard her name being whispered behind her. She found Singing Owl standing there, concern in her eyes. A sudden fear gripped Shanna's heart. "What is it, Singing Owl?" she asked, sliding around to face her. "Why aren't you with Elizabeth?" Her eyes widened. "Lord, Singing Owl, did you leave her alone?"

"No, she is not alone," Singing Owl said. "My daughter Pretty Eagle is watching her. You must come, Shanna. Nothing pleases Elizabeth tonight. My milk seems to displease her. Holding her makes her cry even harder. Please come, Shanna. See if you can do something to make her happy."

Bold Wolf heard this. He leaned over and kissed Shanna on the cheek. "Go on and see what is wrong with our daughter," he said. "Since I am host, I must stay here, but if you need me, send for me. My family is more important than the council."

"I shall," Shanna said, giving him a quick hug and kiss.

Then, breathless with fear, she left the platform and ran with Singing Owl to Bold Wolf's cabin. When she stepped through the entranceway and saw Pretty Eagle rocking Elizabeth back and forth in her arms, she rushed to her and took the child.

She sat down in a rocker that Emily Diepholz had sent as a prewedding gift to Shanna and rocked Elizabeth for only a moment. It was as though a magic wand had been waved over her and Elizabeth, for the child's cries stopped.

"I do not know what caused her to be so unhappy," Singing Owl said, looking at Elizabeth, who was wrapped in a soft blanket. "Shanna, she has never been like this before."

"She just missed her mother, that's all," Shanna murmured, smiling down at Elizabeth, yet feeling guilty over seeing her daughter's tear-streaked face.

But Elizabeth was smiling now, only an occasional leftover sob quivering through her body. "Did you miss your mommie?" Shanna murmured. "I love you so, Elizabeth. I never want you to cry over anything. I want your life filled with sunshine and happiness."

"Should Pretty Eagle and I stay or leave?" Singing Owl asked, glancing toward the door, listening to the excitement outside beside the fire.

"Please go on," Shanna said softly. "Join the others. I shouldn't have asked you to stay so long away from the excitement. Take your daughter. Enjoy yourselves."

"If you are certain . . ."

"I am certain. Go. Bold Wolf will understand if I stay here with Elizabeth."

Shanna watched them leave, then sat down on the bed and lay Elizabeth on it, slowly unfolding the blankets away from her. "Sweetie, just look at you, all fat and pretty," she said. "Were you crying tonight because you missed me, your *mother*?"

"You are not her true mother."

Those words, that *voice,* the flatness in which those words were said, made Shanna's insides turn stone cold.

Scarcely breathing, her eyes wide, Shanna looked quickly up and saw Chief Bent Arrow's wife standing in the doorway.

"You!" Shanna said, her voice barely a whisper.

"You . . . are . . . the one? You coldheartedly left Elizabeth to die?"

"I named her Night Wind," Running Deer said, as she stepped slowly into the room. "Before I left her by the pond, I named her."

Shanna's heart thundered inside her chest, making her breathless. She stood up beside the bed and purposely blocked Running Deer's view of the child. "You say you named her . . . yet you left her there, surely to die?" She was ashen with fear that the woman was now going to reclaim the child. Elizabeth was now so much a part of Shanna, she was not sure if she could live without her.

"I thought she was already dead," Running Deer said blandly. "When I left her, I thought she . . . was not breathing."

"You *thought*?" Shanna said, her voice rising to match the loathing she felt for this woman. "You thought she was dead and you . . . you just left her there, alone?"

"I went there to have my child with . . . with plans already to leave her," Running Deer said, lowering her eyes. "Whether or not she was dead."

"How . . . could . . . you?" Shanna asked, hardly able to be civil to this woman who was surely heartless clear to the core.

"I had no choice," Running Deer said simply. "You see, Shanna, my husband, who is a proud Mohawk chief, was injured long ago, which made him unable to plant seeds inside a woman's womb. My husband is *old.* Scarcely ever do we share a bed now. When I became with child with another man's baby he did not even notice the change in my body, it was so slight."

"Another man's baby?" Shanna asked, her voice scarcely a whisper.

"I was so hungry for love," Running Deer said, stifling a sob behind her hand. "I married my husband for all of the wrong reasons. I wanted to be the wife of a powerful chief. Even now I wish to still be his wife. The child would have changed everything. I could not allow my chieftain husband to know about the child."

"And so you just threw her away, as though she were something worthless?" Shanna said, stunned over this woman's callousness.

"My husband is a proud man," Running Deer said, taking slow steps toward Shanna. "I could never reveal to him that I had sought love in another man's arms. I most certainly could never tell him that I bore a child that was not Mohawk. My husband is a man of much dignity. If word spread among his people about my trysts with another man, my husband's dignity would be ruined."

"Dignity?" Shanna said in a hiss. "What about the child's dignity?"

"I have had many sleepless nights worrying about what I did," Running Deer said, her voice breaking. "I was wrong to leave her, yet . . . what else could I have done? I truly thought she was dead. She was so premature . . . so tiny."

"Yes, so very tiny and defenseless," Shanna said softly. "Had I not found her, she *would* have died. Get out of here. I don't want you near Elizabeth."

"I must see her," Running Deer said, tears in her eyes. "I have grieved for her. I have a friend from your village whose cousin is part Mohawk. She comes for frequent visits. Recently, when she was at my village, she told me of the child that you and Bold Wolf have taken in as yours, and told me of the affliction. I realized that it had to be my child. Shanna, I must see her. I . . . I was wrong to leave her."

"No," Shanna said, backing closer to the bed.

"Please don't do this to me. I love her so! And . . . I don't trust you. Should you take her away from me, who is to say what you will then do to her? Surely you feel threatened by her presence!"

"I plan to take her nowhere," Running Deer said, swallowing hard. "I would then have to explain many things to my husband. I do not want to lose his love. If he knew about the child, he then would also know about the man who got me pregnant. No. Never will I tell him anything. I do not want to be banished from my husband's home or our village."

"You *should* be banished and left alone to fend for yourself," Shanna said snappishly. "You would at least have more of a chance than the child had!"

Then Running Deer's words sank in. "You aren't here to take her away from me?" she said, her tone softening. "You just want . . . to see her?"

"I want also to hold her," Running Deer said, searching for sympathy in Shanna's eyes.

Again fear gripped Shanna's heart.

"No, I can't let you hold her," she blurted out.

"Just one look, then, is all I ask of you," Running Deer pleaded, reaching out a hand toward Shanna. "Please, Shanna. Just . . . one look."

Though she still felt strongly against it, Shanna saw more and more that Running Deer did seem truly filled with suffering over how she had treated the child. Shanna sighed deeply, then slowly stepped aside.

She stiffened as she watched Running Deer fall to her knees beside the bed. She circled her hands into tight fists at her sides as Running Deer slowly unfolded the blanket until she got a full view of Elizabeth, who was dressed in a soft gown with ruffles at the throat and the hem.

"Oh, she is so beautiful," Running Deer said, then broke into sobs and turned away from the child, her face in her hands. "She . . . is . . . so beautiful. I . . . was so wrong!"

"Yes, she is beautiful," Shanna said, gazing down at Elizabeth, seeing her utter sweetness. "And yes, you were wrong. Oh, so *very* wrong."

Then Shanna placed a hand on Running Deer's arm to help her up. "Please leave now," she said, her voice tight. "You have seen Elizabeth. Please leave now and forget her. She was no longer yours the day you abandoned her."

Running Deer stumbled to her feet. She gazed with despair into Shanna's eyes. "I shall not trouble you again over Elizabeth," she murmured. "Please do not tell Bold Wolf about this . . . that I am the child's true mother."

"*I* am Elizabeth's true mother," Shanna said, her voice drawn. "And no, I won't keep what you told me from Bold Wolf. Elizabeth is also *his* child now."

Running Deer gazed in a long, deep silence at Shanna, then lowered her eyes and ran from the cabin.

Stunned, Shanna could hardly believe what had just transpired between herself and the Mohawk woman. Then relief flooded her. She realized that she no longer had to worry about someone coming to claim the child. It was as if someone had lifted a heavy weight from her shoulders.

Now she knew! Oh, Lord, now she knew. And it no longer mattered!

Bold Wolf came into the cabin almost immediately after Running Deer left. "I saw Running Deer here," he said, looking over his shoulder to where Running Deer had joined her husband again beside the large outdoor fire.

"Wait until I tell you all that she told me," Shanna said, sighing as she settled into a chair. She held Elizabeth over her shoulder and softly patted her back.

Bold Wolf sat in a chair opposite her. "Tell me," he said, reaching over to run a hand over the child's soft head.

"Chief Bent Arrow's wife is Elizabeth's birth mother," Shanna blurted out.

Then she explained it all to him.

34

I believe love, pure and true,
Is to the soul, a sweet immortal dew
That gems life's petals in its hours of dusk.
                    —MARY ASHLEY TOWNSEND

The afternoon sun was waning. The great council house was filled almost to bursting with Bold Wolf's people and friends who had come from their villages to witness Bold Wolf's and Shanna's *niba-wagan,* marriage.

Bold Wolf and Shanna were sitting on a platform in the center of the Penobscot council house, while everyone else sat in a wide semicircle around them and dancers performed to the music of various instruments.

The music leader was shaking a cow's-horn rattle, while others performed on drums as dancers circled about counterclockwise inside the semicircle of people, singing, in a series of high cries, *"Ta-ho, ta-ho."*

The dance, performed by both men and women, was an alternating step and shuffle, although there was also much individual variation. At certain changes in the song, the facing lines would reverse their positions, those advancing forward moving backward, and vice versa. Shanna noticed that the most distinctive feature in these dances was that at the end of each song, the leader would shout the word for "marriage," echoed by the rest.

The dance was the publication of the union, and

once it stopped, in the eyes of the community the couple was considered bound together in marriage.

So proud that the day had finally come when she would be Bold Wolf's wife, Shanna beamed as she watched the dancers from her platform strewn with flowers.

She looked at various guests and recalled the gifts they had brought to her and Bold Wolf. Many of them had brought dried meat, pemmican, berries, and blankets, all of which would feed them and keep them warm during the Moon of Long Nights, winter. The nights were already crisp with the promise of the cold moons soon to come.

Shanna could hardly refrain from giggling out loud when she recalled other gifts that had been meant more for amusement than practical purposes. One of the gifts had been a back scratcher made from a piece of thin ash, fourteen inches long, with a bend an inch wide, notched and carved. With the long handle, one could reach far down the limbs and back without removing clothes. She knew that to display such a scratcher always produced laughter. It was only given mischievously, for the back scratcher was a relic of the past, when people dressed solely in skins and were infected with lice.

Another gift mischievously given by one of Bold Wolf's best friends caused Shanna's face to flood with color. It had been a toothpick made from a raccoon's penis bone!

Casting that embarrassed remembrance from her mind, Shanna gazed with much love toward Emily and Samuel Diepholz, who had come to the wedding with gifts that would make Shanna's home more beautiful. She could hardly wait to hang the beautiful sheer curtains at the windows and spread the large braided rug on the floor before the fireplace.

Emily and Samuel had gone further with their gifts than just bringing something for the bride and groom. They had brought Elizabeth a wooden rocking horse that Samuel had made specifically for the child in his spare time. Shanna had owned a rocking horse when she was a child and spent hours rocking back and forth as her mother embroidered beside the fire.

Bold Wolf now reached over and took Shanna's hand. She turned wondering eyes to him, so very handsome on their wedding day. He wore a shirt and leggings decorated with beads and feathers, and his best moccasins were adorned with porcupine quills.

Shanna felt beautiful herself. White columbine petals were braided through her long red hair. Her white, fringed doeskin dress was adorned with row after row of tiny shells and delicate feathers. She also wore a necklace of woven red beads several rows wide, the weave being that of wampum strips.

Shanna again looked out toward the crowd and saw that all of Bold Wolf's people and their visitors were dressed especially fine today in their best garments. She was relieved that Running Deer and Chief Bent Arrow had not attended the wedding, although Bent Arrow had told Bold Wolf he and his wife would be there.

She grew suddenly solemn when she thought of someone else who was missing in the crowd. Jennie. She and Jennie had been fast friends for so long it seemed wrong that Jennie wasn't there to share Shanna's happiness on her wedding day.

Even Shanna's parents! Though they did not approve of the man Shanna was marrying, it seemed wrong that they could go so far in their resentment that they would not attend her marriage ceremony. She would only get married once in her lifetime. How could her parents not want to give her their blessings, especially now realizing just how much she loved Bold Wolf, and how much he loved *her*?"

She would try not to harbor a deep resentment inside her heart over her parents' coldness toward her. It was not in her nature to hold grudges. Yet this? Yes, this would be hard to forgive them!

She looked through a window of the council house. From this vantage point she could see hers and Bold Wolf's cabin. She hoped that Elizabeth was content, yet how could she not be when her mother was so intensely radiant? Surely Elizabeth had felt Shanna's happiness this morning when she had held her and talked to her.

As Shanna recalled those moments with her daughter, she was bubbling over inside, knowing that soon she would finally be Bold Wolf's wife! Soon she hoped to give Bold Wolf a son or daughter. Elizabeth would not be raised alone. She would have brothers and sisters to play with.

Thinking of all of her blessings, Shanna was filled with such joyous bliss she felt as though she were melting inside from happiness. She scooted closer to Bold Wolf, sighing when he gave her a soft, warm, loving smile that made her heart sing.

"I love you," she whispered, shivering sensually when he mouthed the same words back to her.

When the dancing and singing suddenly stopped and silence vibrated around the huge council house, all eyes were transfixed on Shanna and Bold Wolf. Shanna knew that meant there was only one final formality and she would finally, *gloriously,* be Bold Wolf's wife.

She smiled over at him as he reached for a robe made from the white pelts of rabbits, draped it over his arm, then stood up and stepped from the platform. He turned to Shanna and reached a hand out for her.

Her heart pounding, her knees weak from excitement, Shanna gave Bold Wolf a radiant smile, took his hand, then stepped down from the platform and stood before him.

Shanna's pulse raced as Bold Wolf eased his hands from hers, then unfolded the robe and held it out between them. Taking the corners, he drew the robe around both of their shoulders, enveloping both in a single cloak, to signify the finalization of their marriage.

"To you I give my life, my love, my devotion," Bold Wolf murmured, his eyes holding Shanna's. "Today you are as one with me. You are as one with my *people.* I promise you a lifetime of happiness, my Shanna."

Tears of pure joy streamed from Shanna's eyes. "To you I give my all, my everything," she murmured as she continued to look deeply into his eyes. "I promise you that I will always be here for you, through sickness, through health, through trials and tribulations, and through times of joy. Whenever you need me, I will be there. My love for you, Bold Wolf, is like the kiss of the sun on a cold winter's day. I promise *you* a lifetime of happiness, my Penobscot chief, my Bold Wolf."

The robe falling around them, fully enveloping them, Bold Wolf drew Shanna into his arms and gave her a long, deep kiss, his mouth urgent and eager.

In her passion, Shanna clung to him, his kiss filling her with a sweet, painful longing.

Then he drew away from her and pulled the robe from around them.

She was stunned when she found that everyone had noiselessly slipped out of the council house. Someone had even gone around and dropped the buckskin pelts down across the windows and the door, giving Bold Wolf and Shanna complete privacy.

"Everyone is gone," Shanna gasped, looking quickly up at Bold Wolf.

"The council house is now ours for the rest of the day and the full night," Bold Wolf said. He lifted her into his arms and carried her to the back of the huge room, where she now noticed that someone had spread many beautiful pelts and blankets across the floor, around which lay many beautiful wildflowers. The aroma wafting from the flowers was a mixture of sweetness, sage, and pine. Not far from the pallet were huge platters of prepared meats and vegetables, as well as fruit.

"It's so beautiful," Shanna said, trembling with ecstasy as Bold Wolf laid her down on the pallet of furs and as quickly lay down over her, his hands molding her breasts through the soft doeskin of her dress.

"*You* are beautiful and you are my *wife*," Bold Wolf said huskily, then gave her a frenzied kiss, his tongue surging through her lips.

A spinning sensation rose up and flooded Shanna's body as she arched her body against his. "I want you," she whispered as he slid his mouth from her lips, to kiss her eyes closed. "I have never wanted you as badly as now, Bold Wolf. Please . . . oh, please . . ."

His heart pounding, his need for Shanna deep and passionate, Bold Wolf rose and stood over her. He started yanking off his clothes, while she just as desperately removed hers, hungrily watching his flesh being revealed as each piece of clothing was tossed aside.

Then Bold Wolf knelt over Shanna, his knees straddling her. He reached for one of her hands and placed it on his throbbing manhood. She didn't have to be

told what to do. As she moved her hand on him, she
watched his eyes glaze over with passion.

And when he threw his head back and moaned, his
long hair reaching down and brushing against Shanna's stomach, she moved her hand more quickly.

When he stopped her and stretched out on his back,
she straddled him and sighed with ecstasy. He shoved
himself up into her and began his deep, upward
thrusts, each thrust magnificently filling her even
more deeply.

Her breasts high and taut, Shanna gasped with rapture when he reached up and filled his hands with
them, his thumbs tweaking the pink, soft nipples to a
tautness. She rode him, and the pleasure spread
through her body in crashing, hot waves.

Then he placed his hands at her waist and lifted her
from him. He slid over her and entered her with one
eager, smooth, strong movement. Thrusting hard, his
mouth eager and hot on her lips, he pressed her body
into the soft pelts beneath her.

Her legs opened wide to him, Shanna writhed, only
half aware of the whimpering sounds she made as she
felt herself reaching the ultimate of pleasure.

She then watched in wonder as he moved away
from her and knelt down between her legs, exploring
her soft and swollen place with his lips and tongue.
This way of making love was so foreign to Shanna, it
even seemed forbidden. She scarcely breathed as she
watched him burrow his face deeper into her soft
fronds of hair. Then Shanna closed her eyes and cried
out with pleasure when his wet tongue stroked her
woman's center, making soft explosions of ecstasy go
off inside her brain.

Twining her fingers through his thick black hair,
Shanna drew him closer, unable to fight off this need

that was suddenly there, building, spreading, lighting her on fire inside!

But when she felt the threat of going over the edge without him inside her, she framed his face between her gentle hands and brought him up so that their eyes could meet and hold. She did not have to voice aloud what she wished from him. He took her hands from his face, slid his body upward, then shoved his manhood deeply into her folds. In only two thrusts, they both experienced the wonders of their lovemaking as they moaned and clung and rocked and swayed.

Afterward, totally satiated, Shanna lay beside Bold Wolf, panting. When he reached over and slid a flower into her hair, she smiled at him.

"I still taste you on my mouth," he whispered, then brushed his lips across hers. "Now you also taste yourself."

Shanna ran a finger across her lips, then smiled up at Bold Wolf. "What you did was so different from how you have made love to me before," she murmured. "It seems so . . . so primitive."

"It is something quite naturally done between a man and a wife," he said, gently kneading one of her breasts. "Did it not give you intense pleasure?"

"Yes, and so much that it was somewhat frightening," Shanna said. She closed her eyes with renewed rapture when he bent low and swept his tongue around her nipple.

He then stretched out beside her again. "Nothing we share should ever be frightening, for however I choose to make love to you, it is done with much love and caring," Bold Wolf said huskily. "So it is with how you choose to love me."

"I only know of two ways to pleasure you," Shanna said, propping herself up on an elbow as she gazed at him. "One is by using my hand, the other is by how you make love to my body."

"There are other ways," Bold Wolf said, giving her a slow, teasing smile.

"Like *what*?" Shanna asked, sitting up next to him.

"You truly wish to know?" Bold Wolf asked, questioning her with his eyes.

"I want to do what I can, *always,* to make you happy," Shanna murmured. "So, yes, tell me what you want of me. I shall do it."

He took her gently by her arm. "Sit beside me like this," he said, guiding her. "Then, Shanna, place your lips . . ."

When he guided her lips to his manhood, which was again swelling as a result of their conversation, she wasn't quite sure what he was asking of her.

But recalling how he had made love to her in such a way, she had to believe that somehow she could make him feel the same sort of pleasure with her mouth.

"Slowly . . . gently . . ." Bold Wolf said as he guided her lips to his waiting manhood. He sucked in a wild breath of pleasure when her tongue gently touched him there. "Open your lips for me. Then . . . then . . . move your tongue as you know how to move your hands on me."

So badly wanting to please him, already aware of how this way of making love made one feel, she swept her tongue around him, then slowly lowered her mouth over him.

When his body stiffened and he groaned, she jerked quickly away from him for fear of having hurt him.

"I'm sorry," she murmured, her eyes wide.

He looked up at her and laughed softly. "Sorry for what?" he said huskily. "For giving me such pleasure I feel as though I am floating?"

"Then what I did didn't hurt you?" Shanna asked, her eyes innocently wide. "You . . . stiffened. You groaned."

"It is a natural response from a man whose body is turning to hot ecstasy," he said, sighing and closing his eyes when she returned her mouth to him and slowly stroked him.

With pleasure throbbing through him in such heated splashes, Bold Wolf caught his breath, hardly daring to breathe. When he could hardly bear the intensity of the pleasure any longer, and wanting to be inside her again when he reached the ultimate of passion, he eased her away from him, led her beneath him, then entered her in one quick thrust.

"I will hold off until you have reached your own level of passion," Bold Wolf whispered into her ear. "I can never be selfish in my lovemaking. I want always to share it with you, equally."

"You do not have to wait long," she whispered back, her face hot with the building pleasure. "My darling, oh, my darling, how I love you."

Again they went over the edge into ecstasy together, then rested in each other's arms.

"We shouldn't stay here for too long," Shanna said, brushing a kiss across Bold Wolf's stomach. "I'm so anxious to be with Elizabeth for the first time as a family."

"I want also to be with our daughter, but we will not see anyone now until tomorrow," Bold Wolf said. He smiled at her as she looked quickly up at him. "Do you not see the food? The flowers? The wood that has been brought in for the night fire? It is for us to enjoy the whole night through, my wife. The council house has been turned into our lover's lair."

Shanna sat up and looked around her, then looked down at Bold Wolf. "It is all so wonderful, but I didn't tell Singing Owl that we would be gone for that long," she murmured.

"That has been taken care of," Bold Wolf said, taking her by her wrists, bringing her down next to him again. "Like I said, my wife, tonight is ours, totally ours."

He drew her close to his hard body and gave her a long, deep kiss.

She twined her arms around his neck and reveled in these moments that she had for so long dreamed about, and had too often feared were an impossible dream.

"Say it again," she whispered against his lips.

"Say what?" he asked, gazing into her eyes.

"Call me your wife," she whispered, running her fingers through his thick, long, black hair. "Please let me hear it again, my love."

"My wife," he said huskily. "You are my wife."

"My husband," she said in turn. "Oh, darling, you are now my *husband*, truly, truly my *husband*."

Again they kissed, long and sweet.

Shanna smiled a secret smile, for tonight she had a special tidbit of news that she had not yet shared with her husband. She only realized today that she had not yet had her blood flow for this month.

That could mean that the very first time they had made love she might have become pregnant!

She would not tell him just yet. She would wait until she was sure, for she never wanted to disappoint him over anything.

Ah, it was such a delicious thing, to suspect that a child might even now be growing inside her womb!

35

How do I love thee? Let me count the ways.
I love thee to the depth and breadth and height
My soul can reach.
                    —ELIZABETH BARRETT BROWNING

It was *kik-ai-gizus,* Planting Moon, the month of May.
Through the entire nine months of her pregnancy,
Shanna had been pampered so much, she was glad
that finally today she was well into her labor pains.
She had found early on, shortly after she had told
Bold Wolf of her pregnancy, that it was the custom
of the Penobscot people to give their pregnant women
constant attention. Anything Shanna wanted had been
given to her, especially whatever food she craved.
Shanna had been watched closely by everyone, making
sure she didn't look at anything ugly, for if she did,
the child might also be ugly.

But now, while she was moving toward the moment
of delivery, it was just a midwife and the village shaman who were with her. Bold Wolf was not even allowed to enter the cabin until she had given birth to
their child.

Lying on a soft layer of blankets, her body racked
in pains, and wearing nothing but a sheen of sweat,
Shanna fought against crying out when the pains were
now only seconds apart.

"I want Bold Wolf," she said, giving Cloud Racer,
the Penobscot shaman, a pleading look.

As he had moments before when she had requested

Bold Wolf's presence, the shaman, with his long and flowing black hair and his loose buckskin robe, ignored her. He stood over her, shaking his rattle and chanting, while White Rain, the village midwife, knelt beside the bed, gently stroking Shanna's large abdomen.

Shanna gave White Rain a soft, pleading look. "Is Elizabeth all right?" she murmured, feeling comfortable with this round-faced woman, for her sister was Singing Owl.

White Rain was just as gentle and sweet as Singing Owl. Shanna felt assured that White Rain would help make Shanna's childbirth an easy one.

"You must not think of Elizabeth at this time," White Rain said softly. "Concentrate now on pressing down. As I push on your abdomen, shove, Shanna. Shove. It is time for the child to make its entrance into the world. It is ready. You must help it."

Shanna gripped the sides of the bed and closed her eyes. She pressed her lips tightly together to keep from screaming, then pushed with all her might as the pain came in great leaps of fire inside her.

"It is almost here!" White Rain cried. "I will reach up inside you and help the child. Bear with me, Shanna, for what I will do will cause you more pain, but only briefly. The child needs just a little encouraging."

When she felt herself being stretched as White Rain slid her hands up inside her, the pain was so severe she felt as though she might faint. Shanna thrashed her head from side to side, her lips tightly pursed.

"It is coming!" White Rain said. "I have the child's head and now . . . and now . . . all of it!"

Shanna felt an instant relief when she felt the child slide from inside her. She started to look down to see the child, then grew wide-eyed with wonder when the pains gripped her again and she felt something else moving inside her.

White Rain cut the navel cord and, as Shanna's firstborn gave off its first cries of life, White Rain handed the baby quickly to the shaman and was there for the second child—just in time, as he popped his head out and then slid into White Rain's waiting arms.

"Two!" White Rain cried. "You have two children instead of one, and they are both boys!"

Shanna was so taken aback by the news, she was at a loss of words. Although she had gained an exorbitant amount of weight, never had she suspected she was carrying twins within her womb. She had blamed the weight on the amount of food that was constantly urged on her by the pampering women of the village.

"Twins?" she murmured, struggling to sit up to see them. "Bold Wolf . . . and I . . . have two sons?"

Her question was ignored. White Rain was too involved in cutting the second cord while the shaman stood by holding the other child, no longer chanting, just gazing in wonder from child to child.

And then Shanna felt more movement inside her. She was again overwhelmed with excruciating pain.

Wide-eyed and stunned, she stretched out again on the bed, thinking that a third child was going to enter the world. "It's coming," she cried as she felt something else sliding from within her. "Another child!"

"No, it is not another child," White Rain said, laughing softly, laying the twin she was holding up next to Shanna. "Shanna, it is only the afterbirth."

Shanna scarcely heard what she said, for she was totally mesmerized by her first look at her adorable, tiny bundle of joy who lay beside her. His dark eyes so like his father's, he gazed trustingly back at her.

For a moment Shanna was transported back to

when she had found Elizabeth, so tiny and defenseless that day by the pond.

"You are so beautiful," Shanna whispered, as she ran a trembling hand across the copper skin of her son.

She sighed with wonder when her other child was placed next to his brother. "Oh, just look at *you,*" she murmured, seeing that *his* skin was as pink as *hers.* Even his eyes and his slight shock of hair were the color of hers.

"One in your father's likeness," she whispered proudly. "And one in your mother's."

The shaman went outside the cabin and got Bold Wolf.

Bold Wolf hurried inside, stood over the bed, and stared, mesmerized by the sight of his wife and his *two* sons lying next to her. He was so awestruck that he had fathered twins, and so relieved that Shanna had come through the deliveries all right, he could find no words to express his deep gratitude and joy.

"Bold Wolf, Elizabeth has not only one, but *two* brothers," Shanna said, laughing softly. "I shouldn't have been so surprised, for my parents also had twins."

The thought of her brothers and her parents made her sad, for today was something they should have shared with her. She fought back tears, knowing they might never see her children. She would not allow that to spoil these precious moments with her beloved husband and their newborn children.

"You have seen and now you must leave again," White Rain said, gently touching Bold Wolf on the arm. "Step out for a moment while I bathe both Shanna and the children."

"But he hasn't held them yet," Shanna said, surprised that Bold Wolf had to leave so abruptly after having just seen his sons.

"He has forever and ever to hold them," White Rain said. White Rain smiled at Bold Wolf, and he knelt down to give Shanna a kiss. Shanna returned the kiss, then watched him leave.

"It will not take long to do what is required after birthing," White Rain said, bringing a basin over next to the bed, setting it on the floor.

Shanna watched as the children were bathed.

She then turned and watched what the shaman was doing, her eyes widening when she saw that he was cutting up the children's removed navel cords.

"Why are you doing that?" she asked.

"The cords must be cut, wrapped up, and burned, then buried," Cloud Racer said matter-of-factly. "If this is not done, the children will grow up with a tendency to snoop, habitually prying as if searching for something."

Seeing this as quite peculiar, yet realizing it was a Penobscot custom that she would have to understand, Shanna didn't question him further. She watched him leave with the wrapped-up pieces, then again turned her attention to her sons. One was already bathed and dressed in a soft white cotton gown. The other began crying as White Rain bathed him.

"Don't you think they are hungry?" Shanna asked, aware now of how her breasts seemed hot and throbbing.

"They cannot feed from your breasts until you drink what I have prepared for you," White Rain said, now slipping a gown on the other child.

Shanna ached to hold her children again, but would wait patiently until White Rain was through with what was customary. She had been told earlier about what she would be required to drink after giving birth.

After delivery, all Penobscot women were given a concoction of boiled yellow ash leaves, which was thought to cleanse the new mother's insides before the children nursed from her breasts.

"First, though, you must be bathed on the outside and dressed in a nursing gown," White Rain said. She emptied the basin of water outside, then came in with another basin of fresh, warm water for Shanna's sponge bath.

Anxious to get through all of the required rituals, wanting to hold her children again, eager to feed them, and so badly wanting Bold Wolf to be there sharing all of these firsts with her and their sons, it was hard for Shanna to lay there as White Rain bathed her.

Finally that was over and Shanna wore a soft cotton gown. She took a wooden cup from White Rain and placed it to her lips. Because Shanna had been told that the concoction was bitter and strong, she tried to hold her breath while she drank it. But it was so horrible, she could not help but gag and choke on it.

"You have done well today," White Rain said, placing a gentle hand on Shanna's arm. "For having not cried once during your labor and while giving birth to your sons, you have proved that you are a courageous woman. Bold Wolf will boast of you forever while discussing matters of family with his friends."

Shanna didn't feel so proud at this moment. The vile-tasting concoction was making her stomach churn. She gladly relinquished the empty cup to White Rain.

"Gently, now," White Rain said, lifting one child and placing him in Shanna's left arm, close to her left breast. She then placed the other child in Shanna's right arm, then slid both of Shanna's breasts free of the gown and placed the children's lips to each of the nipples.

"I shall now go for Bold Wolf," White Rain said, gathering up her paraphernalia and walking toward the door.

"Thank you, White Rain, for everything," Shanna murmured, a quiet joy rushing through her as she felt the wonder of her children suckling, their tiny hands softly kneading her breasts.

"When you have another child, I will be there, also, for you," White Rain said, smiling at Shanna over her shoulder, then left the cabin.

Bold Wolf hurried inside again and scooted a chair close to the bed. Evening was approaching, with the soft warble of birds in the trees. Shanna could see through the window that the sky was pink from the sunset.

"My wife, oh, how proud I am of you," Bold Wolf said thickly. He wanted to hold the children, but knew he could be patient for a while longer. It was enough to be able to sit there and see his sons feeding from their mother's breasts, Shanna's contentment showing in her gentle, sweet smile and the radiance of her violet eyes.

"Bold Wolf, I never knew that holding my very own children could give me such a deep, wonderful feeling of satisfaction," Shanna murmured. "Oh, darling, I must be careful never to show any partiality between Elizabeth and our sons. I never want her to feel second to them just because they were born of our special love for one another."

"You, who are a woman of such deep compassion, will know how to spread your love three ways so that none of them will ever feel chosen over the others," Bold Wolf said softly. "We are now three times blessed, Shanna."

Shanna thought back to her mother when she gave birth to her twins. From the very moment the boys came into the world, it seemed that her mother complained and was annoyed by their presence. Shanna had to believe that was why they had turned into troubled children who fussed and feuded with each other as soon as they were old enough to know how.

"I never want our sons to behave like my twin brothers," Shanna blurted out. "Tommie and Terrie aren't happy little boys. We must make certain our sons always feel wanted."

Bold Wolf took one of her hands in his. "My wife, you were not born in your mother's image," he said thickly. "There is not one thing about her that is seen in you. That she resents her sons does not mean you will resent yours. Your love is genuine; hers is false. Is not that enough for you to know that you worry for naught?"

"I know that I worry needlessly over so many things," Shanna said, laughing softly. She gazed down at first one son, then the other. "And I must stop that, mustn't I? I have no worries in the world, do I?"

Just as she said that, her thoughts went to Jennie. She looked quickly up at Bold Wolf. "I so wish that Jennie could know about the children and could come to Indian Island and see . . . and hold them," she said, her voice breaking. "Can you find a way, darling, to tell her?"

"Yes, she will know," Bold Wolf said, nodding.

"Thank you, darling," Shanna said. "Jennie means so much to me."

She gazed down at her babies, then smiled up at Bold Wolf, as she eased one away from a breast. "I think the children are fed enough for now," she said, finding it hard to manipulate both children at once, yet knowing that she would only learn by doing. "I think it's time their daddy holds them."

Bold Wolf stiffened as he lifted one of the children

away from Shanna. He laughed softly when the child emitted a loud burp as he drew him over and cradled him in his arms.

"I forgot to burp him," Shanna said, giggling. "I have so much to remember . . . to *learn.* I'm somewhat luckier, though, than most new mothers. I watched my mother with my brothers, and Emily with Elizabeth. I know how much of it is done."

Bold Wolf gazed down at the child as he slowly rocked him in his arms. "And so we have one that is pale-skinned and one whose skin is like his father's," he said, taking in this child's violet eyes and pink skin, laughing softly over the shock of hair that favored his mother.

"Yes, and I believe, in our excitement of the moment, that we failed to name our sons," Shanna said, laying the other child out on the blankets at her side so that she could watch him as he looked slowly around him, familiarizing himself with his new surroundings.

"Names, ah, yes, names," Bold Wolf said, smiling over at Shanna.

"You wouldn't go over names with me before the children were born because you said you thought that was bad luck," Shanna said. "Well, now, darling, I think you can see our luck is quite good today, so let's think of names that will fit these two tiny precious sons of ours."

"We agreed that it would be something Penobscot, not white, did we not?" Bold Wolf said, questioning her with his eyes.

"Yes, and I still feel that way," Shanna said softly. "Even Elizabeth should be given a name that your people will feel more comfortable with."

Bold Wolf laughed throatily. "And so today is name-giving day," he said.

Then he grew serious and became lost in deep thought. "Let me name Elizabeth first," he then said. "You found her beside the water, so let us name her Dancing Water."

"That is beautiful," Shanna said, sighing. "Yes. From now on we will call her Dancing Water."

Bold Wolf looked from son to son. "And now for our sons," he said. "I want something that will be with them proudly into their adult years, something like Wild Spirit for one and . . . and Fire Wolf for the other?"

"Wild Spirit . . . Fire Wolf . . ." Shanna said, again marveling over how quickly Bold Wolf could come up with names that pleased her. "Yes, those are wonderful, brave, courageous-sounding names, Bold Wolf. They truly match how our sons' personalities will be."

"The child whose skin matches mine will be Fire Wolf," Bold Wolf said softly. "The child whose skin matches yours will be called Wild Spirit."

Shanna gave Bold Wolf a slow smile. "Admit to me, Bold Wolf, that you did not just now come up with such intriguing names." She laughed softly. "You've been sorting through names in your mind for a while now, haven't you?"

His twinkling eyes were all the answer she needed to know that she was right.

"Now that the name-giving is finished, I must leave for a moment," Bold Wolf said, easing the child in his care back up next to Shanna, resting peacefully in the crook of her left arm.

"Why are you leaving?" Shanna asked, a keen disappointment entering her eyes as she watched him walk determinedly toward the door. "Why must you go *now*? I was so enjoying being with you as a family."

"One member of the family is not here," Bold Wolf

said, giving Shanna a look over his shoulder just before lifting the entrance flat and stepping outside.

"Oh, yes, dear, dear Elizabeth," Shanna murmured, always anxious to see her, even when they were separated for only moments at a time. She giggled. "I mean dear *Dancing Water*."

She passed the time until Bold Wolf's return by watching the babies and caressing them. Both were contentedly asleep now, their tiny lips sometimes moving, as though they thought they were still at her breasts, suckling.

She heard movement at the door and expected to see Bold Wolf returning with Elizabeth. But instead she had to take a second, quick, unbelieving look.

"Jennie?" Shanna said as her friend rushed across the room and bent low to kiss Shanna on the cheek.

"Oh, Jennie, how did you get here?" Shanna asked, her excitement causing her heart to race. "Do my parents know?"

"I no longer live with your parents," Jennie said somberly. She sat on the chair next to the bed. "They weren't the most pleasant people to live with. When a new music instructor came and took over Roscoe Lovett's position, and he saw the strain I was living under, he and his wife offered me a room at their home. I have been there ever since."

"Did Bold Wolf know this?" Shanna said, arching an eyebrow. "He must have, to know where to send word to you about me being in labor today."

"No, it was by sheer accident that I happened to come today to see you and tell you the news that I was free now to come and go as I please," Jennie said, laughing. "Lord, when I arrived here and I was told that you had just given birth to twins, I could hardly believe it."

"I'm so glad you are here," Shanna said, taking one of Jennie's hands and squeezing it.

"Are you going to tell your parents about the babies?" Jennie asked guardedly.

"Bold Wolf sent a message to them today that I was in labor," Shanna said, her voice breaking. "As you can see, they couldn't care less, or they . . . they would be here now."

"The babies are so adorable," Jennie said, clasping her hands excitedly on her lap. "I won't ask to hold one because I am not all that good with children. Even though there were several much younger than I at our home, I never took time with them. I . . . was too busy defending myself against my abusive father. I scarcely noticed anything else."

"Jennie, you said that a new music instructor has come to Old Town," Shanna said softly. "Does that mean Mr. Lovett quit?"

"No. No one has heard from Roscoe Lovett," Jennie said gloomily. "I have no idea where he is, or if . . . if he is even still alive."

Giggling and the pattering of tiny feet into the cabin drew both friends' eyes to Elizabeth as she ran unsteadily into the room. Only recently she had taken her first true steps. Bold Wolf followed her into the room.

"Oh, Elizabeth, wonderful little Elizabeth," Jennie said, sweeping the child up into her arms. She hugged her, then showed her the twins. "See your brothers, Elizabeth?"

Jennie looked quickly over at Shanna. "What are their names?"

Shanna told her their names, then explained how Elizabeth had just acquired an Indian name herself.

"You are so lucky," Jennie said, rocking Elizabeth in her arms. "Perhaps one day, after I tire of playing my violin, I might find a man of my dreams and get married and have my own brood of children."

"Brood?" Shanna said, giving her an amused look, then laughed happily along with Jennie and Bold Wolf.

But then Jennie grew quiet and tears welled in her eyes. She fell to her knees beside Shanna's bed. "I cannot help but be worried sick over Roscoe Lovett," she cried. "What *do* you think has happened to him, Shanna? When I go into the music studio, I feel his presence everywhere, yet he is not there."

"I'm sure one day you will hear from him again," Shanna said, smoothing a fallen lock of hair back from Jennie's eyes. "Just go on with your life and be happy. If he is meant to be a part of it, then in time he will return. If not, then, Jennie, don't let it ruin what you have going for you. I see you even now, Jennie, standing on that vast stage before a crowd with a roaring applause after you have finished a concerto with a world-famous orchestra."

"Truly?" Jennie said, wiping tears from her eyes with the backs of her hands.

"Yes, you are going to be a star," Shanna said softly. "You will have your dream as I have mine."

She and Bold Wolf exchanged sweet, knowing smiles.

Jennie sprang to her feet. "I don't know what I was thinking, bringing my trouble to your doorstep," she exclaimed. "I'm sorry, Shanna. I'm truly sorry."

Shanna reached for Jennie's hand. "Dear friend, our home is your home. Anytime you need to talk to me about anything, please feel free to do so," she said. "I would do anything for you, Jennie. Surely you know that."

Bold Wolf drew Jennie into his arms. "Jennie, you

are always welcome in our home," he said. "Come often."

Jennie returned his hug, then turned on her heel and smiled down at Shanna. "I truly must go now," she said softly. "I must return home and practice my violin. But the next time I come, I will stay longer."

"And don't wait too long for that next visit," Shanna said.

"I won't," Jennie said, backing away from the bed. She blew Shanna a kiss, then hurried from the cabin.

Shanna frowned up at Bold Wolf. "I can't help but be afraid for Jennie," she said, her voice drawn. "Who *are* those people she's living with? Can she truly trust them? And where is Roscoe Lovett? I still see him as Jennie's true salvation."

"Only if he is alive to *be* there for her," Bold Wolf said blandly.

Shanna noted the doubt in Bold Wolf's words. Hearing that, she knew there was most certainly something to worry about, for he was one who always thought positively about things and encouraged her not to worry.

Now Shanna *was* truly worried about both Jennie's and Roscoe Lovett's welfare!

36

Not as all other women are
Is she that to my soul is dear;
Her glorious fancies comes from far,
Beneath the silver evening star.
—JAMES RUSSELL LOWELL

The twins, now two moons old, and Elizabeth, who
now answered solely to Dancing Water, now already
a raving beauty at the age of three, had been left with
Pale Star as Shanna joined Bold Wolf on a moose
hunt. Although Shanna was the only woman on the
hunting expedition, she did not feel out of place
among the hunters who were paddling silently up the
river in their canoes. Bold Wolf had invited her.

She never turned down a chance to go with him
anywhere, for it always meant she not only would be
with him during the long hours of the day, when most
women sewed or cooked, but would also have the opportunity to learn more about ways of the Penobscot.

Bold Wolf sat even now at Shanna's side. He was
sharing his cape of buckskin with her. He had it
draped over them to ward off the approaching chill of
evening, as an oarsman took their canoe in swift
strokes toward home.

It was the middle of September, when the moose
were in their prime. The bulls were in their rutting
mood, and the cows were at their fattest. And this
time of year the moose, deer, and caribou were driven
to seek refuge from the flies that molested them by

fleeing to the lakes and rivers. Here the hunters in canoes easily sought and killed the large animals.

Shanna had been told that the rules for the distribution of the game were that the first man of the season to kill a deer or moose must divide the meat among the villagers as far as it would go. He would not eat of it himself, or he would damage his luck in the next hunt.

Likewise, two hunters traveling together in the same canoe must give each other their first kill, whatever it may be, before keeping either meat or pelts of their own. This was called *ada-be-gwaha,* gift.

It was just growing dusk now and the many canoes, in single file, were making their way back upriver toward Indian Island. The hunt had been good. Large slabs of moose and deer meat were piled high in each canoe. They were covered with sheets of buckskin until they arrived at the village, where the women would immediately start preparing the meat for smoking.

Shanna had seen this done each year now since she had married Bold Wolf. Whatever meat was not consumed fresh in camp was cut up into strips several inches thick and hung over a horizontal pole supported by two upright crotches, under which a fire was built lengthwise.

The meat was always smoked until it was dried like leather.

Sometimes a roofing of birch bark was built over the rack to keep off rain and to confine the heat and smoke.

This smoked meat could be kept indefinitely. It was eaten just as it was, or simmered in a stew.

Bold Wolf reached beneath the warm cape and took one of Shanna's hands. "My wife, did you enjoy your first hunt with your husband?" he asked, his eyes twinkling as he recalled how she had, without hesitation, helped him go after his first moose of the hunt after he had shot it with an arrow. If the arrow penetrates almost anywhere between the ribs, the animal will lie down after he has run awhile and roll on the arrow to dislodge it, driving it in farther until the result is fatal. When they had found the large, downed moose, it had already taken its last breaths and lay quietly waiting to be claimed. Bold Wolf would never forget Shanna's dismay in seeing that only one small arrow could kill such a large creature.

"I must say these two days have been quite interesting," Shanna said, laughing softly, interrupting his thoughts. "And yes, it's been wonderful being with you like this. Now when you tell me you are going on a hunt, I will be able to imagine, while you are gone, what you are doing."

"It is not always as simple a kill as today's was," Bold Wolf said, gazing proudly at the huge pile of fresh meat in their canoe.

Shanna followed his gaze and then looked over her shoulder at the many other canoes that were just as filled with meat.

"It will be a good winter for our people," she murmured. "No one will be hungry in our village."

"It is always good to hear you say 'our' people and 'our' village when you speak of the Penobscot," Bold Wolf said, squeezing her hand affectionately.

"Even though it has now almost been three moons since we spoke our vows, I still marvel over being with you among your people and knowing that I am your wife," Shanna murmured, gazing warmly into his eyes. "I never take it for granted, Bold Wolf, for I shall never forget the obstacles that once stood in our way."

"It is all behind us," Bold Wolf said, easing his hand from hers, sliding his arm around her waist. He drew her close to his side. "We have nothing now but sunshine ahead of us."

"My time with you as your wife *has* been all sunshine and laughter," she said, hardly worrying anymore about her parents, who still had not accepted her marriage to Bold Wolf and had not even seen their grandchildren. Shanna didn't allow herself to dwell on her past, for if she did, it would hurt too much.

But there *was* someone of her past she *still* could smile about: Jennie. Jennie was now on a world tour, playing her violin for concert audiences. The Dennisons', the people who had taken Jennie in, had seen that Jennie's dreams came true. Jennie had mastered the violin rapidly.

"What are you thinking so hard about *now*?" Bold Wolf asked.

"Jennie," she murmured, smiling. "Sweet Jennie. I am so happy for her. Just think, Bold Wolf. Finally she is following her dream all over the world."

"There is one thing missing in that dream," Bold Wolf said, his voice drawn.

"Yes, I know," Shanna said, sighing. "Roscoe Lovett."

She forked an eyebrow. "I wonder what happened to him, Bold Wolf," she murmured. "How could a man just up and disappear like that, unless . . . unless he is *dead*?"

The sight of their village only a short distance away caused them both to become quiet, looking for those who would be waiting on the banks of the river to see how successful their warriors were at the hunt these past two days.

Shanna could hardly wait to see her children, to *hold* them. Nothing was more important to her than being a wife and mother. She adored every minute with her twins and her darling Dancing Water. This had been the first time she was away from them for so long. She did not want to join hunts again unless she could take her children with her.

But she could not help but smile when she thought back to the hunt, and the excitement when they had finally found signs of moose. Bold Wolf had paddled his canoe noiselessly near the shore, where the game was known to come. Bold Wolf and his warriors had already been aware today of the scent of the moose.

"Scenting" had to be explained to Shanna. When a moose was alarmed, it emitted a scent that the hunters could recognize. The source of this scent lay in glands between the hind knees of the animal. The Penobscot said this was truly for *man's* benefit, so that the game could be scented out by him.

Once the moose had been scented, a man in each canoe, at frequent intervals, gave a call with a horn of rolled birch bark, taking advantage of the bull's autumnal passion. When the moose answered, the men put an appealing note into the call to make it sound like a female.

As the bull was lured to the bank by the fake call from the bark horn, where he thought a cow was feeding, the paddling in the canoes had stopped.

Shanna had watched, breathlessly, as Bold Wolf bent to his knees in the canoe, dipped some water in a canoe bailer, and poured it out to make a sound like a cow raising her dripping mouth from the stream, or urinating.

The bull, hearing this, came into view and proceeded to the spot, deviously and noisily, in order to frighten away or challenge a possible rival that might be bent on the same objective.

Shanna was in awe of the large moose as it came into view, searching desperately for the cow, even going knee-deep in the water, growing furious when he could not find the animal he wished to mate with.

While the bull stood in the water, Bold Wolf released the arrow into its side.

They all kept their canoes at a safe distance until the bull left the water and ran into the thicket, bellowing. Then they all paddled ashore and followed him.

Yes, it was exciting, somewhat even frightening, when Shanna saw the size of the downed animal. She had experienced the thrill of the hunt.

But she decided not to pursue hunting any further. She much preferred her role as mother. Her curiosity about hunting was satisfied.

They were now close enough to Indian Island to make out the faces of those who stood along the shore. When she saw Dancing Water and the twins standing with Pale Star, she began waving.

"My woman has not missed her children, has she?" Bold Wolf teased, chuckling as he watched Shanna's exuberance.

"Very much," Shanna said, so glad when the canoe was beached.

She jumped into the ankle-deep water, waded quickly to shore, and fell to her knees and gathered her children into her arms.

"My arms need to be larger," Shanna said, laughing as her three children snuggled against her. "Oh, Dancing Water, oh, Wild Spirit and Fire Wolf, have you missed your mommie?"

But Pale Star spoke Shanna's name solemnly. Seeing the look on Pale Star's face, made Shanna freeze inside.

"What is it, Pale Star?" she asked, easing her children away from her and standing.

"Word was brought from Old Town that your mother's health is failing her," Pale Star said. "Only moments ago your father was here, Shanna, asking for you."

Shanna paled. Her heart seemed to stop still, for she had not even seen her father since her marriage to Bold Wolf. And now he had come to the island asking for her?

"Oh, Lord, Mama must be terribly ill for Papa to have come to Indian Island," she cried. She gave Bold Wolf a desperate look as he now stood beside her. She grabbed his hands and clutched them tightly. "It's my mama, Bold Wolf. Papa came to our island. He came for *me*."

Bold Wolf's eyes widened. Then he frowned. "And what are you going to do?" he asked, feeling her hands trembling in his.

"I must go, Bold Wolf," Shanna said. She searched his eyes, wanting him to approve of her decision. Although her parents had treated her and her husband coldly and had not even cared to see their own grandchildren, it was not in Shanna's heart to return such callousness, especially not if her mother's health was failing.

"Then go," Bold Wolf said, sighing deeply. "Do you want me to accompany you there? Or do you want to go alone?"

"I so badly want you to be with me, should I discover that Mama is dying," Shanna said, swallowing hard. "Papa had to know that if he came for me, you would be included also."

She gazed down at her children, who were now farther up the riverbank, laughing and playing and rolling in the tall, green grass. "Even the children should accompany us there," she said softly. "I . . . I think it's time that my parents finally realize they have grandchildren. And if Mama is gravely ill, it is important that my children know her before she dies."

Bold Wolf reached up and framed her face between his hands. "Wife, you are again looking into the future and seeing things that just might not be," he said thickly. "It has been a while since you have done this. Do not do it now."

"I know," Shanna said, tears splashing from her eyes. "But, Bold Wolf, you *know* that Papa would not have made that trip across the river unless . . . unless my mama's illness is serious."

"Perhaps," Bold Wolf said, "he has only needed an excuse to come for a long time, and he has finally found it."

"I hope you are right," Shanna said, then flung herself into his arms and hugged him. "Oh, Bold Wolf, how awful it is of me to say that I fear going among my family again more than I might fear my mama dying. I cannot help but be so hurt by how they have treated me, and also you and our children. How am I to behave now toward *them*?"

"You are a woman with a big heart and much compassion, so do not fret so much, my wife, over how you might behave," Bold Wolf said, holding her. "Your heart will guide you into what is the right thing to do and to say."

"Mommie, Mommie." Dancing Water yanked on Shanna's skirt.

Shanna bent to her knees, drew her daughter into her arms, and hugged her.

"Mommie, a man came today and told me that he was my grandfather," Dancing Water said, a soft questioning in her dark eyes.

Shanna's heart seemed to stop still, knowing that her father had opened his heart in such a way to this child. It was hard to believe that he could have changed, yet perhaps he had missed Shanna enough to do anything now to have her back in his life.

Shanna smiled and gazed into Dancing Water's eyes. "Do you want to see your grandfather again?" she asked softly. She swallowed hard. "Do you want to see your grandmother?"

"Grandmother?" Dancing Water said, a puzzled look on her face. "Grandfather? Mommie, tell me about them. Father has talked of his to me. Why haven't you ever talked of yours?"

Shanna paled, for she only now realized just how wrong she had been not to teach her children about their grandparents. Yet she would not feel guilty about this. She had never known that her parents would ever own up to the title of grandparents.

"My darling, sometimes life can become confused," Shanna said, reaching up to smooth a fallen lock of black hair from her daughter's brow. "*People* can become confused."

37

His heart in me keeps him and me in one;
My heart in him his thoughts and senses guides.
                                        —SIR PHILIP SIDNEY

As Shanna entered her mother's bedroom with quiet footsteps, a kerosene lamp's soft wavering lit her way. A strong scent of medicine hung heavily in the room, so strong it made her throat sting.

Then she stood directly over her mother's bed and saw just how ill her mother was. She stifled a sob of despair behind her hand.

"Mama," she said, choking on a sob that quickly rose in her throat. "Oh, Mama."

When her mother didn't respond, her eyes remaining closed, Shanna's gaze swept over her mother's face and saw how flushed it was from the raging fever. She fell to her knees beside the bed and took one of her mother's hands in hers, flinching at the heat from her mother's hand.

"Doc Klein says that if your mother's temperature doesn't lower in the next few hours, she won't make it," Jordan said as he stepped up beside the bed. His eyes wavered as Shanna looked quickly up at him. "I thought you needed to be here, Shanna, should the worst happen."

"You should have sent for me well before now," Shanna said, her voice breaking. "Papa, should Mama

die and I don't have a chance to make peace with her,
I . . . will . . . never forgive you."

Jordan pulled a chair up beside the bed and
slumped into it. "I know that I'm guilty of things you
don't understand," he said sullenly. He gazed into
Shanna's eyes. "But, Shanna, how could *you* have
abandoned your *family*?"

"Me . . . abandon . . . my family?" she gasped,
paling. "Papa, it was you who abandoned me."

She turned her eyes quickly from his and swallowed
hard. "You know that is true," she murmured. She
paused and sighed. "Anyhow, Papa, my family is now
my husband and children," she said thickly. "Not
you . . . and Mama."

"Shanna—"

"Papa, now is not the time to talk about our
problems . . . yours and mine," she said. She gave him
a cold stare. "I don't want to disturb Mama. Although
she's in a strange sort of sleep, she just might be able
to hear us. It would be dreadful if the last thing she
heard before . . . before dying was her husband and
daughter arguing."

"Of course you're right," Jordan said, wiping tears
from his eyes. "Shanna, I do need to ask you one
more thing."

Shanna frowned at him. "Papa, *please*?" she softly
insisted.

"Why didn't you bring the children with you?" Jordan asked. His eyes misted again with more tears.
"Why didn't Bold Wolf come with you? I sent not
only for you, but also your husband and children."

"And they were going to come, but . . . I decided
at the last minute that they shouldn't," Shanna
murmured.

She was stunned to see something in her father's
eyes that she hadn't seen since he had discovered her

devoted love for Bold Wolf. She could actually see a deep hurt! He was finally feeling what she had felt when he had turned his back on her and her family!

Torn with emotion, wanting to think that his feelings were sincere and that he truly did feel remorse, Shanna looked quickly away from him, her heart pounding.

Oh, how she had so badly wanted to have contact with her parents and her twin brothers these past years. Yet only now, with her mother possibly on her deathbed, was her father reaching out for her, for all of the wrong reasons.

Surely it frightened him to think of losing his wife and being without his soul mate, his truest friend. Now he wanted to open relations again with Shanna and her family only because *he* didn't want to be alone in the world.

Of course, he had his twins, but she knew they wouldn't be enough for him. Yes, he loved them, but they would not be enough for him for companionship. The truth be known, she imagined the twins rankled his nerves even more now than they did when they were smaller.

It made her heart sink even now to remember how they had shunned her moments ago when she had entered the house. She hadn't seen them these past years. To them she was nothing more than a stranger! As were they to her. She had hardly recognized them. Their legs were so long, they had lost their baby fat, they were dressed like young men in suits that matched their father's.

"Shanna, answer me," Jordan said, his voice more firm. "Why did you not bring your husband and children with you today?"

Shanna turned to him. Their eyes locked. "Papa, it wasn't because I wanted to play the same heart-wrenching games you play," she said, her voice tight. "I didn't ask them to stay at Indian Island to cause you hurt. I did it because I thought it was best not to bring them into a home filled with sickness. You didn't say what was wrong with Mama. How could I know whether or not it was contagious? In fact, Papa, after I mentioned that concern to Bold Wolf, he didn't want even *me* to come."

"But you did come," Jordan said thickly.

Shanna turned wavering eyes to her mother. "Yes, I came," she murmured. She swallowed hard and wiped tears from her eyes. "I had to come, Papa," she said, sobbing. "I love Mama. I . . . have missed her so much."

When she felt his hand on her arm, she turned quick, questioning eyes to her father.

"Daughter, don't you know how much both your mother and I have missed you?" he said, a sob almost choking him as he drew her up from her knees and pulled her into his arms. His body was racked with sobs as he desperately clung to her. "Shanna, Shanna, I was so wrong. Can you . . . ever forgive me?"

She had not been aware of how much she longed for those arms around her, longed to hear those words from her father. Shanna knew *now,* for she clung to him with a desperation that matched his. Her cheek pressed against his chest, her tears soaked into the coat of his black suit.

"Never again will I do anything to hurt you, Shanna," Jordan sobbed. "Oh, please, Shanna, forgive me. Please, Shanna, bring your family here and be a part of my life."

Again she thought of just why he might be asking this of her now, and stiffened against him.

"Shanna, what's wrong?" Jordan asked, his eyes

questioning her as she drew slowly away from him. "What did I say?"

"Papa, do you want me now only because . . . because you fear loneliness should Mama pass away?" Shanna asked, her voice wary.

"Shanna, please don't think that," Jordan pleaded. "I'm opening my heart and soul to you. I'm wanting to be a part of your life again. Please do not suspect things that are not there. I love you, Shanna. I've missed you."

Hoping that he was sincere, Shanna leaned into his arms again, reveling in her father's love again, having thought she had lost it forever.

"Shanna . . . ? Is . . . that . . . you?"

Her mother's faint voice caused Shanna's heart to leap inside her chest. She eased from her father's arms and fell to her knees again beside the bed, smiling when she saw that her mother's eyes were open and looking at her.

"Mama, oh, Mama, yes, it's Shanna," she said, reaching a gentle hand to her mother's cheek. "I'm here, Mama. I'm here."

Bernita lifted a tremoring hand from beneath the blankets, took Shanna's hand, and held it. "My fever isn't causing me to imagine you here at my bedside?" she murmured. "Shanna, it is truly you? You are here?"

"Yes, and I'm not going anywhere until I know you are all right," Shanna said, suddenly realizing that her mother's hand was not as hot as it was only moments ago. Surely that meant that her fever had broken and that she was going to get well.

"Your children?" Bernita asked through dry lips. "They are here? Is . . . Bold Wolf . . . ?"

"No, Mama. Since you were so ill, only I came,"

Shanna murmured. "But when you are strong enough, do you want them to come for a visit?"

Bernita looked past Shanna and gazed at Jordan. "If your . . . father . . . allows it, yes, Shanna, please bring your family and allow us to *all* be family," she said. Then, exhausted, she closed her eyes.

"I'm so thirsty," Bernita whispered. "My lips. My tongue. They are so dry."

"I'll go for some fresh water," Jordan said, lifting an empty pitcher from the bedside table. "I won't be long."

"Shanna . . . Shanna," Bernita whispered, her lips tremoring into a slow smile. "Finally you are here. Finally . . ."

"Yes, I am here," Shanna murmured. "I love you, Mama."

A commotion outside below the bedroom window drew Shanna's attention. She could hear the sound of excited voices and the racket of an approaching horse and wagon. Shanna glanced at her mother and noticed that she had fallen asleep again.

Curious about who had arrived and why there was such a turmoil, Shanna rose quietly from her knees, went to the window, and slowly lifted the shade.

She stared down at the wagon as several men helped Shanna's father take a body from it. She recoiled when she got a better look, the blood on the man's face and body proving that someone had shot or knifed him not only once, but several times.

Shivering, she quickly lowered the blind and sat down on the chair beside her mother's bed.

"The water," she whispered, remembering now that her father had left to get water for her mother. He had been sidetracked by the sudden arrival of the dead man.

"Mama," she whispered, gently touching her cheek. "I'll go for your water. I won't be long."

Closing the bedroom door behind her, Shanna walked down the long corridor, then slowly made her way down the staircase, wanting to avoid seeing any of the men who had brought the body to her father's mortuary. She had seen enough to know that they were a seedy bunch who were probably direct from a gambling house.

When she reached the foot of the stairs and made a turn to go toward the kitchen, she stopped. Her father hadn't yet made it back to his preparation room with the body. For some reason, her father and the men had gone on into the preparation room without the body, surely to prepare a table for it.

Her knees trembling as she stared at the man on the floor, the blood from his clothes and wounds soaking into a layer of sheets that her father had spread beneath him, up this close Shanna was able to make out the man's features.

"George Anderson!" she gasped, her feet feeling frozen to the floor upon her discovery. "It's . . . Jennie's father!"

"Good Lord, Shanna, what are you doing?" Jordan asked, rushing toward her. He stepped between her and the body. "Lord, Shanna, I didn't want you to see—"

"It's Jennie's father," Shanna said, looked wide-eyed up at Jordan. "Someone killed Jennie's father!"

"Yes. While he was gambling, someone caught him cheating," Jordan said. He placed an arm around Shanna's shoulder and led her into the library. He turned her and placed his hands on her shoulders. "Are you all right, Shanna? You are so pale. You aren't going to faint, are you?"

"No, it's just that I . . . I was so stunned to see that

it was him," Shanna said, trembling uncontrollably. She closed her eyes and swallowed hard. "I never liked that man, but . . . but no one deserves to die like he died."

"No, no one," Jordan said, drawing her into his arms, comforting her. "And that's not all he's suffered lately, Shanna."

"What do you mean?" Shanna asked, easing from his arms, gazing up at him.

"His wife left him a short while back," Jordan said thickly.

"She *did*?" Shanna found it hard to believe. The woman she knew had never seemed to have the backbone to do anything that might be in her best interests.

"Now maybe Jennie's brothers and sisters will be able to have a better life," Shanna murmured.

"No, I doubt that," Jordan said, sighing heavily.

"Why not, Papa?" Shanna asked.

"Before Bonnie Anderson left, she sent the children far away," Jordan said thickly.

"What do you mean, far away?" Shanna asked, finding this hard to follow.

"She divided the children up and sent them to various orphanages," Jordan said, sliding his hands into his front breeches pockets. "She had saved back money her husband never knew about. When she had enough, she sent some children on the train in one direction, the others elsewhere. She made sure they were so scattered, her husband would never be able to find them. Then she took off on a train to parts unknown. Who is to say where she is, or what sort of life she has now?"

"The children were just . . . given away?" Shanna said, remembering how she had found Elizabeth. Until that day she had never known just how cruel the world could be. As she grew older, she discovered that all

sorts of atrocities could be done to unsuspecting, innocent children.

"Shanna, let's not talk anymore about such things,"
Jordan said, again holding her, hugging her. "You take
your mother some fresh water. I'll get George into the
preparation room. I'll return to your mother's room as
soon as I can."

"The twins?" Shanna asked as she left the protective warmth of her father's arms. "Where are they?"

"Shanna, they've recently discovered a love of reading," Jordan said, smiling. "They're up in their rooms.
Shanna, I've never heard such silence in our house
as I hear now when they've got their noses stuck in
their books."

She laughed softly, then went to get the water.

When she entered her mother's bedroom with a
fresh pitcher of water, she found that Doc Klein had
slipped into the house. He was bending over Shanna's
mother with a stethoscope, listening to her lungs.

Shanna moved silently over to the bed and placed
the pitcher on the table, then smiled at Doc Klein as
he turned his dark eyes to her, eyes that were almost
hidden in the thick, shaggy gray brows that hung
over them.

"Well, if it isn't pretty little Shanna," Doc Klein
said, holding the small of his back as he straightened
up. He slung the stethoscope across his shoulder. "I've
got some good news for you, darlin'. Your mother is
fast on the road to recovery."

Shanna's heart warmed with those words. She gazed
down at her mother. Her mother smiling up at her
gave Shanna a gentle peace she remembered from
her childhood.

Shanna leaned over to kiss her mother's brow.
"Mama, did you hear what Doc Klein said?"

"I just wasn't ready to say good-bye yet," Bernita said, hugging Shanna.

"Just make sure she gets a lot of rest," Doc Klein said, snapping his satchel closed. "And, Bernita, drink lots of fluids. I don't want a repeated episode of bad kidneys."

"Kidneys?" Shanna asked, turning to the doctor and walking him to the door.

"Yep, as far as I can figure out, that's what caused the raging temperature," Doc Klein said. "I tried out one of my new homemade remedies on 'er. Seems to have worked well enough."

"Thank you," Shanna said, giving the short, squat doctor one of her widest smiles. Doc Klein nodded, then walked away.

Beaming with happiness, everything now finally falling into place again with her parents, Shanna sat down beside her mother's bed and helped her take slow sips of cold water from a glass.

"Shanna, I heard someone arriving shortly before Doc Klein," Bernita said, gently shoving the glass away from her lips. "Was someone brought for burial?"

"Yes," Shanna said, still having a hard time believing that Jennie's heartless, cruel father was dead. She received wires from time to time from Jennie. No one ever truly knew where she was until a concert was advertised in the *Bangor Daily News*.

Shanna wasn't sure if Jennie should even know just yet about the changes in her family. Jennie seemed so content now. Why tell her things that might upset her?

"Tell me about your children," Bernita said, taking Shanna's hand, twining her fingers through Shanna's.

"There is so much to tell," Shanna said, pride showing in her beaming eyes. "Mama, you should see the twins. Oh, Mama, you should see sweet Elizabeth. Did

you know that she now goes by an Indian name? We
have named her Dancing Water."

Shanna talked and talked of her family. It was wonderful for Shanna and Bernita, this sharing again between daughter and mother after what had seemed
like a lifetime of silence and heartbreak.

38

I love your eyes when the lovelight lies lit
with a passionate fire.
                                    —ELLA WHEELER WILCOX

It was late September, when the evening air had a
cool nip to it. An outdoor fire's flames reached high
into the darkening sky, reflecting on Shanna and Running Deer, who sat together on the riverbank on a
blanket, the other women from both tribes scattered
around the fire also on blankets or warm pelts.

Shanna had never been able to warm up to Running
Deer, for she could never get past the terrible thing
Running Deer had done to her daughter.

But Chief Bent Arrow was now dead and Brown
Buffalo, a younger man closer to Bold Wolf's age, was
now the Mohawk's acting chief. Bold Wolf and Brown
Buffalo forged close alliances, and now Shanna had
no choice but to be involved with Running Deer, if
only socially—for Running Deer had married Brown
Buffalo.

The two chiefs were almost inseparable. When Bold
Wolf hunted, Brown Buffalo hunted with him, their
wives thrown together as they awaited their return
from the hunt.

When Bold Wolf celebrated, Brown Buffalo celebrated with him, their wives again together.

And tonight, there was a clambake, both Bold Wolf
and Brown Buffalo together enjoying the fun.

Shanna had to make an effort to enjoy herself tonight. She sat on the blanket with Running Deer when it looked important to Bold Wolf that she make this sacrifice. Shanna and Running Deer were sitting somewhat away from the others because Running Deer's two-month-old baby was asleep in her arms, and when she awakened she would want immediate feeding.

Shanna, however, was ignoring Running Deer, for she did not enjoy small talk with her. Too often it drifted to Dancing Water. . . .

Shanna's eyes and heart were with her husband. He was resting on his haunches with the Penobscot and Mohawk warriors, his voice rising above the others as he told an amusing tale, Brown Buffalo admirably hanging on his every word.

The warriors were circled around the glowing embers of a fire that had been built separate from the large, central outdoor fire, while waiting for the clams to cook. The Penobscot people held this feast annually after a sufficient quantity of clams, crabs, lobsters, corn, and various cuts of fish were accumulated.

As Shanna adoringly watched her husband, she became lost in thought. She could hardly believe she had now been married for ten years. The years had passed so quickly it was as though she had blinked her eyes and they were gone, yet those years had been filled with much happiness.

She and Bold Wolf had shared not only their love, but that of their four children.

When the fourth child, a daughter, had arrived, they had moved into a larger home so that at least the sons and daughters could be separated into bedrooms to assure them the privacy they deserved as they developed into young men and women.

So proud of her family that she could burst, Shanna moved her eyes from Bold Wolf and searched through

the crowd for her children. Her heart warmed through
and through when she found her twin sons, who were
filling out at their age of nine moons into handsome
young men. The muscles of their bare legs corded as
they joined in race games with the other children farther down the riverbank, away from the adults.

Pride swelled within Shanna as she watched her
sons mingle with their friends, laughing and running,
their eyes revealing their utter contentment.

She was glad that no one had ever seemed to notice
how one brother's skin color differed from the other
brother's, as no one ever seemed to notice that Shanna's skin was not the Penobscot's color. Since her first
day among them as Bold Wolf's wife, she was as one
with his people. They were as one with her.

As is Raven, she thought, her five-year-old-daughter,
who sat in the sand building sand castles with children
her age. Hers and Bold Wolf's daughter had been
born with Shanna's skin and hair coloring, but with
the darkest eyes of all midnights, which matched her
father's.

"And, ah, Dancing Water," Shanna whispered, sin-
gling her out from the others. She gazed with much
love at her adopted daughter, who was sitting primly
and properly with the other girls her age, comparing
the colorful strings of shells and beads they had just
strung, which would be used one day soon on a fancy
purse, a blouse, or moccasins.

Although Dancing Water's one lame hand hindered
her somewhat, she had learned well the skills that all
of the other young Penobscot girls learned. It had
been hard at first for Shanna to watch Dancing Water
struggling to position her hand so that she could make
things as pretty as her friends' creations.

Shanna had not interfered. She had sat back and
allowed Dancing Water her privacy while battling

something as private as this. One day she would be a woman and would be expected to do things all women knew in order for a man to notice her as someone who would make a good wife. And Dancing Water had succeeded well in her private lessons.

Shanna had known long ago that even if Dancing Water hadn't mastered the use of her lame hand, it would not have mattered. Her sheer beauty, her sweet personality, were all that would be needed to attract any young brave to her. Young men were drawn to her like bees to honey, always surrounding her, some even fighting over who would sit with her at celebrations and social functions.

"She *is* so beautiful, is she not?"

Shanna was drawn out of her deep thoughts by Running Deer's voice, her child now awake and suckling at a breast.

Shanna looked over at Running Deer. "Yes, and she gets more beautiful each day," she murmured, her and Running Deer's eyes holding, the secret now old between them.

Shanna slid her eyes downward to Running Deer's baby, unable to see much of her because of the blanket wrapped around her. "And I see that Moon Beam is awake," she said, fighting inside herself to be friendly with Running Deer. "She's adorable, Running Deer."

Running Deer took her child from her breast, dropped the buckskin nursing flap down over the breast to cover it, then stretched her legs out before her and lay the child on them.

Slowly she unfolded the blanket from around the baby. "Moon Beam is hungry all of the time," she said, laughing softly. She looked past Shanna at Dancing Water. "Did Dancing Water eat as much when she . . . was this size?"

Shanna's insides tightened, as always when Running Deer brought Dancing Water into the conversation.

She had now mentioned Dancing Water twice in only a matter of moments. Shanna saw this as a threat. She always wondered if Running Deer had told her new husband about the child that she had left for dead, yet Shanna had never gotten the nerve to ask her. She wasn't sure if she really wanted to know.

Surely Running Deer had kept the secret to herself, knowing that to tell her husband could mean the end of Running Deer's abilities to marry chiefs. She would be banished from her husband's life, as well as her people's.

"Dancing Water has always had a big appetite," Shanna said, just not being able to be cruel enough to forbid talk of her daughter with the woman who had given her birth. Although Shanna could not help but resent the woman's curiosity, she knew she would have to tolerate it. At least until Chief Brown Buffalo finally caught on to his wife and knew the deceitful woman she was!

Then a thought came to Shanna that made her heart skip a beat. Since the marriage between Brown Buffalo and Running Deer came so soon after Bent Arrow's death, could that possibly mean that Brown Buffalo was the man who had fathered Dancing Water? Could he be as deceitful as Running Deer?

The thought terrified Shanna, for if this Mohawk chief, who claimed to be Bold Wolf's best friend, was guilty of such a deceit against his very own chief, what might he eventually do to deceive Bold Wolf?

Shanna turned wondering eyes to Brown Buffalo. As he laughed and talked to Bold Wolf, sometimes placing a hand of friendship on Bold Wolf's shoulder, Shanna tightened inside. Her husband was such a trusting man, sometimes too innocent for his own good. This Mohawk chief could be playing games even now, while in his deceitful mind he could be plotting against Bold Wolf!

Against the Penobscot tribe as a whole!

Shanna could not help but feel bitter over thinking anyone might take advantage of her husband in such a way! And if Dancing Water were Brown Buffalo's birth child, who was to say that he might not come one day and demand her as part of the Mohawk tribe?

Running Deer noticed the way Shanna was suddenly staring at Brown Buffalo. "Shanna, my husband Brown Buffalo doesn't know," she murmured, drawing Shanna's eyes quickly to hers. "Never will I tell him about Dancing Water, Shanna. It is still our secret, yours and mine."

"Then he isn't the father," Shanna said, paling. "*He* wasn't the man you were in love with while you were married to Bent Arrow."

"No, it is not that way at all," Running Deer said, folding the blanket back around her child. She brought Moon Beam up against her bosom and slowly rocked her. "It was another man, a man whose skin is the same color as yours."

"A . . . white man?" Shanna gasped, her eyes wide, yet so relieved to know that her thoughts about Brown Buffalo were wrong.

"It is a man you know very well," Running Deer said, turning to gaze at Old Town. "At the time I first met Roscoe Lovett, I thought I loved him. But not until I married Brown Buffalo did I discover what true love is."

"Roscoe . . . Lovett?" Shanna said, shocked to her core over this revelation.

Running Deer turned to Shanna. "Shanna, at first it was not so much the man that intrigued me, but his music. I often took canoe trips upriver from my village and enjoyed walking alone through the forest outside of Old Town. I communed there often with the Great Spirit. One day when I was there, I heard beautiful music. It lured me. I found this white man in the forest playing a flute. After that I met him many times so that I could listen to him play his music. It was far more beautiful than birdsong. One day, not only did his music seduce me, but also did the man. I was easily seduced. I wanted him as badly as . . . he wanted me. I was so lonely. My husband wasn't . . . a husband in the romantic way. I missed that, Shanna. I . . . I am so young."

Running Deer lowered her eyes. "When I discovered that I was with child, I knew it had to be Roscoe's," she said, her voice drawn. "But even then I was no longer meeting him. I knew the wrong in having given my body so willingly to him. I never told him about the child. I never told anyone. I carried the secret inside me like a dark sin, for it, only it, could prove my betrayal to my husband."

"Dancing Water is truly . . . Roscoe Lovett's child?" Shanna said, so stunned her throat had gone instantly dry.

"Yes, she is the white man's child," Running Deer said. "I knew that I could never keep her, for looking at the child every day would be a reminder of my sin of adultery."

She grabbed Shanna's arm. "Now do you understand better than before why I did this hideous thing to my child? Until I met Roscoe Lovett, I was an honorable, good woman. He changed me into someone I never knew any longer. Before my husband died, because of Bent Arrow's deep love for me and because of his charitable ways, he changed me back to the woman I was before my mistake."

She glanced at Brown Buffalo. "And my husband

Brown Buffalo . . ." she said, a sob lodging in her throat. "If he ever knew about . . ."

Her words died on her lips. She hung her head to hide the tears that were streaming from her eyes.

"And all along I thought Roscoe loved Jennie," Shanna said, finding this story so incredible. "But I should have known he didn't when he left Old Town so suddenly and never returned for her. At the time, it was as though he had disappeared from the face of the earth."

Running Deer's head jerked up quickly. She gazed intensely at Shanna. "It is because of me that he is gone," she said, her jaw tightening. "After Dancing Water was born and I left her beside the pond, and . . . I had much time to think, and guilt almost swallowed me whole over all the wrong that I had done, I grew to hate Roscoe Lovett for how he had changed my life into a horrible nightmare. I went to him one day."

She laughed ironically. "Yes, I went to him and saw that someone had been there before me who hated him as much, for his nose was broken and his lip was swollen and cut," she said in a low hiss. "Scornfully I told him that I knew someone who would do worse to him, that all I had to do was say the word *rape* to my chieftain husband and Roscoe would be dead. I told him to leave the area or risk having dozens of arrows sink into his chest when he least expected it."

Running Deer laughed again. "Of course he was very confused about my change in attitude toward him," she said. "Never would I tell him that he had fathered a child. Never!"

Shanna was stunned anew. She thought back to the day she had hid in Roscoe's office and had listened to the men beating him. She thought back to when she had found the note on Roscoe's door, saying that he had gone out of town for business.

Shanna had thought that he had left because he might have been guilty of setting the fire to the brothel, and *worse*. She thought he might have even killed Al Adams!

None of that had been right. He had fled because a powerful Mohawk chief's wife had threatened him!

"I just don't know what to say," Shanna murmured. She looked quickly over at Dancing Water. "And Dancing Water has none of Roscoe's features. She is Indian in all respects."

"That only proves how little a man Roscoe Lovett is if our child has all features of her mother," Running Deer said, laughing scornfully. "Tell me, Shanna, does any of this change things between you and I? Could you find it in your heart to understand just a little bit about why I did what I did those long years ago? I feel less burdened now, Shanna, having told you everything."

Shanna gazed at Running Deer for a long moment, then, sighing, reached over and took her hand. "I shall try much harder to understand," she murmured. "I can tell that you have lived through much regret. Yes, Running Deer, I will be your friend. As long as our friendship does not affect Dancing Water, that is," Shanna quickly interjected. "I love her so very much. She is such a special child."

"That is because she was so deeply loved by you and Bold Wolf," Running Deer said.

She looked quickly up when her husband came to her with a large tray of baked clams and corn on the cob. "My wife, are you hungry for a feast?" Chief Brown Buffalo said, his eyes twinkling as he sat down beside Running Deer.

Bold Wolf followed close behind and sat with Shanna, sliding a huge wooden platter of food onto her lap. "This is the best clambake we have had in years," he said. But his smile faded when he looked into Shanna's eyes and saw something far less than exuberance. "What is wrong, Shanna? What has happened?"

Shanna forced a smile. She knew this was not the time to reveal all of what she had just been told to her husband. "I'm hungry. That's all," she said, trying to make her voice sound lighthearted. "I'm ready for clams, darling." She reached for an ear of roasted corn. "And, ah, this corn smells so good."

She shucked the corn as her husband pried open several clams, yet her mind was spinning with the truths that she had been told. She still found Roscoe Lovett's treachery hard to believe!

Oh, Lord, that made the news that Jennie had wired to her today from Boston something more questionable than wonderful.

Jennie had written to Shanna that she had run across Roscoe while touring for concerts.

Jennie had married Roscoe Lovett two weeks ago!

39

Dreams of the summer night!
Tell her, her lover keeps
Watch! While in slumber tight
She sleeps!
—HENRY WADSWORTH LONGFELLOW

Deliciously warm in bed and in her husband's arms,
their children all safely tucked into their own beds,
Shanna snuggled closer to Bold Wolf. "Tonight was
such fun. Except for—" she said, then stopped short
of telling Bold Wolf about her serious talk with Running Deer.

"Except for what?" Bold Wolf said, propping himself up on an elbow to look at her. The sheen of the
moon spilling its softness through the window gave
him enough light to see Shanna by, and he could see
she was bothered by something, as she had been earlier at the clambake.

He smoothed her hair back from her eyes. "We're
alone now," he said softly. "Want to tell me what is
on your mind?"

"It's so hard to believe," she said. Then she sat
up and rushed through everything Running Deer had
told her.

"Roscoe Lovett fathered Dancing Water?" Bold
Wolf gasped. He placed his hands on Shanna's shoulder. "Does he know?"

"No, she never told him," Shanna said. She flung
herself into his arms. "Oh, Bold Wolf, he's married
to Jennie. If she ever knew the truth about him and

Running Deer, it would devastate her. Bold Wolf, she's already had too many traumas in her life. She doesn't need any more."

He held her close, then leaned back and lifted her chin with a finger. He gazed intently into her eyes. "There is nothing we can do about Jennie," he said thickly. "Jennie has made her choices. We have made ours. We must not allow what was told to you today to alter our lives in any way. We will forget what Running Deer said about Roscoe. We will put it from our minds, as we did when we did not know who fathered her. *I* am her father. You are her *mother*. My beautiful wife, that is how it shall remain until we say our good-byes to this earth and those who live on it."

"Yes, and I just know that we have nothing to fear from Roscoe should he ever discover the truth about Dancing Water," Shanna said, sighing. "If he came to claim her, then he would surely lose Jennie."

She sighed heavily. "And as for Jennie, the terrible thing that happened to her when her father sold her to the brothel . . . that can never happen again to any innocent young lady in Old Town," she said. "I am so glad that at the recent town meeting they decided to ban all brothels. The brothel tent is gone. The other buildings that were used for brothels are being renovated into decent establishments. Everyone can relax now when they walk through Old Town."

"So you see, there is always sunshine where there was once gloom," Bold Wolf said thickly. "And although no one will ever truly know who burned the one brothel and sent threats to the owners of the others, it does not truly matter. Even Al's death. It was all a warning to the town that something had to be done. Now Old Town is a place of respect and peace."

He drew her closer, kissed her on the tip of the nose, then smiled down at her. "Shanna, like my father, I now have visions," he said, a keen excitement in his voice.

"Visions?" Shanna said. "When? How? What did you see in them?"

"My woman, yesterday, while I was alone on the far end of the island before the clambake, I suddenly felt a presence," he said, his eyes gleaming. "I stopped, looked around me, and then suddenly there before me was *you.*"

"Me?" Shanna said, her eyes widening. "How could that be, Bold Wolf? I was with our children all day until just before the clambake. I was in our cabin."

"It was not that you were actually there," Bold Wolf said. "It was as though I were seeing you in a picture that one draws on paper, yet you were moving."

"What . . . was I doing?" she asked, so intrigued now by what he was telling her, she was breathless.

"You were walking, hand in hand, with Dancing Water," he said, even now seeing it in his mind's eye as he had seen it then. "Our twins suddenly appeared running after you, and when you turned to wait on them, I saw that you were big with child again."

"Truly?" Shanna breathed out in a small whisper, sliding her hand down to her stomach. She *was* pregnant again. Tonight she had planned to break the news to Bold Wolf!

He saw her hand resting on her stomach. Then he looked up at her. "You *are* with child again, aren't you?" he gasped. "What I saw was true!"

"Yes, my darling," Shanna said, marveling still over how he could know. "I . . . was going to tell you tonight."

"I am so proud," Bold Wolf said, squaring his shoulders.

"Over the child?" Shanna murmured, herself thrilled so much over the pregnancy.

"Over both the child and my ability to see visions as did my father," Bold Wolf said, laughing throatily. He reached for her wrists and brought her down on the bed beneath him. "My woman, I have waited all day to blanket you with my body. Do you think the child growing inside your womb will mind?"

"I believe the child lying there, so safely cocooned in my womb, will welcome you, his father, because the child knows it makes his mother happy," Shanna whispered, sucking in a wild breath of pleasure as he shoved his manhood deeply inside her soft folds.

"You are calling our child a 'he,'" Bold Wolf whispered, his hands filled with her breasts, kneading them.

"Yes, even though I do not have visions, I already know the child will be a boy," Shanna whispered back, her face hot with passion as his thrusts moved within her so powerfully and rhythmically.

"And how would you know this?" Bold Wolf asked, chuckling.

"Just because I know," Shanna said, giggling.

"That is enough for me to know that the child will be a son, then," Bold Wolf said with passion.

Aflame with longing, Shanna clung to him. "Kiss me," she whispered, her breathing ragged. "Oh, my love, kiss me."

His mouth hungry and urgent, he did as she asked. Sometimes when they kissed and when they came together so sweetly and passionately, he was reminded of those long years they were kept from one another.

But now was now, and the past was past.

And the future?

Ah, what a future their love had created for them. He needed no mysterious vision to tell him that the promise of all tomorrows with his Shanna would be beautiful and never-ending.

She was his vision!

Bold Wolf gave one last, deep shove inside her.

Shanna sighed as ecstasy swam through her in bone-weakening intensity, an ecstasy that she had never known until Bold Wolf had held her that first time.

And then, ah, then she had known that never could there be anyone but him to hold and love her!

Their love for one another was total and complete. It would endure always!

Dear Reader:

I hope you enjoyed reading *Bold Wolf.* The next book in my Topaz Indian Series, which I write exclusively for Penguin Putnam, is *Lone Eagle. Lone Eagle* is an exciting book about the Crow Indians. It will be in the stores six months from the release date of *Bold Wolf.* This book is filled with much emotion, passion, and adventure! I hope you will read it and enjoy it!

For those of you who are collecting the books in my Topaz Indian Series, and want to read about my backlist and my future books, please send a legal-sized, self-addressed, stamped envelope to the following address for my latest newsletter and bookmark:

Cassie Edwards
6709 N. Country Club Road
Mattoon, IL 61938

Thank you for your support of my books. I truly appreciate it!

Always,

Cassie Edwards